P9-DDC-482

THE SPYMASTERS

ALSO BY W.E.B. GRIFFIN

HONOR BOUND

HONOR BOUND
BLOOD AND HONOR
SECRET HONOR
DEATH AND HONOR
(with William E. Butterworth IV)
THE HONOR OF SPIES
(and William E. Butterworth IV)
VICTORY AND HONOR
(and William E. Butterworth IV)

BROTHERHOOD OF WAR

BOOK I: THE LIEUTENANTS
BOOK II: THE CAPTAINS
BOOK III: THE MAJORS
BOOK IV: THE COLONELS
BOOK V: THE BERETS
BOOK VI: THE GENERALS
BOOK VII: THE NEW BREED
BOOK VIII: THE AVIATORS
BOOK IX: SPECIAL OPS

THE CORPS

BOOK I: SEMPER FI
BOOK II: CALL TO ARMS
BOOK III: COUNTERATTACK
BOOK IV: BATTLEGROUND
BOOK V: LINE OF FIRE
BOOK VI: CLOSE COMBAT
BOOK VII: BEHIND THE LINES
BOOK VIII: IN DANGER'S PATH
BOOK IX: UNDER FIRE
BOOK X: RETREAT, HELL!

BADGE OF HONOR

BOOK I: MEN IN BLUE
BOOK II: SPECIAL OPERATIONS
BOOK III: THE VICTIM
BOOK IV: THE WITNESS
BOOK V: THE ASSASSIN
BOOK VI: THE MURDERERS
BOOK VII: THE INVESTIGATORS
BOOK VIII: FINAL JUSTICE
BOOK IX: THE TRAFFICKERS
(and William E. Butterworth IV)
BOOK X: THE VIGILANTES
(and William E. Butterworth IV)

MEN AT WAR

BOOK I: THE LAST HEROES
BOOK II: THE SECRET WARRIORS
BOOK III: THE SOLDIER SPIES
BOOK IV: THE FIGHTING AGENTS
BOOK V: THE SABOTEURS
(and William E. Butterworth IV)
BOOK VI: THE DOUBLE AGENTS
(and William E. Butterworth IV)

PRESIDENTIAL AGENT

BOOK I: BY ORDER OF THE PRESIDENT
BOOK II: THE HOSTAGE
BOOK III: THE HUNTERS
BOOK IV: THE SHOOTERS
BOOK V: BLACK OPS
BOOK VI: THE OUTLAWS
(and William E. Butterworth IV)
BOOK VII: COVERT WARRIORS
(and William E. Butterworth IV)

THE SPYMASTERS

W.E.B. GRIFFIN

AND WILLIAM E. BUTTERWORTH IV

G. P. PUTNAM'S SONS
NEW YORK

PUTNAM

G. P. PUTNAM'S SONS
Publishers Since 1838
Published by the Penguin Group
Penguin Group (USA) Inc., 375 Hudson Street, New York, New York 10014, USA • Penguin Group (Canada), 90 Eglinton Avenue East, Suite 700, Toronto, Ontario M4P 2Y3, Canada (a division of Pearson Penguin Canada Inc.) • Penguin Books Ltd, 80 Strand, London WC2R 0RL, England • Penguin Ireland, 25 St Stephen's Green, Dublin 2, Ireland (a division of Penguin Books Ltd) • Penguin Group (Australia), 250 Camberwell Road, Camberwell, Victoria 3124, Australia (a division of Pearson Australia Group Pty Ltd) • Penguin Books India Pvt Ltd, 11 Community Centre, Panchsheel Park, New Delhi–110 017, India • Penguin Group (NZ), 67 Apollo Drive, Rosedale, North Shore 0632, New Zealand (a division of Pearson New Zealand Ltd) • Penguin Books (South Africa) (Pty) Ltd, 24 Sturdee Avenue, Rosebank, Johannesburg 2196, South Africa

Penguin Books Ltd, Registered Offices: 80 Strand, London WC2R 0RL, England

Published simultaneously in Canada

ISBN 978-0-399-15751-6

Printed in the United States of America
1 3 5 7 9 10 8 6 4 2

THE MEN AT WAR SERIES
IS RESPECTFULLY DEDICATED
IN HONOR OF

Lieutenant Aaron Bank, Infantry, AUS,
detailed OSS
(Later Colonel, Special Forces)
November 23, 1902–April 1, 2004

Lieutenant William E. Colby, Infantry, AUS,
detailed OSS
(Later Ambassador and Director, CIA)
January 4, 1920–April 28, 1996

It is no use saying,

"We are doing our best."

You have got to succeed in doing

what is necessary.

—Prime Minister Winston S. Churchill

When you get to the end

of your rope,

tie a knot, and hang on.

—President Franklin D. Roosevelt

THE SPYMASTERS

I

[ONE]

Between Rzeszów and Blizna
German-Occupied Poland
2145 25 May 1943

"There! It's coming!" Kapitan Mordechaj Szerynski announced at the faint chugging sound of the small steam-powered locomotive. The twenty-six-year-old resistance fighter in the Armia Krajowa, the Polish Home Army, had a wiry five-foot-eight medium build, light skin, and thick bushy black hair and eyebrows.

He turned to the twenty-one-year-old guerrilla beside him. Porucznik (Lieutenant) Stanislaw Polko looked like Szerynski, though was a head taller. They were hiding under a loose layer of downed limbs and leaves next to the narrow gauge railroad track that wound through the dense forest of the Carpathian mountain foothills in southern Poland.

"Pass the word for everyone to move on my command," Szerynski ordered, "not a second sooner!"

"Yes, sir," Polko said, and touched the tips of his right index and middle fingers to his forehead, the two-finger Polish Army salute signifying Honor and Fatherland.

Polko crawled over to the other five guerrillas—the majority of them, like Polko and Szerynski, Jewish and in their twenties—spread out to their right. All were dressed in clothing that they had acquired from farmers who for months had been supplying the

Armia Krajowa with details of Nazi activity in the area. And all were armed with weapons smuggled to them by the Allies—the U.S. Office of Strategic Services working in London with the Government of the Republic of Poland in Exile.

As Polko crawled back beside Szerynski, and the train chugged closer and louder, Szerynski thought he could hear in the cool night air the sound of men singing.

Jesus! he thought. *That's not "Horst-Wessel-Lied," is it?*

Hearing Polko mutter "bastard pigs!" seemed to confirm that there indeed was singing—and probably that of the Nazi anthem.

After another moment of listening, Szerynski then thought: *And the bastards sound drunk!*

"I swear I kill first Nazi pig," Polko muttered as he smacked the magazine of his Sten 9mm submachine gun, the cold fury in his voice unmistakable.

Is he going to follow orders? Szerynski thought.

Or just start shooting?

Szerynski knew that if not for the dark night he now would see in Polko's deep-set coal-black eyes the same anger he'd often seen at the mention of German soldiers.

"Keep your damn head, Porucznik."

Polko grunted.

Only a month earlier Szerynski and his men had been in the Zydowska Organizacja Bojowa—the Jewish Fighting Organization—bravely, but futilely, battling the Nazis in the ghettos of Warsaw, about a hundred kilometers to the north.

Szerynski had seen the brutality inflicted by the Schutzstaffel—the German SS—including last December the torture of his little brother and two other Boy Scouts caught running ammunition to the ZOB. The teenagers had had their testicles torn out, their eyes gouged, and their teeth pulled before being killed and thrown into the snow-covered street as a message to others.

That Szerynski and his men weren't among the thousands of other Poles who were mass murdered after being forced into Warsaw's slums was nothing shy of a miracle. And they had avoided being packed in freight train boxcars for what the Nazi soldiers announced was simply a "relocation" to the SS-run *konzentrationslager.*

Instead, they had fled the city, finding refuge in the forest.

The resistance fighters, after having joined up with the Armia Krajowa, then discovered the truth about the relocations. At the heavily armed concentration camps, the passengers were made prisoners—the SS called them *sonderkommandos*—put in striped outfits, and within weeks worked to their death.

When the farmers alerted the Armia Krajowa that a new camp was being built by slave laborers outside the village of Blizna, Szerynski and his men moved south through the forest to investigate.

The conditions they found at the construction site staggered the mind. Under the cold eyes of SS guards, hundreds of malnourished prisoners struggled at hard labor—hewing timber, pouring concrete, cutting stone, even digging their own graves. Nearby, the slave laborers also worked at carving out of the woods a small airstrip for light aircraft to reach the remote area. They saw the SS summarily beat—and execute on the spot—those judged not to be working hard enough.

And twice weekly the boxcars came on the narrow gauge railway to deliver sonderkommandos, many of the prisoners from Warsaw, as replacements for the dead.

Kapitan Szerynski had told his men: "If we cannot stop the Nazi pigs, we damn sure can rescue some of our people."

"As we planned," Kapitan Szerynski now ordered, "after the train comes to a stop, follow my lead. Maintain discipline. No shooting unless absolutely necessary."

Porucznik Polko was quiet for a long moment.

He thought back to the previous two days, when they had practiced the ambush of the train inside a deserted barn. Using bales of hay as a mock-up for one of the thirty-foot-long freight cars, Szerynski had drilled the discipline into their heads. Each boxcar—it sickened Polko to call them what they were, foul-smelling cattle cars—would be packed with at least fifty prisoners, and possibly as many as a hundred or more, with a shared bucket or two being the only method for the disposal of human waste. Szerynski had cautioned his men that a single stray shot at some Nazi bastard could also easily kill or injure others—and, as they had seen during ambushes with the ZOB in Warsaw, an anxious, undisciplined shooter could almost instantly empty his weapon's entire magazine.

Polko grunted.

"Understood," he said, then looked over his shoulder and motioned for the men to await his signal.

To force the train to a stop, the resistance fighters, using explosive Primacord that resembled a thick bootlace, felled two mature black alder trees across the tracks just past a curve. They trimmed the limbs, then manhandled the trunks so that they were between the narrow gauge rails; the heavy V-shaped "pilot" metalwork on the front of the locomotive would not be able to push the trees off the tracks. Instead, the locomotive would become wedged on top of the heavy timbers, and they could storm the train's freight cars that carried the prisoners.

As they had practiced in the barn, each resistance fighter then would run to a particular door on a boxcar, unlatch its lock, swing it open, then repeat until all doors were open. It was expected that the guards would be either dazed or injured or both from the sudden stopping of the train, and that the guards could then be disarmed and secured—or, if necessary, killed.

The prisoners, once helped out of the boxcars, would be led deep into the forest to where another dozen guerrillas waited to split them up and, later, absorb them into their resistance cells. They knew that each train arriving at the camp near Blizna had averaged three boxcars, and that that meant there could be anywhere from 150 to 450 prisoners to rescue. (The long trains leaving Warsaw for the initial "relocating" had fifty boxcars carrying upward of five thousand people to the death camps.)

The sounds of the steam locomotive and the singing continued getting louder.

The bastards celebrate bringing our people here to die! Szerynski thought bitterly.

But if there is any good news it is that their being drunk should make this ambush easier.

The locomotive's carbon arc headlight, heavily masked so as not to project its full brilliance, could now be seen bouncing a dim beam through the trees by the curve in the train track.

The beam grew bigger as the train approached the curve at a fast clip. The sound of singing grew louder. Then the nose of the train—and the masked headlight—were visible. The locomotive steamed on into the turn, its beam of light sweeping the forest of trees on the far side of the track as it did so. Then, just as the beam of light squared with the train track, it illuminated a huge obstacle on the tracks—and the conductor slammed on the train's full brakes.

Something about this train is different, Szerynski suddenly thought, straining to make out its shape in the darkness.

But what?

At once a stream of sparks began to spray out from where the locomotive's heavy steel wheels slid on the iron rails and the air filled with an ear-piercing high-decibel metallic screech. There then came a deep dull thud that was caused by the underside of the locomotive impacting the tree trunks. The pitch of the screech lessened somewhat, and the trees now could be heard thumping together under the pressure of the still moving train.

It looks to be a shorter train. Maybe only one car?

And it is a smaller car, almost half the size of a boxcar . . . a passenger car? . . . why?

What happened next did not go according to plan.

The locomotive, grinding along the tree trunks, did not stop. It did not appear to slow very much, either. Instead, its right wheels stopped screeching and sparking as they rode up onto one, then both, of the tree trunks.

And then the locomotive veered off the tracks.

Holy mother of God!

He felt the ground shudder repeatedly as the locomotive hit the shoulder, then the coal car followed, then the small passenger car.

That is a small passenger car! What the hell?

The pilot metalwork plowed ground as the locomotive continued to the treeline, where it sheared off a half-dozen trees before finally coming to a stop. The locomotive then rolled onto its left side. The coal car immediately crumpled behind it, then rolled onto its side. And then the passenger car, after impacting the coal car with a deafening crunch of steel and wood, rolled over, too.

"Damn it!" Szerynski said, jumping to his feet from under the ground cover.

"Where is the prisoner boxcar?" Polko said.

"How the hell do I know? Let's go!"

Polko was on his feet instantly. He made a shrill whistle to his men, then hand signaled them to follow their lead. Polko turned in time to see Szerynski leap across the narrow rails, then run in a crouch, his Sten machine gun trained on the passenger car.

Flames began to rise from inside the locomotive, lighting the night, and the steam engine's boiler made a strange pulsating hissing sound.

When Szerynski looked in that direction, a man he immediately decided had to be the engineer appeared on top of the rolled-over locomotive. The engineer struggled with a long-barreled weapon—*Damn it! He's got a shotgun!*—and Szerynski smoothly took him down with a three-round burst of 9mm from the Sten.

Polko and Szerynski then carefully approached the rear of the passenger car. There was no more singing to be heard.

A young Nazi soldier, bleeding heavily from the nose and mouth, then came crawling out the back door, grunting at the effort. Szerynski saw that the collars of his gray-green SS field tunic bore the insignia of a master sergeant. The *hauptscharführer* looked to be maybe nineteen, somewhat younger than the SS they had seen guarding the sonderkommandos.

With the Germans suffering staggering casualties on so many fronts—nearly a million killed or taken prisoner in the Battle of Stalingrad alone—a new conscription law in January had ordered men between ages sixteen and twenty-five and women between ages seventeen and forty-five open to mobilization.

The hauptscharführer was going into shock—though not so severely that when he saw Szerynski he couldn't turn on his side to pull at the flap of the holster on his belt.

Polko saw what was happening and quickly covered the distance between them. He slung the strap of his Sten over his left shoulder while slipping a Colt .45 ACP semiautomatic from his waistband. He aimed the pistol and fired once, hitting the hauptscharführer square in the chest and causing him to roll almost into a fetal position. Then he reached down and put another round in the base of his skull.

Polko glanced over his shoulder. He saw the rest of their men running up as Szerynski signaled for them to provide cover.

Szerynski and Polko then stepped closer to the passenger car.

There were no sounds—human or other—coming from it.

Szerynski peered around the corner of the doorway that the young hauptscharführer had crawled out of. But even with the flames from the locomotive he saw nothing inside but dark shadows. He could, however, smell the interior of the car. It reeked of peppermint—*schnapps!*—and cheese.

As he reached for his flashlight, he looked over his shoulder at Polko. He saw him pulling the dead bodyguard's pistol from its leather holster. Polko put his .45 back in his waistband, then worked the action of the Luger. A 9mm round ejected. It landed at Szerynski's feet. He saw it was a live one.

Well, that one sure as hell would have had my name on it.

Szerynski flicked on his flashlight and, pistol ready, shone the yellow beam inside the passenger car.

A parlor and a forward sleeping compartment . . .

This is a wealthy man's transport!

The luxurious interior—rich carpet and draperies, leather-upholstered seating, and highly polished wooden paneling and heavy tables—was a shambles. Two more baby-faced young SS *scharführer* bodyguards lay crumpled against the door to the sleeping compartment, one sergeant atop the other. The one on top, whose head was turned at an impossible angle, suggesting a broken neck, had a drinking glass impaled in his blood-soaked face.

Szerynski's flashlight beam next found the high-peaked black uniform cap of an SS officer—light reflected off its silver skull-and-crossbones *Totenkopf* and, above that, SS eagle insignias—then found the officer himself. He lay sprawled on his back against the crushed ceiling of the car. One of the highly polished wooden tables had sheared free and smashed into his upper body. A cut across his forehead had coated his face in blood.

So who the hell could he be?

Szerynski waved the flashlight beam around the interior one more time.

No one else in here . . . he's got to be the one.

He turned to Polko and said, "Let's get him the hell out of there."

Polko signaled for two of his men to come closer.

He pointed with the Luger toward the SS officer and rapidly ordered: "Get that Nazi pig the hell out of there!"

The two men immediately crawled in through the door opening and then went to the SS officer. Szerynski was somewhat surprised when Polko also crawled in behind them, but then wasn't when he went over to the two bodyguards, put the muzzle of the Luger to their temples, and fired a single round into each.

Then he spat on them.

When the two men pulled the heavy wooden table off the chest of the SS officer, he made a deep groan.

The bastard is alive!

Szerynski's men, with some obvious effort, then dragged the overweight SS officer out the door, stopping about fifteen feet away from the passenger car. As the taller of the two removed the officer's Luger from its holster and stuck it in his waistband—the checkered wooden grip was inlaid with a silver skull-and-crossbones *Totenkopf*—the shorter one yanked open the officer's tunic and roughly searched inside. After a moment, he made a face of self-satisfaction.

He pulled out a black calfskin wallet, then walked over and handed it to Polko, who then passed it to Szerynski.

"The Nazi pig's papers," Polko officiously announced, needlessly.

Szerynski opened the wallet, unfolded the SS identity booklet, and shone his flashlight on it. After he studied it, he glanced at the fat officer lying on the ground, then back at the ID.

An SS-sturmbannführer? he thought, then whistled lightly.

"What?" Polko said.

Szerynski ignored him. He walked over to the SS officer. The Nazi had his eyes closed. Szerynski nudged him in the hip with his boot.

"Herr Sturmbannführer, what is the purpose of your trip?" Szerynski said in German evenly, shining the flashlight on his bloody face.

The SS officer, who looked dazed, stared back but did not reply.

Polko quickly walked up and aimed his Luger at the officer.

"I shoot Nazi pig with Nazi pistol," Polko said.

"No!" Szerynski said, as he pushed away the arm aiming the Luger. "Not yet."

Szerynski reached to his shoulder holster, thumbed open the snap securing his semiautomatic, then aimed the .45 at the officer.

Szerynski looked back at the officer. "The purpose of your trip?"

The officer, after trying to wipe blood from his face, nodded once.

"I . . . I cannot say," he said thickly, clearly in great pain.

"Cannot or will not? Tell me the purpose of your trip here!"

After a moment the SS officer answered, "I . . . I do not know. I was sent here on orders."

"What do you mean, you do not know? And sent here by who?"

The SS officer, apparently considering his options, coughed once but did not answer.

"Who the hell are you?" Szerynski pursued.

He coughed again, then said, "SS-Sturmbannführer Klaus Schwartz."

"No shit!" Szerynski snapped, waving the identity card in front of his bloody face. "It is on your *ausweis*! Right above your photograph and across from Himmler's signature. So, did Herr Reichsführer personally school you in mass murder?"

As head of the SS, Heinrich Himmler had, with Hitler's encouragement, created a powerful state within the state of the Third Reich that was answerable to practically no one. It had its own secret service—the Sicherheitsdienst, or SD—and its own secret police force—the Geheime Staatspolizei, or Gestapo—and its own army—nearly a million troopers in the Waffen-SS. The SS looted everything from cash to gold dental fillings of the millions sent to their deaths in the hundreds of SS-controlled konzentrationslagers.

Despite Himmler's dumpy body and shifty appearance—he had a small head, beady eyes, and wore round spectacles—the cold-blooded *reichsführer* was a force to be feared.

"I am not a mass murderer," Schwartz said defiantly.

"Is that true?" Szerynski said. "How do you explain the boxcars of sonderkommandos sent here from the KL?"

The SS officer's face showed surprise at the mention of the slave laborers from the konzentrationslager. And again he remained quiet as he considered his answer.

Then Schwartz shrugged. "I am merely—how do you say?—an assistant. I am nothing."

That is bullshit!

Then why are you traveling with three SS bodyguards to visit a construction project?

"Bullshit! No SS-sturmbannführer is 'nothing,' you lying bastard."

Szerynski put the muzzle of his .45 to the man's forehead, causing him to involuntarily cross his eyes for a moment.

"And where is tonight's train carrying sonderkommandos?" Szerynski went on.

Schwartz did not answer.

"Where?" Szerynski pursued, applying more pressure to his forehead with the muzzle.

Schwartz, looking past the pistol at Szerynski, still gave no answer.

Szerynski then turned to Polko and in Polish ordered, "Bring the rope. We can get him to talk."

Polko nodded, then barked an order to his men.

The SS officer apparently understood the exchange. He waved his right hand, palm out. "That won't be necessary."

Szerynski pulled back his .45 and met his eyes. "Good."

Schwartz nodded once—then had a sudden coughing spasm. He brought up his hands to his mouth. Szerynski thought that there was something odd about it. Then Szerynski noticed Schwartz fingering the seam of the cuff on his left sleeve—and then tossing something into his mouth and biting hard.

What the hell?

SS-Sturmbannführer Klaus Schwartz started foaming at the mouth. His body began convulsing.

After quickly dropping the black wallet and holstering his pistol, Szerynski bent over and tried to pry open Schwartz's mouth.

"What?" Polko said, leaning over and trying to help.

"I think he swallowed a death pill. Maybe cyanide."

Schwartz's body then went limp, and there came a deep gurgling from his stomach.

Szerynski let loose of Schwartz's head, and the chunky body fell to the ground with a dull *thump*.

"Damn it!" Szerynski said.

Polko then casually stepped forward and with the Luger pumped four rounds of 9mm into Schwartz, two into his chest, one into his groin, and the fourth into his forehead.

Then he spat on him.

That leaves only one round in your Luger, Stan.

Szerynski looked back to the passenger car and pointed at it.

"If you're finished wasting ammo here," he said, "get the men to collect everything they find in there. Leave nothing—especially ammo. You're down to your last shot."

Polko looked at the pistol, then back at Szerynski. His expression showed he hadn't been counting.

Szerynski reached down for the black leather wallet.

"This should come in handy, especially if we find another SS uniform in this bastard's suitcase."

He gestured with it at the dead SS bodyguards.

"Make sure you get all their papers, too," he said, then slipped it into his coat pocket.

"And what about bodies?" Polko said.

Szerynski, the flames from the locomotive lighting his face, pointed at the wreckage of the passenger car.

"Drag them back in there and then we burn everything," he said.

Szerynski then pulled from his coat pocket a wool sock that contained two pounds of malleable Composition C-2 high explosive. The sock looked as if it were stuffed with a fat link of sausage. An eighteen-inch length of Primacord snaked out of the overhand knot at the top of the sock.

"Remember what to do with this?" Szerynski said.

"Mold it around one of the rails at a track tie," Polko said. "Then cover it with as big a pile of rock as possible to concentrate the explosion on the rail."

"Right. And don't set it off till we're ready to get the hell out of here."

He held out the plastic explosive to Polko, who suddenly turned his head at the faint sound of another steam locomotive.

"It's the train carrying the prisoners!" Polko said.

Szerynski strained to hear the sound, then thought for a moment.

"We cannot ambush it now," he said. "We have lost the surprise element."

"But . . ."

"No but, Porucznik," Szerynski said, and thrust the sock of explosive toward Polko. "Hurry, damn it! We cannot stop them from what they're doing to the prisoners. But blowing the track will slow them down."

Polko considered that, then grabbed the sock of C-2, made a casual two-finger salute, and trotted toward the train track.

Not quite ten minutes later, after his men had returned the dead to the passenger car and doused the interior with kerosene from a can used to fuel its heater, Szerynski tossed in a wooden match. The flame caught slowly and began to spread.

He started moving toward the edge of the forest, signaling all to follow.

As he and his men disappeared into the thick of the trees, behind them came a sudden *whoosh* and they were momentarily brightly illuminated by the flames engulfing the passenger car.

A moment later, the plastic explosive went off, and, a long moment after that, with Szerynski and his men now running toward where the other resistance fighters waited, dirt and small rock rained down.

[TWO]
OSS London Station
Berkeley Square
London, England
0910 30 May 1943

"Yes, Mr. Ambassador, I said I understand," Colonel David Kirkpatrick Este Bruce, chief of the Office of Strategic Services London Station, said into the telephone, struggling to keep his tone civil. "I'll see what I can do. Good-bye."

Bruce—who had intense eyes set in a chiseled face, his dark hair starting to gray at the edges—was a distinguished-looking forty-five-year-old lawyer from a prestigious Virginia family. He had made his own fortune before marrying one of the world's wealthiest women and—like his father-in-law, Andrew Mellon—had been a high-level diplomat.

"Damn him!" Bruce said as he slammed down the receiver.

An attractive brunette in her thirties suddenly appeared in the open doorway.

"Sir?" Captain Helene Dancy, Women's Army Corps, said, the concern in her voice apparent. "Anything that I can do?"

Without looking up at his administrative assistant, Bruce barked, "Get Ed Stevens in here! And now!"

Dancy's eyes went wide.

"Yes, *sir*!" she said, and spun on her heels to leave.

Her reaction wasn't lost on Bruce, and he called out, "Helene?"

She stopped and turned. "Yes?"

"I'm sorry about snapping. Please accept my apology."

She forced a smile, and turned again to leave. "Of course. It's quite all right."

Bruce added, "And bring some coffee, please. We are going to need a fresh pot."

"Right away," Bruce heard her call back as he turned in his high-back leather chair to look out the window at the gray day. He thought over the conversation just now that had triggered his uncharacteristic outburst.

I don't know what aggravates me more—his arrogance, or me letting his arrogance get under my skin.

There was the sound of knuckles rapping on the wooden doorframe. David Bruce spun his chair back around.

A tall, thin, silver-haired forty-four-year-old wearing a perfectly tailored worsted uniform of a U.S. Army officer stood in the doorway.

"Helene said you wanted to see me a week ago yesterday?" Lieutenant Colonel Edmund T. Stevens, deputy chief of OSS London Station, said. "What's going on, David?"

Unlike Bruce, Stevens was not a diplomat with an assimilated military rank. He was a graduate of West Point, and had been personally recruited by the head of the OSS, William "Wild Bill" Donovan.

Before the war, Stevens had resigned his commission so that he could live with his family in England and help his wife run her wholesale food and wine import-export business. Part of Stevens's duties had been to serve as the face of the business when dealing with the difficult upper-crust English businessmen. When Donovan had seen that Stevens handled them with remarkable ease, he decided those skills would well serve the OSS. Having military experience was icing on the cake.

Bruce waved for his deputy to come in, motioning for him to take one of the wooden armchairs in front of his desk.

He glanced at the phone and said, "I just got off the line with Winant."

There had been no love lost between David Bruce and the Honorable John Gilbert Winant. Bruce held himself to the highest standards—some suggested impossibly high standards—and had no patience for those who did not meet the same. He considered Winant, the ambassador extraordinary and plenipotentiary to the Court of Saint James's, to be a weakling of the first order, which he believed was the absolute last thing they needed during wartime. But Winant was the personal representative of the President of the United States of America—the embassy at One Grosvenor Square was a few blocks from OSS London Station's Berkeley Square headquarters—as well as one of FDR's buddies, and accordingly had long enjoyed FDR's generosity.

Bruce realized that what really annoyed him about Winant was the fact that having an ineffectual envoy in such a high-profile position—especially after FDR essentially had called home Winant's immediate predecessor, Joseph P. Kennedy, for being a defeatist—reflected poorly not only on America but also on its other representatives.

David K. E. Bruce, for example.

Bruce believed that America had a long history of fine ministers to the Court of Saint James's—beginning in 1785 with its first, John Adams, who would become President of the United States—and it needed another strong one. And needed it now.

Bruce had old friends in the State Department who out of school told him that the Brits had approached FDR about the subject, whispering that they would be happy with Donovan assuming the position. But Bruce knew that there was no way in hell Wild Bill would give up being spymaster, and certainly not to be tied to an embassy desk and making cautious happy talk.

Donovan can be diplomatic. But as a rule Medal of Honor winners don't suffer fools gladly. Wild Bill would much rather unleash that Irish temper and, borrowing his language, ream someone a new anal orifice than attempt to kill them with kindness.

"Winant," Bruce said, "called inquiring what the hell is going on with General Sikorski. Apparently the Polish Government-in-exile is making it known at the embassy that it doesn't feel it's getting its due from the Allies."

The sixty-two-year-old Wladyslaw Sikorski, who had served as commander in chief of the Polish Armed Forces and chief of the Polish General Staff, was prime minister of the Polish Government-in-exile in London.

Stevens raised his eyebrows. "After being trampled by the Germans and the Russians, I cannot say that I blame the Poles. But telling Winant anything about what we are doing to support Sikorski and the resistance is the last thing we need to do. Ironically, despite his position, he simply cannot keep his mouth shut."

"Agreed," Bruce said. "And Sikorski is tough. He smells Winant's weakness and knows he can pressure him. To what end he will be successful, however, remains unclear. Because Winant, after the diplomatic firestorms that Joe Kennedy caused, won't do anything without FDR signing off on it personally. And likely not even then."

"Which is why he called you? To find out what we're doing, and then tell Sikorski that that's all he's going to get?"

"That's my take, except I'm not going to tell him because Sikorski has been valuable to us. We obviously want to keep it that way."

He took from his desktop a decrypted message from OSS Bern Station and passed it to Stevens.

"This is the response to my message to Allen Dulles about those SS identity papers."

"The ones Sausagemaker got when they tried rescuing that trainload of prisoners?" Stevens said.

He noticed that Bruce made a face when he used the code name for the Polish resistance leader, Mordechaj Szerynski, and decided it was because it reminded Bruce that Major Richard M. Canidy had come up with it. Stevens knew that the diplomatic-minded Bruce was solidly in the camp of those who considered Canidy a reckless agent, and Canidy's choice of flippant code names—among other unconventional acts—seemed only to reinforce that opinion.

Stevens, however, because his background was military and not diplomacy, understood Canidy's actions as an OSS operative and thus held a far higher opinion of him.

Bruce nodded. "The ones that Sikorski passed to us two days ago."

Stevens read the message:

TOP SECRET
OPERATIONAL IMMEDIATE

X STATION CHIEF
FILE
COPY NO. 1
OF 1 COPY ONLY

30MAY43 0730
TOP SECRET
FOR OSS LONDON
EYES ONLY COL BRUCE
FROM OSS BERN
BEGIN QUOTE

DAVID,

MY ABWEHR SOURCE CONFIRMS THAT THE SS IDENTITY CARDS LISTED IN YOUR MESSAGE OF 28MAY ARE IN FACT GENUINE.

THE SS-SCHARFUHRER BABYSITTERS, WHILE LEGIT, ARE OF COURSE SMALL FRY.

BUT SS-STURMBANNFUHRER KLAUS SCHWARTZ -- SS MEMBERSHIP NO. 3,154, NSDAP NO. 10,654 -- IS A VERY BIG FISH. WITH VERY BIG TEETH.

THIS IS ONE OF THOSE RARE APPROPRIATE TIMES ONE CAN INVOKE THAT NEW FIGURE OF SPEECH THAT IT DOES NOT TAKE A ROCKET SCIENTIST TO UNDERSTAND THE IMPORTANCE OF SCHWARTZ HAVING SERVED AS CHIEF

ASSISTANT TO SS-STURMBANNFUHRER WERNHER VON BRAUN -- SS MEMBERSHIP NO. 1,254 -- SINCE JANUARY 1943.

THEIR SS RANKS AND MEMBERSHIP NUMBERS ARE HONORIFIC, PERSONALLY MADE BY HIMMLER. AS A POINT OF REFERENCE, HITLER'S RIGHT HAND MAN, MARTIN BORMANN, HAS SS MEMBERSHIP NO. 555, ALSO HONORIFIC AND ASSIGNED BY HIMMLER.

SCHWARTZ, PRIOR TO JOINING VON BRAUN IN JANUARY, WAS HEAD OF RESEARCH AND DEVELOPMENT AT CHEMISCHE FABRIK FRANKFURT A.G. -- A MAJOR PRODUCER OF AGRICULTURAL CHEMICALS, PARTICULARLY PHOSPHATES FOR PESTICIDES -- FOR THREE YEARS.

CHEMISCHE FABRIK FRANKFURT IS OWNED BY RUHR VALLEY INDUSTRIALIST WOLFGANG KAPPLER, WHO I BECAME WELL ACQUAINTED WITH IN THE EARLY 1930S AT SULLIVAN AND CROMWELL BERLIN. I AM PRESENTLY TRYING THROUGH MY CHANNELS TO REACH KAPPLER TO GET HIS INSIGHTS ON SCHWARTZ. WHEN I KNOW SOMETHING, YOU WILL KNOW.

YOU DID NOT ASK, BUT AS TO SCHWARTZ'S PRESENT WHEREABOUTS, THEY ARE UNKNOWN. HE HAS GONE MISSING, OR AT LEAST NO ONE IS TALKING IF THEY DO KNOW WHERE HE IS. MY SOURCE WILL PROVIDE UPDATES AS AVAILABLE.

I MUST SAY YOU HAVE MY ATTENTION WITH THIS. CAN YOU TELL ME WHAT OUR INTEREST IS IN SCHWARTZ? YOUR LAST

MESSAGE WAS QUITE CRYPTIC, EVEN BY OUR HUMBLE OSS STANDARDS.

FONDLY,

ALLEN

END QUOTE

TOP SECRET

"You know that this," Stevens said, holding up the message, "is one of those instances where we provided the weapons and C-2 and—"

"I do know," Bruce interrupted, nodding.

"And not only to Sausagemaker," Stevens went on, "but to the Sikorski Tourists who smuggled it in as well."

"Yes. And it was through their pipeline that the SS identity papers were brought back here. And Sikorski fed them to us—after, I'm sure, making detailed copies for himself."

When Germany invaded Poland in September 1939, Sikorski and his troops escaped through Hungary and Romania while the Polish Navy sailed the Baltic Sea for Britain. The routes of escape were kept open for his men—who, in a respectful nod, called themselves Sikorski's Tourists—to go back in and support the resistance.

"That we're supplying them with as much as a stick of chewing gum is something Winant doesn't have the need to know," Bruce said. "I'm certainly not going to give him any information that he'd use to rub in Sikorski's face."

"How are you going to handle his request, then?"

"By adhering to something that Winant would appreciate, the unofficial maxim of the Corps Diplomatique."

"I'm confident I can make a reasonable stab at that, but I'll ask anyway: Which is?"

David Bruce said: "Quote *Take no action on absolutely anything today that can be reconsidered tomorrow—or next month* unquote."

Stevens nodded.

"Yeah, particularly with Winant, that would've been one of my first guesses," he said, then looked back at the message.

"The magnitude of this just gets worse by the moment," Stevens said after a moment.

"Unfortunately so. As Allen rather drily notes, you don't have to be a rocket scientist to connect von Braun's work with this Schwartz's."

Major Wernher von Braun was thirty-one years old, a darkly handsome German of aristocratic heritage. His mother traced her royal heritage to France's Philip III, England's Edward III, and Scotland's Robert III. In his finely tailored suits, von Braun looked more like a well-to-do corporate businessman than the absolutely brilliant scientist that he was.

It was well known that even before the war von Braun had been working on new technology involving rockets—including having discussions with Robert Goddard, the top American physicist—and that he now was making major advances for Adolf Hitler's Thousand-Year Reich.

The OSS—through Allen Dulles's source in the Abwehr, the German military intelligence service—had been told that one of von Braun's projects was running the manufacturing and testing facilities for a range of new, almost secret weapons of his design. The self-propelled flying bombs were being called "aerial torpedoes"—the latest of which were reported to be able to carry a ton of TNT-based high explosive for two hundred miles at more than three thousand miles per hour.

They were "almost secret" weapons because Nazi Propaganda Minister Joseph Goebbels already was threatening that the V-1 and V-2—*Vergeltungswaffe*, or retaliation weapon—would first target London, wiping it out as payback for the Allied bombings that were devastating German cities.

"Before Ike went back to AFHQ last week," Bruce said, referring to General Dwight D. Eisenhower, commander in chief at Allied Forces Headquarters, "he told Donovan and me that he was extremely concerned about the impact, if you will forgive the poor choice of words, of these new bombs."

"Goebbels is broadcasting that the attacks will begin this coming December," Stevens said.

Bruce shrugged.

"Let's say, for the sake of argument, that that time frame is pure propaganda at this point."

"But our intel tells us that the first, smaller version of these bombs is being tested."

The Fieseler Fi-103 had a thirty-foot-long sheet metal fuselage, wooden wings, and a new jet engine that pulsed fifty times a second, creating a buzz sound. The Luftwaffe had flown—and crashed—the first one under its own power in December 1942.

"And that's what worries Ike. He's afraid that London under siege—whether six months from now or early next year, which would be far worse—will severely interfere with the cross-channel invasion now set for May."

In 1942, then–Major General Eisenhower had written the plans for OPERATION ROUNDUP that he tried to get approved as the spring 1943 invasion of northern France. The British, however, wanted nothing to do with it. Prime Minister Winston Churchill favored attacking the Axis through the Mediterranean, what he called "Europe's soft underbelly." Now that that was happening—the Allies, having just captured North Africa, expected to have Sicily and Italy taken within a matter of months—additional plans were being hammered out for the invasion of France, this time at the coast of Normandy in spring 1944.

"Ike says keeping secret an operation on the massive scale that they're planning—they're building on his Roundup, mobilizing more than a million troops—is a challenge in and of itself. It follows, then, that the actual invasion would be impossible to ramp up and launch from England if London is being leveled at the same time."

Stevens nodded solemnly.

"Now," Bruce said, motioning toward the message, "getting back to Allen's point of connecting why Schwartz has been working for von Braun. Those agriculture fertilizers he mentioned use concentrated amounts of phosphoric acids—"

"As do incendiary bombs," Stevens interrupted.

"Exactly. And the same plant making chemicals for firebombs can make a high explosive like TNT. So call that Connect One."

David Bruce then tapped his finger on a manila file folder on his desk.

"And here's where it gets worse. I had Helene dig out this background on nerve gas that Professor Rossi put together before he left for the States," he said, referring to the University of Palermo scientist whom Dick Canidy recently had rescued from the SS in Sicily. "Rossi writes that thanks to a Herr Doktor Gerhard Schrader, who developed the industrial process for mass production of T-83, any facility capable of producing such chemicals can easily be converted to produce components for the nerve gas." He paused, then added, "Thousands of metric tons of it."

Tabun, code-named T-83, was colorless, mostly odorless, and, as far as chemists were concerned, relatively easy to make. It also was effective. It quickly attacked the central nervous system, causing intense convulsions, restricted breathing—and painful death.

"And thus the possible Connect Two," Stevens said, meeting Bruce's eyes as he handed back the sheet. Then, without thinking, he suddenly added, "Canidy called this."

David Bruce looked at Ed Stevens with a face of resignation.

"Canidy *suggested the possibility* when Donovan was here," Bruce clarified.

Stevens said: "What I recall he said was, 'It's possible, but is it probable?' "

Bruce looked at him for a long moment.

"Right. None of these bombs can be allowed to strike here, period, no matter what they might carry. Where is he, by the way?"

Captain Helene Dancy came in with a wooden tray that held a pot of coffee and four china mugs.

"Where's who?" she said as she put the tray on a table beside the couch.

"Canidy," Stevens and Bruce said almost simultaneously.

"Either on his way to see Stan Fine in Algiers," she said, reaching for the coffeepot, "or already there. Said he had unfinished business."

Stevens and Bruce exchanged glances.

"Ed here will pour us the coffee, Helene," Bruce then ordered, "while you go grab your message pad. We have an urgent for General Donovan."

[THREE]
OSS Algiers Station
Algiers, Algeria
0923 30 May 1943

"That lying sonofabitch!" Major Richard M. Canidy, United States Army Air Forces, who was a big-boned, six-foot-tall twenty-six-year-old with close-cropped dark hair and deeply intelligent dark eyes, said, angrily waving a decrypted secret message. "Why is he saying that the Nazis never had a yellow fever lab in Sicily? I saw the damn thing, Stan. I blew it up."

Canidy looked at Captain Stanley S. Fine, USAAF—a tall, ascetic thirty-five-year-old who had a thin, thoughtful face framed with horn-rimmed glasses—sitting across from him on the main balcony of La Villa de Vue de Mer. The "Sea View Villa," an 1880s French Colonial–style four-story mansion built high on the lush hillside, served as OSS Headquarters, Mediterranean Theatre of Operation.

The villa belonged to Pamela Dutton, the wealthy widow of one of Wild Bill Donovan's law school buddies. Wentworth Danfield Dutton had served in the United States legation to Algeria. Mrs. Dutton had made her own fortune in New York City importing Italian shoes for women. With Donovan's promise that the villa would be preserved and protected, she had let it to the Office of Strategic Services for the sum of ten dollars per annum.

Fine was wearing a U.S. Army tropical worsted uniform. Canidy—under his brown horsehide A-2 aviator's jacket with the gold leaves of a major pinned to its epaulets—had on a tan button-down shirt, brown woolen trousers, and calfskin chukka boots that he had pulled from the wardrobe in the master suite. It wasn't the first time he'd helped himself to the diplomat's clothing made at a local haberdashery—he'd done that for the missions to Sicily—and it wouldn't be the last.

Two piles of the typewritten messages were next to a dented stainless steel thermos on the massive Mediterranean teak table. Fine picked up the battered thermos.

"I know," he said, pouring rich aromatic Algerian coffee into one of Mrs. Dutton's fine china cups. "And that's not the first message to contradict what you did in Palermo."

Canidy shook his head as he looked out. The view was absolutely stunning. The capital city spread out below on a gentle slope that ended at the port some ten kilometers away. Beyond that, the vast Mediterranean Sea sparkled to the horizon. At anchor and moored at the docks in the circular harbor were military man-o'-wars flying the flags of the U.S. and England, and recently arrived American Liberty ships either off-loading their cargo or awaiting their turn to do so. Silver barrage balloons floated above the harbor, their steel cable tethers discouraging enemy aircraft from strafing the harbor and ships.

Major Canidy and Captain Fine each had an AGO card—a sealed identity card issued by the Adjutant General's Office—that stated they were members of the U.S. Army Air Forces. If anyone questioned their status, and checked military records, their names would be duly listed.

But of course both were attached to the OSS.

Fine, despite an appearance that some mistook as being possibly frail, was in fact absolutely fearless. And he efficiently accomplished his job—in and out of channels—using a creative ability that Canidy described as "beating back the rear-echelon bastards and their endless red tape and bureaucratic meddling."

Canidy would know. He, too, was expert at bending—and often

outright breaking—rules in order to get done what had to be done, damn those who got in the way.

Until being sent on the missions to Sicily, he had served as chief of OSS Whitbey House Station—commonly known to the agents training there as *Canidy's Throat Cutting and Bomb Throwing Academy*—which was an ancient, massive eighty-four-room stone structure on a twenty-six-thousand-acre country estate outside London. That position had made him the OSS's number three man in England, after the chief and deputy chief of OSS London Station.

For the missions in Sicily, however, Canidy had reported directly to OSS Washington, to Director William "Wild Bill" Donovan himself. He knew that that had not moved him up to number two in all of the OSS—but it damn sure put him pretty high in the pecking order.

Which in itself was a remarkable achievement. Because Canidy had not exactly been a willful recruit into the world of espionage.

Dick Canidy's dream had been to be a pilot, and he'd attended the Massachusetts Institute of Technology, paying his way with a Navy scholarship. He graduated in 1938, cum laude, with a bachelor of science degree in aeronautical engineering.

He wasn't particularly excited about having to pay back the Navy with four years of service. It was no secret he felt constrained by the military and its starchy rules and regulations. Still, he pledged that he would honor his obligation—but not serve a single second longer. Having accumulated, in addition to his MIT degree, a commercial pilot's license, an instrument ticket, and 350 hours of solo time, he already was entertaining job offers, one in particular from the Boeing Aircraft Company in Washington State.

After three years in the Navy—with barely a year left on his obligation before he could pack his bags for Seattle—Lieutenant (Junior Grade) Richard M. Canidy, USN, was at Naval Air Station Pensacola when he was approached by a grizzled man named General Claire Chennault.

It was June 1941, and Canidy, an instructor pilot in the backseat of single-engine bi-wing Kaydet trainers, was with fledgling naval aviators day after day flying a mind-numbing circuit around the skies of the Florida Panhandle and southern Alabama.

Chennault was a legendary general known not to mince words with his gravelly voice. In short order, he bluntly laid it out to Canidy that the United States could not stay out of the world war much longer, that when it did join in the fight there would be an enormous demand for aviators, that there was no way the military was going to let skilled pilots out of the service—and that he, Canidy, would then be front of the line, assigned to flying missions God only knew where.

But, the general told him, there was an option.

Chennault—with FDR's approval, if not discreet direct order—was pulling together a group of volunteer pilots, really good pilots. Their mission would be flying Curtiss P40-B fighters to defend the two-thousand-mile-long Burma Road that was the critical route for getting Western aid to China from Japanese attack.

The contract with the Chinese was for one year, Chennault explained, and monthly pay came in at six hundred dollars—twice what Canidy got from the Navy. As further incentive, the general added, Canidy would also pocket a five-hundred-dollar bonus for each Jap he shot down.

Canidy, always quick to take care of Number One first, signed up. He could not decide which was better—making more money or getting an honorable discharge from the Navy that came as part of the package.

Being a Flying Tiger with Chennault's American Volunteer Group (AVG) in Kunming, China, turned out to be damn dangerous. But Canidy rose to the challenge. And he proved that not only had he been born to fly but—with five kills on a single sortie, making him a certifiable ace—he was a natural fighter pilot.

About the time he was counting out his twenty-five-hundred-buck bonus, a self-important bureaucrat type showed up on the AVG flight line. His name was Eldon Baker, and he wasted no time showing that he was a consummate prick. But when he produced from his suit coat pocket his orders personally signed by the President of the United States, Canidy paid attention.

It was December 1941, and Baker announced that with America now in the war, he was there to recruit Canidy into an outfit so secretive that he couldn't tell him anything about it, only that it was important enough for the President to send him clear across the world to bring Canidy back.

That did not exactly convince Canidy to go along—for starters, he did not like the fact that he would be leaving his buddies alone to keep shooting Japs out of the sky.

He was, however, realistic enough to know that, no matter how good of a fighter pilot he was, odds were that eventually he'd meet his match—or that he'd screw up or that a Jap just got lucky, or all of that—and he'd be sent to meet his maker courtesy of a hundred-plus 7.7mm rounds from a Mitsubishi A5M machine gun. And, getting back to taking care of Number One, accepting the asshole Baker's offer would mean he would be another step closer to being done with his military service obligations.

He soon discovered he was dead damn wrong.

Back in Washington, D.C., Baker finally revealed to him that the outfit was something called the Office of the Coordinator of Information, and its director, a Colonel Donovan, was answerable only to Roosevelt himself. Baker said COI needed Canidy—and certain of his connections—to help smuggle out of North Africa a French mining engineer who the Germans also were after—an engineer who both sides knew was critical to the building of a nuclear bomb that would win the war.

When Canidy idly inquired as to what would happen if he now decided that he didn't want any part of the COI in general, and the mission in particular, Baker practically shoved the answer down his throat.

"You either agree to this 'mission of considerable risk,'" Baker coldly replied, "or, now that you're privy to information that's classified as Top Secret–Presidential, you could be institutionalized for 'psychiatric evaluation' for a period of time—habeas corpus having no bearing on the mentally disturbed being protected from themselves—which, in the interest of ensuring that our secrets stay secret, will last for at least the duration of the war."

Canidy was furious at himself for being caught in what he considered was little more than a high-level government con game. Yet intellectually he knew that what Baker said was more than a loosely veiled threat. He really had no option but to choose the mission—and then decided that, assuming he survived the damn thing, he could somehow figure a way to get the hell out of COI afterward.

Soon thereafter, Canidy was assigned the assimilated rank of a major in the United States Army Air Corps and given credentials that stated that. He also was given other credentials—ones to be used as a last resort—declaring that he worked for the Office of the Coordinator of Information, which carried a presidential priority.

Baker's "considerable risk," Canidy soon learned, was something of an understatement. The mission had required life-or-death decisions, ones that were cold and ruthless. And ones, somewhat surprising him at first, that he found himself perfectly capable of carrying out.

And Canidy then came to the realization that his experience in

COI was not unlike what he'd had in Chennault's AVG. Which was to say, Canidy not only rose to the challenge of being a spook, but was damn good at it.

Wild Bill Donovan also recognized that Canidy—having proven expert at espionage and sabotage, at the "strategic services" needed to win the war—was an extraordinarily natural operative. And over time, Canidy was given greater responsibility.

More missions included grabbing other engineers and scientists out of German hands, smuggling uraninite for those scientists to use in building the nuclear bomb in the President's Manhattan Project, modifying B-17 Flying Fortress bombers as explosive-filled drones, even getting involved with the head of the New York City Mafia, Charles "Lucky" Luciano, leading Canidy to discover that the Germans held weapons of chemical and biological warfare in Sicily.

Donovan was said to be of the opinion—one which Stanley Fine agreed with—that Canidy had become almost the perfect spy.

Almost, because Canidy had managed to put himself in a position that no spy was supposed to be in: absolutely indispensable.

Canidy handed the message back to Fine, then gestured toward the taller of the two stacks on the massive teak table.

"And all of those are from Tubes?" Canidy said.

"All from Tubes," Fine confirmed.

The first week of April, Canidy had set up in Palermo a clandestine OSS wireless telegraphy station, code-named MERCURY STATION. Its operator was twenty-four-year-old Jim "Tubes" Fuller.

"Well, at least all are from Mercury," Fine went on. "Those, and there are others in the commo room files, a couple of which state that the crates you found with the nerve gas never existed either."

"No shit?"

"No shit."

Fine held up the thermos toward Canidy, making a *more?* gesture with it. Canidy glanced at his cup, made a face when he saw that it was empty, and pushed it to him.

"This is insane," Canidy went on. "The station clearly is compromised. Because whoever is running it does not realize that Tubes would know that I was involved with destroying both. I just don't understand why they're denying that either was there in the first place."

Fine took a sip of coffee, then offered: "Damage control? The SS knows that it was blown up—maybe not that you did it but that it did get destroyed—so the lie becomes it never existed to try to make all of it secret again."

Canidy considered that for a long moment. Then his eyebrows shot up.

"And the reason to make it secret again," he said, "is because they brought more in? Nerve gas and/or yellow fever?"

Fine met his eyes, then slowly nodded.

"That is a real and distinct possibility," he said. "There is no doubt more Tabun—both stockpiled and being manufactured—and there certainly has been time for more shipments to arrive."

Canidy looked out across the Mediterranean Sea, in the direction of Sicily, and sighed audibly.

"Not fucking again!" he said.

[FOUR]

Almost two months earlier, on the moonless night of March 22, Canidy had smuggled Professor Arturo Rossi out of the Port of Palermo aboard a forty-foot wooden fishing boat, the *Stefania*. To suggest that Rossi—a metallurgist carrying a suitcase that contained no clothing but was instead packed with all his scientific papers from the university—was anxious to leave Sicily would have been akin to suggesting that the Pope might be a little bit devout.

Rossi was under no delusion as to what he could expect from the Nazis should he in some fashion disappoint them. He had seen one colleague executed by SS-Sturmbannführer Hans Müller of the SD and watched another die slowly and painfully in the SS's yellow fever experiment that Müller oversaw.

Canidy, with the *Stefania*'s engine idling and her lines already let loose, then learned from Rossi that the rusty ninety-foot-long cargo ship tied up alongside at the dock had arrived that morning with nerve gas munitions in her hold. Canidy made the split-second decision to sink the ship at its mooring, and had quickly rigged it with C-2 plastic explosive and a time-delay fuse.

When Wild Bill Donovan had read Canidy's after-action report, then met with President Franklin D. Roosevelt to relay the information that the Nazis had sent nerve gas munitions to Sicily, FDR became furious. He wanted absolute proof. And so, nine days after seeing the moonless sky glow with the flames of the burning cargo ship, Dick Canidy, at the direct order of the President of the United States, was headed back to Sicily, this time leading a three-man team.

Aboard the submarine *Casabianca*, Canidy had briefed his team that their main mission was to find out if nerve gas had indeed been on the boat that he'd blown up at the dock and, if so, what damage had been caused by it.

"We're supposed to get in, get the intel, and, if the place is nothing but rotting corpses, get the hell out."

But it turned out that there had not been mass casualties. Canidy's team found only two dead in the harbor area. Agents of the Sicherheitsdienst had tortured a pair of Sicilian fishermen—bashed out their teeth with the steel-plated butt of a Mauser Karabiner 98 and gouged out their eyes with its bayonet—and left them hanging from a yardarm.

The mission then became threefold: One, to find out what had happened to the nerve gas munitions. Two, to ensure that the villa with the yellow fever experiment had been destroyed. And three, to establish MERCURY STATION—a clandestine wireless telegraphy station—that would send intel to OSS Algiers for developing underground connections in Sicily and building a resistance that could rise up when the Allies arrived with OPERATION HUSKY.

It had been Stan Fine's idea to use Roman mythology for the mission's code names—"There's so much of it here, who would think twice about it?" Thus, they code-named the radio station after the messenger god, Mercury, and the submarine *Casabianca* after the god of the sea, Neptune. Dick Canidy became Jupiter (the supreme god of Italy and Rome), Jim "Tubes" Fuller was Maximus ("the greatest"), and Franciso Nola was Optimus ("the best").

Canidy had first met Franciso Nola—a solidly built thirty-five-year-old with an olive complexion, thick black hair cut close to the scalp, a rather large nose, and a black mustache—in New York City, where he'd fled with his family mostly because his wife was Jewish but also because his cousins had been imprisoned by Mussolini's secret police. A commercial fisherman, he still owned boats in Palermo that worked the Mediterranean waters. He not only offered Canidy the use of these but volunteered to personally help fight the fascists in any way he could.

It had been through Nola that they learned what happened with the howitzer rounds with the Tabun in Palermo. The warehouses that Nola's fishing boats used for his import-export business were overseen by a pair of dense longshoremen. When Canidy met the Brothers Buda—Giacomo and Antonio were in their early thirties, around five-five and two hundred pounds, with bad bowl haircuts and belly fat rolls that stretched tight their dirty overalls—he quietly nicknamed them Tweedle Fucking Dee and Dumb.

With some effort, the Budas explained that their crews had off-loaded wooden crates of what they called *"buh-lets,"* pallets of fuel, and field rations from the rusty ninety-foot-long cargo ship that Canidy had asked about—but of course had not said that he'd sunk with the plastic explosive.

Shortly thereafter, they said, two SS officers had arrived at the warehouse, had an argument with SS-Sturmbannführer Müller, and then Müller had ordered the Brothers Buda to make certain that the wooden crates of *buh-lets* with the painted stencil marking of SONDERKART.6LE.F.H.18 T83 10.5-CM would get loaded aboard another cargo ship that was en route.

When Canidy had read through his binoculars the stencil markings, he decided that the "10.5-CM" signified the crates contained 105mm howitzer rounds. He sent that information via wireless message to Professor Rossi at OSS Algiers. Rossi confirmed that they were howitzer rounds—and, more important, that the "T83" was the code for Tabun.

Having finally met the mission's main objective—finding conclusively that the Germans did have ready munitions for chemical warfare—Canidy made plans to destroy them. Then he blew up the villa where the SS was conducting the yellow fever experiments. And he announced to Frank Nola and Tubes Fuller that they would be staying behind and manning the clandestine MERCURY STATION.

That night, Dick Canidy had been back aboard the *Casabianca,* awaiting the cargo ship now carrying the Tabun howitzers, when Captain Jean L'Herminier dialed it in and gave the command to fire the torpedo that sent the nerve gas to the bottom of the sea.

And the next day, back at OSS Algiers Station, the first of the message traffic from MERCURY STATION began coming in regularly.

Including confirmation that the Germans were furious that the villa and cargo ship had been destroyed.

Stan Fine flipped through the taller stack of decrypted typewritten messages, found what he wanted, and handed it to Dick Canidy.

Canidy read it:

```
TOP SECRET                          X STATION CHIEF
OPERATIONAL IMMEDIATE                 FILE
                                    COPY NO. 1
                                    OF 1 COPY ONLY

26MAY43 0615
FOR OSS ALGIERS STATION
EYES ONLY CAPT FINE
FROM MERCURY STATION
BEGIN QUOTE

1. ITALIAN AND GERMAN FORCES ARRIVING PORT
OF MESSINA DAILY VIA FERRY FROM ITALY
MAINLAND.

ITALIANS -- ELEMENTS OF ITALIAN 6TH ARMY. EXPECT
TOTAL OF 250,000 TROOPS BY END OF MONTH.

GERMANS -- 2 PANZER DIVISIONS WITH 60,000 TROOPS
SPLIT BETWEEN PALERMO AND MESSINA. ANOTHER 4
DIVISIONS WITH 120,000 TROOPS SAID TO ARRIVE BY MID-
```

JUNE AND MOVE TOWARD SOUTH COAST. MESSINA BEGINNING TO LOOK LIKE IT COULD BE DOWNTOWN BERLIN.

SOURCE: OPTIMUS BOAT CREW

2. EVERY DAY 4 HEAVILY GUARDED TRAINS, WITH 25-30 CARS EACH, LOADED WITH MILITARY VEHICLES, TANKS, AND ACK-ACK GUNS LEAVE MESSINA AT 1700 GMT FOR CATANIA AND SYRACUSE, AND 1 TRAIN WITH SIMILAR CARS AND CARGO LEAVES EACH DAY AT 1900 GMT FOR PALERMO.

SOURCE: TRAINMASTER AT MESSINA

MAXIMUS
END QUOTE
TOP SECRET

"That's almost a half-million soldiers," Canidy said, handing back the message. "And a hundred and fifty railcars loaded with tanks and howitzers every day?"

Fine nodded.

Canidy thought for a moment, then said: "It's—what?—two miles across the Strait of Messina to the toe of Italy?"

"A little farther, but not quite three."

"And Sicily is the same time as here—"

"Same, GMT plus one," Fine supplied.

"—so that means they're moving the trains at night. Which would make them harder targets." Canidy paused, then said, his tone incredulous, "A *half-million* men? Those have to be exaggerated numbers. How the hell could Tubes possibly know that?" Then his tone turned sarcastic as he added, "Not from Frank Nola's brilliant boat captains."

"Well, those fishing boats do spend a lot of time in the various ports, and their crews have a lot of connections there—"

"Connections?" Canidy interrupted. "They're all practically related. Tweedle Fucking Dee and Dumb come immediately to mind."

"—But I agree the numbers are likely inflated. It makes perfect sense that the Germans would want us to believe they're putting more forces there, particularly after Mincemeat."

Canidy knew a number of minor *ruses de guerre* had been put in play in anticipation of the Sicily invasion, including British Field Marshal Sir Henry Wilson's army, based in Egypt, making movements that looked like preparations for its invasion of Greece and then the threat of advancing further to the Balkans.

But the biggest deception had been OPERATION MINCEMEAT.

In late April, "Major Martin"—a cadaver in a Royal Marines battledress uniform with a briefcase chained to him—had been set adrift from a British submarine just off "neutral" Spain. Secret and personal papers in the briefcase had been created at OSS Whitbey House Station to suggest the major was a courier en route from the United Kingdom to Allied Forces Headquarters when his aircraft crashed and he washed ashore. After the "most secret" papers—disinformation on the true plans for OPERATION HUSKY—fell into the hands of Spaniards sympathetic to Hitler, they were photographed by German agents and the copies sent up to the German High Command.

ULTRA—the code name given to intelligence that was taken from intercepts of secret messages encrypted by German Enigma cipher machines—quietly revealed every step along the way. Including that German intel personnel in Berlin then judged the content of the materials to be entirely credible.

"According to Ultra," Fine went on, "Hitler has just now—on May thirteenth—announced that he believes the Sicily invasion is a diversion, and that, as Major Martin's Top Secret papers said, Greece is next. Which of course was exactly what he feared, making the whole deception even more believable to him."

"Tell them what they want to hear," Canidy said.

"Right. So Hitler has demanded that 'measures regarding Sardinia and the Peloponnese take precedence over everything else.'"

He gestured at the shorter of the two piles of messages.

"There's traffic in there from the two Sandbox teams that we sent in to support the Greek resistance. As the Germans begin moving armored divisions by train to Greece, the teams will help the resistance in taking out bridges and rails to keep those divisions there—and far away from being able to reinforce Italy and Sicily."

Canidy pointed to the message from MERCURY STATION.

"It would not hurt to have another team go in to see if we can corroborate any of what's in that. And another team to save Tubes's ass. I left the poor bastard there. . . ."

Fine exchanged a long look with Canidy, then said, "Jim wanted to go operational. You know that, Dick."

"Yeah, I do. And he actually did a damn good job while I was there with him."

"And you do know that twice we sent in teams to try locating him and Nola, right?"

"*Twice?* What happened?"

"Each time Mercury Station went off the air. And when it finally returned, it was always with the excuse that Nola had had to go deep underground to evade the Italian secret police, and Tubes went along to keep the station from being detected. Then suddenly the station's back up and he's sending these detailed messages."

Canidy shook his head. "Assuming they are in fact under SS control, we're damn lucky the SS didn't set up a trap for those teams—lure them in to execute them."

ULTRA had revealed one of Adolf Hitler's secret orders, issued on October 18, 1942: *"All enemies on commando missions—in or out of uniform, with or without weapons, in battle or in flight—are to be slaughtered to the last man. Should it be found necessary to spare one or two for interrogation purposes, these men are to be shot immediately after interrogation."*

"Trust me," Fine said, "knowing that Hitler has ordered that all captured spies be executed, we were very cautious about that. That the teams were not ambushed suggests that the Germans value keeping Mercury Station on-air more."

"And if they'd either killed them or made them controlled, too, that would have sent the signal that Mercury Station was compromised."

Fine nodded.

After a moment, Canidy said: "Then Tubes really is being controlled."

Fine said: "John Craig van der Ploeg has been sending Tubes chickenfeed since that first suspicious message he showed you on April tenth."

While the SS was prone to execute captured enemy agents—something they readily did well before Hitler sent out the order to do so—they would spare those radio operators who agreed to transmit under control. Knowing this, Allied agents were trained to use a secret danger signal that let their case officer know they had been compromised—signing off, for instance, as "Will" instead of the usual "Bill." That allowed the transmission of factual but harmless intel—the so-called chickenfeed—to the agents to keep them alive until a rescue mission could be staged or Allied troops overran their position.

But even without the use of the secret danger signal, chickenfeed could prove effective.

Fine went on: "That was more than a month ago, and John Craig says in that time he's only become more convinced that Tubes hasn't independently worked the radio."

Canidy saw Fine's eyes look beyond him, past the pair of French doors that opened onto the balcony, which was off the main living area. He heard the sound of footsteps, and then felt the presence of someone standing behind him.

Canidy turned his head in time to hear John Craig van der Ploeg declare, "And I still am convinced of that."

[ONE]
Old City
Bern, Switzerland
2046 25 May 1943

"That skittish bastard gave us only a two-hour heads-up," the driver of the black taxicab—a somewhat battered 1938 Mercedes-Benz 260D—said to the passenger as he made the turn onto the cobblestones of Kramgasse. "This is our only chance to grab him. Don't screw it up, Eric."

"I won't if you won't," Eric Fulmar replied from the backseat. "Too bad Canidy isn't here. This is right up his alley."

Fulmar was twenty-four years old, blond and blue-eyed, and had a lithe build packing enormous energy and power.

With a slight squeal of brakes, the four-door sedan rolled to a stop one block shy of the medieval Zeitglocke clock tower.

The Zeitglocke—or "time bell," featuring a three-thousand-pound bronze bell struck by a gilded human-sized Chronos, the Greek personification of time—rose almost a dozen stories above the busy Kramgasse. Since the thirteenth century, the baroque-style landmark built of stone had served as a prison, a guard tower, and, now, with its fifteenth-century astronomical clock and nearby shops and coffeehouses, a city attraction popular with those trying to forget a world war threatened their neutral country. That black-out rules were in effect, and the street mostly dark, did not exactly help in that regard.

As the Mercedes's idling diesel engine rattled, Eric Fulmar pulled a Colt Model 1911A .45 ACP pistol from the right pocket of his dark gray woolen overcoat.

The driver—Geoff Sanderson, who was thirty years old, of average build and soft facial features—did not jump or otherwise immediately react when he heard the metallic sound of the semiautomatic's slide pulled back on its spring and then released to slam forward. He was more than accustomed to the sound of a round being chambered. He had done the same with his own .45—which he had on the seat beside him, concealed under a hat—a half hour earlier at the OSS safe house just across the River Aare.

"You're just now remembering to do that?" Sanderson said sharply.

"Better late than never," Fulmar replied matter-of-factly as his thumb clicked down the lever that locked the hammer in its cocked position.

"If you'd thought of it sooner, you'd have had time to feed the magazine another round," Sanderson said, and smugly added, "Like I did."

Fulmar grunted as he slipped the pistol back in his overcoat pocket.

"Unlike you," he said, "I tend to hit what I shoot at with my first shot—*if* I have to shoot."

He then reached inside his left sleeve and pulled from the scabbard strapped under his forearm a Fairbairn-Sykes, a black doubled-edged dagger. He touched the tip of the slender five-and-a-half-inch-long blade to the back of the driver's neck, added light pressure, and said, "Usually this is all I need."

Their eyes met in the rearview mirror.

This time it was Sanderson who grunted.

He then grinned and said, "I thought I taught you never to bring a knife to a gunfight."

Fulmar grinned back. He knew they both subscribed to what was taught in Canidy's Throat Cutting and Bomb Throwing Academy at OSS Whitbey House Station: *If you're close enough to stab them, you're damn sure close enough to shoot them.*

"Besides," Sanderson went on, "you know that orders are not to use either unless absolutely necessary—we want this bastard alive."

Then Sanderson's eyes suddenly darted to the windshield. It took some effort to make out details down the dark, crowded street, but he could see just enough. Then he glanced at his wristwatch, then back out the windshield.

"It's five of nine," Sanderson said. "Almost time. Can you see the tall guy, the silver-haired one with the gray homburg? He's at two o'clock, in front of the café."

Fulmar, carefully sliding his Fairbairn back into its sheath, looked down the block.

Kramgasse was wide and lined on both sides with ancient four-story stone buildings. As was common in Old City Bern, above the street-level shops and restaurants were three stories of apartments. He saw couples and clusters of small groups up and down the street and gathered around the Zeitglocke tower at the far end of Kramgasse.

And standing just outside a shadow of the Zeitglocke was the tall man with the homburg.

The hat was not resting on his head but instead cradled under his left arm. He slowly and meticulously ate an ice cream cone that was in his right hand.

"How the hell can I miss him?" Fulmar said. "Fritz, right? What is he, six-four and two-forty?"

"Yeah, something like that. And to repeat myself, when Fritz turns the hat so that its crown is against his coat it means—"

"I know, I know," Fulmar put in, "it means that he's ID'd our mark, the Sparrow, carrying two white Sprüngli candy bags."

He glanced down at one such paper bag with thin rope handles that was beside him.

"—And if he moves the hat from his left arm to his right?"

"That's the abort signal."

"Yeah. He's spotted someone we can't afford getting involved with."

Switzerland was surrounded by vast territory under Axis control. And with Adolf Hitler wanting to grind his boot heel on its neck, the Swiss were not going to give the belligerent Nazi leader any excuse to even attempt an invasion. Thus, it was the job of the Swiss foreign police—Fremdenpolizei—to keep an eye on those who might violate Switzerland's neutrality.

Their job was without end—the country was infested with spies of all stripes, particularly the German Abwehr's Kriegsorganisation—War Organization—but also the SS's Gestapo, and of course agents from the Office of Strategic Services and England's Special Operations Executive (SOE) and Secret Intelligence Service (SIS, known as MI-6). The vast majority operated with either a diplomatic or commercial cover.

Sanderson went on: "Fritz said this place is crawling with Kraut spies and that Dulles's contacts have ID'd at least fifteen hundred."

Fulmar grunted. "Yeah, it's called the German Fucking Embassy. And I bet Dulles has tried turning all of them."

Sanderson chuckled.

Allen Welsh Dulles, carrying credentials of a diplomat with the United States Legation to Switzerland, was OSS deputy director for Europe.

Sanderson glanced at his wristwatch, then looked over his shoulder. "Two minutes. Be careful, buddy."

Fulmar picked up a soft leather briefcase—one packed with $10,000 in mixed currencies, all counterfeit but $500 in U.S. ten-dollar bills—and the white Sprüngli confectionery bag that was next to it.

"Jawohl, mein Führer!" Fulmar said drily in flawless German, then nodded and continued in equally flawless English: "Don't worry about me. Just make sure you guys grab the bastard after the exchange. See you back at the safe house."

He reached for the door handle, worked it, and swung open the door with a creak of its hinges. A cold gust blew in, and as he stepped out he turned up his woolen coat collar against the wind.

Geoff Sanderson watched as Eric Fulmar more or less casually made his way down Kramgasse. The briefcase and the white Sprüngli confectionery bag Fulmar carried in his left hand. His right hand was in his overcoat pocket, gripping his .45.

A minute later, as Fulmar passed some twenty feet in front of Fritz, Fritz moved his ice cream to his left hand, then used his right hand to turn the homburg so that its crown touched his chest.

Sanderson caught the signal and quickly scanned the crowd as he put the Mercedes in gear. It took him a moment but—*There! Coming out from beneath the tower!*—he first saw the two white bags and then the contact—a man who looked to be in his late thirties and oddly resembled his code name.

The Sparrow had a bony face with beady eyes and a beak of a nose. He had short legs—he stood maybe five-two—and was thin, almost sickly-looking.

The Sparrow stopped, put the bags at his feet, then pulled out a cigarette and lit it. He nervously exhaled as he surveyed the crowd around him. He then noticed a tall blond man approaching with a leather briefcase and a Sprüngli confectionery bag—and immediately looked in the opposite direction.

Sanderson then watched as Fulmar stopped and asked the Sparrow for a cigarette. Then, Sanderson knew, they exchanged their code messages: "I don't know which is a worse habit, the actual smoking or always asking for a free smoke," answered with "Everything must have its price, including chocolate."

Sanderson let out on the clutch and slowly rolled toward the men.

He scanned the crowd for anyone who might be taking unusual interest in Fulmar and the Sparrow, noticed none, then watched as Fulmar placed his leather briefcase and confectionery bag beside where the Sparrow had put his two.

The Sparrow produced a cigarette and, after passing it and then lighting it for Fulmar, exchanged nods, reached down to the bags—and grabbed the handle of only the leather case. He turned and tried to casually walk away, but it was clear that he was motioning nervously with his cigarette as he went.

Sanderson watched Fulmar, his lit cigarette hanging from his lips, smoothly scoop up the three Sprüngli confectionery bags in his left hand, then quickly disappear in the crowd at the foot of the Zeitglocke.

At almost the same time, Sanderson saw Fritz put the homburg on his head and carefully track the Sparrow as he walked up Kramgasse in their direction.

Sanderson maneuvered the Mercedes so that the vehicle would be positioned directly in front of Fritz, with the Sparrow, walking at a good clip, soon to be between them.

As the Sparrow nervously scanned the crowd, then the taxi, and then the crowd again, two men in heavy dark clothing and hats suddenly converged on him from behind. One man held at his hip what appeared to be a snub-nosed revolver.

"Oh, shit!" Sanderson said aloud, then saw the gun raised and aimed at the Sparrow's back.

Sanderson began hammering the taxi's horn as he reached for the .45 on the seat beside him. Fritz saw what was happening and pulled out his pistol as he moved quickly toward the Sparrow's attackers.

It was too late.

Sanderson saw the revolver's muzzle flash at the same time that the gilded Chronos's heavy hammer struck the ton-and-a-half bronze bell at the stroke of nine.

The resonating loud ring startled some in the crowd. They jumped, then applauded. The bell's ring completely masked the sound of the pistol shot. There was only the muzzle flash, and then the Sparrow stumbled forward, dropping the leather case as he went.

Sanderson raised his .45—but immediately knew that neither he nor Fritz could fire without the chance of them hitting each other.

Again Chronos struck his bell. And again there was a muzzle flash from the attacker's revolver.

As Sanderson jumped from the taxi, the gunman snatched the briefcase and tossed it to his partner. The two men in dark clothing then separated and disappeared into the quickly panicking crowd.

Sanderson and Fritz reached where the Sparrow lay on the cobblestones.

"Get the back door open!" Sanderson ordered, then bent over and grabbed the Sparrow.

He picked up the small limp body and threw him in the backseat, on the cab's floorboard.

Chronos hit his bell.

And there then came the wail of sirens in the distance.

Fritz jumped in the front passenger seat and slammed the door shut as Sanderson ran around the car and got back behind the wheel.

"Shit, shit, shit!" Sanderson said as he ground the Mercedes into gear and then raced down the cobblestone street.

And again Chronos struck his bell.

After accelerating heavily for two blocks, Sanderson slowed the battered taxicab to a more normal speed. The police sirens grew louder, and in the next block he saw emergency lights approaching, becoming brighter as they flashed off the walls of the buildings ahead.

"Shit!" he said again.

He spun the steering wheel and pulled into an alley, killing the cab's masked headlights as he entered. He stopped the car and kept an eye on his rearview mirror. A moment later, the police cars sped past, their flashing lights momentarily illuminating the alley and filling his mirror.

"Close," Fritz said, looking at him.

"Yeah, too close." He motioned toward the backseat floorboard. "Can you check on him?"

Fritz reached down and put a finger on the Sparrow's neck. After feeling he had a slight pulse, he put the back of his hand in front of the Sparrow's nose and mouth.

"Still with us," Fritz announced, "but barely."

"Damn it!"

They sat in silence for a few minutes, and once sirens could barely be heard, Sanderson put the Mercedes in gear, hit the headlights, and drove out of the alley.

They wound their way to Aarstrasse, followed that street along the river to the next traffic circle, went through that, and crossed the River Aare on the Dalmazibrücke.

Not ten minutes later, after winding down the heavily treed Schwellenmattstrasse, the taxi pulled up to the massive wrought-iron gate of an ancient masonry-walled estate. Sanderson killed the headlights. The diesel engine rattled on in the dark.

About to tap the horn, he muttered, "Where the hell is he?"

Then a sentry in a long black overcoat appeared from the shadows just beyond the gate. Despite the heavy overcoat, Sanderson could tell that the guard carried a weapon—a Thompson Model 1928A1 submachine gun—concealed underneath.

The sentry walked up to the driver's window and looked in as the window came down.

"Open the goddamn gate!" Sanderson flared. "What are you waiting for?"

Jesus! he thought. *It's always easiest to assign guard duty to those who really aren't bright enough for more difficult work—but then you're stuck having dimwits with weapons guarding the goddamn gates.*

The sentry almost immediately recognized Sanderson—if not

his voice and tone—then trotted to the gate and swung it open inward.

The diesel motor revved, and the Mercedes passed through into a courtyard.

There were two heavy wooden garage doors, and the left one then began to move upward. When it was more than halfway open, Geoff Sanderson saw that the man who was opening it was Eric Fulmar. Beyond him, at the back of the garage, was his BMW motorcycle. And resting on its seat was a single white Sprüngli confectionery bag.

That hadn't surprised him.

But after the wooden door had been completely opened, and Sanderson had moved the Mercedes inside, the interior light gave him a better look at Fulmar.

What the hell?

Why is he covered in blood?

"What the hell happened to you?" Sanderson said as he got out of the car.

"Someone thought they wanted the bag more than I did," Fulmar said with a shrug, then looked at Fritz stepping out of the car and added: "They were wrong. Had to use my knife after all."

[TWO]
OSS Algiers Station
Algiers, Algeria
1003 30 May 1943

"Nice to see you again, Major Canidy!" John Craig van der Ploeg announced, his tone upbeat, as he walked up to the table with a handful of decrypted messages.

"You, too," Dick Canidy said, "but how many damn times do I have to tell you not to call me 'major' or 'sir'? I'll throw you off this balcony if you even think of saluting."

"Yes, si—" van der Ploeg began automatically before catching himself. He absently looked at the sheets of newly decrypted messages he held. "Right."

Van der Ploeg was eighteen, with a youthful energy about him. He had olive skin and an unruly shock of wiry jet-black hair that stuck out at odd angles. He easily could pass as Sicilian—which was what Canidy was looking for in a team member for the second mission that ultimately set up MERCURY STATION—but even better for Canidy was the fact that van der Ploeg was a master at operating the SSTR-1 wireless telegraphy (W/T) set.

He'd readily accepted Canidy's offer to join the mission—but when he showed up dockside at the Port of Algiers and saw the submarine that would be taking the team to Sicily, he admitted that he suffered from acute claustrophobia.

"A train, a plane, a ship—anything with windows I can do," he had said with great resignation, his youthful energy clearly shot. "No one will be happy with me if I board that sub."

With the *Casabianca* ready to sail, postponing the mission was not an option. That had forced Canidy to recruit one of the radio operators from the commo room at the Sea View Villa.

Twenty-four-year-old Jim Fuller was another master at W/T. Before the war, he and John Craig van der Ploeg had learned Morse code in the Boy Scouts and now had become fast friends as they practiced sending coded messages back and forth. The tall and easygoing Fuller, with shaggy blond hair and all-American features, looked and talked like the Californian that he was. He even had a surfer nickname—"Tubes"—which he earned at age ten from riding under the curl of the wave, where it formed a tube.

In early April, Canidy had been sitting in the same seat at the teak table on the balcony reading messages from MERCURY STATION when van der Ploeg came from the commo room and handed him another message that he'd just decrypted. In it, Tubes said that Nola wanted OSS Algiers to send weapons for them to stockpile and more money for bribes. Canidy responded by saying to send whatever they said . . . until van der Ploeg announced that he did not believe Tubes actually had sent the message.

"That's not his hand," he'd explained. "It's Mercury Station's radio frequency, but whoever is operating the W/T has all the finesse of a ham-fisted gorilla. Tubes is silky smooth."

That Tubes had not sent the code for a compromised station only made it appear more suspicious.

"Have a seat," Dick Canidy said to John Craig van der Ploeg, motioning to the chair nearest Stan Fine's. "You should hear for your general wealth of knowledge what I was just telling Captain Fine."

As John Craig van der Ploeg took his seat, he said, "What's that?"

"That what the SS is up to in Poland is every bit as vicious as what I found them doing with the yellow fever experiment in Palermo," Canidy said, then looked back at Fine. "Torture, slavery, slaughter—same as I saw in Sicily. It all boggles the mind. Even as you begin to comprehend what is happening, you are in denial. You can't believe that humans—supposedly civilized man—could treat another with such cruelty."

"And that's in Sicily?" John Craig asked.

"On a smaller scale than Poland, but yes, it's there," Canidy said, then added, "You haven't heard any of this?"

"Read, yes," John Craig said. "As I sent and received the messages about what the SS did to those Mafia prisoners, I tried reading between the lines . . . and wondered. But heard? Not directly from you."

Canidy raised his eyebrows as he took a sip of coffee, then nodded.

"The inside of that old villa they were using for the yellow fever experiment was a cesspool," he began. "The rancid smell of rotting flesh made you sick to your stomach. The men, their bodies bruised and disfigured, were on wooden gurneys. Leather straps secured their wrists and ankles. Dirty gray sweat- and bloodstained gowns more or less covered their torsos. Their arms and legs—with festering wounds oozing dark fluids—were exposed. The bodies all had rashes. The dead ones were bloated."

Canidy looked over the lip of his cup at Fine, and added, "It really was hellish—something out of Dante's *Inferno*. Knowing that the SS does this, I don't know how Francisco and Mordechaj control their rage as much as they do—"

"Who is Mordechaj?" John Craig asked.

"—because if that were happening in my country," Canidy finished, ignoring the interruption, "and I had a family, nothing could hold me back from getting my pound of flesh out of the bastards."

Fine—who was Jewish and did have a wife and three children waiting for him in Santa Monica, California—drained his coffee, then nodded appreciatively as he put the empty cup on the table.

"Trust me," Fine said, an edge to his voice, "that thought has crossed my mind more than a time or two." He paused, then in a more pleasant tone said: "And speaking of family, how is Ann?"

Canidy shrugged. "If she had her way we would be a family right now. I told her that this was not the time to get married. She kept a stiff upper lip, as our Brit cousins would say, but she's not overly happy with me right now."

Twenty-year-old Ann Chambers—a highly intelligent gorgeous blond southerner whose father's empire included nine major newspapers and more than twice that many radio stations—and her girlfriend had been injured in March when Luftwaffe bombs leveled Ann's London neighborhood. The friend had died from head trauma. Ann had suffered amnesia, and she and Canidy had only recently been reunited after Ann was found sixty miles north of London, in a barn that had been converted into a makeshift infirmary.

"I actually meant her health," Fine said.

"She seems fully recovered," Canidy said. "Operative word *seems*. The doctors have told her to take it easy for now. With her flat destroyed and housing tight, we're grateful to you that she could sublet the studio's apartment. She is very comfortable there, and starting to write again for her old man's news service."

Continental Motion Picture Studios quietly maintained a luxurious penthouse apartment in Westminster Tower, which overlooked Hyde Park, and was two blocks from the Dorchester Hotel. When Brandon Chambers heard that doctors said his daughter needed time to recover, cost for her room and board was not a consideration.

"It must have been hell wondering about her," Fine said. "I'm glad you know she's now comfortable."

Canidy clearly remembered the gut-wrenching feeling he'd had when he first saw Ann's flat leveled, and then the overwhelming emotions in Sicily when Tubes Fuller had handed him the message from Stan Fine announcing that Ann had been found—and was safe at OSS Whitbey House Station.

The helplessness I felt at Ann gone missing because of those goddamn German bombs came close to a simmering rage.

The thought of losing someone you deeply love triggers emotions more powerful than I ever imagined.

And then to think how the Nazis so savagely treat prisoners . . .

"Getting back to the goddamn Krauts," Canidy then added, "I saw more compassion, more respect for life and death when they took all of us in Saint Paul's lower school to the slaughterhouse to show us where hamburgers really came from."

Fine knew all about Saint Paul's. It was there that he had first crossed paths with Dick Canidy.

Stanley S. Fine had been a very young Hollywood lawyer—the vice president, legal, of Continental Motion Picture Studios, Inc. His responsibilities included keeping secret from the general public that "America's Sweetheart"—Continental's virginal movie star Monica Carlisle, born Mary Elizabeth Chernick—had not only been married to a German aristocrat and soon thereafter divorced, but that the union had produced a son by the name of Eric Fulmar.

After Eric's father returned to Germany, his mother had decided that Eric was the last thing she needed in her Hollywood lifestyle. She ordered Fine to ship her son to boarding school.

The headmaster of Saint Paul's School, Cedar Springs, Iowa, was one George Crater Canidy, Ph.D, D.D. It was said of the Reverend Canidy, a widower, that he wasn't simply devoted to the Episcopal school—he and Saint Paul's essentially were one and indivisible.

Reverend Canidy had a son about the age of Eric. Dick Canidy and Eric Fulmar quickly became buddies—and almost immediately seemed to be in constant mischief. Or worse.

Once, on the annual fall nature walk, Dick and Eric were horsing around, shooting wooden kitchen matches from toy pistols that were supposed to shoot suction-cup darts. The matches set a leaf pile on fire—and the Studebaker parked next to it went up in roaring flames.

Fine had had to rush to Cedar Rapids. He bought the owner of the destroyed automobile a new one. That calmed everyone, and freed the boys from the clutches of a fat lady at the Juvenile Authority. Even more important, it kept the whole escapade out of the newspapers.

Some six months later, just barely released from school probation, Eric and Dick were allowed—after repeated warnings of what would happen if there was anything but golden behavior—to join a field trip to the Iowa Cattlemen's slaughterhouse.

Reverend Canidy had not been at all thrilled with the idea of this particular educational activity, especially its gore, of course, which he considered beyond grisly. But he was an educated man, and knew that even the Bible depicted the gruesome sacrifices of animals. He also understood that young teenage boys should not be coddled, and finally gave his reluctant approval to the biology teacher who with great enthusiasm had offered to run the field trip.

The boys had indeed been fascinated with the facility, including the actual processing of the cattle, which the biology teacher had pointed out was conducted as humanely as possible. And with the exception of someone having unlatched a holding pen gate and a score of cows having to be herded back in—fingers were pointed, but Dick and Eric dodged all accusations—there had been no real trouble on the field trip.

The only problem had come that night in the school dining hall. By unfortunate coincidence the main dinner course served to students in both the upper and lower schools was spaghetti with a pulpy red tomato and meat sauce.

When Dick, and then Eric, covered their mouths and moaned a long and deep *Mooooo!*—and that got picked up by the older boys, who made it echo in the dining hall—many of the younger boys, their plates untouched, went to bed hungry that night. A couple, having rushed to the restroom when their faces went white, fell asleep with completely empty stomachs.

For the next week, Reverend Canidy saw to it that the chefs left red meat off all menus.

"Who is Mordechaj?" John Craig van der Ploeg repeated.

"Kapitan Mordechaj Szerynski," Canidy said, looking between van der Ploeg and Fine. "Code name Sausagemaker. He's a resistance leader in the Polish Home Army. Lost most of his family—including his teenage brother, who the SS dismembered last Christmas—in the Warsaw ghetto. Before I came here from OSS London, I helped with the team that was working with him. Ever hear of Sikorski's Tourists?"

John Craig shook his head.

"The prime minister of the Government of Poland in Exile is a general—a real warrior—by the name of Wladyslaw Sikorski. When Poland was invaded by Germany in '39, Sikorski fled with his army and navy to regroup. Now the ones who go back and forth to Poland supplying the resistance—with supplies provided by the OSS—call themselves Sikorski's Tourists. They, like the Poles trapped in Poland, revere him. He really is one tough sonofabitch."

John Craig nodded.

"Dick, what do you think are the real chances for the Poles?" Fine said.

Canidy sighed, then shrugged.

"Hell if I know, Stan. In the big picture, I just don't think anyone gives a rat's ass about liberating Poland right now." He waved with his coffee cup uphill, in the direction of Allied Forces Headquarters. "Not with all of AFHQ's effort going into the biggest picture—taking Sicily and Italy and, ultimately, Normandy."

Fine shook his head. "It's been more than five months since the Polish foreign minister gave those details on the concentration camps—and has anything really been done?"

"Done about what?" John Craig van der Ploeg said.

"Count Edward Raczynski," Canidy said, "gave a speech—'The Mass Extermination of Jews in German Occupied Poland'—to the United Nations. The SS runs concentration camps that work the stronger prisoners to death—the rest they send directly to death camps. There're at least a half-dozen camps in Poland alone. I think I brought one of the booklets that a London publisher reprinted with the speech. You should read it for your edification."

Canidy paused, drained his coffee, then added: "The nasty truth is that the Poles are really being screwed. Especially considering it's our Bolshevik buddies taking turns with the Krauts to exterminate every Pole they can when the two aren't bitterly fighting each other and snatching up parts of Poland for their own."

"The Katyn Massacre?" Fine said, making the question more of a statement.

"That's one nice example," Canidy said, his tone bitter. "Our so-called Ally."

"The mass murder of all those Poles," John Craig said. "I heard about that. The Russians really did it, huh?"

Just the previous month, in mid-April, Radio Berlin announced to the world that the Germans had discovered the mass graves of more than twenty thousand Polish intellectuals—army officers, businessmen, priests, and other leaders—executed in the Katyn Forest area of the Soviet Union, territory that Nazi forces had taken. The dates on papers found in the pockets of the dead ended a year earlier, in April 1940—which had been after the Soviet invasion of

Poland and after Joseph Stalin's signing of an order for the execution of the entire Polish Officer Corps.

Reich Minister Joseph Goebbels, relishing the high propaganda value of the horror, declared to the world that what had come to be called the Katyn Massacre was proof that the USSR—and by association its Allies, especially the Americans and the British—were mass murderers.

"Red Joe," Fine said, "took offense at the accusation that the blood is on Soviet hands. He's 'outraged,' and has unequivocally denied any connection whatsoever. It's so blatantly a lie you'd expect him to profess not even knowing a Katyn Forest exists."

Canidy shook his head, disgusted.

"And getting back to all the slaughtering by the Germans," he said. "The evidence is overwhelming. That's bad enough, but now we know there is the threat of them using chemical or germ weapons on the battlefield. While Kappler, the SS-obersturmbannführer in Messina, said that he was ordered to stage the howitzer rounds with the Tabun only as insurance, that hothead SS major in Palermo—the same prick who was running the yellow fever experiment that came from Dachau—*Müller*, that's the sonofabitch's name—he found the gas and had to have plans to use it."

"Fortunately you took it out first," Fine said.

Canidy met Fine's eyes, then went on: "Here's the nice scenario I mentioned to Donovan in London: We know the Germans are testing the Fi-103—those Fieseler 'aerial torpedoes'—and plan to lob them at London. What's to stop another hothead SS sonofabitch like Müller from thinking that with the SS already using gas in the death camps—as Poland's foreign minister unequivocally outlined before the United Nations—and already having it on howitzer rounds, what's the difference with putting the nerve gas on an aerial torpedo and aiming it at, oh, say, Number Ten and Westminster . . . ?"

Prime Minister Winston Churchill was using the annex at 10 Downing Street as his residence. The Palace of Westminster, England's equivalent of the United States Capitol, housed its Parliament.

Canidy added: "I'd be really surprised that that *hasn't* been considered, starting with that sonofabitch Hitler himself."

"Even if the bombs didn't hit directly on target," Fine said, "the scenario is . . ." His voice trailed off as he considered the ramifications. "*Horrific* comes to mind."

Canidy nodded. "It could—it *would*—bring Britain to its knees."

John Craig van der Ploeg's eyes grew wide.

Even John Craig gets the gravity of that, Canidy thought.

He motioned again uphill.

"And then what would the big guns do?"

Fine knew that by "big guns" Canidy meant the full effect of General Dwight David Eisenhower, commander in chief, Allied Forces Headquarters. At AFHQ (pronounced "aff-kew") Ike, with his second in command, General Sir Harold Alexander, had under him nearly five hundred thousand soldiers, sailors, and airmen of the U.S. Seventh Army and the British Eighth Army.

The AFHQ brass had taken over the luxurious Saint George Hotel, which was uphill from the OSS's headquarters. The Saint George was very much like the Sea View Villa, built in the same style in the 1880s, but twice the size and with a brilliant white masonry exterior (Pamela Dutton had her villa painted a faint pink). It was surrounded by well-kept gardens and neat rows of towering palm trees. Its impeccable interior featured grand gilded ceilings and walls adorned by thousands of multicolored hand-painted tiles. If it weren't for all the "guests" wearing military uniforms, it would take some convincing that there actually was a war going on.

The overflow of officers from the Saint George—particularly all the brass's aides—filled a score of nearby buildings. It would have taken the Sea View Villa had Stanley Fine not played the OSS's Presidential Priority card and told one of Ike's flunkies, a pompous ass by the name of Lieutenant Colonel J. Warren Owen, to go to hell.

That the OSS technically reported to the chairman of the Joint Chiefs of Staff—and that Top Secret–Presidential did not directly apply to protect OSS Algiers Station—was something Owen either did not comprehend, or was too afraid—"More like too lazy," Canidy suggested—to confirm with JCS.

The big guns were of course the conventional forces. What the spies, saboteurs, and assassins of the Office of Strategic Services did was anything but conventional. Their unorthodox methods were held in contempt—leaving the OSS to more or less operate all on its own.

Eisenhower only recently had become a cautious believer in the OSS after being impressed with intel from Corsica—an Axis-occupied French island in the upper Mediterranean Sea—that he had not expected.

The OSS's first covert team inside enemy-occupied Europe had established a clandestine radio station, code-named PEARL HARBOR, on the island, and on December 25, 1942, began sending almost daily messages to OSS Algiers Station. Among other things, PEARL HARBOR reported that only twenty-five thousand Italians—and almost no Germans—had taken Corsica and done so with relative ease. The Vichy government, in true French fashion, had ordered its two army battalions on the island not to resist. After waving a white flag of surrender, the battalions were demobilized and their general put under house arrest. Then the Italians, with their limited strength, concentrated their resources on only the west and east coasts, leaving most of the island undefended.

Fine had told Canidy that it had taken some effort, but he'd finally gotten past Lieutenant Colonel J. Warren Owen to personally deliver PEARL HARBOR intel to Ike on a regular basis. Fine insisted on the hand delivery because he did not want anyone else taking credit for it—or, worse, later saying it had been "misplaced" when it in fact had been thrown away in a hotel garbage can.

"Ike likes what I'm feeding him," Fine told Canidy, "but he still wants to keep us on a short leash. With the next ops about to launch, he's anxious about what we and the SOE are up to."

"Speaking of whom," Canidy said. "I'm guessing we still have the same joyful relationship with our spook cousins."

Fine found himself chuckling. He then cleared his throat.

"Sorry," he said. "The last thing I should be doing is laughing. If you asked them, they would look you square in the face and say, 'Everything is bloody brilliant. We're all in this together, old chap!' But the fact of the situation is that it has not improved—and is damn laughable."

Wild Bill Donovan had worked closely with British intelligence—particularly a navy officer by the name of Commander Ian Fleming—when he began forming what eventually would become the Office of Strategic Services. Donovan understood that the Brits were more than mere veterans at the tradecraft of espionage—they arguably were the masters. It certainly didn't hurt that their Secret Intelligence Service had been formed in the sixteenth century.

In 1940, Winston Churchill had spun off the SIS's Section D, what it called its clandestine arm, to help create the Special Operations Executive. The prime minister ordered the SOE to set Axis-occupied Europe "ablaze" with guerrilla warfare.

Donovan had patterned—some said shamelessly stolen—a great deal of the unconventional warfare tactics for the OSS's Special Operations after the SOE, specifically its Research and Development Station IX.

When asked why, Donovan shot back: "Because *they* know what they're doing!"

From the first day that Stan Fine had arrived at OSS Algiers Station, the understanding had been that, in the spirit of Allied Forces cooperation, the OSS agents would train with the SOE agents at the SOE's "finishing school" at Club des Pins. The onetime swank beach resort had telegraphy and cryptography and jump schools, plus courses in the use of plastic explosives to blow up bridges, railroads, et cetera.

It made perfect sense in theory; both were honing the same skills of irregular warfare, and of course both were fighting for the same side.

In reality, inter-service rivalry reared its ugly head.

Fine went on: "As you'll recall, more and more of our guys were being turned away. And then I was told that due to a rush of incoming new SOE agents, there would be no room at all for my men."

"'Thank you very much, and don't let the doorknob hit you in the ass on the way out,'" Canidy said bitterly.

"That pretty much was the message."

"Thank God you started the Sandbox."

The Sandbox was the code name for a deserted Catholic school that was inside a high-walled compound at Dellys, about sixty kilometers to the east. Dellys was sort of a miniature Algiers—really not much more than a very big village—with its own port and ancient casbah. Fine had taken over the school and other property in and near Dellys to create an OSS Operational Techniques School. It had all the training classes that the SOE had at its Club des Pins, plus a half-dozen fishing boats and another dozen rubber boats that they used for putting agents ashore. There also were C-47 "Gooney Bird" aircraft for the agents to practice parachuting.

Fine grinned. "Actually, after you went out there in March and taught that ad hoc course on how the Germans run their Abwehr, we brought in some of the training material you had at Whitbey House. So they're now referring to the Sandbox as the Dick Canidy MTO Throat Cutting and Bomb Throwing Academy. It's everything the Brits have—and, even better, we have complete and total access to it. We wait for no one."

Canidy nodded. "And we damn sure shouldn't. I've had it with the OSS being treated as the redheaded stepchild of this war—by our so-called Allies and by our own military."

He sighed.

"Fuck it. You know what they say: Don't worry about things you can't control. Deal with what you can."

"Getting back to Ike," Fine said. "Every time I take him new intel, he makes a point to remind me of his order that none of our agents are to go into Sicily for fear we will blow Operation Husky."

Canidy grunted.

"Never mind that we have gone in—what?—four times," he said. "That I have twice—*and* destroyed nerve gas that could have been used against us. I don't guess Ike gave the OSS an *Attaboy!* pat on the back for that."

Fine shook his head. "Don't hold your breath waiting for that to come—even if we had told AFHQ about that."

"AFHQ was never told?"

He thought that over as he sipped his coffee.

"Well, I guess that makes sense. Ike's people repeatedly told us that there was no indication that the Krauts had the gas in the first place. So, why would that asshole Owen and Company want to believe us when we say that (a) not only did it exist, but (b) we took it out?"

"And, Dick, Owen would loathe being proven wrong. Which, frankly, would've been next to impossible for us to do without any physical evidence."

"Oh, there's evidence all right. It just happens to be a thousand meters down on the ocean floor."

Fine added: "It just wasn't a battle worth fighting."

"If Ike doesn't want us in Sicily, what are you telling him about Tubes and Mercury Station?"

Fine, stone-faced, looked at Canidy and said, "About who?"

After a moment, Canidy made a face that he understood, then said: "Change of subject: Have they come up with a D-day for Husky?"

"Which D-day?"

"There's more than one? How can that be?"

"Right now, it's next Wednesday."

"Next Wednesday?" Canidy repeated, his tone incredulous.

Fine grinned and looked at John Craig van der Ploeg.

"Tell him, son."

"You've heard," John Craig began, "that 'Three can keep a secret—' "

" 'If two of them are dead,' " Canidy finished. "You probably learned that in my Throat Cutting and Bomb Throwing course."

John Craig nodded. "As a matter of fact, I did. I also learned that Benjamin Franklin—who knew a thing or two about spying, having been part of the Secret Committee created by the Second Continental Congress in 1775—actually said it first."

"Impressive," Canidy said drily. "And this little bit of trivia of yours has what bearing on D-day?"

"Well," John Craig said, "the minute those proverbial three people hear the date for D-day, word spreads. To throw off the enemy, AFHQ is assigning at least four days as Husky's D-day. The first one is Wednesday of next week. It's what's called 'disinformation.' "

"I know what the hell disinformation is," Canidy snapped. "As I'm sure you've been seeding that disinformation in your messages that we assume are being intercepted by our eager enemies. And the closer we get to Wednesday, the heavier your message traffic will become to give the illusion of a pending invasion."

John Craig nodded. "You have no idea. Our commo room is really busy. We've also been spreading rumors around Algiers that that's the date. With any luck the Krauts will man their guns next Wednesday awaiting a beach assault—and be met with only another lovely Mediterranean sunrise. Then we'll repeat all that with the next date that AFHQ gives us. With more luck, they'll think the date for the real D-day is just more disinformation and not show up."

Canidy grunted. "Don't hold your breath that that will happen."

"Dick," Stan Fine then said, "you didn't hear it from me: It's early July. No hard date yet."

"We're invading Sicily in six, seven weeks?"

Fine nodded.

"What about Corkscrew?" Canidy said. "It has to be right about now."

The primary objective of OPERATION CORKSCREW was the destruction of Pantelleria's airfields and radar installations considered a threat to the invasion of Sicily. Pantelleria, a thirty-two-square-mile island that was thirty miles east of Tunisia and sixty miles southwest of Sicily, had a normal population of about three thousand. Italian soldiers had quadrupled that.

CORKSCREW's secondary objective was to gauge just how many bombs would be required to take the island—information that could then be used in the plans for taking Sicily.

"The heavy pounding starts Wednesday of next week," Fine said.

"No shit? Or is that another bogus date?"

"It's actual," Fine said.

John Craig offered: "That makes the other disinformation not seem intentional. They will think they just misread or misinterpreted what we sent. Right date, wrong island."

Canidy looked at John Craig.

"Believe it or not, I do know how that works," Canidy said, then sighed. "Jesus! All this changes everything with Mercury Station."

[THREE]
Aboard the *Sequoia*
On the Potomac River near Mount Vernon, Virginia
1703 30 May 1943

"You might want to check your line there, General," the President of the United States said casually to the director of the Office of Strategic Services, gesturing with his silver-tipped cigarette holder at the fishing rod that had just barely flexed.

It was a warm, cloudless spring afternoon. William Joseph Donovan and Franklin Delano Roosevelt, sipping gin and tonic cocktails from squat fine crystal glasses, were seated in heavily varnished mahogany fishing chairs on the stern of the 104-foot-long *Sequoia*. The wooden motor vessel recently had been replaced as the Presidential Yacht by the 165-foot all-steel U.S.S. *Potomac* and passed to the secretary of the Navy on the condition that FDR, as he did now, could on occasion borrow her to conduct quiet meetings.

"For fishing expeditions," FDR had explained to Navy Secretary Frank Knox, adding with a conspiratorial grin, "maybe even ones that actually involve a rod and reel."

The *Sequoia*—running on only one of her twin diesel engines in order to slowly troll the fishing lures—made her way upriver after having cruised down to where the Potomac River flowed into Chesapeake Bay.

The sixty-one-year-old President, looking gaunt and a little tired, wore a long-sleeved white shirt, its cuffs rolled up to his elbows, and khakis, both starched but well wrinkled. A wide-brimmed floppy canvas hat shielded his pale face and scalp from the sun.

Roosevelt held up his glass in the direction of Mount Vernon, now visible on the southern bank.

"A toast to our first commander in chief," the present commander in chief announced, "and spymaster. I trust you're aware that George Washington set up the Continental Army's first intelligence command."

Donovan, a stocky, ruddy-faced, silver-haired Irishman of sixty, was similarly clothed but with a dark blue button-down shirt and no hat.

He smiled and raised his glass toward Washington's estate and said, "Indeed. Knowlton's Rangers, in 1776. Here's to General Washington, who declared, 'The necessity of procuring good intelligence is apparent and need not be further urged.' "

Not lost on Donovan was the connection that Roosevelt was making between FDR and George Washington.

Two years earlier, FDR had asked Donovan to take leave of his successful New York City law firm and become head of the United States' new intelligence organization. It had the innocuous name of the Office of Coordinator of Information, but the Top Secret COI was anything but innocent or harmless.

As its spy chief, Donovan had been a civilian using the title of "colonel," which he'd been in the First World War. But two months ago, in late March 1943, FDR had given Donovan his new commission. COI had become the Office of Strategic Services, and its director was now Brigadier General William Joseph Donovan, USA, a rank more appropriate for America's spymaster.

Roosevelt, whose long history with Donovan dated back to their days as classmates at Columbia Law School, knew that "Wild Bill" was one helluva soldier. The rare kind of leader who men faithfully followed without question. That had been proven without question on the battlefields of France in World War One. Donovan had been with the "Fighting 69th," the National Guard regiment from New York City.

In one particularly bloody engagement, Donovan, his troops taking great casualties and himself badly wounded by machine-gun fire, continually had exposed himself to enemy bullets as he moved among his men. He reorganized the battered platoons, then led them in assault after assault on the enemy. Refusing to be evacuated for his wounds, Donovan continued fighting until confident that his men could withdraw to a less exposed position.

That had earned him the Medal of Honor—America's highest award for valor.

Despite their many differences—FDR was the product of moneyed privilege, while scrappy Donovan's wealth was self-made—Roosevelt recognized that he and Wild Bill shared more than a few qualities, chief among them being tough, intelligent, shrewd sons-ofbitches.

This wasn't lost on Donovan, either, but being a tough, intelligent, shrewd sonofabitch, he understood that their relationship, based on genuine mutual respect, was far more professional than an actual close friendship. While they did call themselves pals, Donovan knew that FDR used people—indeed was an unapologetic Machiavellian who took great pleasure in quietly playing people against one another—and was careful not to confuse FDR's attention as anything more than FDR working to get what FDR wanted.

And what FDR always wanted—whether for professional or personal reasons, or both—was solid, truthful information.

In 1920, Roosevelt, then serving as assistant secretary of the Navy, attached Wild Bill to the Office of Naval Intelligence and sent him to collect intelligence in Siberia. Donovan, long the world traveler as he managed the interests of his law firm's international clients, found that he enjoyed being FDR's envoy.

Wild Bill had found a new calling—and Roosevelt had found a source he could trust.

In his first term as President, FDR sent Donovan to get him the facts on Italian dictator Benito Mussolini's invasion of Ethiopia. (Donovan reported back that the helpless Africans were being slaughtered in the one-sided "war.") And then, in 1940, Donovan was sent by FDR to do the same as another charismatic European leader—this one the chancellor of Germany—was spreading the evil of Fascism.

Adolf Hitler threatened all of Europe—and, Roosevelt feared, maybe beyond.

After a quick trip to England to answer FDR's question—"Can our cousins beat back that bastard Hitler?"—Donovan said the British could not take on the Nazis alone, but for the present they should be able to protect themselves—if aided by the United States.

That wasn't the good news that Roosevelt wanted to hear. But then that was why he had sent Donovan: to get the facts and deliver them unadulterated.

Roosevelt immediately sent Donovan on a longer trip to gather intelligence in the Mediterranean and the Baltics. Three months later, Donovan's report found FDR, now in his third term as President, calculating how a neutral America could help stop the spreading of Fascism and Communism.

He knew only one thing for sure: It would be anything but easy.

FDR solemnly believed in the oath of defending the Constitution and laws of the United States of America against all enemies, foreign and domestic. Yet in order to protect the U.S.—as well as effectively deal with America's isolationists who vehemently opposed the U.S. getting involved in another world war—he needed not just more intelligence but more solid intelligence.

He was up to his ears in the former. It came from the vast U.S. government agencies—starting with the Federal Bureau of Investigation and its director, the relentless J. Edgar Hoover—set up to collect exactly that. But when combined with intel provided by others, such as the Office of Naval Intelligence and the Military Intelligence Division, a perfectly clear picture rarely came into focus.

The reason for this was because of each organization's first priority: self-preservation. Intelligence provided to the President, they deeply believed, should always shine a favorable light on the agency and, conversely, should never ever make said agency look bad. And the way to do that was to provide the President with what he wanted to hear—thus making the agency appear brilliant—and squash anything that didn't.

Franklin Delano Roosevelt, who from time to time admitted having an ego, thought it remotely possible that he might, key word *might*, suffer some failing—but being a naive fool certainly wasn't one. He understood what was going on, and what he needed, and who could get it for him.

Thus, in July of 1941, using his presidential emergency unvouchered funds, he created the secret new office of Coordinator of Information, and named Wild Bill Donovan its chief. He then quietly announced to the heads of the various intelligence agencies that Donovan's office would collect all national security information from them, analyze it, and deliver his findings directly to the President.

In FDR's mind, this of course would be just as Donovan had done since FDR, as assistant secretary of the Navy, had sent him around the world to serve as his eyes and ears.

The heads of the various intelligence agencies, however, were of a different mind. Put mildly, they were less than pleased. Turf battles reached a fevered pitch. And Donovan found his COI more or less shunned.

After almost a year, FDR relented to the argument of the Joint Chiefs of Staff that highly sensitive military intelligence should not be evaluated by an organization outside the military. The President ordered that the COI become the Office of Strategic Services, complete with the ability to collect its own intel, and that Donovan report to General George Catlett Marshall, chairman of the JCS.

Now it was Wild Bill Donovan who made the expected noises to demonstrate his displeasure. But no more than necessary. Because, being a tough, intelligent, shrewd sonofabitch, he was well aware that his relationship with another tough, intelligent, shrewd sonofabitch really had not changed.

He would always have direct access to the President.

[FOUR]

Roosevelt watched as the tip of Donovan's bamboo fishing rod flexed once more, then the line began screaming off its bulky reel.

Donovan quickly put his cocktail glass on the teak deck and pulled the rod butt from its holder.

"Told you," FDR said with a chuckle, then in a mischievous tone added: "You never listen to me, Bill."

"Please accept my sincere apology, Mr. President, sir," Donovan said drily.

As he raised his rod, both men looked out behind the boat. Some fifty yards back they saw a silver flash at the end of the line—and a large fish broke the surface of the Potomac.

"Looks like it might be the nicest striper yet," the President said with a smile, then bit down on the cigarette holder at the corner of his mouth and began reeling in his line to keep it from getting tangled with Donovan's.

They had been trolling for almost two hours, and in that time both had hooked plenty of fish. Iced down in the cooler that had been hauled below to the galley, where the chef was preparing dinner, were eight nice-sized striped bass, each weighing between fifteen and twenty pounds. FDR had caught five, Donovan three.

Donovan, however, had hooked two other fish. Both had broken off—one in a spectacular display of defiance complete with great leaps and shakes of its head to throw the lure free—and the President was not going to let it be forgotten.

FDR glanced over, and needled him: "Seeing how big it is, if you can actually boat it, I'll allow it to count as two—"

Just as he said that, the huge fish shook its head and threw the lure.

Donovan sighed. He looked at FDR, shrugged, then leaned back in his mahogany fishing chair. He returned the rod butt to its holder, retrieved his cocktail, and took a healthy sip.

Roosevelt, letting line on his reel unspool in order to reposition his lure, then casually said, "Any further word about your loose cannon's actions in Sicily?"

Donovan knew that he was referring to Dick Canidy, and was about to snap: *We've had this conversation, Frank, and he's not a loose cannon!*

But then he saw out of the corner of his eye that Roosevelt, watching his lure get smaller in the distance, was smiling. And he remembered that, when Donovan had defended Canidy as someone who more times than not got things done no matter the obstacles, FDR had replied that he'd heard others call Donovan *his* loose cannon, and felt the name was as unfair to Donovan as it was to Canidy.

Donovan believed that the OSS's successes came from what he called a "calculated recklessness." He preached—and personally practiced—not being afraid to make mistakes, because the OSS had to be unafraid of trying things that had not been tried before.

And Donovan believed that what Canidy had done on the Nazi-occupied island was a perfect example of what defined an OSS operator—secretly going behind enemy lines to smuggle out a Sicilian scientist, then finding that the Nazis had chemical and biological weapons of warfare there, and more or less single-handedly destroying them. All without feeling obligated to go up the chain of command, asking permission to do so—permission that, if not immediately denied, would be delayed for future (fill in the blank) "discussion," "research," et cetera, et cetera, until the window of opportunity to act was slammed shut.

"What happened with the nerve gas?" FDR pursued.

"I talked with Canidy in London," Donovan began, ignoring the loose cannon comment. "This gets a little complicated—"

"Then talk slowly," FDR interrupted. "I'll try to keep up when I'm not catching your fish."

Donovan couldn't help but chuckle.

"Thank you, Mr. President. I do appreciate your magnanimity."

He paused to gather his thoughts, then went on: "Okay, let me back up and bring in Allen Dulles. Among his many sources in Switzerland is a vice counsel of the German consulate in Zurich. That's his cover—he's actually working for Admiral Canaris in the Abwehr."

"He's a German intelligence officer posing as a diplomat?"

"Yes, at least as far as they want the Gestapo—and anyone else paying attention—to believe. What they don't want anyone to discover is what Tiny really is—"

"Tiny?" Roosevelt interrupted again.

"That's what Dulles calls Canaris's agent behind his back, which apparently is enormous. Tiny is a giant of a man."

"Does he have a real name?"

Donovan pretended not to hear the question, and instead said: "What Tiny really is, is a pipeline to those in Hitler's High Command who believe the war is all but lost. Wilhelm Canaris is one, and posted him in Switzerland to reach out to the Allies. He went first to the Brits, but they dismissed him as untrustworthy, mostly due to him having been in the Gestapo. Then he approached Dulles, who cautiously took a chance. And it's paid off. He fed us intel on von Braun. . . ."

He paused to see if Roosevelt recognized the name.

"The scientist who Hitler has building those self-powered bombs," FDR said.

". . . Wernher Magnus Maximilian von Braun," Donovan confirmed. "*Baron* von Braun is brilliant. He's building what they're calling 'aerial torpedoes'—flying bombs with pulse-jet engines and rockets fueled by alcohol and liquid oxygen—the ones that Goebbels is screaming will wipe out London as soon as this December. The intel says that von Braun also is a major player on the team that is developing jet engines for the Luftwaffe's fighters. And because of the von Braun connection, we have been told that both projects are being carried out at the same site. That may or may not be the case, but regardless, we have yet to pinpoint any facility."

Roosevelt puffed on his cigarette, exhaled, then said, "Churchill, while he'd never admit to it, is practically soiling his tartan shorts over London being attacked. If it's only propaganda, then it's damn effective."

"I'm afraid it's more than propaganda. Hitler is mad as hell and wants nothing more than to do to London what our bombs are doing to German cities. Especially if that can lead to the breaking of the Brits."

FDR grunted. "A flying bomb suddenly blowing up in London—"

"*Bombs* plural, Frank," Donovan interrupted. "Potentially hundreds at once. We know that these new aerial torpedoes are being tested. And, if the numbers are accurate, then they are capable of covering two hundred miles in under fifteen minutes. Which means they could launch from France and strike Big Ben—or anywhere in London; Canidy suggested Number Ten as a target—before anyone could begin to respond. And even if there was time, it's practically impossible to intercept something going more than three thousand miles an hour."

Roosevelt, ignoring the informality, nodded and said, "Three *thousand* miles an hour? Is that credible?"

"Call it half that, a third that. The fact is the self-propelled bombs—whatever their speed—are being developed. And each one is said to be able to carry a ton of TNT."

"Now, that would indeed strike terror," FDR said, then was quiet as he pulled on his fishing pole, seemingly checking his lure.

Donovan went on: "There is another possibility with these aerial torpedoes that hasn't been mentioned."

"Another?" FDR turned. "What?"

"Canidy found in Sicily, you'll recall, that one method of delivering the Tabun was with a howitzer round—"

"You're suggesting," FDR interrupted, "that that bastard Hitler now plans to put nerve gas in those flying torpedoes?"

When Donovan reported to Roosevelt that Canidy had discovered not only that the Germans had the capability to fire Tabun in 105mm shells from light field howitzers, causing death on a massive scale, but also that the SS continued a germ warfare experiment with yellow fever that had begun in the Dachau concentration camp, FDR had been furious.

Roosevelt adamantly did not want to fight a war using such cruel weapons. But he was prepared, as he'd threatened the Axis, "to retaliate in kind" should the enemy violate the Geneva Protocol that prohibited their use. To that end the President had ordered the U.S. Army to secretly produce tons of chemical warfare munitions at arsenals in Colorado and Arkansas, then stockpile them in secret locations.

"What I'm saying," Donovan went on, "is that Canidy brought that up as a 'what if' when we spoke in London. As he said, 'It's possible, but is it probable?'"

Roosevelt took a long puff on his cigarette, then exhaled audibly.

"And *that* really would scare hell out of Churchill. And everyone else. But especially Winston. You know what he said . . ."

He met Donovan's eyes.

Donovan said: "That if the Germans use it he would 'in a moment float Berlin away on a cloud of mustard gas.'"

"And we'd have a helluva time stopping him from doing so," FDR said.

"I'm not sure he'd have the opportunity to do so," Donovan said bluntly, "not if London suddenly is leveled and its population dying from nerve gas."

Roosevelt raised his right eyebrow, then said, "Good point. I'm surprised this was not discussed more during Churchill's visit." He paused, then added, his tone thickly sarcastic, "You don't think that

that was intentional on the Honorable Prime Minister's part—that he didn't want us to know what he might be doing about it?"

British Prime Minister Winston Churchill had left Washington two days earlier, after having met with FDR for the Trident planning conference that covered the next strategic moves against Italy and Germany. Churchill now was en route to Algiers to meet with General Eisenhower.

"That certainly cannot be dismissed," Donovan said. "Our cousins, while professing to be our equals in this war, conveniently keep a lot of things to themselves."

"I've noticed," FDR said drily.

"Whatever the case, it has to do with 'the Prof.' He has told Churchill that 'it's absolutely utterly impossible' for anyone—and certainly not the Germans—to have developed such bombs. And because Churchill knows Professor Lindemann's almost maniacal hatred of Hitler is unmatched, and that he would not underestimate the Nazis, Churchill believes him unquestionably. Therefore he doesn't address it."

The fifty-seven-year-old Frederick Lindemann, First Viscount Cherwell, was personal assistant to the prime minister. The highly opinionated physicist wielded an extraordinary influence as the chief adviser on all matters scientific.

"What I do know," Donovan went on, "is that when David Bruce and I spoke with Ike in London, he shared his fear that if any of these new bombs hit there we can forget about any chance of staging the cross-channel invasion. Ike tried to go into France with Operation Roundup, but Churchill would have nothing to do with it because of War One—specifically the memory of sixty thousand Brits dead on the first day of the Somme Offensive still painfully fresh. I know that you are aware that that's why Churchill pushed instead for this Italian Campaign, for the 'soft underbelly.' . . ."

Donovan looked for a long moment at FDR, until the President met his eyes and nodded.

"Frank, without Normandy we very likely could be facing the turning point in the war. Especially if Hitler bombs London and—"

"Damn it, Bill!" FDR interrupted, poking at him with his cigarette holder. "Don't you go and start sounding like Joe Kennedy, too! This is not what I wanted to hear. . . ."

"You know that I'm not a goddamn defeatist, Frank. I agree with Ike; I know we can win this war. We have to win this war. And I'm telling you the truth about what you need to know, not what I think you want to hear. You'll recall that that was why you said you put me in this job."

FDR, silently staring off into the distance, puffed on his cigarette until it burned down to the holder. He turned back to Donovan and met his eyes.

"Do whatever necessary to stop those flying bombs, Bill. Keep Canidy on it—sounds like the perfect job for a loose cannon—and anyone else . . . *everyone* else."

Donovan nodded. "As to the rockets, we've already been in contact with Professor Goddard—"

"The famous physicist? That Goddard?" He gestured toward the east. "Isn't he over in Annapolis?"

"That's the one. Robert H. Goddard. He has a lab in Annapolis, where he's doing research for the Navy. Before the war, von Braun contacted Goddard, whose scientific papers he admired, to discuss the concepts of the building of rockets. Goddard has nothing but praise for von Braun—for his great ability as a scientist, that is."

The President grunted, then took a sip of his cocktail.

"I started by asking about Sicily," the President said. "Get back to that."

Donovan said: "I know I'm probably repeating myself here, but in short, after Canidy blew up the yellow fever lab, he made sure that the cargo ship transporting the Tabun was destroyed. Specifically, it was sunk by torpedo."

FDR nodded.

Donovan added: "There has been no known fallout from either event."

"What I really want to know," Roosevelt then said, gesturing *give me more* with his hand, "is what do we know about *why* the Tabun was in Sicily?"

Donovan said: "What we know comes from two sources. One, from Canidy, whose connections in Palermo had access to the SS office there. And, two, from the Abwehr, from Admiral Canaris's agent Tiny, who told us that SS-Obersturmbannführer Oskar Kappler, the number two SS man in Messina, knew about all the SS operations on Sicily, including the secret plans for chemical and biological weapons. Their information was the same: that the gas was never meant to be used offensively. It was staged only for insurance."

"Who exactly is this Kappler? Can his word be trusted?"

Donovan nodded again.

"We have no reason to doubt it. Kappler comes from a wealthy Ruhr Valley family with a lot to lose. Among other companies they own, Kappler Industrie GmbH is the chief provider of coke and other key engine-building materials to Mann and Daimler-Benz. His father, Wolfgang, was a business associate of Fritz Thyssen—"

"I know Thyssen," Roosevelt interrupted. "He's the steel industrialist."

"Right."

"Years ago he approached my cousin Teddy with a business deal in South America—you know how much time Teddy spent in that part of the world. Thyssen had—*still has*—companies all over, which turned out to be smart planning considering that Hitler nationalized his German companies, especially his steel plants in Ruhr. That was after Thyssen soured on Hitler's vision of a Thousand-Year Reich and fled the country with his family. Teddy said that, despite the mistake of supporting Hitler early on, he was a decent man."

"Well, it all ties in," Donovan went on, "because Canaris also is tight with Wolffy Kappler. I would say that Kappler wants his businesses operating again during peacetime—as well as ending the destruction of the Fatherland—and would be willing to help Canaris and his group take out Hitler to accomplish that. And, failing that, to help Canaris land on his feet after the Thousand-Year Reich collapses. Before the war, Thyssen had been seen with Wolffy Kappler inspecting the industrial docks at Buenos Aires."

"Is that so? Now, that's interesting. Argentina was one of the countries Teddy said was involved in Thyssen's business offer."

"That would not surprise me; there is a lot of interest in quote neutral unquote Argentina. But getting back to the Tabun. SS-Obersturmbannführer Kappler had no intention of allowing the gas munitions to be used—and hid them—because, we believe, he doesn't want the war to become any worse—he, too, believes it's all but over—and because he's making plans to get the hell out of Dodge."

"Explaining his father being sighted in Argentina."

"Exactly."

"Let's just hope that's the case with all the other stockpiles of Tabun."

"We can try and find out," Donovan said.

"Do it. You're one of the few I can tell, Bill, that that gas scares the hell out of me. Even the gas we're stockpiling. One mistake and . . ."

Donovan nodded solemnly.

"We're already working on it, Mr. President."

"Okay, now what is it you said you wanted to tell me about Poland?"

Donovan reached into his shirt pocket and pulled out two folded sheets. He unfolded them, then handed them to FDR.

"You can see for yourself."

The President looked at it and began reading:

TOP SECRET

30MAY43 1000

FOR OSS WASHINGTON

EYES ONLY GEN DONOVAN

FROM OSS LONDON

BEGIN QUOTE

OUR SOURCE SAYS SAUSAGEMAKER AND TEAM SPENT FOUR DAYS RECONNING AREA AND FACILITY NEAR BLIZNA. CONSTRUCTION OF CONCENTRATION CAMP -- WHICH APPEARS ALMOST HALF COMPLETE -- IS OVERSEEN BY ELEMENTS OF SS USING FORCED LABOR. THESE PRISONERS, DIVERTED FROM SS-RUN CONCENTRATION CAMPS, ARE STARVED AND WORKED TO THEIR DEATH. BOXCARS BRING NEW PRISONERS EVERY OTHER DAY.

SAUSAGEMAKER'S TEAM STAGED A NIGHTTIME AMBUSH TRYING TO RESCUE A TRAINLOAD OF INCOMING PRISONERS.

BUT THE TRAIN THEY ATTACKED TURNED OUT TO BE A VIP TRAIN WITH ONLY A SINGLE LUXURY CAR. ITS PASSENGERS WERE AN SS-STURMBANNFUHRER AND HIS THREE SS BODYGUARDS. ALL NOW DEAD. SS-STURMBANNFUHRER SWALLOWED SUICIDE PILL.

WE ARE HAVING IDENTITY CARDS CHECKED BY TINY AT OSS BERN. WILL SEND FOLLOW-UP MESSAGE WHEN ID CARDS ARE CONFIRMED.

SAUSAGEMAKER TORCHED TRAIN WITH DEAD SS ABOARD THEN BLEW UP TRAIN TRACK. TEAM LAYING LOW TO AVOID ANY SS PAYBACK.

BRUCE
END QUOTE
TOP SECRET

Roosevelt looked up from the message, took a gulp of his gin and tonic, then said, "Jesus Christ! Another concentration camp? Is there no end to the heinous crimes these goddamn Krauts commit?"

Donovan shook his head.

"Who is Sausagemaker?" FDR said.

"He's a Pole—explaining where Canidy came up with his code name—a young man of twenty-two or -three. And he's in the Polish Home Army, leading the resistance in southern Poland. He barely escaped the Nazi slaughter in the Warsaw ghetto uprising. The rest of his family wasn't so fortunate."

"What is the significance of this SS officer?"

"Other than the obvious—that he was in some capacity in

charge of the new camp the SS is building in southern Poland—we don't know yet."

"The sabotage of the track should help, no?"

"A little. Depending on the damage, the Germans have been able to make repairs in as little as four hours."

"Then what is it that you want to do?"

"More sabotage. A helluva lot more. We're already supplying some of General Sikorski's guerrillas. I want to give them the means to take out these camps and the trains supplying them. The Germans are building more death camps because all the others are at capacity." He paused, then added, "Frank, it's become a logistical problem for Hitler. His SS simply cannot 'cleanse' fast enough. And the killings have only gotten worse since Count Raczynski spoke to the United Nations."

The President shook his head in disgust.

"How the hell can I say no to that? Do it, Bill. But with this caveat: keep our fingerprints off it. I fear that if Hitler gets the idea we are targeting these camps—as opposed to it being just guerrillas—he will make an extra effort to kill those poor people faster. Just as happened after Raczynski's UN speech."

"Understood. Done."

Roosevelt then looked down, turned to the second message, and began reading:

```
TOP SECRET

29MAY43 1750
FOR OSS WASHINGTON
EYES ONLY GEN DONOVAN
FROM OSS BERN
```

BEGIN QUOTE

1. NAMES OF REDS ACQUIRED FROM THE SPARROW SAID TO HAVE INFILTRATED THE NEW MEXICO SANDBOX ARE BEING INVESTIGATED THROUGH TINY'S SOURCES.

2. TINY SAYS THAT YOUR BOSS'S DECLARATION OF ONLY AN UNCONDITIONAL SURRENDER LEAVES NO ROOM TO NEGOTIATE WITH THOSE WHO COULD BE IN CHARGE OF TAKING OUT HITLER.

DULLES

END QUOTE

TOP SECRET

Roosevelt poked his index finger at the sheet.

"What the hell!" the President blurted. "Does that say what I think it does? 'Reds' in 'New Mexico sandbox'?"

"We are checking it out. But, yes, Allen says our Russian friends have spies in the Manhattan Project."

Donovan noticed that the President seemed to stiffen at the suggestion of his Top Secret–Presidential project not being absolutely secret.

The OSS was deeply invested in the MANHATTAN PROJECT, FDR's race to build the atomic bomb before Nazi Germany developed its own. A number of highly distinguished scientists—many Jewish, such as Albert Einstein and Niels Bohr—had fled the horrors of Nazi Europe. In a letter signed by Einstein and sent to Roosevelt in August 1939, they convinced the President that they believed that the scientific community could soon discover how to create the world's most powerful weapon—one producing the explosive equivalent of twenty thousand tons of TNT—by harnessing the power of a nuclear reaction.

FDR quickly understood that whoever was first to build such a weapon would win the war.

Thus, the OSS's first priority became the acquisition of whatever the MANHATTAN PROJECT needed—uranium ore, smuggled scientists, matériel, et cetera—as well as depriving the Germans of the same.

The President angrily shook the message.

"I'll have the bastards lined up and shot!" he said. "When those names come, I want a copy of them immediately!"

"Yes, sir. But if we do find that there are indeed Russian spies, they'd be worth more to us alive than—"

"Who the hell is this 'Tiny,' Bill?" Roosevelt interrupted. "We are getting one hell of a lot of information from one source. And I can only gather that he's also involved with where the Russian names came from."

"First, he is far from being our only source—it was the Sparrow, an American citizen whose parents are Russian, who sold us one short list of purported spies in Los Alamos, which Allen says Tiny is checking against Abwehr lists. Second, while it is a lot from one source, everything he has given us has been good. *Everything*, Frank. Tiny is even writing a book documenting how he's helping bring down Hitler. He lists who's who in the German High Command, what war crimes they're committing, et cetera, in anticipation of them being brought to justice after the Reich collapses."

"A book, you say?"

"A book," Donovan confirmed. "He works on it in Dulles's office, and keeps it locked up there for safekeeping. And of course Allen uses it for a reference."

"So then these Russian names are from the Abwehr," FDR said.

"Canaris, as you would expect of the head of German military intelligence, has his agents keeping a close eye on Stalin. And, in the course of that, it's logical that the Abwehr could come across such information."

"What's Tiny's real name?" FDR pursued, handing back the messages.

Donovan, stalling, folded the messages and put them in his shirt pocket. Then he took a sip of his drink, put it down, and took his fishing rod out of its holder. He raised the tip as he checked on his fishing lure.

FDR turned to him and repeated, "What's his real name, General?"

Donovan, the formal tone and use of his rank not lost on him, met FDR's eyes.

"Mr. President, I believe you will agree that what Tiny has told us thus far has proven to be invaluable. As Allen Dulles will tell you, it is extremely difficult for us to get anti-Nazi Germans to stick out their necks to help us when all they hear is that the Allies will not make any separate peace."

"So *that* is what the line about 'unconditional surrender' being a problem is about?" FDR pursued, his tone now icy. "That if Germany must surrender, any negotiations as to who takes over will be rendered null and void? You're telling me that this Tiny—or even Admiral Canaris—has no desire whatsoever to become head of a post-Hitler Germany?"

"What I know is that there are Germans who fervently believe that Hitler has lost the war and that the most important thing that they can do is remove him to stop the destruction of Germany and its people." He paused, then went on, "Mr. President, the fewer people who know of Tiny, the better. With all due respect, if I do not tell you, then it would be impossible for you to accidentally reveal his identity. And we cannot afford to lose him. I promise to share more as soon as possible."

FDR grunted, broke off eye contact, then silently turned his attention to his fishing lure. He looked to be in deep thought.

Ten minutes later, with not another word uttered between them, FDR suddenly pointed toward a twenty-two-foot-long Chris-Craft luxury motorboat. It was moving down the Potomac at full speed. The captain of the vessel and two other men waved to the *Sequoia.*

I think I know that boat, Donovan thought.

FDR said: "With your luck, Bill, that Chris-Craft is going to get close to your lure and scare off all your fish."

As the boat passed, the gold lettering painted on its transom came into view:

CIRRHOSIS OF THE RIVER

GEORGETOWN

Yeah. I do know that boat.

Wonder who's aboard and where they're going?

Just as Donovan was going to reply to FDR, the brightly varnished red mahogany vessel made a sweeping U-turn and began to bear down on the stern of the *Sequoia.*

"Who the hell is that?" FDR idly wondered. "And who the hell would name their boat that?"

Jimmy Whittaker would, Donovan thought.

U.S. Army Captain James M.B. Whittaker (Harvard '39) was on an OSS mission in the Philippines. He had attended Saint Mark's prep school with Dick Canidy, and came from family wealth beyond imagination.

He who calls you "Uncle Frank" and owns not only the Georgetown mansion that we use as a safe house but God Only Knows What All Else. And who is unafraid of pissing you off.

That's who, Mr. President.

But I'm damn sure not going to bring him up now.

Three Secret Service agents, cradling Thompson submachine guns, suddenly appeared on the deck and went to stand at the starboard and stern railings, putting themselves between the President and the approaching vessel.

Donovan got up and stood beside the tall agent at the starboard railing. He now saw a man in a suit and tie standing at the stern of the Chris-Craft. In his right hand the man carried a black briefcase. The left hand had what looked like a death grip on the chrome railing that ran the length of the low cabin roof.

When the man saw Donovan at the railing, he put down the briefcase and saluted him.

"Friend of yours, Bill?" FDR said. "Are you getting picked up so you can avoid our fishing contest?"

After a moment, Donovan said, "Yes, sir. That is, about him being a friend. He works for me."

"You're absolutely sure of who this man is, sir?" the taller Secret Service agent said as he adjusted his grip on his Tommy gun.

Donovan, knowing that at least one M2 .50 caliber Browning machine gun—*and maybe even an antiaircraft 40mm Bofors cannon*—was trained on the approaching watercraft, looked at the President.

FDR put in: "Son, you heard the General. Let him aboard."

The agent looked over his shoulder, said, "Yes, sir, Mr. President," and passed the order for the crew to prepare to receive a visitor.

As the Chris-Craft slowed its approach, two lean U.S. Navy seamen apprentices, who Donovan thought looked to be all of fifteen, went amidship and put heavy bumpers made of hemp over the side, then tied them off so that they rested against the hull just above the waterline. The smaller boat then slowly came in alongside the *Sequoia*. Lines were tossed and cleated, and then the man in the suit was helped aboard the *Sequoia*.

Donovan turned to Roosevelt.

"If you'll excuse me, I'll be right back."

As Donovan started walking to intercept his OSS man, FDR, clenching his cigarette holder in his teeth, checked the line on his fishing reel.

He said, "And I'll be right here catching your fish."

Three minutes later, Donovan, holding a manila envelope and reading an unfolded sheet of paper, walked up to FDR. The Chris-Craft, with the courier back aboard, then could be seen dropping back behind the *Sequoia* and pulling away.

"What is so important?" Roosevelt said.

Donovan handed him the paper.

"A follow-up message from David Bruce concerning those aerial torpedoes. I think that, considering our conversation just now about London, you'll find this interesting."

[ONE]
OSS Algiers Station
Algiers, Algeria
1023 30 May 1943

Stan Fine motioned with his hand for John Craig van der Ploeg to pass him the new messages.

"Tell me why you're convinced about Tubes," Canidy said.

"It's mostly from the chickenfeed."

"I get that," Canidy said. "But what kind of chickenfeed?"

"For example," John Craig van der Ploeg said, "when President Roosevelt in his Fireside Chat announced he was significantly raising war production numbers—those hundred and twenty thousand additional fighter aircraft—I added another fifty percent and messaged 'a hundred and eighty thousand Lockheed Lightnings' along with news that Bizerta and Tunis were captured on May seventh and we had taken more than a quarter million German and Italian POWs. And I mixed in mindless information—weather forecasts, sports scores. All things that the Germans either already knew or that they could cross-check elsewhere. There's no question that the Krauts analyze every word FDR utters, so those aircraft numbers were easy to confirm, and the extra sixty thousand either made them think there'd been a keystroke error—or that the message was actually more accurate. And they of course are well aware of their own losses here in North Africa."

"Nice work."

John Craig van der Ploeg smiled. "Thank you. But the part of the chickenfeed that tells me whoever is running Tubes's W/T isn't really Tubes comes from the personal stuff I send him. We exchanged a lot of information when we practiced—including, of course, about . . ."

"About what?"

Canidy could see that John Craig was embarrassed.

"For Chrissake, the man's life is at stake. What the hell can you be embarrassed about?"

"Well, we used to message back and forth about girls. And then, right before you came back from Sicily, he messaged me about that girl he met there in Palermo."

Canidy looked at him for a long time.

Jesus, he's talking about Andrea Buda.

And Tubes was more than smitten with her.

And why wouldn't he be? Twenty years old, maybe five-seven with a perfect curved figure. Inviting, doe-like almond eyes. Rich chestnut brown hair that fell to her shoulders. And those perfect, magnificent breasts . . .

Yeah, small wonder he had a hard-on for her.

Wait. That one afternoon she just disappeared—is she the reason Tubes got caught by the SS?

That can't be possible. She hid from the SS.

Professor Rossi's sister taught her to pray the rosary in church.

And her father's a fisherman on one of Nola's boats.

Not to mention those morons Tweedle Fucking Dee and Dumb are her brothers. Stupid as a box of rocks, yes, but they did tell me where the Tabun was stashed. . . .

"Andrea," Canidy furnished.

John Craig van der Ploeg nodded.

"She is stunning," Canidy said.

"That's what he said. That and really . . . uh, horny."

Really!

Well, no surprise there. She exuded sex from her every pore.

"And?" Canidy said.

"Well, uh, he told me certain things that she liked, uh, when they were getting, well, you know, doing things only he would know."

I can only imagine what those were, Canidy thought. *And I told that sonofabitch to keep his hands off her—that thinking with the little head could get him killed.*

Shit. Maybe that is what happened . . .

"And when I alluded to them in the chickenfeed," John Craig went on, "whoever was working the W/T did not have a clue what I was talking about. Then there was talk about a brothel, which made no sense. Why would he pay for hookers if he had something as hot as Andrea? And for free."

"Don't kid yourself," Canidy automatically replied. "One way or another, you pay for the companionship of women. As a rear admiral at Pensacola once told me, 'Son, if it flies, floats, or fucks—rent it!' I'm not a hundred percent onboard with that. Deep inside this hard-ass persona is an old-school romantic who doesn't share women. But now, John Craig, you, too, are privy to that distinguished old sailor's sage advice and may apply it as you see fit."

Canidy glanced at Fine, who he saw was grinning, then said, "Anyway, so you created your own danger signal for a compromised station. Very nicely done."

"John Craig is good," Fine put in. "That's why I made him our station signal officer."

Canidy could see John Craig's face brighten at that.

"Tell him, son," Fine said.

"I'm in charge of all commo," John Craig said. "I maintain the facilities and the message center, oversee all the traffic from the agents, the procedures and ciphers, as well as the security, and the training of the agents at the Sandbox in W/T commo."

"Impressive," Canidy said, "but after what you just told me, not surprising. Clearly you're doing a fine job."

"Thank you," John Craig said. "But, uh . . ."

"But what? Spit it out."

"But . . . I want to go operational. I want to help find Tubes."

Canidy grunted.

"What about you being station signal officer here?"

"I've already established all the procedures and protocols. I have two candidates who easily can step in and follow them."

Canidy glanced at Fine, who just perceptibly shrugged and nodded, then looked back at van der Ploeg.

"That's all well and good, John Craig, but what the hell about your claustrophobia? You're suddenly miraculously cured?"

"Not suddenly. I've been working on that. I've been forcing myself to stay locked up in the commo room—you've seen it, no windows, no nothing but walls—which has helped. And also when I've been out at Dellys, I've been going to your throat-cutting school every spare moment I have. Ask anyone out there. I'm ready."

"Look, why the hell should I take you and not someone else more experienced?"

"Easy. Because no one else is more experienced than me. I can track Tubes's radio."

"How do you mean?"

"Whoever is running his station is accustomed to me at the other end. I can keep him on the radio long enough for us to triangulate on his signal."

Canidy considered that.

If we find the radio, he thought, *there's a damn good chance Tubes is nearby.*

And if he's not, I'm sure I can get whoever is running the radio to talk.

"Won't they know we're close because of your signal strength?"

"I'll have to dial down my transmit power, but that's a piece of cake." He paused, then added, "I really want to go."

Canidy met his eyes.

"Why this all of a sudden, John Craig? Didn't you hear what I said the SS is doing? If you're captured—"

"That's why I want to go," John Craig interrupted. "Because I'm the reason Tubes is there . . . out there somewhere. When I didn't go the first time, he had to go in my place, so now it's 'If not now, when? If not me, who?'"

Canidy glanced at Fine, who was looking up from the stack of messages he'd been handed. Fine made a facial expression that Canidy, having known him since the day he showed up at the boarding school in Iowa, read as *Whatever you decide, I'm with you.*

Then Canidy looked away, out across the harbor, in the direction where Sicily, some six hundred miles away, would be over the horizon.

He felt his throat tighten.

Fine recognized what was happening, and after a long moment changed the subject: "You might want to look at a couple of these, Dick. They are all somewhat related."

Fine handed him the messages.

"The top one's from Dulles to Donovan. Dulles says Tiny is saying the Kriegsmarine is about to make major changes."

Canidy, who knew Allen Dulles was OSS deputy director for Europe, raised his eyebrows, then looked at the sheet and started to read.

"Jesus!" he exclaimed after a moment.

He looked back at Fine.

"So, Herr Grossadmiral," Canidy said, "is going to order all U-boats out of the North Atlantic? After a campaign of—what?—almost four years? Jesus!"

"Good news . . . ?"

"*Damn* good news," Canidy said, looking down at the half-dozen Liberty ships at anchor in the harbor. "Especially now that we're gearing up for invading Sicily. Can never have too heavy of a supply line."

"Not when, as in last year alone, some seven-point-five *million tons* of critical war matériel gets sent to the bottom of the ocean. Already, we're noticing the difference. More than twice the number of Liberty ships are actually making it here."

The 441-foot-long vessels—known as EC2 (Emergency, Cargo, Large Capacity)—each transported the equivalent of three hundred railroad freight cars in cargo, everything from jeeps and tanks and trucks to munitions and medicine to C rations and soldiers. They were being built—the first in March 1941, with more than three thousand ordered—at eighteen shipyards on every U.S. coast.

Before his first EC2, master engineer Henry J. Kaiser had never built a ship. But using mass-production theories—some that had helped him construct the Bonneville and Hoover dams in record time—he learned, by his seventy-fifth EC2 completed at an Oregon shipyard, how to turn out a finished vessel only ten days after the laying of her keel.

Which became critical, because as the convoys, each with scores of ships heavy with matériel, steamed at eleven knots eastward across the Atlantic Ocean, the Nazi U-boats attacked.

Seeking to choke off the supply line and starve England and the Allied forces, the submarines hunted down the sluggish ships in "wolfpacks," a deadly tactic devised by Karl Dönitz, whom Hitler just months earlier had promoted to grand admiral and named commander in chief of the German Navy.

Wolfpack torpedoes sunk hundreds upon hundreds of the Liberty ships—many within sight of the U.S. coast, made easy targets when silhouetted by the lights onshore—to the point that the Allies considered a Liberty ship had earned back her cost if she completed just one trip across the Atlantic Ocean.

"Thanks to Ultra?" Canidy said.

"Yeah, the tide changed, also last year, thanks to Bletchley Park finally cracking the U-boat Enigma."

Canidy knew that the Government Code and Cypher School, the British code-breaking operation, was at Bletchley Park, forty miles northwest of London. Also known as GCCS, insiders said it stood for Golf, Cheese, and Chess Society.

Different German services used different Enigma machines, the Kriegsmarine's being among the hardest to decode.

"When Bletchley Park did that," Fine went on, "it changed everything. In November '42, the high for our losses was seven hundred and twenty-nine thousand tons. That fell to just over two hundred thousand tons this past January—about the same time Hitler made Dönitz head of the navy."

"Down half a million tons. That is one helluva change."

"And as of this month, we've lost only thirty-four ships in the Atlantic. Even better, the wolfpacks are now the hunted ones. Dönitz, with his subs being targeted and blasted—he's lost forty-three this month, which we're told is twice the replacement rate—is pulling them all back. He's calling this 'Black May.'"

Canidy looked at Fine and motioned with the message from Dulles. "And if Dulles is getting this kind of rich intel from Tiny on what the Krauts are doing next, then . . ."

Fine nodded.

Canidy was deep in thought for a moment, then said: "Okay, we've got to go in there and get Tubes the hell out. I'm not leaving him at the mercy of the SS with Husky's D-day around the corner. We also can see if there's anything from a pack of Hitler Youth to a half-million troops amassing. And if there's any of that goddamn nerve gas."

"We?" Fine said. "And how do you plan to deal with Eisenhower?"

"No one else has been able to find Tubes. I know my way around. And as for Ike, no one knows I've been there twice, so why the hell not a third time?"

"You said 'we.' "

"John Craig and me and whoever we need. Right, John Craig?"

John Craig van der Ploeg's face brightened, and he excitedly said, "Thank you, sir!"

Canidy's eyes narrowed.

"And *that* is the last goddamn time!" he snapped. "You call me 'sir' when we're over the fence, and we'll both get killed."

The look on John Craig's face showed that he understood.

[TWO]
OSS Bern Station
Herrengasse 23
Bern, Switzerland
2250 27 May 1943

OSS Chief of Station Allen Welsh Dulles was in the library of his mansion in Old City Bern, sitting in one of four deep-cushioned leather armchairs. The seating was arranged in a semicircle at a low round marble table before the enormous stone fireplace.

Dulles, who in April had turned fifty years old, had the calm, thoughtful appearance one might expect of perhaps a Presbyterian minister—warm, inquisitive eyes behind frameless round spectacles, thinning silver hair, a neatly groomed gray mustache. He was in fact the son of a Presbyterian minister and grandson of a Presbyterian missionary. He'd joined the diplomatic corps in 1916, right after graduating Princeton University.

He was wearing what members of his social standing called a sack suit, a two-piece woolen garment with cuffed baggy pants and no padding in the shoulders of the jacket. His closet held more than a dozen such suits—all very much of the same cut, varying only in color, either gray or black, with or without pinstripes, and all from the clothier J. Press—which he invariably wore with a crisp white dress shirt and a striped bow tie.

Herrengasse 23 was a four-story classic baroque-style residence that had been built in the seventeenth century. The richly appointed oak-paneled high-ceiling library—dimly lit by the flickering flames of the crackling fire and a single torchiere lamp glowing in a near corner—had the comfortable smell of old leather and fine tobacco. With Bern's blackout rules in effect, and strictly enforced to avoid aerial attacks by Axis forces, the great room's massive crystal chandelier remained darkened and the heavy fabric draperies were pulled tightly across the tall casement windows.

A German-manufactured Braun radio-phonograph combination was tuned to 531 kilohertz to pick up Landessender Beromünster, Switzerland's national public station. Earlier, Dulles had been listening to a news broadcast in German, then a rebroadcast of a BBC-produced report, its reader having the markedly distinct clipped accent of the British.

Now, with the Braun's volume turned low, the radio station was playing a performance of Mozart's *The Marriage of Figaro*. It had been recorded in German at the Stadttheater, which was a half-dozen blocks away, not far from the Zeitglocke, which would sound its massive bronze bell in ten minutes.

Dulles appreciated the works of Mozart; he just could not decide which held more irony during wartime, the playing of a comic opera heavy with sex or the *la folle giornata*—day of madness—story line of the opera itself.

Especially on a radio station whose signal reaches far into Nazi territory, where the penalty for listening to Beromünster's broadcasts gets one charged with sedition—and the death sentence of getting thrown in a concentration camp.

Dulles picked up a Zippo lighter that was on a silver tray on the marble table. The tray also held two bottles of Rémy Martin VSOP cognac and four snifters. One of the crystal glasses was nearly half-full. Beside the tray sat a large wooden humidor heavy with Honduran cigars and a thick manila envelope rubber-stamped in red ink: TOP SECRET.

It would seem all we have now is day after day of madness—and none of it humorous.

Today alone brings Sparrow's killing by parties unknown and confirmation of a link between that chemist Schwartz and von Braun that can only mean more madness.

And now this envelope of photographs showing damage from the Ruhr Valley bombings.

He glanced at the stainless steel lighter and ran his thumb over the emblem on its case that was a miniature representation of the orange-and-black crest of Princeton. Although the dim light did not allow him to see details, he mentally recited his alma mater's motto that was embossed in Latin on the crest: *Dei sub numine viget.*

As he moved his thumb upward, flicking open the top of the lighter, he thought of its translation: *"Under God's Power She Flourishes."*

His thumb then spun the gnarled wheel that sparked the lighter to life. With a practiced flourish, he held its flame to the tip of the foot-long straw-like stick of wood he held in his other hand, then turned the stick vertically so that the flame grew hotter as it burned upward. Then he picked up his favorite pipe, one crafted of exotic burl wood, gently tamped the tobacco in the bowl with his thumb, and finally held the flame over the tobacco.

A purist, he used the wooden stick's flame—and not that of the Zippo—so that the delicate flavor of the tobacco would not be affected by any taste of lighter fluid.

He began to puff. The tobacco caught fire, glowing red. He blew out the flame on the wooden stick and placed it in the ashtray on the table.

He breathed in the thick, sweet smell of the tobacco, put the pipe back to his lips, and took a lengthy, slow draw. After a long moment, as he exhaled appreciatively, he looked up at the oil painting of Old Glory that had recently been hung over the mantel.

Under God's Power She Flourishes indeed . . . he thought.

While Dulles looked and acted every bit the Ivy League–educated diplomat—he presently was registered with the Swiss government as the special assistant to the American Minister, U.S. Legation to Switzerland, where he kept his official office—he of course was the top U.S. secret agent there, quietly conducting OSS business at the mansion on Herrengasse.

The covert meetings Dulles held almost always at night, when the dark of blackout made surveillance of who came and went via the alley leading to the mansion's rear entry practically impossible. The security of his residence—with the notable exception of its telephone lines being tapped, as no suspect telephone in Switzerland went unmonitored, either by the Fremdenpolizei or other organizations, authorized to do so or not—also afforded Dulles the confidence that no one saw or overheard anything said therein.

For Dulles, such security was critical, as he devoutly believed in his mission. He genuinely feared the threat of the spreading of Fascism. He'd at times served as a League of Nations legal adviser, which had allowed him to meet world leaders, among them the Italian dictator Benito Mussolini and the German chancellor Adolf Hitler. Neither man had left him with a good gut feeling then, and everything he had learned of them since only served to support what his gut had warned him.

Dulles had watched the early years of World War Two with a professional detachment—though ultimately he not only joined those who believed the United States should intervene in the war but became a vocal proponent of it. He wrote books arguing against America's neutrality.

And when, after the Japanese attack on Pearl Harbor on December 7, 1941, America finally found itself fully involved, he found himself serving his country in the Office of Strategic Services, working old contacts in Switzerland and establishing new ones to find anti-Nazis—Germans especially but also anyone else—willing to do anything to stop the evil that was Adolf Hitler.

Allen Welsh Dulles, deep in thought as he considered what would be the course of the evening's meeting, took another puff on his pipe, exhaled, then leaned forward for his glass of cognac. He held the snifter so that its large bowl rested in his palm, the body heat from his hand gently warming the cognac through the fine crystal.

He started to rock the snifter, then stared at the slowly swirling cognac as he thought: *The details of these bombings could cause him to tip either way—for us or against us.*

But there's no doubt they will make him furious.

I can only hope he blames his losses on Hitler.

Dulles put the glass to his nose, inhaled the rich aroma of the cognac, then took a sip. As he felt the alcohol warm his throat and then his stomach, there came a tap at the solid wooden door. It began to swing inward. He set his glass back on the table and glanced at his Patek Philippe wristwatch—the elegant Swiss-made timepiece, a gift from his wife, Clover, when Dulles had first served in Switzerland, showed it was shy of 11 P.M.—then he nodded appreciatively at his guest's punctuality and glanced toward the door.

A serious-looking man in his late twenties with an athletic build and wearing the satin housecoat of a manservant—but who in fact was an armed OSS agent—entered the room first.

"Mr. Dulles, may I present Herr Kappler?"

He made a grand sweeping gesture with his right hand, and a tall, erect fifty-five-year-old man entered the library. The agent then quietly slipped back out the door, pulling it shut behind him with a solid *click* of its heavy metal latch.

Wolfgang Augustus Kappler had hawk-like facial features, piercing green eyes, and short dark hair that was graying at the temples. While he carried himself with an air of unquestioned confidence, Dulles knew him to be charming and gracious—a genuinely gentle man. He also knew that he was a devout Roman Catholic and anti-Nazi, one careful to distinguish between those who committed the atrocities in pursuit of National Socialism and its Final Solution for a master race and those who quietly fought the Fascism and racism while trying to save the Fatherland from further destruction.

At least till now maybe, Dulles thought.

Kappler wore a solid gray three-piece suit with a stiffly starched white dress shirt and a silver necktie. The custom-cut woolen garment fit perfectly, which accentuated a bulge in the jacket's left patch pocket.

Dulles, with a warm smile, began to approach him.

"It is a real pleasure to see you again, Wolffy."

Kappler effortlessly strode across the room and, with both hands extended, reached out and vigorously shook Dulles's right hand.

"Allen," Kappler said in his strong, deep voice, "it is always good to see an old friend."

The two had known each other for almost a dozen years, having first met in the Berlin office of Sullivan and Cromwell.

Dulles, after getting his law degree at George Washington University in 1926, had been recruited by Sullivan and Cromwell, the international law firm based in New York City at which his older brother, John Foster Dulles, already had made partner. There was prestige involved with taking the position, certainly, but Dulles quietly admitted that the money was too good to turn down. And, he decided, if necessary he could always return to the diplomatic corps.

Thus, Allen Welsh Dulles came to handle international clients for the firm of Sullivan and Cromwell, and Kappler had come to him at the suggestion of Friedrich "Fritz" Thyssen, a fellow industrialist, for help with his corporate investments.

Like Thyssen, Kappler between world wars had been quietly looking to diversify his holdings beyond Germany and neighboring countries. His main business, Kappler Industrie GmbH, was hugely successful in the manufacture of steel and iron and other key materials for the building of automobiles, heavy trucks, trains, and aircraft. Wolfgang Kappler had sought to expand that business abroad while at the same time very quietly investing in other businesses.

The United States of America came immediately to his mind.

Allen Dulles oversaw for Kappler the setting up of a U.S. holding company in which Kappler, through Dulles's investment banker connections, poured significant funds into blue-chip companies General Motors Corporation, Boeing Aircraft, International Business Machines, and E.I. du Pont de Nemours and Company, as well as a few smaller railroads in which Kappler hoped eventually to secure a controlling interest.

These companies proved to be as Kappler had expected—solid investments that were not subject to the mercurial economies he suffered in Europe, Germany's out-of-control inflation being but one problem.

Yet bringing Kappler Industrie to the United States—and selling its various metal products to GM and Boeing and others for automobile and aircraft manufacturing—had not been the success that he or Dulles had anticipated. Which led Dulles then to suggest that Kappler look south, to the wealthier countries in South America that were hungry for new industry.

In almost no time, Dulles had created additional holding companies in Argentina and Uruguay, with others planned for Chile, Brazil, and Venezuela. These, however, were not like the holding companies Kappler had in North America, ones through which he simply bought shares of existing corporations. These were far superior. The South American properties contained manufacturing and import-export companies that Kappler either wholly owned or held a majority interest in.

And they quickly had begun to pay off handsomely. Even more important—especially with the Nazis squeezing any German company that they wished, from extorting them for money to outright stealing them in the name of nationalization for the Thousand-Year Reich—Kappler had wealth being generated far from Germany and Europe.

[THREE]

Allen Dulles motioned with his pipe toward the low marble table holding the humidor and bottles of Rémy Martin.

"May I interest you in a cigar? And perhaps a taste? The cigars just came in; they're from Honduras. As for the cognac, I'm afraid that VSOP is the best I have to offer. I hope it is to your liking."

Kappler smiled broadly.

"No to the cigar, thank you. But cognac? Of course! I thought you would never ask. And, yes, Very Superior Old Pale is indeed my personal choice. Anything more expensive is simply that—overpriced."

"Agreed," Dulles said, putting his pipe to his mouth.

Dulles then picked up one of the snifters so that its large bowl rested in his palm. He took the open bottle of Rémy Martin and, having tilted the large snifter so that it was almost sideways, then poured cognac till it filled to the rim. He turned the glass upright and offered it to Kappler.

"Thank you," Kappler said, taking it and holding it up. "To old friends."

Dulles, meeting Kappler's eyes, touched snifters, adding, "And always new opportunities."

Not breaking eye contact, they took healthy swallows.

Kappler exhaled dramatically.

"Superb!" he announced.

"Yes," Dulles began, "truly nectar of the gods—"

He stopped when, from afar, there came the sudden striking of the Zeitglocke.

"Ah, and we now hear from the great Greek god of time, Chronos!" Wolfgang Kappler said dramatically.

He held up the index finger of his left hand and added, "Which reminds me . . ."

He reached into the bulging left pocket of his suit coat. With a grand gesture, he produced a small black felt clamshell box wrapped with a simple crimson cord. He presented it to Dulles.

"It would be my great honor, Allen, if you would accept this small token to commemorate our long and deep friendship."

The look on Dulles's face showed he was somewhat uncomfortable. While Kappler almost always came bearing a gift—at their very first meeting more than a decade earlier he had presented him with an exquisitely cut crystal ashtray—Dulles had never become accustomed to his generosity.

Dulles's look was not lost on Kappler, who motioned gently with the box, holding it closer to Dulles.

"Please," Kappler said with great sincerity.

Dulles looked from Kappler's eyes to the box then back to Kappler.

Dulles smiled. "Well, if you insist, but—"

"I do insist, my dear friend," Kappler interrupted, and smiled back. "And don't be ridiculous. It has been through your fine efforts that I have made a handsome fortune."

Dulles took the black felt box and slipped off the crimson cord. The clamshell hinged open, and inside, nestled on a small black silk pillow, was a yellow gold–cased Patek Philippe with a brown leather skin strap. The stylish champagne-colored face, under a high-domed crystal, had black hands for the hour, minute, and second movements, as well as two smaller dials on either side, where the numbers "3" and "9" would have been. On the right side of the case were golden push buttons, one above and one below the knurled knob used to set the time.

"It is absolutely gorgeous. And my favorite, Patek Philippe."

"Our last visit, we spoke of timepieces," Kappler said, nodding toward the simple but elegant Patek Philippe on Dulles's wrist, "and I thought you would appreciate having a more sporty one with complications. It is a 1463 J Chronograph. Eighteen-karat yellow gold."

Dulles caught himself grinning, and heard himself say, "I think my life has plenty of complications without purposefully adding more."

Kappler now dutifully smiled.

"Yes. I understand. As do we all. But of course I refer to the complications—the mechanical functions beyond the hands showing hour, minute, and second—that make watches more desirable to the connoisseurs."

"This is really too nice to wear," Dulles said.

"And did you notice the strap?" Kappler smiled appreciatively. "Hand-sewn hide of crocodile."

Dulles looked at Kappler. "I do not know what to say, except that you shouldn't—"

"You must see something else," Kappler interrupted, ignoring the comment and reaching into the box.

He pulled the wristwatch free of the black silk pillow, then turned it so that the back of the case was visible. A clear crystal there showed all the intricate movements therein—tiny golden gears turning and silver wheels spinning in an orchestrated fashion that was pure precision.

Dulles puffed on his pipe, then said, "I feel compelled to repeat myself: It is absolutely gorgeous. Truly a work of art."

"Yes. And I knew that you would appreciate it. I understand that they make one with twenty complications—one dial showing the date of Easter, another a celestial chart with more than two thousand stars."

Where is he going with all this? Dulles thought.

Dulles looked at Kappler as he replaced the watch on the tiny pillow, then put both into the box.

"Amazing," Dulles said. "I cannot begin to imagine so many options. Nor, for that matter, what one would do with such a magnificent instrument. It must keep perfect time."

"True. Magnificent, it is." He met and held Dulles's eyes. "And, as we all well know, my old friend, life is all about timing."

Dulles, puffing his pipe, thought: *Why do I suspect, Wolffy, my old friend, that that is a reference to something far larger than a fancy wristwatch?*

Kappler went on: "I was pleased to be able to personally select your watch this afternoon, following a very lengthy meeting with Franz Messner and Ernst Schröder that I thought would never end."

Dulles had dossiers thick with intelligence on the forty-seven-year-old Messner, an anti-Nazi who was the general director of Semperit, the century-old international rubber manufacturer based in Vienna, and on Schröder, a confidant of Hitler in his sixties who represented the Reichsbank in its transactions with the Switzerland National Bank.

"More gold laundering?" Dulles asked, but it was more of a statement.

The Allies were well aware—and extremely pissed—that SNB for at least a year had been buying at discount more than one hundred million francs' worth of gold every three months from Germany. Lately it had been foreign-minted gold coins.

The Allies had applied diplomatic pressure, and Switzerland had made the appropriate responses that made it appear it would comply—accounts were closed, fines levied—yet the transactions, too lucrative to turn down, continued.

Kappler nodded. "Before arriving here yesterday, Messner and I spent two weeks in Lisbon arranging for new funds to be channeled as escudos through Banco de Portugal deposit accounts set up under Portuguese subsidiaries of Semperit and Kappler industries."

Dulles grunted.

More money for buying raw materials for Germany's war machine, he thought.

"You know that I am not proud of that," Kappler said, as if reading his mind. "But we are being watched, and if I did not do that which is expected . . ."

Dulles thought he detected an odd tone in Kappler's voice.

Dulles looked at his snifter, swirled the cognac, then took a big sip.

What the hell could that be about?

Well, one way to find out.

He looked back at Kappler and said, "Okay, Wolffy. We have, as you say, been friends a long time—"

"Absolutely," he said, stone-faced.

"—long enough that you can tell me exactly what is on your mind."

They locked eyes for a long moment. Kappler remained stone-faced. Then his eyes glistened, and he suddenly sighed, and his face turned soft.

He took a deep sip of his cognac, then replied, "Allen, I do not want to wind up like Fritz."

"What do you mean? Wind up how?"

"Marty Bormann . . ." Kappler began, then had to clear his throat.

Nazi Party Minister Martin Bormann was an average-looking Prussian of forty-three—pasty-faced, cold dark eyes, his thinning black-dyed hair slicked back against his skull. He came from an average background—the son of a postman—but had risen to a position that was anything but average. Having earned Adolf Hitler's trust, beginning by managing with great success the party's finances and then Hitler's personal finances, the Nazi leader had appointed Bormann as his personal secretary. And thus Bormann, to the great displeasure of those in Hitler's High Command, came to control who had access to the Nazi leader and to personally implement Hitler's wishes.

Kappler drained his cognac snifter.

"What about Bormann?" Dulles pursued.

"At the direct order of Hitler, Bormann had Fritz Thyssen and his wife locked up in a Berlin asylum . . ."

What? They're in a loony bin?

Last we heard Thyssen was living in Cannes, making plans to head for Buenos Aires.

". . . and now Bormann has told me that Göring is planning on sending them to be interned in a konzentrationslager." He crossed himself. "May God save them . . ."

Reichsmarschall Hermann Göring—the close-to-obese, hot-tempered fifty-year-old head of the Luftwaffe and chief of all Wehrmacht commanders who Hitler had designated as his successor—also wielded an almost unquestioned authority in the German High Command. Which of course caused a constant friction between him and Bormann and all others therein.

"What do you think is the purpose of that?" Dulles said.

"I do not have to think what it is. Bormann told me."

"And?"

"Money, gold, artwork. Anything and everything. Göring has been trying to get Thyssen to reveal where he hid assets that the Nazis haven't gotten their hands on. Which is why, after the French turned over the Thyssens to the SS and Bormann locked them up, Göring made an effort to ensure that their accommodations were comfortable. But now Bormann says that Göring has lost patience and is turning the screws, pressuring Fritz to talk by sending them to the KL."

Dulles studied Kappler as he poured him more cognac.

This was not the first time that he had shared stories of Hermann Göring using his position to build a personal fortune. That had happened as Dulles had been helping Kappler hide his own assets: "Bormann told me that when the Nazis first occupied Paris, Göring sent a message to Hitler in which he gloated: 'My sweetest dream is of looting and looting completely.' And he did. When the Nazis took over Baron Rothschild's palace, as an example, Göring swept the place clean. He then presented Hitler with a pair of paintings by Pablo Picasso—and kept for himself almost fifty works by Braque, Matisse, and Renoir to add to his looted collection at his country estate, Carinhall. Göring, whose appetite appears insatiable, gets what he wants."

Dulles now put his pipe to his lips as he met Kappler's eyes.

"And if they know about Thyssen," Dulles said softly between puffs, "then they must suspect you have assets beyond Germany, too."

Kappler, his face somber, nodded.

With his usually strong voice on the verge of breaking, he then finished: "It has already happened. They nationalized my Chemische Fabrik Frankfurt last week."

"They seized Chemische Fabrik Frankfurt?"

Kappler nodded again.

"Last week," he repeated, his voice almost a monotone, "while we were in Portugal. It's as if they sent me there so I would be far away when it happened."

"Only it," Dulles said, "or other companies, too?"

"Only it. So far. But it is only a matter of time before they find an excuse—or create one—to do to all my companies what they have done to all of Fritz's. Bormann even made it a point to inform me that after taking over Thyssen's companies, they had had no trouble running them without him. . . ."

Dulles nodded. After a long moment, he suddenly said, "Could Klaus Schwartz run it?"

He saw Kappler stiffen at the mention of the name.

"Schwartz used to run your company, yes?" Dulles went on. "What can you tell me about him?"

"Herr Doktor Schwartz?" Kappler then said bitterly. "Or SS-Sturmbannführer Schwartz?"

"Are they not one and the same?" Dulles said, more or less rhetorically.

Kappler's eyes narrowed as he shook his head.

"When Himmler gave Klaus that SS rank, he no longer was the man I'd known and worked alongside for almost a decade. The Nazis poisoned his mind. He started wearing that outrageous uniform all the time, barking 'Heil Hitler!' and throwing out his arm every time he entered a new room." Kappler took a sip of cognac, then said, "I was not sorry to have him leave my company."

"He was only at Chemische Fabrik Frankfurt?"

"Yes. He was educated as a chemist, and was in charge of my research and development department. He served me very, very well. That is, until that ridiculous SS persona took over. Now I understand that he is working with that rocket scientist?"

"Wernher von Braun," Dulles provided.

"Yes, that's the one."

"Before he left your company, was Schwartz working on anything unusual?"

Kappler thought that over for a long moment, then said, "Nothing that I'm aware of, but then I was not aware my company was about to be nationalized, either." He met Dulles's eyes. "Why do you ask about Schwartz?"

"We found out that he was working with von Braun, as I said, and we are trying to determine what exactly is the nature of that work. And if there is any connection with the work and Chemische Fabrik Frankfurt."

Kappler nodded thoughtfully, then said with more than a little sarcasm, "While they have nationalized my company, the SS still graciously permits me to run it. At least, I suppose, until such time that Bormann decides otherwise." He paused, then added, "I will make discreet inquiries."

Dulles puffed on his pipe, then exhaled the smoke. He glanced at the manila envelope stamped TOP SECRET.

Jesus! he thought. *And I was worried about his reaction to the bombings?*

He looked back at Kappler, who was staring into the fire.

And that of course is what you're thinking, Wolffy.

You're wondering what the hell Hitler plans to do with the Thyssens in a concentration camp. Make them slave laborers? Or just gas them, too? Or maybe both—especially if Göring squeezes Fritz enough to cough up his hidden assets.

And you're convinced you're about to be sent to share a tent in a concentration camp with Herr und Frau Thyssen—"Bormann decides otherwise" being a euphemism for "internment."

He then glanced at the Patek Philippe in the clamshell box in his hand and snapped it shut. The sound caused Kappler to twitch his snifter.

What did he say—"Life is all about timing"?

Talk about real complications . . .

[FOUR]
2435 27 May 1943

Allen Dulles, standing by the fireplace with his back to the crackling fire, reached for the open bottle of Rémy Martin—which was beside where he'd placed the black felt box containing the Patek Philippe chronometer—and refilled Wolfgang Kappler's snifter and then his own.

Kappler took a sip and then, having recovered some of his strong voice, said: "I so far have been allowed to travel freely—anywhere, anytime—for two very basic reasons: First, with the obvious exception of Chemische Fabrik Frankfurt, my companies have been best run by me—and thus best meet the needs of the war effort. Hitler and Bormann and Göring have agreed with this. Second, my family, particularly my wife and teenage daughter, is constantly kept under close watch by the Gestapo wherever they go.

"That *gottverdammt* Bormann has made it perfectly clear to me that should I seek any sanctuary or exile, then"—he paused, obviously struggling as he sought the right word—"then *great harm* will come to my family. The bastard of course had the arrogance to add, 'I would say that I'm very sorry but you must appreciate that it is in the best interests of the Führer and the Fatherland.'"

He paused, looked at the fire for a moment, then met Dulles's eyes.

Kappler went on: "As you well know, having helped me with the endeavor, I have significant investment in Chemische Fabrik Frankfurt A.G. here, with loose ties to Farben, and in Compania Química Limitada in Buenos Aires and Montevideo—"

"I do well know," Dulles interrupted, and thought: *Because I set that up. I saw to it that the Argentine and Uruguayan compa-*

nies were identical to the Frankfurt one—yet completely separate of Farben.

And the separation was even more important because every single one of Farben's manufacturing plants is on a list to receive a visit from a squadron of Allied bombers.

Now that Chemische Fabrik has been nationalized, I guess that distinction is what we lawyers call moot.

I. G. Farbenindustrie A.G. was a conglomerate that before the war controlled a majority share of the world chemical manufacturing market. Farben now worked around the clock supplying matériel for the Axis war effort. Dulles remembered how difficult it had been keeping the process of setting up Kappler in North and South America secret from I.G. Farben's powerful executives, the vast majority of whom became devoted members of the Nazi party.

Kappler continued: "—and, in view of my present problems, I could not be more grateful for your counsel in seeing that my South America incorporation was—*is*—completely independent of its German counterpart . . ."

Is he reading my mind? Dulles thought.

And he should mean: What's left of its German counterpart. Because Royal Air Force and Army Air Force bombers have been wiping out German refineries.

". . . especially," Kappler finished, "with the Allied bombing missions indiscriminately taking out Farben's manufacturing plants."

There he goes reading my mind again!

And if he's bothered by those bombings, he won't be thrilled with these photographs.

"Not at all indiscriminately, Wolffy. Their targets are 'POL' plants—for Petroleum, Oil, Lubricants. Other facilities may be targets of opportunity or, perhaps, as happens in the fog of war, mistakes. And you are indeed fortunate that your companies in South

America have no link—direct or indirect—to their German counterparts. Because if there was any indication that they in any manner aided the Axis, they would be taken out. Not necessarily by U.S. bombers out of Brazil, of course, but by other quiet and equally effective means."

At Canoas Air Force Base near the southern tip of Brazil—some two hundred miles north of its border with Uruguay—the U.S. Army Air Forces had a detachment of its 26th Antisubmarine Wing, based out of Miami, Florida. The U-boat hunters patrolled the Atlantic Ocean with a mix of light, medium, and heavy bombers—Lockheed A-29 Hudsons, North American B-25 Mitchells, and Boeing B-17 Flying Fortresses—any of which could easily reach a target in Argentina.

While it would be an act of war for the 26th's aircraft to attack a facility in a neutral country, Kappler knew that the OSS had sabotage teams. And he had an image flash in his mind of Augustus Compania Industrial y Mercentil Limitada and Augustus Carbonera Argentina S.A.—his steel and coal manufacturing plants just up the River Plate from Buenos Aires—going up in flames.

He met Dulles's eyes for a long moment.

Dulles, puffing on his pipe, did not blink.

Kappler nodded, then looked away in thought.

After another long moment he said: "There are of course those who are betting the Germans will win the war, and so have no reservations doing business with them. Particularly when it is quite profitable to do so with the cheap laborers supplied by the SS. And there are those who refuse to do so. . . ."

His voice trailed off as he looked at Dulles.

When Dulles was working in Berlin for Sullivan and Cromwell, he had become disgusted with the viciousness of the National Socialist German Workers' Party and Hitler's goal for a *judenrein*—a

Jew-clean—Germany. He had lobbied to have the law firm close its Berlin office and cease doing business with any company conducting any kind of trade with the Nazis. That had represented a remarkable amount of income for the firm, but Dulles declared it to be "blood money," among other just descriptions that would reflect poorly on the firm, particularly its partners.

He ultimately won on both counts. The law office in Berlin was quietly closed. Sullivan and Cromwell then sent letters explaining why the firm was taking such measures to those clients with any connection to the Third Reich. Among them were Thyssen, Kappler, and Gustav Krupp, head of the four-hundred-year-old Friedrich Krupp A.G., the largest corporation not only in Germany but in all of Europe.

"Gustav Krupp von Bohlen und Halbach is an über-Nazi," Kappler said bitterly. "Hitler is his hero—he practically drools in his presence—and so Hitler has no worries about his loyalty. Krupp, after Thyssen fled here to Switzerland, is the main reason that the industry in the Ruhr Valley continues producing at near capacity—he has his plants as well as Thyssen's entire Vereinigte Stahlwerke that Hitler seized. It would not surprise me that it was Gustav who pressured Bormann to seize Chemische Fabrik."

Dulles puffed on his pipe as he listened.

"And," Kappler finished, "he probably wants all of mine nationalized, too—which would explain Marty Bormann's threat."

"What precisely," Dulles then asked, "got Fritz Thyssen in hot water with Hitler? Was it that letter he wrote?"

"Yes," Kappler said, "mostly it was his denouncing of Nazism, particularly after being a high-profile early supporter, which was the same as denouncing Hitler himself. So, after Thyssen left the country with his family, an angry Hitler declared him a traitor, stripped him of his citizenship, and—"

A knock at the door interrupted his thought.

As Kappler and Dulles looked toward it, the door swung open and the OSS agent reappeared.

"Mr. Dulles, Herr Doktor Bernhard?"

Dulles felt Kappler's eyes on him, and when he looked he could see Kappler's expression was that of questioning.

He's wondering who the hell is interrupting what he thought was supposed to be our secret meeting.

Well, this should be as interesting as I thought it would be. . . .

[FIVE]
OSS Dellys Station
Dellys, Algeria
1130 30 May 1943

Major Richard Canidy, USAAF, sitting in the left seat of the UC-81 aircraft—the military designation for the small four-seat Stinson Reliant—applied more throttle to its single 240-horsepower Lycoming radial piston engine. As he put the high-wing tail-dragger into a steep bank, he caught in the corner of his eye that John Craig van der Ploeg, staring wide-eyed out from under his unruly wiry black hair, had a death grip on his seat.

Oh hell . . .

Canidy casually reached over and tapped him on the shoulder. When van der Ploeg jerked his head to him, Canidy formed a circle with his index finger and thumb, then raised his eyebrows, the gesture asking *Are you going to be okay?*

Van der Ploeg suddenly looked at his hands and realized he'd reflexively grabbed his seat. He immediately forced himself to let go. Then he nodded and made an *okay* sign in reply.

Canidy nodded back, but thought, *You damn sure don't look okay. But at least you're trying to force yourself to get over your phobias. Otherwise, this is going to be one helluva long mission. . . .*

Canidy turned his attention to outside the windscreen, to the dirt landing strip beneath them. The rough runway had been carved out on the backside of the ridge from where Dellys overlooked the Mediterranean Sea. At this altitude of 1,600 feet ASL—above sea level—they could still easily see the small city of low white buildings set into the hillside with a small semicircular harbor at the bottom. Canidy was reminded of Stan Fine describing it as a small-scale version of Algiers, which was some sixty-odd miles due west.

At the landing strip's eastern end, next to a Nissen hut, were two olive drab aircraft sitting side by side. The bigger of the two, a twin-engine tail-dragger, was a C-47. A jeep had been parked by the Gooney Bird's nose.

That should be our bird to Sicily. . . .

The second aircraft was another UC-81. Canidy watched as it began moving, taxiing maybe fifty feet, and then turning onto what on an improved runway would have been a well-marked threshold, complete with numbers "27" to indicate the compass heading of 270 degrees. Here, however, it was all just raw dirt. If not for the presence of the airplanes and the orange windsock above the hut, it would've been easy to mistake the strip as nothing more than a wide swath in a crude road that cut through the lush green hillside.

Canidy continued banking his Stinson, going around so that he would touch down almost exactly where the aircraft had taxied now.

As he leveled out and lined up with the strip, they hit a thermal. The wave of hot air rising off the ground tossed the aircraft, causing it to suddenly rise then drop. Although the harness straps kept them snug in their seats, John Craig van der Ploeg immediately grabbed his seat bottom—then almost as quickly realized he had done so, and released his grip, forcing his hands to his knees. He took a fast series of shallow breaths.

Good job, Canidy thought, keeping his focus forward as van der Ploeg's eyes darted his way to see if Canidy had caught him.

Canidy now saw the UC-81 on the ground suddenly kick up a cloudburst of tan dirt as the pilot gave the engine full takeoff power. The plane then started accelerating and almost immediately became airborne. With a climb rate of 1,300 feet per minute, it quickly gained altitude.

Canidy decreased his throttle and, with his airspeed dropping, began lowering his flaps. As the aircraft settled into a smooth, steady descent, and he tweaked the throttle, he now realized that John Craig van der Ploeg had been watching his every move with rapt fascination—and that he was staring with what looked like genuine interest at the altimeter and its needles creeping counterclockwise.

That brought back memories of his time as an instructor pilot at Pensacola Naval Air Station.

I should've let him fly this thing. It would have taken his damn mind off being enclosed.

Well, maybe next time.

No. Definitely next time.

Him knowing how to fly is a skill that could come in handy.

With the altimeter needles indicating they were passing through eight hundred feet ASL, Dellys disappeared behind the ridgeline. Canidy, with the aircraft now quickly approaching the threshold of the dirt strip, brought it in while keeping enough altitude to just pass over the almost dissipated dirt cloud. He then settled the aircraft down, the wheels of the fixed main gear gently touching ground and kicking up their own dirt cloud. The tailwheel then found the runway.

Greased it! Canidy thought, and grinned inwardly.

The Stinson lightly bounced along the uneven dirt strip as Canidy taxied to where the other UC-81 had just been beside the Gooney Bird. Canidy now saw that a guard was sitting in the driver seat of the jeep. He wore a U.S. Army uniform with no insignia. A Colt .45 in a holster hung from his web belt, and a .30 caliber carbine rested across his lap.

He must have gone inside the hut to avoid getting sandblasted by the propwash.

Canidy gave the guard a thumbs-up as he applied the brakes and chopped the power. The propeller slowed as the engine chugged dead. The guard got out of the jeep, grabbed two sets of wheel chocks from the back, then moved toward the aircraft.

In the quiet cockpit, Canidy threw the master switch, then glanced at his Hamilton chronometer wristwatch.

Exactly twenty minutes to cover the sixty miles from Algiers.

Not bad for a little bird . . . could take this to Sicily if we absolutely had no other choice.

But what a long damn ride that'd be.

And we'd have to find a place to hide it, and a way to refuel it. . . .

John Craig van der Ploeg turned to him, forced a smile, and made a thumbs-up gesture.

And I'm not sure he'd make it, Canidy thought as he pulled off his headset.

Despite the sweat on his forehead giving him away, he's trying like hell to put a good face on his fear.

Then he thought: *Damn I miss this! These seat-of-the-pants puddle jumpers are fun—but nothing like flying fighters. . . .*

Canidy gestured with his thumb to the back of the aircraft and said, "Let's leave the gear there until we find out where it—and we—go."

John Craig van der Ploeg glanced back at the hefty black duffel bags and two parachute packs, then gave him another thumbs-up. He nodded, his mop of thick black hair bouncing as he did so.

Canidy, watching the guard start tying down the aircraft, unfastened his harness.

He thought, *Well, we are way ahead of where we were just two hours ago.*

But still just barely getting fucking started . . .

"Bad news," Captain Stanley S. Fine had announced to Canidy and John Craig two hours earlier at his desk at OSS Algiers Station.

Fine had set up his office in what before the war had been the villa's reading room. It was on the second of the Sea View Villa's four floors. In its center, four enormous dark leather chairs, each with its own reading lamp, were arranged around a low square stone table. The walls were lined with bookshelves, complete with a small ladder on rollers to reach the higher shelves. Covering one wall of books were various charts that detailed the OSS Mediterranean Theatre of Operations.

There had been no desk, and Fine had had one fashioned out of a solid door—complete with hinges and knob still attached—placed across a pair of makeshift sawhorses. His office chair had come from the kitchen, which was just down the hall, past the two dining areas. The room also had a view of the harbor beyond the French doors that opened onto a small balcony.

OSS Algiers HQ had a permanent staff of about twenty. Most wore, as did Fine, the U.S. Army tropical worsted uniform, with or without insignia depending on their current duties. Another group of twenty was transient, working mostly with the training of agents, and wore anything except military-issued items as they came and went on irregular schedules.

They all shared the folding wooden-framed cots that filled three of the four bedrooms on the villa's top floor. The fourth bedroom—a windowless interior space—had been turned into the communications room. Its wooden door was steel-reinforced, with a wooden beam and brackets on the inside added as security. Tables held wireless two-way radios and Teletypes and typewriters. There was a nearly constant dull din of the operators sending and receiving the W/T traffic—the tapping out of Morse code and the clacking of their typing the decrypted messages. An armed guard was posted in the hall.

Next level down, the third-floor bedrooms had been made into basic offices for more of the permanent staffers. They held mismatched chairs with makeshift desks and rows of battered filing cabinets.

And the very bottom floor—a huge space, complete with a formal ballroom that prior to the war had been used for entertaining—was a warehouse. The storage area held stacks of crates and heavy wooden shelving. There were the usual office supplies—typewriters, boxes of paper and ribbons, et cetera—and the not so usual office supplies.

Safes contained hundreds of thousands of dollars in gold and silver coins. Rows of wooden racks held a small armory—weaponry of American, British, and German manufacture—as well as stores of ammunition. Other crates contained Composition C-2 plastic explosive and fuses. Clothing racks were lined with a variety of enemy uniforms collected from prisoners of war taken in the North African campaigns. And, stacked in one corner, were cases of Haig & Haig Gold Label scotch.

"What bad news?" Dick Canidy said, looking down at his feet as Stan Fine hung up the telephone that was a secure line to General Eisenhower's AFHQ office at the Hotel Saint George.

Canidy plucked a crisp paper bill that was stuck to his chukka boot. He briefly examined its front and back, then let it flutter back to his feet.

The floor was nearly ankle deep in paper currency. The notes had not been printed by the United States Bureau of Engraving but, instead, by counterfeiters whom OSS Washington had arranged to be released from federal prison into OSS custody. The idea of convicted felons not only free to continue counterfeiting but being encouraged to do so had thrilled absolutely no one at the Treasury Department and had caused FBI Director J. Edgar Hoover to formally protest to the President. But once again Wild Bill Donovan prevailed.

Now more than the equivalent of a million U.S. dollars' worth of bogus 100 Deutsche reichsmark notes covered Fine's office floor. Another million in a mix of French francs and Italian lire filled the floor of the commo room. It was obvious that fresh-off-the-press notes would not pass muster in the field and Fine had decided that the way to more or less gently "age" them was to walk on them.

"That was Owen on the horn," Fine said.

He saw Canidy make a face at the mention of General Eisenhower's pompous aide, Lieutenant Colonel J. Warren Owen. A chair warmer whose sole job seemed to be keeping Eisenhower's schedule—and keeping Ike to that schedule, which could be a formidable task—Owen had a very high opinion of himself. It wasn't necessarily deserved, many believed, especially when he arrogantly would, as a way to quickly establish his bona fides, reference anything that allowed him to boast of being a graduate of *Hah*-vard.

Fine remembered Canidy declaring: "When I was at MIT, I had a helluva lot of bright buddies in Cambridge. How that dimwit Owen got into Harvard, let alone got through it, I'll never know."

Making matters worse, for whatever reason—"It's because he's not bright enough to understand unconventional warfare and the risks required," Canidy further declared—Owen liked nothing more than to say no to damn near anything that the OSS requested.

Fine went on: "Owen said that Ike—he actually said it in that condescending tone he uses, 'Per our Supreme Commander's direct order'—the *Casabianca* was the last submarine they're letting us use 'until further notice.' I won't bore you with all his other reprimands."

Canidy was not only familiar with the Free French Forces submarine *Casabianca*, he considered himself friends with her thirty-five-year-old captain. Commander Jean L'Herminier had extricated Canidy from Sicily on March 25 and then eleven days later put Canidy back in—this second time with Frank Nola and Jim "Tubes" Fuller—before pulling Canidy out alone.

"The last?" Canidy repeated. "Damn it!"

Fine nodded. "And he added that that had been allowed only because the sub is headed back to Corsica. Ike was genuinely impressed with the intel that Pearl Harbor has provided, and now that the station has gone off the air again—it's having troubles with its SSRT transmitting—he said he feels obligated to let us check on it. We're sending in a replacement radio and other supplies. More importantly, we want to make physical contact to ensure the station isn't blown."

L'Herminier—whose submarine was carrying her complement of four officers and fifty men, plus a half-dozen OSS agents—would again use the method he had developed for covert landings. After carefully surveying the coast by periscope, looking for any enemy activity and pinpointing an appropriate landing spot for the teams to go ashore by rubber boat, the sub would slip back out to sea, flood its ballast, and sit on the bottom of the Mediterranean awaiting night.

Then, at dark, with the sub barely on the surface to keep a low profile from enemy patrols, the small boat would be launched.

Casabianca crewmen, armed with Sten 9mm submachine guns, would row the OSS men—carrying W/T radios and weapons and cash—to shore. The team then inserted, the crewmen would return to the sub and the sub would return to the sea bottom until the scheduled times to ascend to periscope depth and receive the signal either to retrieve the team or to leave them.

"But goddamn it!" Canidy blurted. "That is *exactly* the same thing we're trying to do with Mercury Station!"

"Except," Fine said reasonably, "Mercury is (a) on Sicily and (b) no one at AFHQ is aware that the station even exists. Owen took more than a little delight just now in carefully reminding me quote Remember that our Supreme Commander is quite anxious about the security of Husky and thus has ordered there be absolutely no OSS activity there prior to D-day unquote."

Canidy looked ready to explode.

"The sonofabitch doesn't know that I've been in and out of Sicily twice!" he said. "Can you imagine trying to sell this to Ike now? 'General Eisenhower, sir, I realize that no one in AFHQ ever believed that the Krauts had chemical and biological weapons on Sicily. But I went in and found them, then blew them up, and then left behind a clandestine radio team that, despite us now believing it is controlled by the SS, is reporting that up to a half-million enemy combatants are arriving to defend against Husky. Oh, and we also have reason to believe that the Krauts have brought in more Tabun and/or yellow fever. So, sir, can you please allow us a sub to insert one small team?' "

Fine stared silently at Canidy.

"Yeah. And that's exactly what Ike would do, too, Stan. Just stare at me. And then probably have me put in shackles until after Husky—hell, maybe for good measure until six months after the end of the war—for the 'good order and discipline' of the service."

He paused, then sighed. "Jesus!"

Kicking up a trail of counterfeit reichsmarks, Canidy walked across the room to the French doors. He swung them open and for a long, quiet moment looked out at the ocean.

"When did the *Casabianca* sail?" Canidy then said.

"Three days ago," Fine said.

"From here to Corsica," Canidy said, looking out in its direction, "that's right at five hundred nautical miles, making it a four-day run at best to get there. Then another day or two on station, while they deal with Pearl Harbor, then four days to get back here."

He turned, looked at Fine, and said, "That's best-case scenario—"

"Agreed."

"—and I can't wait that long, even if I thought I could convince Jean to turn around and insert us again in Sicily."

"Then what?" Fine said.

"We are in radio contact with the *Casabianca*, no?" Canidy said.

Fine looked at John Craig van der Ploeg.

"Daily, right?"

John Craig nodded.

"The commo room," he said, "has a schedule of four times each day for the *Casabianca* to surface en route to periscope depth and receive our messages. Beyond that, she can transmit to us anytime that she needs to."

"Great," Canidy then said. "Then that's what we'll do!"

"*What* is what you'll do?" Fine said.

"What we'll do is parachute in and get Jean to pick us up."

Both Fine and Canidy knew L'Herminier had the mind-set of a special operator willing and able to make his own independent decisions. Six months earlier, when the SS went to capture the French fleet at the port of Toulon, the admiralty of Vichy France demanded its ships be scuttled. As dozens were burned and sunk at their moorings, L'Herminier ignored orders and, with the *Casabianca* under cannon fire, dived and made way for Algiers.

"I can convince him to do that," Canidy said. "Ike will never know."

Canidy looked between Fine and John Craig.

They said nothing.

"Good. I take it that we're agreed," Canidy then said.

"Hold on, Dick," Fine then said. "Do you really think it's wise for you to go in—especially with all you know?"

"I'll answer that question with a question: Did Wild Bill think it was wise to go into North Africa right before Operation Torch?"

"But, damn it, Dick, Donovan wasn't there."

"You're sure about that?"

Fine thought about it for a moment and said, "Then no one knew he was there!"

Canidy made a smug smile. "Exactly."

Fine pursued: "If the SS finds you—"

"And begins peeling the skin from my pecker?" Canidy interrupted. "I'll do what Donovan always says if he's captured—bite a Q-pill."

Fine looked at John Craig, who appeared to be contemplating the disturbing idea of suicide by cyanide pill.

"You're my witness, son. I don't approve of this." He paused, then added, "That does not mean that I don't understand it. I just don't approve of the damn thing."

"Okay," Canidy then said cheerfully, "now that that's resolved, one last thing."

He looked at John Craig.

"I'm not going to keep calling you 'John Craig,' and I'm damn sure not going to stumble over 'van der Ploeg' over and over. So, if I'm still going by Jupiter, then you can be . . . oh, what the hell . . . you can be Apollo."

"Any particular reason?" van der Ploeg said. "I don't know my Greek gods."

"Apollo was god of all kinds of things—light, sun, truth, healing, even plague."

"Okay."

"I think we're probably going to need all that—particularly the plague."

Apollo grinned.

"Stan," Canidy then said, "would you get on the horn and tell Darmstadter we're on our way out there? Just as soon as Apollo and I go downstairs and load up in the warehouse, then prepare a message for the commo room to send to the *Casabianca*. Tell Hank I'll borrow one of those tiny Stinsons I saw out at Maison Blanche if I have to."

Now Fine grinned. In some circles, Canidy was damn near infamous for stealing airplanes, boats, trucks, whatever—which he declared he was actually only "borrowing," arguing that he always returned whatever he took.

"You wouldn't be borrowing it, Dick. Those birds belong to us."

[ONE]
OSS Bern Station
Herrengasse 23
Bern, Switzerland
2325 27 May 1943

Allen Dulles, keeping eye contact with Wolfgang Kappler, said to the agent, "Yes, please show him in."

Kappler wordlessly raised his eyebrows.

They looked toward the door as a man entered and the agent slipped back out the door and closed it.

Kappler studied the man. Because of the dimly lit room, details were difficult to make out from the distance. But the fact that Dr. Bernhard was massive was unmistakable. He stood six-foot-six and had broad shoulders.

"Come join us," Dulles called out.

As the man approached, walking somewhat hunched over, Kappler could make out that, with the rumpled tweed jacket, unkempt thin hair, and horn-rimmed eyeglasses with very thick lenses, he looked very much like a university professor of about age forty.

An enormous university professor, Kappler thought.

And a familiar-looking one . . .

Reaching Dulles, the man held out his hand and said in a deep, almost abrasive voice, "A pleasure to see you again, Allen. I hope I am not interrupting anything."

I think I know that voice, Kappler thought.

In fact, I know I do!

Then the man turned toward Kappler and seemed to be trying to focus on him through the thick lenses.

He offered Kappler his hand and said, "I am Dr. Bernhard—"

No, I don't think so . . . Kappler thought.

"I know who you are!" Kappler suddenly said, his tone cordial. "Hans, it's me, Wolfgang. We met when you worked for Hjalmar Schacht at the Reichsbank in Berlin. You were involved with providing me funds for the expansion of my coal mine operations in the Ruhr Valley, near Ruhrpott."

There was a moment's hesitation, then he replied, "Wolfgang Kappler?"

He instantly pulled back his great big hand as if he had touched a red-hot stovetop. He glared down at Dulles.

"You asked me here to meet with a messenger of the devil himself?" he said. "This man can go to hell—he is closer to Hitler than Hitler's own mistress!"

Kappler puffed out his chest and declared, "It is you who can go to hell, Hans!"

Then he looked at Dulles and added, "What is this Dr. Bernhard nonsense? And how dare he speak of me that way! I thought that we were friends, Allen."

"It is his code name," Dulles explained evenly. "I think you know for obvious reasons why."

His other code name being Tiny, which is equally obvious.

When Kappler did not respond, Dulles added: "Hans is as much an anti-Nazi as you and Franz Messner."

Gisevius grunted derisively as he looked between Kappler and Dulles.

Then, as Kappler watched with shock, Gisevius casually dropped into one of the deep-cushioned leather armchairs. He leaned forward and poured himself a snifter of cognac, spilling some on the floor as he did so.

He acts as if this is his own home! Kappler thought.

Next, he flung open the humidor, fished out a fat cigar, and slammed shut the top.

Such arrogance!

Gisevius then unwrapped the cigar and ran it along his nose as he inhaled deeply. He grunted again. After dipping the closed end of the cigar in his cognac, he bit a small hole, then spit the piece of tobacco into the fireplace.

And such rudeness!

Finally he put the cigar in his mouth and, using the Zippo with the Princeton crest, lit it, then tossed the lighter back to the table.

He exhaled a massive gray cloud of smoke, grunted again, then said, "Not bad. Would be better in other company." He glanced up at Dulles. "No offense to the host."

But that is offensive!

Kappler quickly looked at Dulles to gauge his reaction—and was surprised to see that he was grinning.

Dulles then chuckled. He turned to Kappler, motioning toward the armchairs.

"Please have a seat, Wolffy. As we say in America, Hans's bark is much worse than his bite."

Gisevius grunted again.

"Or his grunt," Dulles added with a smile.

Allen Dulles had become accustomed to the brusqueness of the forty-year-old Hans Bernd Gisevius shortly after they had first been introduced in early 1943. Gisevius then had carefully—but boldly—announced that he worked for Admiral Wilhelm Canaris, the head of the Abwehr.

Canaris, Gisevius explained, had posted him as a vice counsel of the German consulate in Zurich, with the position serving as his cover for his secret mission of reaching out to the Allies. Then Gisevius had gone on to declare that he and Canaris were part of a group plotting to kill Hitler.

To Dulles, who by profession was trained to be skeptical, it had all sounded like so much hot air braggadocio. Gisevius certainly was not the first self-important German official to present himself at the American Embassy and try cutting a deal that promised, say, to single-handedly deliver the Nazi surrender in exchange for said official to find himself the head of the new German government.

Single-handedly with of course the full support and aid of America.

Thus, Gisevius had had to work hard to be believed. He'd already failed to convince the British, who had turned him away for fear he was a double agent. In 1933, after graduating from law school, Gisevius had joined the Geheime Staatspolizei—the Secret State Police—at its start only to be more or less thrown out for declaring that the organization itself was full of criminals, and the Brits had warned Dulles of that fear based on his having been in the Gestapo.

Despite being a skeptic, Dulles decided to take a chance—a cautious one—on the unlikely secret agent.

Gisevius soon solidified his standing with Dulles by supplying an endless stream of German intelligence, beginning with the fact that a mole had been working in the office of the military attaché in the American Embassy in Bern. When Dulles had questioned that, Gisevius produced a fistful of copies of Top Secret messages that the U.S. legation recently had sent—including one of Dulles's—that had been intercepted by the Nazis and passed to the Abwehr.

Dulles's OSS agents, with a little effort, were able to track the leak to a Swiss civilian who was employed as a janitor. A Nazi sympathizer, the janitor was stealing carbon copy sheets from the trash of the military attaché—copies that were supposed to be put in a secure burn bag and destroyed.

And then Dulles had learned that the Gestapo not only was watching Gisevius, it had given the group plotting against Hitler—including Generaloberst Ludwig Beck, the former chief of the German General Staff, and Count Wolf-Heinrich von Helldorf, Berlin's chief of police—its own code name, Schwarze Kapelle, the Black Orchestra.

"Allen," Gisevius now announced, holding up his snifter in his right hand, "so as not to appear rude to you, I will finish your nice cognac. But I then shall leave the company of one who actively supports Nazism"—he puffed on his cigar, then took it in his left hand and poked it in Kappler's direction, the smoke filling Kappler's face—"one who in fact was one of Hitler's earliest financiers and today is on a first-name basis with Hitler's High Command ring of thugs."

Allen Dulles glanced at Wolfgang Kappler, whose face had turned red. His green eyes were narrow and clearly furious.

"Let me tell you how that happened!" Kappler suddenly snapped, his tone uncharacteristically cold.

"Please do," Gisevius replied.

"Twenty years ago, when Fritz and I first met him, Marty Bormann was a snot-nosed twenty-three-year-old district leader in the Mecklenburg Freikorps Rossbach."

He paused, locked eyes with Gisevius, then added almost bitterly, "I assume you know what that is?"

Gisevius was uncowed.

"The paramilitary organization," he replied evenly, then puffed on his cigar. "The Freikorps that was established in the Ruhr set out to cause trouble for the French, whose military occupied the Ruhr to oversee steel and coal production for Germany, having defaulted on timber and coal deliveries. They were fanatical fighters, primarily against the Communists, but also against others."

"Fanatical is precisely it," Kappler said. "And already Marty—whom I, being twelve years his senior, knew very well, which I will get into in a moment—was showing that he had a cruel streak. He managed an estate by day, and it was there that he met, and came to lead, the Freikorps Rossbach guerrillas, sabotaging anything the French considered valuable and attacking anyone thought to sympathize with the French or the Communists."

"'Attack'?" Gisevius parroted, thickly sarcastic. "I believe the proper word is *assassinated*."

Kappler looked at him a long moment.

"Yes," he said, "I will grant that that is what happened. And it is why Marty spent time in jail."

Gisevius nodded and smiled smugly.

Kappler continued: "Marty was found guilty of aiding Rudolf Höss, who killed Walther Kadow for being the traitor they believed told the French about Albert Schlageter derailing the trains."

"Schlageter was found guilty and executed," Gisevius said.

"Correct. And almost immediately made a martyr for the Nazi party."

Dulles, his face showing no emotion as he took in the discussion, had watched much of what Gisevius and Kappler described, first when serving in the U.S. diplomat service in Switzerland and collecting intelligence against the Austro-Hungarian and German empires, and then between world wars when developing clients in Germany for Sullivan and Cromwell.

During his time in both the government and the private sector,

Dulles had come in contact with many leaders, including an up-and-coming charismatic politician, an Austrian by the name of Adolf Hitler.

"'*Wenn ich Kultur höre entsichere ich meinen Luger!*'" Gisevius suddenly quoted, raising his right hand and mimicking a pistol with his thumb and trigger finger.

"Actually," Dulles put in, "the pistol in question was a Browning—*Whenever I hear of culture, I release the safety on my Browning!* The key dialogue in the stage play on Schlageter's life, dedicated to Hitler, trumpeting the anti-bourgeois of Hitler and Nazism."

Gisevius, poking his cigar at Kappler again, said: "And you were a major supporter of National Socialism—of Hitler and the anti-bourgeois of Nazism—and encouraged others in your industry to support the same. You and Fritz Thyssen and Doktor Emil Kirdorf—"

"Kirdorf was a blind, doddering old fool!" Kappler exploded at the mention of the ninety-year-old industrialist. "But he was immensely powerful—"

"Hitler personally awarded him the Order of the German Eagle," Gisevius interrupted, "the highest honor for a German civilian."

"—yes, and so he influenced us, particularly as we shared a national pride. We all believed that the Treaty of Versailles was belittling our great people."

With the treaty, Germany agreed to take responsibility for causing the First World War. It required that the country make steep reparations as well as to disarm—the aim to make the Germans conciliatory and to pacify them.

"As Kirdorf declared," Kappler went on, "'We will rise again!'"

Gisevius said: "And you embraced that. So much so that in Amsterdam you and Thyssen arranged, through Rudolf Hess, for a three-hundred-thousand-mark line of credit with the Dutch Bank voor Handel en Scheepvaart, which Thyssen happened to quietly own. Hess spent the complete line—which you then personally covered in Dutch guilders—to purchase what would become the Nazi party's headquarters in Munich. . . ."

Kappler did not reply.

He thought: *Did he get all this information from being at the Reichsbank—or from the Abwehr?*

". . . All this while," Gisevius went on, puffing heavily on his cigar, "you and Thyssen were becoming buddies with Bormann and his goon squad. Bormann named his firstborn after Hitler, his second son after Hess, and his third after Heinrich Himmler. All of whom were godfathers to their namesakes. Hitler also served as witness to Bormann's wedding to the daughter of a Nazi party official. And Hermann Göring's five-year-old is Hitler's goddaughter."

He paused to let that sink in, glanced at Dulles, then looked back at Kappler and added in an unpleasant tone, "So, such is the dirty little secret of Herr Kappler being long connected with those goons who now make up Hitler's High Command."

Gisevius, turning and staring at the fireplace, took a deep sip of his cognac, the light from the flames reflecting on his snifter. He puffed his cigar, then turned to Dulles.

"Allen," he said, "I'm afraid that this was not a good idea. I do not believe Herr Kappler is the proper candidate. If that indeed was your intention . . ."

"Proper candidate?" Kappler blurted, his tone clearly indicating that he was offended. "For what?"

He turned to Dulles and repeated, "Candidate for what?"

[TWO]
OSS Dellys Station
Dellys, Algeria
1145 30 May 1943

By the time Dick Canidy and John Craig van der Ploeg jumped to the ground from the Stinson, the guard had it chocked and tied down. Then, with a casual wave of greeting, he had headed back to his seat in the jeep.

They started walking toward the Nissen hut—an inverted "U" of corrugated steel from War One with wooden walls at each end and a single wooden screened door—that was being used as a combination guard shack and base ops building.

The wooden door swung open, and a tall, skinny twenty-two-year-old American with a round friendly face came out.

"Welcome back, Dick!" First Lieutenant Henry Darmstadter, USAAF, called out as the spring on the door slammed it shut behind him. "Stan said you were on the way."

Canidy went to Darmstadter and wrapped his arms around him.

"Damn good to see you, Hank!" Canidy said.

"Yeah," Darmstadter said, trying to wiggle free of the grip, "but not quite that much."

John Craig chuckled.

Canidy then put his hands on either side of Darmstadter's head and kissed him wetly in the middle of his forehead.

"Jesus Christ, Dick!" Darmstadter said, wiping at his forehead with his sleeve. But he was grinning.

Canidy looked at John Craig and said, "This man saved my ass in Hungary, and I will never forget it."

"Really?"

Van der Ploeg then looked at Darmstadter.

"How they hanging, John Craig?" Darmstadter said, dodging the question. "You need another ride over to the Sandbox?"

John Craig van der Ploeg caught Dick Canidy's questioning look.

As John Craig shook Darmstadter's hand, he said to Canidy: "Remember? I told you I've been out here almost every day."

Canidy nodded. "Right. Going through throat-cutting school."

"I hear he's been doing a helluva job," Hank offered, and motioned at the Gooney Bird. "You made three jumps last week, right?"

"Four," John Craig said, "including the night jump. That gives me twenty total. But tell me about saving Dick."

Darmstadter sighed. "Look, the truth of it is I did nothing that Dick wouldn't have done for me."

"But the fact of it is you did it," Canidy said, then looked at John Craig. "Very simply, I was trapped in Hungary, without a single hope in hell of not being captured and either shot on sight or strung up in a cold damp dungeon to slowly die. Then Hank here came flying in on his great white steed—"

"It was a Gooney Bird just like this one," Hank interrupted, shaking his head and gesturing toward the olive drab C-47.

John Craig's head turned to Darmstadter . . .

"—his great *olive drab* steed that was filled up to here"—Canidy went on, holding his hand flat, palm down, index finger touching his forehead—"with enough extra fuel to blow us all to kingdom come—"

John Craig turned to Canidy . . .

"It was just an auxiliary fuel cell," Darmstadter said.

. . . then back to Darmstadter . . .

"—and Hank landed this fuel-packed flying bomb on a piece of real estate that was this big"—he put his index finger and thumb a hair-width apart—"and surrounded by ancient thick forest—"

. . . back to Canidy . . .

"Dick had actually taken down some trees with Primacord."

. . . to Darmstadter . . .

"And then with everyone finally onboard, Hank managed to get his now overloaded olive drab steed airborne, its props actually trimming the treetops as the bird strained to gain altitude."

. . . then, finally, John Craig looked to Darmstadter for his response.

Darmstadter shrugged.

"It was nothing," he said. "You just do what you have to do."

"I'd never heard that story," John Craig said.

"And you wouldn't from Hank," Canidy said. "He's what they call 'modest.' And to think that Hank here almost never made it as a pilot. But that's another story."

"What?" John Craig said.

"It was nothing," Darmstadter said again. "I just had to learn to get over a queasy stomach during aerobatic maneuvers."

"It was more than nothing," Canidy said. "The Elimination Board had him on probation, and he was about to get thrown out for throwing up and becoming disoriented in rough air."

Canidy saw a look of recognition in John Craig's eyes.

He's thinking he's not the first guy to have some obstacle to overcome.

Canidy went on: "Getting booted would've meant that he'd never gotten his wings, which would've meant that he'd never made it into our merry little band of spies"—he paused, after a moment cleared his throat, then finished—"which would've meant that he'd never plucked my sorry ass out of Hungary.

"But," Canidy finished, "he overcame it. And he now is one of the finest pilots I am privileged to know. And a kiss on the forehead is my reminder I have not forgotten my deep debt."

Darmstadter appeared embarrassed.

"So," Canidy said, changing the subject, "what the hell is going on out here?"

After a moment, Hank nodded at the guard and said, more than a little angrily, "For starters, spending far too much time keeping our aircraft from being requisitioned for Husky by anyone at AFHQ who can even spell 'OSS.'"

"What does that mean?"

"I guess they figure if they can take our birds, we can't get into trouble. Everything we're doing is being tightly controlled. We have been assigned a limited airspace for practicing our jumps. And our aircraft now are not allowed to fly more than a mile out to sea."

"What the hell?"

"It's about AFHQ making sure we don't go anywhere that might reveal Husky. Last week, we had a Gooney Bird accidentally stray outside the one-mile limit—the pilot was distracted when he dropped his cigar—and next thing he knew when he looked up, puffing away, there were two Lightnings along his nose. They'd been on coast patrol and sent out to escort him back to base."

"Jesus! Ike really is serious about putting the clamps on things."

Darmstadter shrugged.

"Yeah, but it has actually become a game for us."

"A game?" John Craig said.

"A challenge. You went through Dick's school—our job requires us to figure out how to sneak around obstacles. Eisenhower doesn't know it, but he's actually helping us practice our skills."

Canidy laughed out loud.

"Well, that really answers one of my next questions."

"Which is?"

Canidy glanced at the Gooney Bird, then looked at Darmstadter.

"First things first," he said. "Can you sneak around Ike's obstacles with this to drop a couple agents in Sicily?"

"When?"

Canidy mimed looking at his watch. "Yesterday."

"Who's going in?"

"Who might you think?"

Darmstadter looked between Canidy and van der Ploeg.

"Should I ask?"

Canidy shook his head. "Best not to. That way—"

"I can honestly say I don't know," Darmstadter finished.

"You must have been going to my school, too," he said with a smile.

"I can take you," Darmstadter then said. "But not with this bird."

"Why not?" Canidy asked.

Darmstadter smiled.

"Because I have something better," he said, and gestured to the far end of the dirt strip.

"What's down there?"

"You'll see," he said. "C'mon."

Darmstadter, having booted the guard from the jeep, drove them down the dirt strip. As they neared the runway's far eastern end, Canidy could begin to make out that a pocket had been carved into the side of the hill and covered in desert camouflage netting.

It's a revetment.

With something big inside.

Somethings, plural.

Darmstadter stopped the jeep to one side of the revetment, then hopped out and waved for Canidy and van der Ploeg to follow.

As they stepped closer, Canidy said, "You're hiding aircraft?"

Darmstadter smiled and said, "Yep. Here. Give me a hand."

He untied two lengths of rope, and the three of them began rolling back the netting. Canidy then saw two identical C-47s, both unlike any he had seen.

A version of the Douglas DC-3 airliner, the twin-engine C-47 was an Army Air Forces workhorse, reliably transporting everything from troops to cargo to towing gliders. The Douglas manufacturing plants were producing them by the thousands, nearly one every half hour.

Canidy knew that the C-47's fuel-efficient twelve-hundred-horsepower Twin Wasp radial piston engines gave the aircraft a cruise speed of 160 miles per hour and a top speed of 224. With a range of more than two thousand miles, it could without adding an auxiliary fuel cell—as Hank had done for the Save Canidy's Ass Mission in Hungary—easily make the Dellys-Sicily round-trip.

Assuming, of course, it wasn't shot down.

Darmstadter's Gooney Birds were painted a flat black. And while, like conventional C-47s, they had USAAF insignia—a star in a circle over a bar—under each wing and on either side of the rear of the fuselage, the insignia was painted a matte gray, as were the tail numbers on the vertical stabilizer, just ahead of the rudder.

"I don't know much about airplanes," van der Ploeg said, "but I don't think I've ever seen any like that."

"What the hell, Hank?" Canidy said. "What's the story?"

"Aren't they beautiful? I got the idea from the 492nd Bombardment Group at Eighth Air Force."

"At Harrington Airfield."

"That's it. Outside London. After they're done fixing up a bunch of shot-up B-24s they've salvaged—patching the bullet holes, removing ball turrets—their plan is to drop our OSS guys behind the lines in France. They're painting the Liberators this same dull black so that they deflect light from the ack-ack's search beams. The black makes them damn-near invisible in the dark of night."

Canidy looked back at the Gooney Birds. "And so you had these painted, too. Interesting. Anything else?"

"Flame dampeners on the engine exhaust. And . . ."

Darmstadter started walking toward the tail of the one on the right.

He stopped near the rear of the left side of the fuselage, at the troop doorway. The door had been removed. He pointed inside.

Canidy followed him and looked.

"Jesus!" he said. "A Browning?"

"Yeah, I wanted a fifty-cal but could only get my hands on the thirty-cal," Hank said. "It's a modified M1919."

"Who modified it?"

"Who do you think? I added a heavier barrel for full-auto—that's five hundred rounds a minute. And I mounted it on this quick-release track, so it's easy to move out of the way for jumps, then move it back in place. There's a second Browning onboard as backup."

As they walked out of the revetment, Canidy surveyed the aircraft and nodded appreciatively. "That is one helluva special bird."

They pulled the netting back in place.

"No one beyond Stan Fine knows that I have them. I brought them in after midnight, and only take them up after oh-dark-hundred."

"How do you avoid not getting picked up on radar? You don't—"

"Stay on the deck? Sure. Sometimes. Why not? But I've got another trick."

Darmstadter got in behind the wheel of the jeep.

"Which is?" Canidy said, as he and van der Ploeg hopped in.

Darmstadter engaged the starter and the engine ground to life. "You'll see tonight. Your bags are packed, right?"

Canidy nodded. "Just waiting on you."

[THREE]
OSS Bern Station
Herrengasse 23
Bern, Switzerland
2345 27 May 1943

Wolfgang Kappler, uncharacteristically, raised his voice: "I asked, Allen, a proper candidate for what?"

Allen Dulles made a dismissive motion with his hand in the direction of Gisevius.

He said, "Before we get into that . . ." and took the manila envelope stamped TOP SECRET from the round marble table. He pinched its brass clasp, then opened the flap.

"My old friend," Dulles then said, "the reason I asked you here tonight was to share some important, but possibly upsetting, information."

"What upsetting information?" Kappler said.

Dulles pulled out a stack of black-and-white eight-by-ten-inch photographs and handed the top few to Kappler.

"And these are?" Kappler said as he looked down.

"Photographs shot only days ago, before and after Operation Chastise. We received them this afternoon. The ones you hold were taken by a photo-recon Spitfire aircraft at first light two days before the mission."

Kappler noted that the first photograph had a time stamp in the lower right-hand corner. It read: 0715 14 MAY 43. The photograph showed the bold rays of the early morning sun painting the bucolic valley in warm tones. The low angle of the sun cast long, dramatic shadows from the tall trees and church steeples.

"Yes, the Ruhr is wonderfully peaceful at that hour," Kappler said. "Before the war, it was among my favorite times, simply sitting and enjoying my *strudel und kaffee mit crème* as the day came to life. I very much miss it."

Dulles then handed him another few photographs.

"These were taken three days later," he said simply.

Kappler looked, quickly turned them toward the light for a better look—and caught himself in a gasp.

"Ach du lieber Gott!" he whispered.

Under the layer of industrial haze, what looked like a blanket of morning fog, with only the treetops and steeples rising above, was actually the morning sunlight reflecting on a torrent of floodwaters.

"The western Ruhr Valley, it is flooded!"

"Yes. The dams were bombed."

"How is this true? How did they get past the German defenses? And past the underwater torpedo netting that protects the dam itself?" He paused, then added, "And why have I not heard about this?"

Gisevius answered: "The British used a new 'bouncing bomb' dropped from specially modified Lancaster Mark III aircraft."

"'Bouncing bomb'? How do you know of this?"

Gisevius, with a flip of his hand, gestured for Dulles to answer.

Dulles explained: "As I understand it, somewhere around twenty Royal Air Force bombers descended almost to the surface of the reservoirs, and then released these new bouncing bombs, after first spinning them backward, so that they skipped stone-like across the surface until they hit the dams. The Lancasters managed to get in and out of German airspace by flying at treetop level to avoid being picked up by radar or spotted by antiaircraft. Which of course was extremely hazardous; at least one aircraft crashed after striking power lines. Three of the Lancasters in the first wave of eight either were shot down or crashed."

"It is unbelievable," Kappler said.

"That is what the Nazis want everyone to think," Dulles said. "But, as you see, the mission was highly successful."

"And," Gisevius said, "that is why you have not heard about it. It is a black eye for Hitler that they want kept quiet."

Dulles added, "Beyond the success of bombing of such critical German assets—once considered untouchable—this act also keeps Hitler on the defensive, holding back troops that could be put, for example, on the offensive in Russia."

And on the French coast, Dulles thought but would never mention, *in anticipation of a cross-channel invasion.*

Kappler nodded, then turned to the next photograph.

He made a face and shook his head in shock. The picture showed the 112-foot-tall limestone Möhne dam—and the enormous jagged gap in its middle. The three-thousand-acre lake, surrounded by gnarled oak and ash trees, looked to be at least half-drained. Water still cascaded over the lip of the hole.

"This breach in the Möhne," Kappler said softly, "it looks to be about eighty meters wide and at least that deep."

Kappler rapidly flipped through the stack.

"Do you have any information on my properties?" he said as he scanned each image. "Thyssen and Krupp had their steel plants closest to the dams."

Here it comes, Dulles thought.

Kappler flipped back to the photograph showing the torrent of floodwater reflecting the morning sunlight.

"Judging by how high the water is on the church steeples,"

Kappler said, "the flooding stream appears to be some ten meters deep."

He looked up at Dulles.

"That is the disturbing news I mentioned," Dulles said. "To the best of our knowledge, all but two of your plants were lost."

"All *but* two? I lost *five* manufacturing facilities!"

Dulles nodded solemnly.

"Possibly others," he said. "Krupp lost everything it had in the Ruhr, including what was previously Thyssen's. Because, as you note, they were all closest to the dams."

"Everything?"

Dulles nodded again.

"That floodwater was powerful—more than three hundred million tons. For fifty miles downstream, it flooded mines and wiped out more than a hundred factories, a thousand houses, and rail lines, roads, bridges. Farms were washed away—crops, livestock, everything."

"And people?" Kappler asked, but it clearly was an obvious statement.

Dulles nodded solemnly.

"Ach du lieber Gott!" he again whispered.

"It is our understanding," Dulles said, glancing at Gisevius, "that the German reports are listing casualties of nearly thirteen hundred killed, most French and Belgian POWs and forced laborers."

Kappler crossed himself.

"Sorry that you lost your *sklavenarbeiter*?" Gisevius said, his tone caustic.

"Hans!" Dulles snapped.

Dulles had heard Kappler complain about having to witness the cruelty inflicted on the slave laborers, and had written reports on them that he had sent to General Donovan, who then shared the information with President Roosevelt and others in the OSS.

Gisevius went on: "No more exploitation of slave labor for your mines? Fear not. The SS will bring more."

"That's enough!" Dulles said.

"I do not exploit!" Kappler said, his voice rising. "One cannot be found guilty of a crime when another holds a gun to his head forcing him to cause such an act! I have no choice but to use them because the SS demands both the money I pay for them and the increased productivity they provide." He paused, then added: "I will have you know, however, that we are, as delicately as possible, running the plants far from peak production. Delicately, because anyone even remotely suspected of intentional slowage—and especially sabotage—is dealt with immediately by the SS."

"And," Dulles put in, "I can vouch that Wolfgang has seen many of the Jewish slaves smuggled out."

"Many?" Gisevius challenged.

"More than a hundred in the last six months," Dulles said.

"How do you know that?"

"Beyond saying that the OSS has provided their false papers, I cannot tell you more at this time."

Gisevius grunted.

Dulles then handed over to Kappler another series of photographs. All were mostly black with vaguely recognizable landmarks that were faintly lit by moonlight.

"These recon shots were taken at night."

Kappler looked at Dulles, then asked, "The hydroelectric output from the dams—there were, I believe, a pair of five-thousand-kilowatt power plants . . ."

"Destroyed," Dulles said.

"Then it is with no surprise that the valley," Kappler said, his voice almost a whisper, "is completely without lights."

"And will be until the hydroelectric power returns. Also not surprising, there are of course crews already working to repair them."

Dulles passed another photograph. "The Eder dam also took hits."

"That's the largest masonry dam in Germany," Kappler said. "Its reservoir holds more than twice that of the Möhne."

Dulles nodded, then passed two more photographs.

"And also the Sorpe and Ennepe dams."

As Kappler looked at them, Dulles said, "Because the overall success of the mission will be a great morale booster for the Allies, the story is going to be widely reported beginning tomorrow." He gestured toward the Braun radio. "Landessender Beromünster, for example, will break the news in German and, using BBC reports, also in English. And it will run—with a map but not these photographs—in England's newspapers and in every other newspaper we can get to publish it."

He pulled from the envelope a copy of the *Berner Zeitung*.

"This is an early copy of tomorrow's edition," Dulles said.

Kappler took the *Berner Zeitung* and glanced at the front page. The largest headline read in German: BOMBERS DESTROY STRATEGIC GERMAN DAMS.

Dulles went on: "We also have prepared leaflets to drop in German-occupied countries reporting that the taking out of the dams has caused widespread panic. That there's no water available for anything from drinking to fighting fires should the Allies follow up with an incendiary attack. That without the electricity generated by the dam's power plant, homes are dark and industries idle. That there is hysteria over what little water remains being tainted and causing deadly diseases."

Wolfgang Kappler crossed himself again.

He said, "When Fritz Thyssen quietly fled Germany with his wife, daughter, son-in-law, and grandson in September of 1939, the rest of us who had even considered leaving were stuck. Now, at least thank God that my wife and daughter have been staying in our Berlin home. Otherwise . . ."

Dulles said, "What if I said we could get your wife and daughter out?"

Kappler stared at him for a long moment, then shook his head.

"Danke schön, meine freund," Kappler said softly. "Let me think about that. But my first reaction is no, because that would not stop Hitler, not stop the madness. And, also, because my son—SS-Obersturmbannführer Oskar Kappler, who is second in command in Sicily—he would then be hunted down and hung by wire from a meat hook."

Dulles nodded.

Kappler took a sip of cognac as he looked into the flames and considered his next thought.

He swallowed, then inhaled deeply and exhaled audibly.

"Well, then," he went on, his words measured, "so I have just had one of my companies stolen from me. I have lost five plants—possibly more—to a bombing that Hitler believed was impossible. And Marty Bormann has threatened to nationalize all the rest of my properties."

He turned and looked for a long moment at Dulles, then continued: "And the companies you helped me set up in the Americas now are essentially useless to me.

"As you and I have discussed time and again, Allen, I believe someone has to do something to stop the madness—the destruction of lives, of property, of our very souls—before nothing is left of Germany but rubble. Up until now, I simply had to play the good German, running my companies as required. I cannot complain about that; my family and I live a very comfortable life. But conditions have gravely changed to a point where in good conscience I cannot continue the charade."

"I understand," Dulles said.

"Do you?" Kappler challenged. "I must tell you that it took me a long time to understand, to truly understand. And because of that I stand before you"—he looked up toward the high ceiling, gesturing grandly with his right hand—"and before our Almighty God deeply ashamed."

He paused, then met Dulles's eyes.

"Now I am desperate. I am tired of being held hostage, tired of being forced to participate in an evilness that no God-fearing man should. I often feel as trapped as those pitiful *sklavenarbeiter.*

"Allen, I must be that someone we discussed who does something. I must escape these invisible shackles that Hitler has put on me and bring honor and sanity back to my country."

Dulles nodded, then sipped his cognac.

Kappler finished: "I am willing to devote everything I have left."

He looked at Gisevius and added: "Just as Thyssen and I funded the resistance that gave rise to Hitler and, as you say, his goons—"

"I also said thugs."

"—goons and thugs of his High Command, so shall I fund the resistance that now takes him down."

Dulles looked at Gisevius.

"Well, Hans, do you still believe Wolfgang not to be our man?"

Gisevius looked between them, grunted, then refilled his snifter.

Kappler looked at Dulles and said, "I've about had enough of this man's arrogance. I'm asking you, Allen, as a friend, what are you talking about? What is it that I'm to do beyond what I've offered?"

Dulles let out a long sigh.

"We need you to reach out to Krupp," he began, "and convince him that he has a choice."

"Which is?"

"To join those of you working to bring down Hitler."

"But I told you that he's an über-Nazi! He's not even a Krupp by blood—Hitler allowed him to change his name when he married that idiot Krupp girl. That's how crazy this all is."

Dulles nodded.

He said, "I understand the odds are indeed great—"

"They are impossible!"

"—but what harm is there suggesting to him that he can quietly sabotage his own facilities that are building weapons and know that they will survive the war or"—Dulles tossed the photographs of the flooded Ruhr Valley on the table—"he can do nothing and watch them be destroyed now."

Wolfgang Kappler met Allen Dulles's eyes for a long moment, then nodded.

Dulles watched as Kappler then took the bottle of cognac that Gisevius had, refilled his snifter, and took a healthy gulp.

Dulles wasn't certain due to the dim lighting, but he thought that he saw Kappler's hands shaking.

[FOUR]
OSS Dellys Station
Dellys, Algeria
1750 30 May 1943

"Mother Roo One," First Lieutenant Hank Darmstadter said after touching his AIR-TO-AIR microphone switch, "this is Joey."

"Go ahead, Joey," the male pilot's voice replied.

Dick Canidy, who was hearing the radio traffic in his headset, grinned at the mother and baby kangaroo code names.

"Mother Roo One" and "Mother Roo Two" were the olive drab

C-47s at the threshold of the Dellys dirt strip. Aboard each plane were two dozen OSS agents from the Sandbox in parachute gear. "Joey" was the number three aircraft—a matte black C-47—waiting just off the dirt strip.

Both olive drab Gooney Birds had navigation lights burning on the wings and atop the vertical stabilizer. The only lights illuminated on the dull black Gooney Bird were inside, on the control panel before the pilot, Darmstadter, and the copilot, Canidy; otherwise the aircraft was completely dark as it sat with its engines idling.

Darmstadter keyed his microphone and said, "Ready when you are, Mother Roo One. Get us the hell out of here."

The pilot chuckled, then said, "Roger that, Joey."

The air-to-air radio frequency went quiet, and Canidy then heard the pilot's voice of Mother Roo One transmitting on the control tower frequency.

"Algiers Control, Sandbox Four Four Three," he said.

"Four Four Three, Algiers Control, go ahead," the air traffic controller replied with a British accent.

"Sandbox Four Four Three at Dellys, departing to the east for local flight plan. Note that we are one of two C-47 aircraft and that we will be dropping sticks. Acknowledge."

"Four Four Three, Algiers Control understands you are at Dellys and one of two aircraft departing to the east for paratrooper activity. There is no other air traffic in your area. You are cleared for takeoff. The sky is yours. But do remember that you are ordered to remain within your restricted airspace. Acknowledge."

Canidy smiled as Darmstadter gave the finger in the direction of Algiers Control.

"Understood," Mother Roo One replied in an annoyed tone.

The aircraft's bright landing lights came on and its Twin Wasp engines roared.

"Sandbox Four Four Three rolling."

After a moment, Mother Roo One rumbled past the nose of Joey in a flash.

Then Canidy heard the other pilot's voice in his headset.

"Algiers Control, Sandbox Niner One Two."

Canidy noticed that the second C-47—with its navigation lights still lit but not its landing lights—did not move forward on the threshold of the dirt strip.

"Go, One Two," the Brit controller replied, now sounding annoyed or bored or both.

"We are at Dellys with Four Three."

"One Two cleared for takeoff. Have a nice flight. Stay in your box."

"Roger that. One Two rolling."

Canidy, expecting the second olive drab aircraft to flash past, was caught off guard when Darmstadter's voice came over the air-to-air.

"Mother Roo Two, Joey hopping in."

"Roger that, Joey."

Darmstadter lined up with the dirt strip. He locked the brakes, checked the magnetos, and then ran up both engines to takeoff power. The Gooney Bird began trembling. He released the brakes, and the aircraft moved in darkness down the runway, then became airborne.

Darmstadter made turns to follow the nav lights of Mother Roo One as she made a slow circle above the airstrip. Canidy then saw below that Mother Roo Two had turned on her landing lights and was taking off.

Five minutes later, the three aircraft had joined up. Joey was five hundred feet below and another five hundred feet behind Mother Roo One. And Mother Roo Two was five hundred feet below and behind Joey.

Exactly ten minutes later, after hopping the ridge and passing the coastline, the three aircraft continued out over the sea for one mile.

"Godspeed, Hank," the voice of the pilot of Mother Roo One came over the air-to-air.

"See you shortly," Darmstadter replied.

At a cruise speed of 160, Darmstadter had calculated that they could be back at Dellys in six or so hours, faster if he decided to burn more fuel.

Canidy watched as Mother Roo One and Two then quickly broke off from the formation, gaining altitude as they turned back toward the coast to prepare to drop their parachutists.

Joey, invisible under the radar, descended to six hundred feet ASL and settled in on a course of due northeast.

Canidy switched to INTERCOM, keyed his microphone, and said, "Very clever."

In the dim light of the panel, he saw Hank turn to him and nod.

"It works every time. And we reverse the process when I come back. The controllers just think they're seeing radar echo onscreen, not a third bird. After another ten minutes, I'll take us up to eight thousand. They won't care at all what we are then. And this black bird will really disappear in the sky."

"I damn sure hope so," Canidy said, then began unstrapping his harness. "What's the guy's name in back?"

"Kauffman. Good guy."

"I'm sure he is. You okay here for a moment? I'm going to go back and make sure Apollo isn't bugging Kauffman to help him repack his parachute for the tenth time and/or about to jump out the door."

[ONE]
Schutzstaffel Provisional Headquarters
Messina, Sicily
1330 30 May 1943

"I wasn't aware you knew anyone in the Abwehr," SS-Standartenführer Julius Schrader said, his pious tone making the statement sound somewhat suspicious. "But then you've always been rather well connected, haven't you?"

The portly thirty-five-year-old colonel was of medium height, with pale skin and a cleanly shaved head. He was sitting in the high-back leather chair behind the polished marble-top desk that dominated the large office, and absently wiping at something on the tunic of his uniform.

"But I didn't personally know anyone!" SS-Obersturmbannführer Oskar Kappler snapped. "That is, beyond knowing, as you also well know, that the Abwehr has a new agent in the Trade Ministry here."

Kappler, a lieutenant colonel thirty-two years old, was tall and trim and athletic. He had a strong chin, intelligent blue eyes, and a full head of closely cropped light brown hair.

Kappler looked at Schrader a long moment and went on: "And, for the record, I don't appreciate your inference. We've been friends too long for that bullshit."

He thought: *Did I lay that on too heavy?*

Oh, to hell with him! Despite his insistence otherwise, he has always been envious of my background.

I don't appreciate his pious tone and his inference.

Until this morning, I did not know anyone here in the Abwehr.

But I sure as hell cannot tell him the truth about our meeting. . . .

Scheisse!

Kappler and Schrader were in the Sicherheitsdienst; the SD was the intelligence arm of the Schutzstaffel. The SD—which was to say SS-Reichsführer Heinrich Himmel—did not trust the German military intelligence agency—which was to say Admiral Wilhelm Canaris, under whom Himmel once had served—any more than it trusted any of the British or American intelligence agencies.

Kappler and Schrader had served in the Messina SS office for the last eighteen months. But they had been friends far longer, going back nearly fourteen years, when they were university students in Berlin and playing on the school's polo team.

"He asked me down to coffee under the pretense of 'a matter of great urgency,'" Kappler explained. "Turned out he only wanted to talk shop."

He waved toward the telephone on Schrader's desk, knowing that as a matter of course they tapped all the SS office lines. "Check the tape if you do not believe me!"

"You need to calm down, Oskar," Schrader said as he got up from his desk. "That won't be necessary, and you know it."

Kappler thought: *Maybe that was over the top . . . or perhaps just right.*

He watched Schrader, hands stuffed in his pockets, casually cross the highly polished stone floor and stop at one of the half-dozen floor-to-ceiling windows with the heavy burgundy-colored drapes pulled back to either side.

Schrader looked out at the sickle-shaped Port of Messina—which the previous night had been busy with a troopship off-loading German and Italian soldiers—and across the emerald green Strait of Messina. The toe of the boot that was mainland Italy was five kilometers away.

Kappler knew that Schrader stood at the window to project a quiet image of one in deep thought, but felt that he overdid it to the point that it appeared pretentious.

"There is not time to calm down," Kappler went on. "We almost had a disastrous experience with these nerve gas weapons, and now they are sending more this week?"

Schrader, still looking out the window, said, "I expected you to be troubled by that, which is why I'm sending you to Palermo this afternoon to ensure all the necessary safeguards are in order."

"And now this Abwehr agent is asking about the nerve gas," Kappler went on, "which of course I lied about any knowledge of."

Schrader turned to look at Kappler.

"He asked—what is this agent's name?—about the Tabun?"

"Beck. Ernst Beck is his name. And, yes, he asked. I said I had no idea what he was talking about."

Schrader met Kappler's eyes for a long moment, nodded thoughtfully, and said, "Interesting."

Then he turned to look back out the window.

Well, I think that convinced him, Kappler thought.

Or at least threw him off the scent for now . . .

At nine o'clock that morning, SS-Obersturmbannführer Oskar Kappler had been seated on the patio of Café Alessandro that overlooked Piazza Salvatore. It was a warm, sunny morning, and a little more than half of the dozen small round wrought-iron tables were occupied. Kappler had picked one that was in an empty corner with a good view of the piazza.

He was sipping a black coffee and admiring the attractive Sicilian girls making their way to the nearby University of Messina when a man in an ill-fitting rumpled suit approached his table. The man looked to be maybe thirty years old, five-foot-nine, and 190. He had a friendly face with dark, inquisitive eyes and thin black hair that went to his collar and could use a trim. A small white rose was pinned to his lapel.

"Herr Kappler?"

"It is that obvious?" Kappler said, standing and offering his hand.

"The uniform was my first clue."

"I see."

"It is my pleasure to finally meet you. I am Ernst Beck," he said as he shook Kappler's hand, impressed with his firm—but not crushing—grip and the fact that he maintained eye contact throughout.

Beck then added, "Actually, the uniform was my second clue. We of course have a quite detailed dossier on you back at the office."

Kappler made eye contact again.

Would that have anything to do with who my father is? His companies and connections with the High Command?

Or perhaps because I am not exactly blindly faithful to Der Führer and his crumbling Reich?

I didn't exactly throw out my arm and bark "Heil Hitler!" just now. . . .

"Yes, of course you do, Herr Beck. You are, after all, with the German Trade Ministry," he said, slightly sarcastic.

I've known the ministry was your cover since the first day you set foot in Sicily.

"Please, call me Ernst," Beck said, ignoring the sarcasm.

Kappler gestured toward the other seat at the wrought-iron table and said, "Please join me. Coffee? A pastry perhaps? Being so close to the office, I do happen to come here regularly. It is most excellent."

"Thank you, but I'm fine," Beck said.

Kappler sipped at his coffee as he let his eyes wander across the piazza. He then found another two young women, well built and in tight clothing, and watched as they approached then passed the café.

Picking up on what Kappler was following, Beck offered, "You know, you'd have far more luck with the locals if you lost that SS uniform."

Kappler's eyes darted back to Beck, who he saw was smiling.

Am I being tested?

"You would think for all we're doing for them," Kappler said, "they could be more appreciative of a man in uniform. They should be grateful. Throwing themselves at us would be a nice start."

Beck met his eyes, and with dripping sarcasm said, "And by that you would mean showering them with the fine ideals of Der Führer and the Thousand-Year Reich? Surely they must be giddy with anticipation to die for a lost cause."

He believes as I do!

Or . . . is that part of the test?

"That is quite a bold statement to make to an officer of the SS," Kappler said evenly.

Beck shrugged. "Not just any SS officer."

What does he mean by that?

Beck looked at Kappler for a long moment and said, "I appreciate you taking time to meet with me."

Kappler glanced across the busy Piazza Salvatore. It was two blocks up from the port and offered a stunning view of the Mediterrean Sea. Café Alessandro was one of four restaurants on the piazza. And around the corner was the Schutzstaffel Provisional Headquarters.

Kappler then said: "You chose a rather conspicuous place to meet, wouldn't you say? My office is a block away."

Even the Gestapo's thugs could stumble across us here—and probably have.

"Yes," Beck said, "I would agree that it is quite conspicuous."

"And you're not worried what someone might think? Or say?"

"Someone?"

Kappler smiled. He grabbed both lapels of his tunic and tugged at them in an exaggerated fashion.

"Of all people," he said, "I would expect that someone in your line of work would have noticed there are quite a number more of these around town."

"Ah, yes. And I have. But if we have nothing to hide, why should we hide? Should anyone ask, I can say that I'm making a simple professional courtesy call as the new head of the Trade Ministry."

Kappler grunted.

But we are hiding something . . . perhaps our allegiance?

And here is my test, Herr Beck.

He said, "While that of course is a quite logical line of thought, I'm afraid to say that it cannot be applied to the SS. They can be irrational, and they project the same on others."

"'They'?" Beck repeated.

"They," Kappler confirmed.

"So, then everyone is an enemy of the Reich until proven otherwise?"

Kappler nodded.

"Yes," he said, "although sometimes not even then. I did say they can be irrational."

Beck smiled. "That you did."

Okay, let's cut the bullshit.

"And may I ask what it is that we are not hiding here in this conspicuous place?" He sipped his coffee. "What is it that I can do for the German Trade Ministry that, as you said on the telephone, 'is a matter of most urgency'?"

"Nothing," Beck said. "But I appreciate your kind offer, Herr Kappler. I suspect that at some point I will take you up on it."

"Then this urgent matter . . . ?"

Beck reached inside his suit coat, into the left pocket that was behind the flower.

"Curiosity overwhelms," Kappler said. "Why the white rose?"

Beck glanced at it, then said, "The white rose stands for many things. For some, it is purity and innocence. In our line of work, it's silence and secrecy." He paused, then grinned and added, "That, and the pretty ladies really like it. Perhaps for all those meanings."

Beck produced an envelope.

"This came in very early this morning."

He handed it to Kappler.

There was a folded typewritten sheet inside. Kappler opened it, and as he began to read, he inhaled deeply.

Ach du lieber Gott!

"Karlchen"?

He warned me that he very well one day might have to use it!

Kappler looked back at Beck and tried to gauge if his shocked reaction was as obvious as it felt. Kappler then made a thin smile, and feebly said, "It is from my father."

Beck, stone-faced, nodded.

Trying not to appear anxious, Kappler turned his attention back to the page:

```
HIGHEST SECRECY


TO—

SS-OBERSTURMBANNFUHRER OSKAR KAPPLER

SS PROVISIONAL HEADQUARTERS SICILY
```

THROUGH—
HERR ERNST BECK, DIRECTOR
GERMAN TRADE MINISTRY, MESSINA, SICILY

BEGIN MESSAGE
MIDNIGHT, MAY 27TH, IN THE YEAR OF OUR LORD, 1943

DEAR OSKAR,

FIRST, MY KARLCHEN, YOUR MOTHER ASKS THAT I SEND TO YOU HER LOVE AND YOUR SISTER'S LOVE.

SECOND, AS YOU MAY HAVE HEARD, THERE RECENTLY HAS BEEN SIGNIFICANT DESTRUCTION IN THE RUHR VALLEY. KNOW THAT OUR FAMILY SUFFERED NO PERSONAL HARM, AS WHEN IT HAPPENED I WAS OUT OF THE COUNTRY ON BUSINESS AND YOUR MOTHER AND SISTER WERE IN BERLIN.

KAPPLER INDUSTRIES, HOWEVER, DID LOSE FIVE OF OUR SEVEN OPERATIONS THERE. IN DUE COURSE, I WILL SHARE MORE DETAILS ON THIS, BUT FOR NOW THE DAMAGE IS DONE AND BEING DEALT WITH AS EXPEDITIOUSLY AS POSSIBLE.

THIRD, AND I THINK PERHAPS MOST IMPORTANT, YOU SHOULD BE AWARE THAT I HAVE BEEN ASKED TO PERFORM SOME EXTRAORDINARY TASKS. THESE ARE ONES THAT I DEVOUTLY BELIEVE OUR ALMIGHTY GOD HAS CHOSEN FOR ME TO DO. AND I HAVE AGREED TO DO SO.

BECAUSE THEY ARE OF THE HIGHEST SECRECY, I KNOW THAT YOU UNDERSTAND THAT THEY ARE DANGEROUS, AND MAY NOT END WELL FOR ME.

I AM SHARING THIS WITH YOU NOW BECAUSE IF SOMETHING SHOULD HAPPEN TO ME, YOU WILL NEED TO TAKE YOUR OWN EXTRAORDINARY ACTIONS. ONES TO SAVE YOURSELF FROM A POSSIBLE SIMILAR FATE BUT ALSO ONES TO SAVE YOUR MOTHER AND SISTER.

TO THIS END, YOU WILL BE APPROACHED BY A GENTLEMAN OF POWERFUL RESOURCES WHO FROM THE START HAS HELPED ME WITH ALL OUR FAMILY BUSINESSES AND INVESTMENTS IN THE AMERICAS. THESE NOW CONSTITUTE OUR FAMILY'S ENTIRE WEALTH, AS ALL KAPPLER INDUSTRIES IN GERMANY HAVE BEEN OR ARE ABOUT TO BE NATIONALIZED. THIS IS THE SAME THAT BORMANN HAS DONE WITH FRITZ THYSSEN, WHO YOU SHOULD UNDERSTAND GORING PRESENTLY IS MOVING FROM A BERLIN ASYLUM TO A KONZENTRATIONSLAGER.

YOU WILL KNOW THIS GENTLEMAN IS LEGITIMATE IN THE SAME MANNER AS YOU KNOW THIS MESSAGE YOU NOW READ IS LEGITIMATE.

I CLEARLY APPRECIATE THAT THIS SUDDENLY PLACES AN UNFAIR BURDEN ON YOUR SHOULDERS, BUT KNOWING YOUR FINE CHARACTER THERE IS NO QUESTION IN MY MIND THAT YOU UNDERSTAND SUCH DESPERATE TIMES REQUIRE SUCH GREAT SACRIFICES.

LASTLY, AND SADLY, I AM AWARE AND ASHAMED THAT I HAVE BEEN REMISS ALL YOUR LIFE IN SAYING THIS ENOUGH TO YOU, BUT PLEASE KNOW HOW VERY PROUD OF YOU I AM, MY SON, AND THAT I LOVE YOU.

PRAY WITH ME THAT THIS WAR SOON ENDS, BEFORE MORE MINDLESS HARM IS DONE, AND THAT WE ALL WILL AGAIN BE TOGETHER AS A FAMILY.

STAY STRONG. MAY GOD BLESS YOU.

YOUR FATHER
END MESSAGE
HIGHEST SECRECY

Kappler, his eyes beginning to water, felt his throat constrict. He looked out across the piazza and drained his coffee.

"I'm sorry," Ernst Beck said softly.

Kappler looked at him.

"Yes," Beck said, "I of course read the letter. It's my job. But know that I am under orders to provide you with whatever you need."

"My father," Kappler said, "he is working with the Abwehr?"

Beck nodded.

"That is all I know," he added, then nodded at the message. "But considering the urgency I was instructed to get that to you, something tells me this is all going to get very interesting very quickly."

[TWO]
Latitude 37 Degrees 15 Seconds North
Longitude 4 Degrees 13 Seconds East
Over the Mediterranean Sea, North of Tigzirt, Algeria
1820 30 May 1943

Stepping slowly away from the flight deck—the only lights burning on the aircraft were on the control panel, and these had been dimmed as low as possible—Dick Canidy moved in the dark toward the bulkhead door. He glanced up at the astrodome, the clear Plexiglas bubble used for celestial navigation. Some—not much—natural light was coming through it from the twinkling blanket of stars and the sliver of a crescent moon. He then heard the droning of the Twin Wasps grow slightly louder and at the same time felt the angle of the aircraft nose up. Hank Darmstadter had started his slow ascent, headed for eight thousand feet.

Canidy went through the bulkhead door and closed it behind him.

It was noisier than hell in the back. The aircraft's walls weren't insulated, of course, and he essentially was standing between—and within feet of—both engines, albeit separated by the thin skin of aluminum alloy that was the fuselage. The trooper door aft had been removed, and the slipstream was howling at the opening.

The temperature at Dellys had been just above ninety when they had taken off, and the salty-smelling sea air in the plane was still humid and hot. That would soon change as they gained altitude. The temperature of air dropped five-plus degrees with every thousand feet of elevation. Reaching eight thousand feet, they would lose forty or so degrees. Chilly, but not unbearable, especially considering everyone was wearing an extra layer of clothing—black coveralls.

Standing at the bulkhead, Canidy strained to make out shapes.

It's damn-near darker back here, if that's possible.

After grabbing a rib of the fuselage for balance, he took a step forward—and immediately tripped.

Damn it!

He caught himself, then looked around trying to see what his boot had found.

While the folding metal seats lining either side of the fuselage were capable of holding twenty-eight parachutists, Canidy knew there were only two people in the back of the C-47—and he'd just found one of them.

Twenty-four-year-old Second Lieutenant Jeffrey Kauffman was the beefy copilot—he stood six-foot-two, 230—who would relieve Darmstadter after serving as jumpmaster and making sure Canidy and van der Ploeg had safely exited the aircraft over the LZ.

Kauffman was now curled up against the foot of the bulkhead, lying on a woolen blanket and resting his head on one of the four big black duffel bags stacked there under the cargo netting. He was in the process of bending his knees, pulling his feet closer to him—*That's what I hit, his feet*—but otherwise not paying any attention to Canidy.

Smart guy—getting some shut-eye while he can.

Sorry to disturb your slumber.

Canidy looked at the bags of gear, with parachutes attached, and that brought back the memory of earlier in the day, when he found out what John Craig van der Ploeg planned to bring.

While Dick Canidy and Stan Fine remained at the teak table on the villa balcony and went over last-minute details concerning who to message about the mission into Sicily—and more importantly who the hell not to message—John Craig van der Ploeg had gone downstairs and begun pulling together what gear to take.

He had been there an hour by the time Dick Canidy entered the vast storeroom and found him in a far corner.

John Craig was looking at a sheet of paper with a neatly hand-printed list. Near his feet were four well-worn Italian leather suitcases. All were open and empty. A variety of clothing and gear was spread out on the floor around the suitcases.

"What the hell is this?" Canidy said.

"The suitcases?" John Craig said. "Francisco Nola's fishing boats have been smuggling families here from Sicily. We bought their suitcases—and what clothes they would sell us—so that we'd blend in when we went there."

"No . . . what the hell is *all* this?"

"What do you mean?" John Craig said, holding up the sheet of paper. "This is what we always did in Boy Scouts before a trip. We made a packing list, then laid out everything before packing, checking it off the list as we went."

Canidy looked at him—*Jesus! We're not going to Camp Two Teepee to roast marshmallows*—then walked over to where everything was spread out.

In front of one suitcase, John Craig had put a mess kit, two bath towels, a package of handkerchiefs, a toilet kit—and his clothes.

Canidy reached down and counted six pairs of socks, six boxer shorts, six T-shirts, six outer shirts, and six pairs of pants.

How the hell long is he planning on staying?

He then looked at what was next to the second suitcase. There was an olive drab canvas musette bag and, beside it, a web belt and harness and a Colt .45 ACP pistol and two extra magazines with two boxes—a hundred rounds—of full metal jacket ball ammo. And there was a blackjack. And gold Swiss coins and what looked to Canidy to be some of the OSS "aged" Italian paper currency.

"That's fifty thousand dollars in gold," John Craig offered. "And another hundred grand in lire."

In front of the third suitcase there was another towel, a raincoat, and a sleeping bag. Next to this was a second .45 with two extra magazines and two boxes of ammo, a first-aid kit, a canteen, a compass, a flashlight, a gas mask, a dozen K rations, and finally a pack of playing cards and a box of Hershey chocolate bars.

"What?" Canidy said. "No marshmallows and graham crackers?"

John Craig's eyes brightened.

"To make s'mores! We have any?"

Canidy grunted.

"That was a fucking joke," he said, then swept his hand in the direction of all that was on the floor. "Much like all this."

Canidy walked over to the suitcases and glanced at each of them.

"The radios are in which ones?"

Van der Ploeg pointed to the first and third suitcases.

Canidy went to the first one, reached in, and after a moment found the false bottom. He then carefully removed it, revealing three black boxes. The transmitter and receiver of the SSTR-1 wireless telegraphy set were nearly identical black boxes, each about ten inches long and four inches wide and tall. They had black Bakelite faceplates with an assortment of knobs, dials, and toggle switches. Each weighed five pounds; the similar-sized box that was the power supply weighed ten.

He pointed at the third suitcase and said, "Same in there?"

"Exactly."

"You tested them?"

John Craig nodded. "Touch them."

Canidy did.

"They're still warm," he said.

"They just came down from the commo room."

Canidy made a satisfied face, then put the false bottom back in place.

He turned his attention to what was in front of the suitcase.

"Everything we take is going to fit in two suitcases. Got it?"

John Craig didn't look convinced.

Canidy reached down and grabbed four pairs of pants and four shirts, then tossed them in the nearby corner.

"What?" John Craig said.

Canidy looked over his shoulder and said, "Were you planning on visiting—or moving to Sicily?"

Then Canidy did the same with the four T-shirts, four pairs of socks, the handkerchiefs, and one of the towels. Finally, he threw out the sleeping bag and gas mask and mess kit.

Canidy then walked over and scanned the items on the shelving. He took a quick inventory and then pulled four cartons of Camel unfiltered cigarettes from one section. He tossed two cartons in each of the suitcases that had a W/T.

"I didn't think you smoked cigarettes," John Craig said, visibly surprised.

"I don't. Those are for what's known as bribery. They're worth their weight in gold in most places."

Canidy looked back to the shelving and pulled more packages off and tossed them in the suitcase.

"Women's hosiery?" John Craig said.

"Even better than gold. Especially if you're interested in getting laid."

John Craig looked as if he might blush.

Canidy then went to the cases of Haig & Haig and pulled out two bottles.

He carried them over to the musette bag.

"Wrap these bottles in those towels of yours—and anything else that will protect them—and put them in this bag. Do not pack them in a suitcase. As much as I'd hate to have a bottle break when we jump, I'd hate even more for the scotch to ruin the radios."

"Got it," John Craig said, and noted that on his list.

Canidy pointed to a stack of wooden crates.

"That's C-2 plastic explosive," he said, then added mock-seriously: "Unlike your boxer shorts—which may well be explosive—you can never have enough C-2. That's taught in my throat-cutting and sabotage school; I'm deeply disappointed that you failed to absorb such a critical point."

John Craig avoided eye contact as he wrote "C-2" on his list.

Canidy said: "Grab two crates, plus primers and det cord."

John Craig noted that.

Canidy then put his hands on his hips and surveyed his work.

"All right. That and a few other items I have should be all we need."

Starting with Q-pills for all. . . .

Canidy turned away from the gear at the bulkhead and glanced around the darkened C-47 interior.

Now, where the hell is John Craig?

He started aft, careful of any other obstacles as he went. Halfway down, he began to make out the vague shape of the Browning machine gun by the trooper door—and then the human form behind it.

What is he doing?

As Canidy reached the rear of the aircraft and inhaled, there was no question what John Craig van der Ploeg was doing.

Oh, Christ! he thought, getting an even stronger whiff of the vomitus that almost triggered a sympathetic gag. *That's what. He's airsick!*

The closer Canidy stepped to van der Ploeg, the stronger the foul acrid odor became.

And the stupid bastard is sitting in the worst place.

Please don't tell me he tried to hurl out the door.

Canidy got a better look at him, and around him. John Craig was sitting next to a dozen olive drab ammo cans stenciled with 200 CARTRIDGES .30 CALIBER M-1919 in yellow. He was leaning against the aft bulkhead, his eyes closed and his head drooped toward the open door. The recent contents of his stomach were widespread.

He did try to hurl out the door—and the slipstream fed it right back to him.

"Hey!" Canidy said over the roar. "You okay?"

John Craig's eyes cracked open.

"I've been better."

Kauffman's going to love this but . . .

"Come sit up at the forward bulkhead. Back here in the tail is where you feel the most motion."

"I'm okay here. I need to see out."

"But I don't want you fucking *falling* out!"

John Craig then held up a static line. Canidy saw that one end was tied to his waist and the other was hooked into the deck rail that held the machine gun. He also saw that there was virtually no slack in it.

Well, he won't be slipping out the door.

"You know how to use the Browning?"

Canidy saw John Craig's mop of hair bob, indicating that he had nodded. He also thought he saw some chunks of vomitus fall out.

"We don't want to attract any attention up here. There will be one helluva lot of muzzle flash, even with that suppressor. So do not—repeat do not—engage unless we are fired on first. Is that clear?"

The mop of hair bobbed again.

Canidy added: "It's critical to the mission we stay invisible. Got it?"

More bobbing.

"All right, then. Can I get you anything?"

He held up his canteen and said, "I'll survive."

I'm not so sure about that. . . .

"Hang in there, Apollo. Work on being the god of healing. I'll check back in a bit."

John Craig didn't say anything. He just let his head drop back to the bulkhead. Canidy saw him close his eyes.

What a way to start . . .

What the hell could possibly happen next?

[THREE]
German Trade Ministry
Messina, Sicily
1010 30 May 1943

Oberleutnant zur See Ludwig Fahr removed his suit coat, put it on a hanger, then hung that on the hook behind his office door, taking care not to damage the small white rose pinned to the lapel.

Fahr's modest office, on the second floor of the ministry building, held little more than an old wooden desk, a pair of wooden armchairs before it, and another wooden chair, this one on metal rollers, behind it. His window overlooked the Port of Messina where the ferryboats arrived adjacent to the commercial fishing dockage.

He went behind the desk and took his chair. Only two of the chair's four wheels actually rolled, and it made a grinding sound as he pulled it closer to the desk and turned to use the typewriter.

On the desk next to his portable Olivetti typewriter was a pair of Kriegsmarine-issued high-powered Zeiss binoculars. He had taken them off the submarine after he had reluctantly agreed to give up his command of U-613. Fahr now used the fine optics to keep watch on activities in the port—especially the pretty young Italian women as they disembarked the ferryboats. If he liked the looks of one enough—and usually there were two or more candidates—he could run down and intercept them, offering coffee or, if the hour was right, something stronger.

Fahr had to admit that he missed commanding the submarine and his men and a life at sea. Those feelings flooded back every time a *U-boot* called on the Port of Messina, which was every week now.

But he also had to admit that this wasn't exactly a bad life, either. And, besides, he knew there was no going back. When Admiral Canaris had come to him a year ago and explained that the war was changing and that Fahr had more important things to do for the Fatherland, starting with again working under Canaris, Fahr knew that that was exactly what he would do.

Canaris was the kind of leader one followed without question.

Ludwig Fahr rolled a fresh sheet of paper into the typewriter, tapped his fingertips together as he glanced out at the harbor and composed his thoughts, then began typing:

HIGHEST SECRECY

TO—

BRIGADEGENERAL HANS OSTER, DEPUTY DIRECTOR

ABWEHR HEADQUARTERS, BERLIN

FROM—

HERR ERNST BECK, DIRECTOR

GERMAN TRADE MINISTRY, SICILY

1125 HOURS

1943-05-30

BEGIN MESSAGE

AS PER YOUR DIRECTION, URGENT MESSAGE
FROM FATHER TO SON WAS DELIVERED THIS DATE
AT 0800 HOURS.

I PERSONALLY WATCHED HIM READ MESSAGE.

THERE IS NO QUESTION (A) THAT THE MESSAGE WAS IN FACT BELIEVED TO BE FROM THE FATHER AND (B) THAT THE DETAILS OF THE MESSAGE ITSELF WERE BELIEVED TO BE GENUINE.

ADDITIONALLY, THERE DID NOT APPEAR TO BE ANY REAL SURPRISE -- SUCH AS ANGER OR DENIAL -- ABOUT THE GRAVITY OF WHAT THE FATHER WROTE.

```
THE REASON FOR THAT, I THINK, IS THAT IN THE COURSE
OF OUR CONVERSATION IT BECAME CLEAR THAT THE SON
ALREADY BELIEVED AS THE FATHER DOES.

FINALLY, SON UNDERSTANDS THAT THIS CHANNEL IS NOW
OPEN AND AWAITS FURTHER WORD.

STANDING BY.

BECK
END MESSAGE
HIGHEST SECRECY
```

Oberleutnant zur See Ludwig Fahr tugged the sheet of paper from the typewriter, read over what he had typed, penciled two corrections, then noisily slid his chair back.

He stood, and took a long look at the harbor and then the sea. Out in the strait, he saw that a sleek Kriegsmarine *Schnellboot*—literally "fast boat"—was reducing its speed between the outer channel markers, making an approach to enter the mouth of the port. He grinned appreciatively.

What beautiful lines she has!

Fahr, having briefly commanded one before moving to U-boats, was quite familiar with the fast-attack S-boats. Built in slightly different designs, they all were about one hundred feet long with wooden hulls and massive engines—one variant packed triple two-thousand-horsepower Daimler-Benz diesels—and were capable of hitting more than forty knots.

S-boats were heavily armed with 4cm Bofors, four-barrel 2cm

flaks, and 53.3cm torpedoes. To deliver the torpedoes on target, it would wait in the dark to ambush a submarine or ship, then strike quickly. Then it would run, as it carried only the fish in its tubes. The weight of additional torpedoes would slow the boat's fast attack—and faster departure.

Fahr looked beyond the S-boat and saw an unarmed, unattractive bulky barge-shaped vessel—and grinned even more broadly.

A ferryboat was following the S-boat into port.

If I hurry, I can have this sent and be back here in time to watch the ferry unload!

He quickly walked out of his office and marched the message up to the radio room on the top floor.

[FOUR]
Latitude 37 Degrees 81 Seconds North
Longitude 10 Degrees 96 Seconds East
Over the Mediterranean Sea, West of Sicily
2010 30 May 1943

A loud noise suddenly shook Dick Canidy out of a deep sleep, and he slowly realized that it had been his own snoring that had awakened him. He quickly scanned around him and in the glow of the instrument panel lights saw that he was strapped in the copilot seat and that Hank Darmstadter still had the left seat.

Canidy turned back the left sleeve of his black coverall to check his Hamilton wristwatch. According to the chronometer, they had right at two hours behind them.

So, another hour plus or minus . . .

He sniffed, then cleared his throat.

He thought he could still smell vomitus but figured that had to be a product of his imagination.

Wonder how John Craig is doing back there.

With any luck, he's slept the entire time.

Canidy then thought he saw that Darmstadter had glanced his way. That was confirmed when he heard Hank's voice in his headset.

"You might want to give it a little longer, Dick."

"Give what?" he said, yawning.

"That beauty sleep of yours didn't take."

Canidy balled his fist and raised his index finger in Darmstadter's direction.

Canidy then said: "Anything exciting happen while I was out?"

"Nothing since you came back and filled the flight deck with that delightful barf odor."

"I thought that was my imagination. Sorry."

"How do you think he's doing back there?"

"I was just wondering that myself. With any luck, he's been passed out the whole time."

Darmstadter then pointed out the windscreen at about three o'clock.

"Pantelleria is about sixty miles that way," he said. "I'm sure we've been picked up on the Freya RDF, but maybe the Krauts won't bother with just one blip way out here. If we don't get any action from Pantelleria, it'll likely come at Sicily."

When Canidy had studied the photo-reconnaissance images of Sicily—taken from thirty thousand feet by USAAF P-38 Lightnings with the belly painted sky blue—he'd also viewed the images of Pantelleria.

While the photos had shown no massing of troops or matériel on Sicily—which could have meant that there were none . . . or none yet . . . or that they were being very well concealed—the photos did show that Pantelleria, a solid forty-two-square-mile rock in the middle of the Strait of Sicily, was heavily fortified.

Ringing the island were at least fifty easily recognized concrete gun emplacements, some seventy-plus Italian and German fighters and bombers at Marghana Airfield, and U-boats and S-boats almost daily calling at the two ports. The recon images also pinpointed the distinctive tall antennae of the Freya radio direction finder stations.

There was no argument among the AFHQ brass that Pantelleria in Axis hands would cause serious problems with the invasion of Sicily and, conversely, that Pantelleria in Allied hands would be a great asset for staging fighter aircraft to provide close air support during OPERATION HUSKY. Thus, Eisenhower laid on OPERATION CORKSCREW, with its secondary purpose being to gauge the amount of high explosive needed to pound the enemy into submission. Knowing how much HE it took there would help them prepare enough HE for Sicily. The first attack by air had occurred on May 18.

The heavy round-the-clock bombing of Pantelleria begins "next Wednesday," Canidy thought, recalling John Craig van der Ploeg's announcement. Major General Jimmy Doolittle's Northwest African Strategic Air Forces would begin sending more than a thousand bombers each day.

Over the intercom, Canidy said, "Maybe we should have waited a week. Then they really will be too busy to worry about us."

"Yeah," Darmstadter said with a chuckle, "but damage is done. All we can do is hope they can't find us up here."

Canidy scanned the night sky but saw only the sea of stars above and, below, the stars reflecting on the sea itself.

A few minutes later, Darmstadter's voice was back.

"We're about an hour out from Marsala. I'll get back down on the deck when we're twenty miles out. Then, crossing the coast, I'll pop up to seven hundred AGL for putting you in the DZ. After you guys jump, I'll continue eastward, making three or four turns to throw off anyone who might figure out we were over your LZ. And on the way out, I'll pass over Palermo while Kauffman scatters those psy-op leaflets. Then we head home. Sound good?"

He glanced at Canidy and saw that he was giving him a thumbs-up.

We should be fine, Canidy thought. *Their ack-ack couldn't hit shit over Tunisa, and judging by the aerial recon photos of Sicily, the Krauts haven't even put in any antiaircraft defenses yet.*

And all the Me-109s and FW-190s were at the Messina airfield. None at Palermo.

Of course, there's always the possibility that that all could have changed an hour ago. . . .

Darmstadter finished: "With any luck, no one will ever know we were here. And if they do see us coming in low, they'll think I'm an idiot who had trouble finding Palermo just to drop a bunch of flyers."

The OSS Morale Operations Branch produced psychological warfare—everything from radio broadcasts to leaflets designed to cast doubt—and despair and worse—that the Axis did not have a snowball's chance in hell of winning the war.

Back at Dellys, Canidy had seen Kauffman loading boxes of the "psy-op" matériel on the aircraft. It had come from a print shop in Algiers that Stanley Fine had taken over.

"You gotta see what they're coming up with," Kauffman had said to him, cracking open a few boxes and pulling out samples. "It's great stuff."

The first eight-by-ten sheet Kauffman handed him showed a sketch of a wooden cross with a German helmet on top and the single word: *You?*

The next one had a sketch of a leering Nazi SS storm trooper with his boots on the throats of a young man and woman holding Sicilian flags. In Italian were the words: *How Much Longer?*

Another simply read: *Why Die for Hitler?*

"And here's the best," Kauffman said, handing Canidy a stack of very thin paper squares that he realized was meant to be toilet paper. Each sheet was imprinted in German with: "Let's stop this shit, Comrades! We do not fight for Germany—but only for Hitler and Himmler. The Nazi Leaders lied to us, and now they are saving their own skin. They send us to die in the mud, saying hold out until our last bullet. But we need our last bullets to free Germany from this SS shit! Enough! Peace!"

Canidy asked Darmstadter, "Did you get a look at those leaflets?"

"Yeah, they're pretty good—" He suddenly pointed out the windscreen, above them at ten o'clock. *"Shit!"*

Canidy quickly leaned over and looked past Darmstadter.

He saw that they were closing in on an airplane.

Exhaust glow! Multi-engine.

That's one big sonofabitch . . . a transport?

And we almost ran right up its ass—

No! We're about to!

"It's fucking descending on us!" Darmstadter announced, and automatically began an evasive maneuver, pulling back on the throttles as he banked the aircraft to the right.

Canidy watched as the enormous aircraft filled the windscreen, hung there a moment, then very slowly started to grow smaller.

Damn that was close!

And in another moment they would've seen us alongside.

And then what?

With the Gooney Bird standing on its starboard wing and slipping away to the right, there suddenly came from the rear of the aircraft a familiar heavy vibration.

What the hell?

That feels like automatic gunfire!

In the next instant, long flames began to light the sky above them. Canidy could now make out that the big and boxy aircraft had a swastika on the vertical stabilizer.

Then came more heavy vibration, a steady endless stream of it.

That sonofabitch!

It's the Browning!

And damn he's burning through ammo!

The flames grew longer across the sky—*That's fuel that's catching fire! He hit a fuel cell!*—and then suddenly the German aircraft's starboard wing was engulfed in flames.

Then came a bone-rattling *BOOM!*

Darmstadter and Canidy shielded their eyes, the intense, sudden light nearly blinding them.

The explosion sheared off the burning wing. The airplane, its fuselage now rapidly burning away, pitched violently left—and began to spiral downward.

Darmstadter yanked the yoke to level out the Gooney Bird, then slammed the yoke and throttles forward.

The nose dropped and the airframe began making a louder and louder hum as the airplane rapidly lost altitude.

Canidy watched the airspeed needles spin.

"Airspeed two-twenty," he called out as the aircraft approached its top speed of 250 miles per hour.

"Two-forty . . .

"Two-sixty . . .

"Two-eighty-five . . . *Hank*?"

Darmstadter did not reply.

"Three-ten, Hank!" Canidy called.

He's going to tear the goddamn wings off!

Just then, shy of 325 miles per hour, Darmstadter pulled back on the throttles.

The hum of the airframe was deafening—but it slowly began to ease.

"Two-seventy," Canidy then called out.

It took him a moment to realize that the heavy, steady vibration from the Browning had stopped.

Canidy rubbed his eyes and tried to focus on the control panel. They were still losing altitude but not nearly as fast. The altimeter indicated 5,500.

"Airspeed two hundred," Canidy announced, "and we're dropping through fifty-five hundred feet."

Darmstadter, scanning the night sky, eased back on the yoke. The aircraft began leveling off. Canidy saw that the altimeter was now indicating 5,100 feet, the airspeed 180, and he called that out.

Darmstadter maintained that level and speed for five minutes, quietly scanning the sky. Then he turned and looked at Canidy.

"Nice flying," Canidy said.

"What the hell was that, Dick?"

"Goddamn big. And goddamn close."

"I noticed."

"And goddamn German, for sure. I saw the enormous swastika on the tail."

"Yeah, so did I," Darmstadter said, his tone sarcastic. "It was nicely lit, I recall." He paused, then repeated, "What the hell was that?"

Canidy answered with a question: "Did you count six engines?"

"Yeah. Pretty sure I did. So, a Giant? What the hell is a Giant doing out here alone?"

"Trying to wipe us out of the sky, for one. A Giant would explain how the Browning ate up the wing and maybe the fuselage, too. They're fabric."

The six-engine high-wing Messerschmitt Me323 Gigant had an airframe built of lightweight tubing and covered in doped canvas, giving the aircraft a twenty-ton payload. It had clamshell doors that formed its nose, through which it could quickly load and unload everything from 88mm flak cannons to half-tracks to Panzer IV tanks to 120 troopers.

"Maybe it's one of those that got away," Darmstadter said after a moment. "Last month, some P-40s and Spitfires scrambled after a couple dozen Giants that were being escorted not far from Pantelleria. We shot down all but six or so." He paused. "Maybe that was one of the six."

Darmstadter was quiet a long moment. Canidy noticed that he still had his hand firmly on the throttles, and now that he finally was letting go, and flexing his fingers, he saw why.

His hands are trembling. . . .

Canidy said, "Well, beyond there being one fewer Giant for the Third Reich, there is good news."

"What?"

"You get to paint your first kill on the nose of this bird."

Darmstadter didn't respond to that. Instead, he said: "Speaking of that, do you want to go back there and kick his ass? Or do you want me to do it?"

"Why?"

"Damn it, Dick, those Giants have four thirteen-millimeter machine guns!"

"Five, normally," Canidy offered.

"Okay, then five! To our one!" He scanned the sky again. "And what if there'd been escorts?"

"I don't know that John Craig is fully at fault, Hank."

Darmstadter turned to look at Canidy.

"Meaning?" he challenged.

"I was thinking that you may have been as responsible for that as him."

"How in hell do you figure that?"

"When you stood us on the starboard wing, you put that giant aircraft right in John Craig's sights. Who wouldn't take a great shot like that? I'm tempted to go back there and tell him if you can find him four more, and he shoots them down, he will become a certified Ace."

Darmstadter shook his head in disgust.

After a moment, he added more than a little throttle.

"I just want him off my damn airplane, and the sooner the better."

[FIVE]

Thirty minutes later, Darmstadter began a slow descent for the deck.

Canidy heard his voice, a much calmer voice now, come over the headset: "About that time, buddy."

Canidy nodded, then unfastened his harness.

"I'll check back with you shortly," Canidy said.

He removed his headset and left the flight deck.

It was still noisier than hell in back. And now very chilly.

Canidy found the beefy Kauffman moving the first of the gear—two large duffels and the two wooden crates of Composition C-2—from the bulkhead to the aft door. He was impressed by how Kauffman carried his bulk with a casual ease. And how he came across as completely self-confident. Nothing seemed to bother him.

When he came up on the flight deck after we took out the Giant, he acted like that was a daily thing for him.

The anchor-line cable ran the length of the ceiling, from the bulkhead at the flight deck all the way back to the aft bulkhead at the troop door.

Canidy, sliding his hand along the cable, casually walked aft, then suddenly stepped on something small and round, and immediately felt both feet start to go out from under him. He caught himself with the anchor-line cable, dangled for a moment, then regained his footing.

He looked down.

The fucking deck's awash in a sea of spent .30 cal!

He really let loose with that Browning. . . .

Canidy kicked at the brass shells as he walked to the back. He found John Craig van der Ploeg now sitting in the last seat on the port side, next to the troop door. The smell of vomitus remained, but only slightly.

The Browning machine gun had been moved backward on its track, clearing the doorway. In a pile next to it, their hinged lids open, were four empty .30 caliber ammo cans.

That's eight hundred rounds.

How the hell did he quickly reload three times?

And without melting the barrel?

Or maybe he did melt it. . . .

Van der Ploeg looked up at Canidy and saw him staring at the ammo cans.

Between the sound of the propellers and the engine exhaust and the whistle of the slipstream, the noise at the troop door was close to a roar. Van der Ploeg had to almost shout to be heard.

"They shot first," he announced in a dazed monotone.

"What?"

"They shot first," he said in an even louder dazed monotone. "So I shot back."

Canidy looked at him.

They did? Or did he get excited and imagine it?

I didn't notice any muzzle flash.

But everything happened so damn fast, it's possible I missed it.

And he had to have one helluva view of that bird.

"That was one helluva shot," Canidy finally said.

John Craig shrugged. "Hard to miss something that big that close."

Canidy chuckled.

Which was what I told Hank.

Canidy said, "Ready to jump?"

He nodded.

"I'm ready to get the hell off this airplane!"

Which, interestingly enough, is what Hank told me.

Kauffman was putting the two big black duffel bags in line at the doorway. Each had its own parachute, and Kauffman then hooked up their static lines to the anchor-line cable. Next, with some effort, he used the sole of his boot to push the two wooden crates behind the duffels, and hooked up their static lines.

"Better get your chute on," Canidy said. "I'll be right back."

Canidy—having shared van der Ploeg's version of events with a doubtful Darmstadter and then saying they'd be in touch—had returned strapped into his parachute. He now was sitting in a port-side folding seat just forward of van der Ploeg's.

The Gooney Bird had crossed over the coastline of Sicily ten minutes earlier, and as far as they knew the invisible black bird had evaded any notice—and certainly any flak from antiaircraft welcoming committees.

The pitch of the Twin Wasps changed, and the aircraft bled off speed. Kauffman, now prepared to serve as jumpmaster, was leaning against the bulkhead, arms crossed, and looking out the open door as if he could actually see the drop zone in the dark.

A light above Kauffman's head came on, glowing red, and he looked at it for a second.

Coming up on the DZ, John Craig thought, as he felt his pulse start to race.

Stay calm. You've done this.

Breathe in . . . breathe out . . .

"Stand up!" the jumpmaster called out.

John Craig, with more than a little effort under the weight of his pack, pulled himself up using the ribs of the fuselage. He continued holding on with his right hand to keep steady on his feet.

"Hook up!" Kauffman called out.

John Craig reached up and clipped his static line hook onto the anchor-line cable.

"Check static lines!" Kauffman called out.

As Canidy confirmed that van der Ploeg was properly hooked up, Kauffman stepped over and did the same with Canidy's.

"Stand in door!" Kauffman then called out.

This last command they did not take literally. The first to exit the aircraft would be the duffel bags and wooden crates of C-2. The jumpers would go last.

That had been Canidy's order. He said that he did not want to jump first and be floating blissfully to earth while, say, the chute failed on the C-2 and a hundred-pound wooden crate plunged onto his head.

The red light was replaced with green, and Kauffman kicked the first duffel out the door. After a moment, its static line went taut, popping the parachute. Kauffman, using one-second intervals, was already kicking out the second duffel and following it with the first of the two crates of C-2.

Kauffman had his foot on the second crate as John Craig van der Ploeg now literally stood in the doorway.

Deep breath in, then breathe out . . .

Kauffman could sense his anxiety.

"Don't you worry one bit!" the jumpmaster shouted, his voice strong and encouraging. "For you, jumping in the dark will be just like jumping during the day."

Van der Ploeg looked over his shoulder and shouted back: "How is that? I've done this—"

"You close your eyes during both—so either way it's dark!"

Kauffman then laughed heartily at his own joke as he kicked the second crate out the door.

John Craig thought he heard Canidy chuckling behind him.

He stared out into the star-filled night sky.

And then he did close his eyes for a moment.

"Our Father, Who art in Heaven—"

"Go!" Kauffman shouted.

John Craig at once felt Kauffman give him a hard slap on the back—*That was a push!*—and the sudden sensation of being thrust into the hundred-mile-an-hour rushing air of the slipstream.

"Hallowed be Thy name . . ."

Feet together, knees bent . . .

He almost immediately came to the end of his static line. There was a slight tug, then it popped his chute, and as the canopy quickly filled he was violently yanked upright—then, nearly as quickly, was gently and slowly floating downward.

"Thy Kingdom Come, Thy will be done . . ."

Breathe!

Inhale . . . exhale . . .

Above and behind him, the sound of the airplane became smaller and smaller. He began to make out what few sounds there were around him—mostly rushing air making his parachute lines vibrate—and heard that there was absolutely no sound coming from the ground.

"On Earth as it is in Heaven,

"Give us this day our daily bread

"And forgive us our trespasses

"As we forgive those who trespass against us."

He saw down past his feet the parachutes of the gear. Beyond them, he could make out a couple roads—the asphalt reflecting light, causing it to look like a river—and a very few lights from what he guessed were houses.

And then he saw the canopies of the gear collapse, telling him that they had found the ground.

Okay. I'm next.

Feet together, knees bent, get ready to roll . . .

"And lead us not into temptation

"But deliver us from evil . . ."

He thought he could now vaguely make out parts of the ground.

"For Thine is the kingdom,

"And the power and the glory

"For ever and ever . . . Amen."

Something smacked his legs—"Goddammit!" he cried out—and next came the sensation of being beaten by a thousand canes.

The thrashing was intense, and he automatically shielded his face with the crook of his arm.

Something then ripped at his right foot, and there immediately came a burning sensation.

Then suddenly he was jarred to a stop, and felt a great burning as the webbing of his harness dug into his thighs.

And then he was hanging in the dark, with all quiet.

And then the burning in his foot became intense.

And then he passed out.

VI

[ONE]
OSS London Station
Berkeley Square
London, England
1020 31 May 1943

"Pull that door shut, please, Helene," Chief of Station David Bruce said, standing by the window of his office and sipping at a steaming china mug of coffee, "and see that we're not disturbed."

"Yes, sir, Colonel," Captain Helene Dancy, Women's Army Corps, replied over her shoulder as she left carrying the tray that had held the fresh coffee service.

The door clicked shut, and Bruce looked at Lieutenant Colonel Ed Stevens, who wore his usual perfectly tailored worsted uniform and sat on the couch and poured coffee.

Bruce walked over to his desk, picked up a sheet, and handed it to Stevens.

"Wolfgang Augustus Kappler," Bruce announced, pronouncing each syllable pointedly. "Until yesterday, I had hardly known the man. And now he is suddenly the focus of everything I'm supposed to do?"

Stevens took a sip of coffee as his eyes went to the message:

TOP SECRET

OPERATIONAL PRIORITY

31MAY43 0810

FOR OSS LONDON -- COL BRUCE

OSS ALGIERS -- CAPT FINE

COPY OSS WASHINGTON -- GEN DONOVAN

FROM OSS BERN

BEGIN QUOTE

DAVID AND STANLEY,

AS PROMISED IN MY MESSAGE OF 30MAY43, I SHARE WHAT I HAVE JUST LEARNED FROM MY MEETING WITH WOLFGANG KAPPLER. TO WIT:

1. FRITZ THYSSEN. WE KNEW THAT THYSSEN FLED GERMANY WITH HIS FAMILY AND THEN HITLER NATIONALIZED HIS STEEL WORK INDUSTRIES. WE NOW KNOW THAT FRITZ IS NO LONGER HEADED TO ARGENTINA, THAT INSTEAD VICHY FRANCE TURNED HIM AND HIS WIFE OVER TO THE GESTAPO, THAT HITLER HAS HAD THEM LOCKED UP IN A

BERLIN ASYLUM, AND THAT THEY SOON WILL BE INTERNED IN A CONCENTRATION CAMP.

2. WOLFGANG KAPPLER. MARTIN BORMANN HAS ESSENTIALLY THREATENED KAPPLER WITH SAME FATE AS FRITZ. TO START, HITLER HAS NATIONALIZED HIS CHEMISCHE FABRIK FRANKFURT. AND BORMANN HAS THREATENED HARM TO KAPPLER'S FAMILY IF HE TRIES TO FLEE GERMANY AND/OR HIS DUTIES TO THE THIRD REICH. THE WIFE AND DAUGHTER -- HANNAH, 53, AND ANNA, 19 -- ARE LIVING IN BERLIN. SON OSKAR, 32, AN SS-OBERSTURMBANNFUHRER, IS SECOND IN COMMAND AT SS PROVISIONAL HQ IN MESSINA. I OFFERED -- AND WOLFGANG DECLINED -- FOR OSS TO GET WIFE AND DAUGHTER OUT OF GERMANY. KAPPLER WORRIES THAT SHOULD THAT HAPPEN, BORMANN WILL TARGET SON. IT IS CRITICAL TO THE SUCCESS OF WOLFGANG'S MISSION THAT HE NOT WORRY ABOUT THE SAFETY OF HIS FAMILY. TINY IS REACHING OUT TO SON TO GAUGE HIS COMMITMENT TO NAZISM. IF IT IS DETERMINED THAT SON MUST BE TERMINATED -- WE COULD LAY BLAME ON SS OR ITALIAN SECRET POLICE -- SO BE IT. TO THAT END I AM REQUESTING (A) THAT DAVID PUT TOGETHER A CONTINGENCY PLAN THAT WOULD HAVE MOTHER AND DAUGHTER DISAPPEAR TO SAFETY AND (B) THAT STAN PUT TOGETHER SAME FOR SON -- AND HIS POSSIBLE TERMINATION -- IN SICILY. BOTH OPS SHOULD BE ACTIONABLE WITHIN SEVEN (7) DAYS OF THIS DATE.

3. SS-STURMBANNFUHRER KLAUS SCHWARTZ. KAPPLER SAYS HE WORKED FAITHFULLY FOR HIM AS CHIEF

```
CHEMIST AT CHEMISCHE FABRIK FRANKFURT FOR TEN
YEARS BEFORE HIMMLER QUOTE POISONED HIS MIND
UNQUOTE AND SCHWARTZ RADICALLY EMBRACED NAZISM.
WITHIN LAST WEEK SCHWARTZ WAS KNOWN TO BE
TRAVELING UNDER ORDERS OF HIS BOSS, WERNHER VON
BRAUN, BUT HIS WHEREABOUTS ARE BEING KEPT QUIET
DESPITE INQUIRIES BY TINY'S SOURCES. KAPPLER IS
LOOKING INTO WHAT IF ANY UNUSUAL PROJECTS
SCHWARTZ MAY HAVE HAD WORKING AT CHEMISCHE
FABRIK FRANKFURT BEFORE HE LEFT TO ASSIST VON
BRAUN.

4. STATION CHIEFS LONDON AND ALGERS REQUESTED TO
ACKNOWLEDGE RECEIPT OF THIS AND COMPREHENSION OF
CONTINGENCY PLANS.

FONDLY,
ALLEN
END QUOTE
TOP SECRET
```

The tall, thin Stevens, after putting the message on the coffee table, leaned back on the couch and crossed his outstretched legs.

"With Kappler's connections in the High Command, I can understand why Allen seems anxious," Stevens said. He then chuckled and added, "Think we should tell him the reason they can't find Schwartz is because he's dead?"

"Who the hell does Dulles think he is, Donovan himself?" Bruce suddenly said, coldly furious.

Ed Stevens raised his eyebrows.

"'Station chiefs requested to acknowledge receipt'!" Bruce quoted, gesturing at the message on the table by Stevens. "'Ops actionable within seven days'! We're just supposed to drop everything? And he copies Donovan on the message so it in essence becomes an order, a *fait accompli*."

Bruce then looked thoughtful as he sipped his coffee.

"I suggest that he's playing to Donovan," Bruce said.

"In what way?" Stevens said.

"Clearly Donovan also floated his idea of an 'extra-legal' contingency plan with Dulles."

"Which is?"

"A code word for wholesale assassination. The elimination of Axis sympathizers, a hit list of those who would be the next Hitler. Starting with taking out the top one hundred Nazis. Summarily execute them. Donovan told us about it when he was just here. And if he told us, he certainly bounced it off Dulles, who now is running with his own version of it."

"Okay," Stevens said after a moment, reasonably, "I can see how that's playing to Donovan."

"It would not surprise me if Dulles has this industrialist Kappler, with all his connections, being groomed for something like that."

"I suppose that has to be considered."

"As Donovan joked—and I'm pretty sure he did not mean it seriously—'Shoot them all and let the Lord sort them out.' Because he then admitted that the downside of that was they wouldn't be tried as war criminals."

Stevens nodded, then said, "So, what do you want to do with this? We can get to Kappler's wife and daughter reasonably easily. But it's getting out of Germany—and especially out of Berlin—

with two grown women watched by the Gestapo that's going to be the challenge."

Bruce nodded thoughtfully. He was about to open his mouth to speak when he heard a knock at the door.

"We are not to be disturbed!" Bruce said instead, his voice angry and impatient.

Captain Dancy's voice came from the other side of the door: "Harrison has an Operational Immediate Eyes Only for you, Colonel."

Bruce looked at Stevens.

"Oh, hell," he said, "now what?"

Stevens shrugged.

Bruce raised his voice. "Bring it in!"

Dancy opened the door and held it open as Captain Tom Harrison, the five-foot-one ninety-nine-pound thirty-two-year-old chief of the commo room, purposefully marched in and stopped before the desk. He saluted crisply.

"Colonel, sir," he said, "an Eyes Only Operational Immediate for you."

"So I hear. Let's see what you've got," Dulles said, gesturing impatiently with his right hand *Let me have it.*

Harrison first extended a clipboard with a sheet titled "Receipt for Classified Document." When Bruce had signed it, Harrison handed him a document with a TOP SECRET cover sheet on it.

"That'll be all, Harrison, thank you," Bruce said.

"Yes, sir, Colonel," Harrison said, saluted, turned on his heels, and marched out. Dancy pulled the door shut.

Bruce scanned the message, made a face, then thrust the sheet at Stevens.

Stevens took it and read:

TOP SECRET X STATION CHIEF

OPERATIONAL IMMEDIATE FILE

COPY NO. 1

OF 1 COPY ONLY

31MAY43

OFFICE OF THE DIRECTOR OSS WASHINGTON

FOR OSS LONDON EYES ONLY BRUCE STEVENS

QUOTE

1. OSS LONDON DIRECTED AS HIGHEST PRIORITY TO SUPPORT WITH ALL MEANS AVAILABLE OSS BERN'S REQUESTED CONTINGENCY RESCUE PLAN.

2. RESCUE WILL BE ATTEMPTED AT EARLIEST POSSIBLE TIME AT OSS BERN'S DISCRETION.

3. OSS LONDON ALSO DIRECTED TO SUPPORT OSS ALGIERS IN WHATEVER WAY POSSIBLE WITH ITS CONTINGENCY PLAN.

4. ADDITIONAL ORDERS TO FOLLOW THIS DATE.

5. STATION CHIEF LONDON WILL ACKNOWLEDGE RECEIPT OF THIS MESSAGE.

END QUOTE

DONOVAN

TOP SECRET

David K. E. Bruce then drained his coffee, slammed his china mug on his wooden desk, and said, icily sarcastic, "Did I mention Dulles's *fait accompli*?"

[TWO]
Palermo, Sicily
2050 30 May 1943

John Craig van der Ploeg, his mind foggy, felt weightless as he floated freely through a warm darkness that was absolutely peaceful.

He turned his head to the left and had the sensation of something tickling his right ear. He turned his head the other way, and then something tickled his left ear. He turned back to the left, felt the tickle again, then right, then shook his head—and found himself suddenly awake.

And dazed.

And completely confused.

Gone was the peaceful, warm darkness. Now it was just damn dark. His whole body ached. His ears rang. And his right foot felt as if he had put it in a searing fire.

The slightest movement caused his whole body to sway.

So I'm floating?

Where am I?

He looked around and slowly began to get his bearings. There were limbs surrounding him, poking and scratching. He could smell the leaves.

Is that what was tickling my ears?

There was intense pressure—a squeezing sensation—at his upper thighs and buttocks, and it took him a moment to realize that it was being caused by the webbing of his parachute harness.

He looked up and saw his collapsed parachute, its lines all fouled in the limbs.

I landed in a tree?

Damn I hurt . . .

He looked down and around and still could see nothing in the darkness but more limbs and leaves.

Did I break my foot?

And why can't I move?

How long have I been here?

And then he panicked.

I'll never get found up here!

"Help!" he called out in Italian. "Up here! Someone! Help me!"

There then came a bright light in his eyes, and he immediately stopped.

The beam of light moved down to his torso, and he felt a hand yanking at his harness, then heard the metallic rattling of the harness release.

The next sensation that John Craig van der Ploeg felt was that of falling forward—and then down.

More limbs slapped at him as he fell.

"*Ugh!*" he grunted as he hit the ground, landing faster than he'd expected.

Then he heard a familiar voice.

"Knock off the yelling!" Dick Canidy said with more than a little disgust. "You were only five feet off the ground, for christsake."

John Craig caught his breath, then said, "What happened?"

"What the hell do you think happened? You landed in a tree! A huge chestnut. The damn thing must be sixty feet tall." He grunted. "You sure like hitting huge fucking targets."

John Craig moaned, then reached for his right boot.

"You okay?" Canidy said, shining the beam back to his face.

He saw John Craig wince.

"My foot. It feels like it's on fire."

The flashlight beam moved to the booted foot—on the way illuminating some dried vomitus on John Craig's black coveralls—and Canidy knelt to get a better look, grateful the foul odor was mostly gone.

He carefully grasped the boot and slowly moved the toe of it up and down.

"That hurt?"

"A little. Some burning."

"I don't think it's broken. You'd have a helluva lot more pain if it were."

Canidy then started to slowly roll his foot side to side.

"Stop! That burns like hell!"

"Let's see if you can put any weight on it," Canidy said, then stood and offered his hand.

John Craig hopped up on his left leg, then tried to take a step. He screamed in pain as his ankle gave way and his right leg collapsed beneath him.

Once again on the ground, he crab-crawled over to the thick trunk and leaned against it.

Canidy looked at him.

"Well, shit! This certainly changes things. . . ."

He looked up, and then around them.

"Stay put," Canidy said. "I need to pull together our gear and get rid of the parachutes so no one sees them." He looked up again. "Especially yours, which is going to be a bitch getting out of there."

John Craig, his head spinning, watched Canidy start to climb the huge chestnut tree. Then he closed his eyes.

John Craig heard fast footfalls approaching and opened his eyes wide. He had no idea how long he'd been out. He started to move—and instantly felt the burning sensation in his right foot.

He reached for his .45 and began to raise it in the direction of the sound.

Then he heard the footsteps stop.

Then Canidy's voice: "Put that damn thing down before you cause us even more trouble."

John Craig let out a sigh as he lowered his weapon.

"Feeling any better?" Canidy said, catching his breath.

"Not really."

"Shit."

"Where's the gear?" John Craig said.

"Stashed with the parachutes in two places. Took me twenty minutes, but I found some nice rock outcrops up the hill to put it in."

"Why?"

"So if one stash is found—which is unlikely, but you never know—they will think they hit the jackpot. And we will have a backup hidden."

"No, why stashed?"

"Because I sure as hell cannot carry the gear and you."

"Oh yeah. Sorry."

"Right now our Plan B options are less than lousy. One is for you to sit tight while I go find a motorcycle, a car—something that can haul your ass into town. But if someone saw us jump, and you stayed here, then you'd literally be a sitting duck when they came. So the other option is for you and me to have a three-legged race to town, and once we get you comfortable there, I'll come back and grab the gear."

"Three-legged race?"

"You hold on to me and we walk together."

Canidy started peeling off his black coveralls. Underneath he wore more of Wentworth Danfield Dutton's tailor-made clothing.

John Craig, under his coveralls, had on brown pants and vest and a tan collarless shirt bought from a Sicilian who had been smuggled to Algiers aboard one of Frank Nola's fishing boats.

"Get out of your coveralls," Canidy said, "and I'll stash them with mine."

I wonder if the vomit soaked through, he thought.

Make that I'll stash it near mine. . . .

John Craig struggled to stand.

He said, "We're on the outskirts of Palermo, right?"

At OSS Algiers, Canidy had mapped out the route they would take from the Landing Zone to the port, complete with landmarks.

"Yeah," he said, "the LZ's a little more than a mile west of the port. I saw the road as we landed. It's not far."

"Oh yeah," John Craig remembered. "So did I."

"Hurry up. We need to get moving. We've already been in one place way too damn long."

John Craig van der Ploeg had his right hand on Dick Canidy's left shoulder. Canidy had his left hand on John Craig's right shoulder.

"Inside foot first . . . and go!" Canidy said, and stepped forward with his left.

John Craig, putting weight on Canidy's shoulder, swung out his right boot. As he eased pressure onto the hurt foot, he grunted with pain.

"Good?" Canidy said.

"Just keep going."

They took another step. John Craig immediately fell forward.

Canidy tried to catch them before they both went down. He failed.

They were lying on the ground when Canidy heard John Craig moan—and then chuckle.

"That hurt," John Craig said, then chuckled again. "But that was pretty damn ridiculous."

Canidy couldn't help himself. He chuckled, too.

Then he said, "What the hell else can go wrong?"

"Don't ask," John Craig said. "With my luck anything is possible."

Then they both chuckled, and that turned into hearty laughter.

After a moment, they composed themselves.

They got up, shakily.

"Okay," Canidy said once they had regained their balance, "let's try it again . . . and go!"

Progress over the uneven ground was slow. Finding a comfortable rhythm seemed impossible, even as they quietly counted out a cadence—"One . . . two . . . three . . . four . . . and one . . . two . . . three . . . four . . ."

They pressed on, more or less stumbling forward, and almost a half hour later came to the narrow road. They turned to follow it downhill. The smooth surface made finding a rhythm a little easier. They were making better time despite John Craig moaning that the pain was becoming worse.

They heard a dog barking ahead.

Then John Craig suddenly exclaimed: "Damn it! Stop! I need to stop!"

They shuffled to the side of the road.

"It just hurts too much," John Craig said. "Just leave me."

He moaned as he collapsed under a squat tree.

Now what? Canidy thought, and inhaled deeply.

He noticed that the tree had a strong, familiar smell. He reached up to one of the limbs, felt an equally familiar shape growing there, and plucked it.

Lemon, he thought, then remembered the landmarks he had marked on his map. *This is part of that citrus farm.*

The dog barked again.

"There's a farmhouse just down the road," Canidy said. "I wasn't sure if it was inhabited, but that dog means it probably is. I'm going to go have a look. You should be fine. We're far enough away from the LZ. And there's been no sign that someone has seen us, or at least is coming after us."

"Go," John Craig said, curling up in a fetal position.

Nice, Canidy thought. *This just keeps getting fucking better . . .*

Canidy shook John Craig's shoulder fifteen minutes later.

"Wake up!" he said. "You can sleep when we get to town."

"What? How do we get there?"

"Let's go," Canidy said, then put his hand under John Craig's right arm and pulled him to his feet. Then, with great effort, he got him to the road.

"A bicycle?" John Craig said. "I can't pedal with this bad foot."

"You're not going to. Just sit on the seat."

It took another great effort to get John Craig on the bike seat and balanced. Canidy found that the real challenge came next, when he mounted the bike just in front of John Craig.

"Put your hands on my shoulders," Canidy instructed.

John Craig did so.

Canidy, his left foot on one pedal, then started pushing the bicycle forward with his right. When he went to get that foot on its pedal, he found that their combined weight made the bike terribly unbalanced, causing the front tire to wobble wildly.

Canidy was convinced they were about to go down—and hard.

Behind him, he heard John Craig begin to chuckle.

"Don't you dare fucking start with that now!" Canidy said, but he chuckled when he said it.

He managed to get in a couple strong rotations of the pedals, and with more speed the wobbling tire evened out and the bicycle became more stable.

Just like a damn airplane, Canidy thought as he stood somewhat triumphantly and steered along the dark road.

They coasted downhill, picking up speed, and after a couple minutes passed the farmhouse.

John Craig noticed that there had been no barking.

Is that because the dog didn't hear us?

Or because Dick had to do something so he could steal this bike?

Then he felt sick at that mental image. And then guilty.

Damn it! None of this would've happened if I hadn't landed in that tree and screwed up my foot.

Thinking it would ease his conscience, he was about to ask Canidy about the dog, then decided that it was a really long shot that Canidy would even answer the question—and, if then, answer truthfully—and John Craig decided he really didn't want to hear his fear confirmed.

[THREE]
Schutzstaffel Field Office
Palermo, Sicily
1830 30 May 1943

This is the last place I want to be right now, SS-Obersturmbannführer Oskar Kappler thought as the driver turned off the engine, *but at least I'm out of Messina. And I'm ready to get out of this goddamn car.*

Starting before noon, Kappler had been almost desperate for an excuse to leave the SS headquarters. He knew painfully well that he was disturbed by the contents of the letter from his father, and feared that his distraction was apparent to anyone and everyone—and particularly obvious to SS-Standartenführer Julius Schrader.

Schrader took an odd pleasure in boasting that, having known Kappler so long, "I can read you like an open book, my friend."

Kappler did not buy that—and often took offense at what he considered Schrader's prying into his private life, especially his family's wealth and privilege—but that did not stop Schrader from trying. Thus, Oskar did not want to be around Juli all damn day, and tomorrow, and very likely the next, constantly having to fend off what he knew would be Schrader's persistent proclamations as to why Kappler was behaving in such an unusual manner.

When Kappler had heard Schrader mention checking on Müller and his SS field office operations, he had had to restrain himself from appearing overly eager. Schrader knew Kappler loathed Müller. Thus, Kappler had gone to his office and passed a couple hours—a time frame that seemed much longer—then finally stood in the doorway to Schrader's office and, in a tone he hoped came across as casual if not bored, announced that he would be leaving to drive to Palmero.

Schrader had made a *harumph* sound, and said, "I think not."

What the hell? Kappler thought.

"Otto will drive you," Schrader had then announced. "That is not open for discussion. That is an order, my friend. I can see that you are mentally distracted over this morning's meeting with the Abwehr agent and the topic of nerve gas. I do not want to find myself sending out a team for search and rescue because you lost your way and drove off a cliff into the Mediterranean Sea. The trip will give you the opportunity to ensure that Müller continues making proper amends. And a nice three-hour drive and change of scenery will be mentally cleansing."

Otto Lieber was Schrader's newly arrived SS-scharführer bodyguard. He was slight of build, a fresh-faced, blue-eyed blond seventeen-year-old Weisbadener whose peach fuzz cheeks convinced Kappler that he'd yet to have his first shave.

Schrader glanced at his wristwatch.

"It is now just after three o'clock," he said. "Otto should have you arrive around six, in time for Müller to treat you to drinks and a nice dinner."

"I'll be fine driving myself," Kappler protested.

Schrader held up his hand, palm out.

"You'll be better being driven, my friend. I will send for Otto to bring around my personal vehicle. Nothing but the best for you!"

Kappler thought, *I despise that little car!*

He looked Schrader in the eyes and sighed audibly.

"Very well, Juli. I surrender. I suppose I should be saying, 'Thank you.' "

"Yes, you should."

The next thing Kappler knew, the scharführer was pulling up

outside the headquarters building in Schrader's two-year-old Fiat 1500.

Kappler put his overnight bag in what passed for a backseat and his black leather briefcase on the front floorboard. Then he made a tight-lipped smile at the driver as he squeezed his tall, athletic body into the cramped two-door Italian sports car.

SS-Scharführer Otto Lieber, after the initial twenty minutes of forced small talk about weather and how great the war was going, quickly got the message that SS-Obersturmbannführer Oskar Kappler had no desire to spend the trip chatting.

"If you don't mind, I have a few things to consider before we reach our destination," Kappler said.

"*Jawohl*, Herr Obersturmbannführer! I fully understand," Lieber said, and turned his attention to the winding coastal two-lane road, running the Fiat up and down its gears.

There was nothing to see but ocean and the waves pounding the rocky shoreline, and Kappler gazed out at it in deep thought.

That morning, after shaking hands with Ernst Beck and leaving Café Alessandro, Kappler had reread his father's letter a half-dozen times, at the very least, and now had it memorized.

Father always used my full name when I was a child—especially when he was angry as hell. I can hear it now, his voice growling: "Oskar Karl Kappler, you will do as I say or else!"

And when he was speaking to me about something very serious, he always called me "Karlchen" in a calm, commanding voice to get my full attention.

Well, he sure as hell has it now.

I do not think that there is any significance to be found in his sending the love of my mother and sister, other than that simply being a method not to draw attention to the "Karlchen" code so that it can be used again. Especially because he did state that Mother and Anna were unharmed and in Berlin.

I had wondered what, if anything, had happened to the family businesses in the Ruhr dam bombings. There have been no details of that in any news reports, suggesting that something big did happen and that Berlin is keeping that quiet.

What has been surprising to me is that the messages I sent Felix asking what he knew about the bombings have gone unanswered. That could mean that he did not get them—which is very doubtful, as he's never not gotten my messages and not answered them—or that he does not know—doubtful again, considering his position in the SD—or that he has been ordered not to tell me.

This last one I have come to believe, though if it is correct I do wonder why Felix then didn't reply that he did not know and was looking into it.

His not answering any of the messages . . . does that mean something?

Perhaps not.

Regardless, what happened to the Ruhr operations would appear to be a trivial point now. Even if all seven were lost to the bombings, it does not matter—not if Hitler has stolen them from us.

Just as he stole Fritz Thyssen's.

And why is the bastard throwing the Thyssens in a concentration camp?

Is Hitler that paranoid? That revengeful?

Or is the war, contrary to Otto's happy talk, that lost?

Or all the above?

My father and mother did not do as the Thyssens—give Hitler and his Thousand-Year Reich the finger in front of all their fellow Germans and then leave the country. As far as I know, my father has done all that's been required of him.

Yet it is absolutely crystal clear that Father fears that our entire family is in danger.

He said to take "extraordinary actions to save yourself from a possible similar fate but also ones to save your mother and sister."

Then he suddenly thought: *Jesus Christ!*

He turned and looked out the side window so that the scharführer would not see his expression.

Am I being watched?

Is that why the hell Juli ordered me to take this kid on the trip?

The bastard's keeping an eye on me!

He looked to the floorboard, to where he had put his black leather briefcase. Inside the case, among his official papers, was his Luger and four extra magazines of 9mm. He then glanced at Lieber. The peach-faced Otto stared straight ahead, seemingly oblivious to anything except the dotted lines on the macadam.

Using a clueless kid would be a clever way for me not to suspect he's actually watching me and reporting on what I'm doing.

And did anyone pay any attention that after I called and left a message for Müller to expect my arrival, I called Beck and told him that I would be out of town overnight in Palermo?

Oh, hell . . . now I am becoming paranoid!

"Calm down, Karlchen," as Father used to tell me. "You must always think thoroughly before acting."

This kid's not capable of babysitting an infant, let alone keeping up with me.

Still, as Felix said when we were in intelligence school: "Even the paranoid have enemies."

He'd laughed, that Felix, but he'd meant it seriously.

Otto suddenly stood on the brakes and downshifted.

Kappler jerked his head to look forward. He saw that a herd of forty or more goats blocked the road. A farmer carrying a long wooden staff was trying, and failing, to hurry them across.

"Sorry," Otto said, then tapped the horn.

The honking caused the animals to run in circles and around the car.

"I'd suggest just running them over," Kappler said, "but I don't think this flimsy little car is much of a match against even those small animals. And we don't want to be stuck out here."

Jesus! Kappler thought. *Stuck out here indeed.*

My family's very existence is at grave risk and I'm stuck in a joke of a vehicle surrounded by a damn herd of crazed goats?

Otto hit the horn again, impatiently revving the engine.

This time the farmer prodded at the animals with his staff and after a moment managed to part the herd.

Otto shot through the gap.

Okay, think, Oskar. Think!

Getting back to those "extraordinary actions" . . . what am I supposed to do with Mother and Anna? Do I try to get back to Berlin now? Try to prepare them for whatever happens next?

No. Father wrote "if something should happen to me, you will need to take your own extraordinary actions."

And in that case I would be approached by a powerful man, someone who was involved with the family enterprises that Hitler cannot touch.

I wonder if Hitler even knows about them?

I've known about them, known they exist—I even remember Father going to Argentina with Thyssen—but never knew details of exactly what we have there in South America and in the United States.

Father always said that he would tell me "in due time."

And—ach du lieber Gott!—*what a "due time" it is!*

He shook his head.

I never thought that those properties would one day "constitute the family's entire wealth." It certainly appears to have been a brilliant business strategy, particularly in light of Hitler stealing all we have in Germany.

Yet Thyssen did the same—and it's all utterly worthless to him locked up in a konzentrationslager.

And what the hell will I do if the same happens to Father?

And what if the bastards decide "like father, like son" and throw me in, too, for good measure?

Father writing that he prayed the war will soon end, and that we will soon be together as a family—that read like his last words. Ones in vain, especially considering he said those secret, dangerous tasks that God chose "may not end well for me."

So, what to do? I'm just supposed to wait? For what? And for how long?

That Beck said he thought it was "going to get very interesting very quickly."

Does he know something?

Kappler felt his heart race. And he suddenly realized he had no idea how long he'd been holding his breath, and now found himself making rapid, shallow breaths.

He could hear his father's voice: *"Calm down, Karlchen!"*

I may never hear my father's voice again. . . .

He turned to look out his side window when he caught his throat tightening and felt his eyes glistening. He did not want the scharführer to see that.

"Everything all right, sir?" Otto Lieber said, glancing at him.

Kappler after a moment cleared his throat, then nodded.

"Just something in my eye," he said. "I'm fine."

Otto Lieber nodded, then quietly returned his attention to the road.

[FOUR]

SS-Obersturmbannführer Oskar Kappler reached down for his leather briefcase as he looked at the massive white masonry building that served as the SS's Palermo field office. It had been built in the "four corners" city center—the Quattro Canti Quarter—by the Normans nine centuries earlier. It was four stories high. A dozen stone steps led up to the huge heavy ornate metal door of the main entrance.

Seeing the field office building brought back memories—none of them good—of the times that Kappler had been forced to come to Palermo.

I tried to get those Tabun howitzer munitions lost here, so no one could use them. But that bastard Müller found them—and could have killed us all when he decided that he had plans for them.

As the supervising officer of SS-Sturmbannführer Hans Müller—a high-strung twenty-eight-year-old major who had a violent temper that matched, if not surpassed, that of Adolf Hitler—Kappler was responsible for what Müller did. Or failed to do. And when Kappler wrote up the report detailing Müller's intended use and then loss of the nerve gas, and in it demanded that the reckless Müller be demoted and reassigned, Julius Schrader had squashed it.

"I am going to do you a favor, my friend, and tell you that you really do not want this incident to go any further," Schrader had counseled Kappler as he put the report in his desk drawer. "Remember, someone in Berlin reading this could suggest that blame lay with you for poor training and supervision of Müller. Give him another chance. Just keep a closer eye on him."

Or that blame lay with Juli—and so he left the bastard in his job.

And that left me walking a damn tightrope with the bastard, because Müller knows I do not wield the authority over him that I should.

"Well," Kappler said to Otto, "we got here in one piece. I don't know about you, but first thing I need to do is relieve the pressure on my bladder."

"*Jawohl*, Herr Obersturmbannführer!" Otto Lieber said, then quickly got out from behind the wheel.

Kappler watched as Lieber then bolted up the stone steps and went inside the building.

I guess he has to go worse than I do.

Kappler squeezed out of the car, swung the car door closed, and casually went up the steps. When he opened the huge metal door, there in the entryway stood Otto Lieber, gesturing to the left, toward a door.

"I've located the gentlemen's facility, sir," Lieber said. "It is through this door and to the right."

You really are that wet behind the ears, aren't you, Otto?

And you're probably convinced that your service just now is as important to winning the war for the Fatherland as is being on the front lines and actually dodging bullets.

"Thank you, but I have been here," he said drily. "If you want to be genuinely useful, see if you can find Sturmbannführer Müller now and let him know I'm here."

"*Jawohl*, Herr Obersturmbannführer!"

Five minutes later, Kappler reappeared in the entryway and found Otto standing with a young man in uniform.

Oh, for Christ's sake! Another one?

"Heil Hitler!" the young man barked as he stiffly held out his right arm in a Nazi salute. "Scharführer Günther Burger at your service, sir!"

SS-Scharführer Günther Burger was almost a mirror image of

SS-Scharführer Otto Lieber. Kappler vaguely remembered seeing his name on the field office manning chart, very far down at the bottom.

Kappler looked at Otto, then back at his twin.

"I was expecting to see Sturmbannführer Müller," Kappler said, ignoring the Nazi greeting.

"*Jawohl*, Herr Obersturmbannführer! The sturmbannführer has asked me to take you directly to the hotel where you will be staying. With the sturmbannführer's compliments, sir."

Is the bastard blatantly ignoring me?

"But where the hell is he? I thought it was clear that he was supposed to be expecting me."

"*Jawohl*, Herr Obersturmbannführer! And he is. At the Hotel Michelangelo. After we get you checked in."

Burger then gestured somewhat nervously to the door, and added, "It is right around the corner, Herr Obersturmbannführer. Just two blocks, sir."

Interesting, Oskar Kappler thought after unpacking his overnight bag and taking a long look out the window of his suite on the top floor of the Hotel Michelango. *I don't know what Müller is up to, but it's clear he's trying to make amends with this very nice room.*

The suite had a wide view of the harbor. Kappler saw that there were mostly commercial fishing boats moored there. And at the end of one of the T-shaped piers—newly rebuilt, he knew, to replace the pier that had burned when the cargo ship blew up just after off-loading the Tabun—were a pair of *Schnellboots*.

Still, I don't trust the bastard one bit, he thought as he went into the hall and pulled the door shut.

Coming down the stairs, Kappler saw that Günther Burger and

Otto Lieber were seated on facing couches in the center of the wide tile-floored lobby. They appeared to be conversing with the ease of old friends.

When Burger noticed Kappler coming down the wide stairs, he popped to his feet. Lieber automatically followed suit.

Kappler scanned the lobby. He saw that the cocktail lounge was at the front of the hotel, just off the lobby and beyond a wide arched passageway that had two large potted palms on either side. He walked to the scharführers.

"I have alerted Sturmbannführer Müller that you are here," Burger said. "He said he is coming right away."

"Good," Kappler said, and looked to the lounge. "I'll be in there. Otto, you are free until nine tomorrow morning, when I'll see you right here. Try to stay out of trouble."

Kappler took a seat at a cocktail table in the far corner with a view of the lobby through the arched passageway. The lounge was empty except for two older men drinking at the wooden bar. When they glanced at Kappler as he entered, he thought they looked intelligent and educated—if not exactly thrilled to see an SS uniform—and guessed they might be university professors.

The bartender—a short, fat Sicilian whose coarse skin and hard features made Kappler think he would be better suited as, say, a fishmonger—waddled across the room to him.

When it immediately became clear that the bartender did not speak German or English, Kappler pointed to a wall where a wine advertisement had been tacked up as decoration. It had a sketch of a bottle of red wine.

Kappler pointed to it, said, "Bottiglia rosso," then used his index finger to indicate "one."

The bartender grunted, left, and shortly thereafter waddled back to him carrying a heavy, tall water glass and a bottle of red wine.

As Kappler watched the bartender struggle with the corkscrew in his sausage-shaped fingers, he became more convinced the man wasn't meant to serve drinks. And when he botched the ritual of offering the cork and then a taste of the wine before completely filling the glass—and the man did indeed fill the glass, right to the lip—Kappler really began to suspect something very strange was happening.

The bartender then, without a word, turned with the open bottle and started back for the bar.

Kappler was about to stop him, then looked at the glass and thought, *Hell, this should last me quite some time—if I can figure out how to drink it without soaking my uniform.*

He had just bent forward to start very carefully sipping at the wine when he noticed someone was entering the lounge. He glanced up and saw two attractive young Sicilian women in tight, revealing dresses.

When he saw that they were leading a man in an SS uniform, he sat up.

Müller!

SS-Sturmbannführer Hans Müller was of medium build with a slight paunch. He had dark eyes that were not necessarily pleasant, puffy cheeks, and thinning black hair that he purposefully had cut to resemble that of Hitler's.

Kappler saw that Müller's hair now was mussed and his tunic not completely buttoned.

It looks like he just pulled it on!

And who are these women?

They were both about five-four with full, curvy figures and olive skin. One had very short brown hair and big almond eyes. The other, with her rich wavy dark hair touching her shoulders, had warm dark eyes. They appeared to be somewhat tolerating their escort.

Kappler saw that the two men at the bar glanced at the women, then, seeing the SS uniform, made a face and immediately turned away.

Müller took a long moment to look around the lounge, then found Kappler in the far corner and nodded for the girls to follow him.

Has the bastard been drinking? Kappler thought.

Müller came closer, and Kappler then thought, *No, not just drinking. He is drunk!*

Kappler was going to keep his seat, but at the presence of the women he automatically got to his feet.

"Heil Hitler!" Müller began thickly, his words slightly slurred as he thrust out his arm.

Kappler simply stood staring at him.

Müller dropped his arm and went on in German: "It is so very good to see you again, Herr Obersturmbannführer. I trust your room is to your satisfaction?"

Kappler, who realized from Müller's forced tone that he was working at being hospitable, looked him in the eyes.

And his drunkenness is an outrage! he thought.

I should run these women off and have him locked up for dereliction of duty!

But . . . this behavior is absolutely nothing compared to what I tried to have him punished for the last time. And look what I accomplished with that—not a damn thing.

Müller made a thin-lipped smile.

And, you smug bastard, you know that!

Well, I have much bigger problems to concern myself with. I cannot be distracted by this unprofessional behavior.

So, okay, I shall play along with you, you bastard . . . which could very well confuse the hell out of you.

"I asked about your room?" Müller said. "Is it not to your liking?"

"It is quite a nice room," Kappler said.

"Very good," Müller said.

Müller then waved to get the bartender's attention and made a circling motion over their table to order drinks all around. The bartender nodded.

"Shall we sit?" Müller then said, and when the women did not move, he impatiently motioned at them individually, instructing them to sit on the outside of him and Kappler.

They don't speak German, Kappler thought, looking at them.

Meine Gott, they are indeed quite attractive. . . .

"Allow me to present Lucia," Müller said, gesturing first to the long-haired one, "and Maria."

They smiled at Kappler.

They at least understood their names and the gesture.

What do I say?

Kappler nodded and smiled, then decided to keep it simple and said, *"Ciao."*

The bartender appeared with Kappler's open bottle of red wine, two others, and three more glasses. He drained the open bottle and a second one in the glasses, then turned to leave with the empties.

"Send Signore Palasota!" Müller called after him in German.

The bartender looked back and nodded, then disappeared from the room.

Does he understand German? Kappler thought. *Or he just recognized the name?*

"I want you to meet the fellow who runs our place," Müller said, and leaned closer to Kappler, putting his hand on his shoulder.

"Our place"? Kappler thought, looking at him, then at the hand on his shoulder.

"I am aware," Müller said, "that we may have had our differences in the past. And I am glad that that is where they are—in the past."

Kappler looked at him.

What the hell is he doing?

Müller made a thin smile and held up his glass in a toast.

"Here's to our making a fresh start and moving forward," Müller said. *"Salute!"*

He tapped his full glass to Kappler's very full one, causing some wine to spill. Müller did not seem to notice, or did not care, as he took a sip of his wine.

Kappler shrugged, then carefully sipped his wine.

"Of course."

"And as an olive branch," Müller went on, laughed, then said, "or perhaps, as is the case, an olive-skinned branch, you'll allow me to treat you?" He glanced at the big-eyed young woman. "Do you like Lucia?"

Kappler looked at Müller.

What the hell are you talking about?

"Treat"?

So these are whores?

Kappler realized that the girls were looking provocatively at him. Lucia batted her big brown eyes and made a well-practiced smile. He caught himself automatically smiling back.

Then he felt an involuntarily stir in his groin, and hated himself for it.

They are!

I don't care how attractive they are. I am not going to degrade myself by following some miserable prick who was able to come up with . . . with . . . however the hell much a whore costs!

He looked at Müller, who was looking toward the arched passageway.

And, you bastard, I certainly do not want you believing you've done me any favors—and not one such as this.

Scheisse!

"Ah!" Müller suddenly said. "Here comes Signore Palasota!"

[FIVE]
Palermo, Sicily
2255 30 May 1943

Dick Canidy and John Craig van der Ploeg rolled into Palermo proper. The city was dark and eerily quiet. The few people they passed—the bicycle allowed them to approach quietly and quickly—ducked down alleys or found other shadowy spots when they realized they'd been seen.

Why? Canidy thought. *Is there a curfew?*

If so, we're screwed if we're stopped.

After ten minutes, getting closer to the western side of the port, Canidy made sure they kept clear of the train station at Via Montepellegrino in case troops were arriving. Canidy then turned onto Via Altavilla and, looking intently, found the familiar side street that was lined with two-story apartments.

"We're ten blocks up from the port," he said quietly. "Which is where we go tomorrow and visit the Brothers Buda."

John Craig van der Ploeg, even in the dim light, could see that the neighborhood was run-down. Trash littered the street. And the shabby buildings were not at all maintained.

Dick's had to have been here before. But why?

"Where are we?" John Craig said.

"Our home away from home, I hope. I'll tell you more once we're inside."

Canidy skidded the bicycle to a stop at an apartment midway down the street. Its wooden door was a faded yellow, the paint peeling. Mounted above it, in a small space, was a small, weathered wooden crucifix. Four empty clay flowerpots painted bright colors were in a wrought-iron rack in front of the lone window.

Canidy planted his feet on the ground as he steadied the bicycle.

"Can you get off by yourself okay?" Canidy said over his shoulder.

Canidy immediately felt John Craig put more weight on his shoulders and then the bike shudder as he slid off. Canidy thought that the bicycle, free of its burden, could almost float. He then leaned it against the wall under the clay pots. He pulled the clay pot that was painted red out of its holder and reached in under it.

He triumphantly held up a small object toward John Craig, and with a tone of satisfaction said, "Thank God for old habits."

Canidy moved to the yellow door.

The key, John Craig figured out when he heard Canidy working the knob. *So, he has been here before.*

Canidy then exclaimed: "I'll be damned. It's been kicked in."

Canidy pulled his .45 from the small of his back, then pushed at the door with his boot. It swung inward, its hinges making one long, low squeak.

There were no lights burning in the apartment, and when Canidy reached inside and slapped at the switch, none came on.

"Damn it," he said, then carefully entered.

John Craig saw the beam from Canidy's flashlight sweeping the room.

A moment later, he was back at the door. He rolled the bicycle inside, then said, "Get in here."

John Craig winced with pain as he shuffled through the door. He pushed it shut behind him, then had to push it twice more before it stayed shut.

It was pitch-dark inside, but he could just make out that they were in the kitchen—and that the place had been trashed. Something crunched under his feet as he walked. And there was a faint fetid odor, as if something had been left to rot a long time ago.

"Wait here," Canidy said. "I'm going to check the rest of the house."

"Okay," John Craig said, pulling out his .45 and putting his weight against what felt like a tile-covered counter by the front window.

As he strained to make out any objects in the kitchen, he could hear Canidy moving quickly through the apartment. First there were the sounds of Dick opening and closing doors on the first floor, then ones of him pounding up the wooden stairs and searching the second floor end to end.

He's spent almost twice as much time upstairs.

Then John Craig saw the yellow beam of Canidy's flashlight filling the stairwell and heard the sound of him bounding down the stairs.

As he entered the kitchen, the yellow beam briefly swept the room, then went out. In that short time John Craig could see that the place was more than just a sloppy shambles. It had been demolished. The table was overturned, the chairs broken, cupboard doors torn from their hinges, plates and drinking glasses shattered on the floor.

"What the hell happened here?" John Craig said.

"Nothing good, that's for goddamn certain."

"Is the place empty?"

"Yes and no."

"What's that mean?"

"It means I've got some bad news, which could be good news, and some really bad news."

"And what does that mean?"

"Nothing that can't wait another few minutes until I can get some damn lights burning."

It took Dick Canidy a good twenty minutes to find the rat's nest of wires that was the main fuse box and then determine that the glass fuses—most of them anyway—were not blown or otherwise broken. Then he spent another ten minutes going methodically through both floors, flicking switches on and off, until he finally found a light that came on.

It was on the first floor, in what had been a living room at the opposite end of the apartment from the kitchen. It was a lone bulb in an overhead fixture that somehow had survived the almost total destruction of everything in the apartment.

It's disturbing how—what? furious? psychopathic?—they had to be to destroy this place, Canidy thought as he unscrewed the bulb and the room went dark. *I'm surprised they didn't firebomb it for good measure.*

He then carefully cradled the bulb, flicked on his flashlight, and went back upstairs. This time, John Craig followed, pulling himself up the stairs using the handrail.

John Craig was just reaching the top step when Canidy got the bulb installed. It lit the area fairly well, and John Craig now could see that the whole upper floor had been a bedroom.

Then he gasped.

In the middle of the room, with wrists and ankles tied by fabric to a wooden armchair that lay on its side, was the bloated corpse of a naked dark-haired man.

"That's the bad news I mentioned," Canidy said matter-of-factly.

"That's not Tubes!"

"No, of course not. But I'm not sure who the hell it is."

John Craig looked around, saw the bathroom door, and shuffled as fast as he could through it. The tiny room reverberated with his loud retching.

Not so much throwing up as it is dry heaves, Canidy thought.

There can't be anything left in his stomach after all he threw up in the airplane.

Canidy turned and got a better look at the dead man. He looked like he could be maybe thirty. He had a large nose and a black mustache. His thick black curly hair was matted with caked blood from the single bullet hole in the center of his forehead.

He's the spitting image of Frank Nola, just not as tall.

Has to be his cousin Whatshisname . . . Mariano.

I wonder if he was working with Frank? Or with the mob? Or is there really a difference?

Almost every inch of the dead man's olive skin was deeply bruised.

He got the shit beat out of him.

They must have started at his feet and worked their way to his face.

Canidy then saw the man's fingers.

Correction.

They started with pulling his fingernails, then probably went to his feet.

Jesus did they work him over!

Canidy saw that John Craig was standing in the door to the pisser, bracing himself on the doorframe as he stared at the body.

"What is this place?" John Craig said.

"It's supposed to belong to Frank Nola's cousin. I'm guessing that that's who this guy is. They look alike, present condition notwithstanding." He paused, then added, "Then again, maybe we will find Frank looking like this. . . ."

"Jesus!"

"Yeah, it's one thing to read about this shit," Canidy said, "but not so nice up close and personal, is it?"

"You warned me," John Craig said quietly. "You said it at the table with Captain Fine."

Canidy ignored his use of military rank.

"Don't try to understand it," he said. "I sure as hell can't."

John Craig nodded meekly.

"Is this what happens because of that Hitler order?" he said. "The one ordering the killing of 'enemies on commando missions'?"

"'In or out of uniform, with or without weapons,'" Canidy recited. "'Slaughtered to the last man.' The operative word being *slaughtered*."

He looked down at the dead man and added, "And this is a clear example of what Hitler meant when he said 'should it be found necessary to spare one for interrogation,' they're to be shot immediately afterward."

John Craig, bent at the waist, made a sound that suggested he might have to throw up again. He somehow held it back.

"What mission was he on?" he then said.

"I don't know. None. At least that's my bet. But he could have been working for Frank and/or in the Mafia. Bottom line is that the SS believed him to be, and that was that. I don't think it's any coincidence that's why he's tied up with that. To make a point to whoever found him."

John Craig looked at the ivory-colored fabric knotted at the wrists and ankles.

"I don't understand," he said. "What's the significance?"

Canidy reached down and picked up from the floor a length of the fabric. He tossed it to John Craig.

He saw that it was about four feet long and a foot wide, with a couple inches of its edges stylishly frayed. He gently rubbed it between his fingertips. It was soft, and felt vaguely familiar.

"So it's a scarf," John Craig said. "Probably a woman's?"

"It's a silk scarf. There's more in the closet."

John Craig looked, and saw a very familiar pile of ivory-colored silk.

"A parachute! We air-dropped the money and everything that was asked for in the messages. So, the scarf is cut from it. . . ."

"Right," Canidy said.

He thought, *What did Nola say his cousin's wife's name was?*

Doesn't matter . . . though "Idiot" comes to mind.

"I'm guessing that this guy's wife found the parachute and made herself that scarf from it. Then she paraded around Palermo with it, and some SS shithead saw it—or someone else saw it and snitched to the SS. So the SS made a little courtesy visit."

"And then they did this . . ." John Craig said, looking at the dead man.

He stared at the dead man's hands.

"His fingernails . . ."

"Pretty bad, huh?"

". . . They tore them out?"

"No. They pulled them out. Slowly. It's torture. Then, judging from the shape of the bruises, they beat the shit out of him with a cosh."

In addition to daggers and garrotes, John Craig's training at OSS Dellys had had him practicing close-combat using a cosh. The limber paddle made of leather had a heavy lead ball sewn in its head. One smack alone caused deep pain; multiple hits, particularly to the temples, led to death.

"Why?" John Craig said, his face looking ill. "Because he didn't tell them what they wanted to know?"

"That is possible, even probable, considering his bruises. But I'm thinking it's because he couldn't."

John Craig raised his eyebrows.

"And that," Canidy added, "is what might be the bad news that could be good news—good news for us."

Canidy walked over to the overturned and broken bed frames. They were against the far wall, which had a window. The mattresses had been shredded. It took him a minute to clear a large area of the wooden floor there, pushing the torn sheets and mattress pieces to either side of the room.

"Keep your fingers crossed," Canidy said.

John Craig shuffled over to get a better view in the light of the lone bulb.

Canidy shined his flashlight up and down the floorboards, pushed at a couple places with his fingers, then found what he was looking for and started to pull up a thin board. When that was out of the way, he tugged on a wider one until it started to come up.

John Craig now saw that it was the edge of a larger piece that had been cut in the floor.

A hidden door!

As the large section of flooring came up, John Craig saw Canidy nod.

He looked up at John Craig and said, "My son, let this be a lesson to you. To paraphrase Matthew, 'Live a life as pure and righteous as mine, and blessed be your luck all your days.' Or maybe it was Mark or Luke who said that."

"What did you find?" John Craig said.

He looked around the makeshift door. He saw that there were dead spaces between the long joists that supported the floor of the second level and the ceiling of the first floor.

And then he saw that there was a suitcase in one dead space.

Canidy said, "If my clean living is any indication, this is the backup W/T that Tubes and I brought."

Canidy looked at John Craig and could tell that he mentally was putting the pieces together.

"So," John Craig then said, "this guy's wife wears a silk scarf. That brings the SS here, where they find the parachute and maybe the money and whatever else we air-dropped before Mercury Station was compromised. And a parachute for a supply drop means that there had to be a radio to arrange for the airdrop."

Canidy exhaled audibly, then nodded.

"That's my guess. It fits. And because this poor bastard Mariano had no idea where the radio was, it got him killed." He paused, then added, "Not that the SS bastards weren't going to kill him if he knew and told anyway."

"And then they trashed this place."

"Let's say they completed the job with a crazed enthusiasm. The place wasn't exactly a model home the first time I came here."

Canidy reached down inside the floor. When he pulled out the suitcase, he saw what had been put beneath it.

"Ah, I was hoping to see this again."

"What?"

Canidy pulled out a Sten 9mm submachine gun and slid it across the floor in John Craig's direction.

"That one's yours."

He reached back in and pulled out another machine gun, this one with a longer barrel. It looked substantially better built than the stamped-metal Sten.

"My Johnny gun," he announced. "Officially a Johnson Model 1941 Light Machine Gun. This has real meaning to me."

"Why? And what's it doing in there?"

"It's what I used to blow up the villa where they had the yellow fever experiment. I got it from a guinea mobster. When I left here to get on the sub, I gave it to Tubes. Figured he'd need it more than I did."

"You got it from the Mafia?"

"You haven't heard that story? When I met Frank Nola in New York City? That's how the hell you and I ultimately wound up right here, right now."

John Craig shook his head.

Canidy looked at the suitcase.

"First things first," Canidy said, and pointed at the window. "That is where Tubes first set up our W/T, running the antenna out there. Time for you to earn your keep and remind me why the hell I brought you in the first place. Starting with trying to make contact with Tubes and Algiers. You ready?"

John Craig shrugged.

"I'll give it my best. I think as long as it doesn't involve my damn foot, I should be fine."

"Okay, then I'll try to cobble together some kind of table for you to work at."

John Craig looked askance at the dead man.

Canidy caught that, and added, "Right. And do something with him. . . ."

VII

[ONE]
Hotel Michelangelo
Palermo, Sicily
1915 30 May 1943

SS-Obersturmbannführer Oskar Kappler watched a rugged-looking man of maybe forty approaching the cocktail table where he and SS-Sturmbannführer Hans Müller sat with the two hookers. The man was about five-nine and muscular, with a warm face, a somewhat pronounced nose, and a full head of brown hair. He was casually but nicely dressed, and Kappler noted that he did not walk as much as he sauntered.

The man stopped before the table.

"Giovano said you asked for me, Hans," he announced in passable German as he met Kappler's eyes and nodded once.

Müller put his arm around Kappler and said, "So I did. I wanted you to meet a very important person, Obersturmbannführer Oskar Kappler, who I told you was coming."

The man offered his hand, and in German said, "Jimmy Palasota. It is a genuine honor to have you here."

"The pleasure is mine," Kappler said, shaking the hand firmly.

"Jimmy runs our little hotel," Müller announced.

There he goes with "our" again, Kappler thought.

Maybe it is simply one of those boastful "our favorite place"–type expressions.

"When Hans here told me that you would be our guest tonight," Palasota went on in German, looking between Müller and Kappler, "we made sure the top suite was available."

Kappler saw that Palasota appeared very relaxed and comfortable with himself—*He's not at all intimidated by Müller*—and that his intelligent eyes missed nothing.

What does he mean by making sure the suite was "available"? Kappler wondered. *They threw out the guest who was using it?*

"It's quite fine," he said.

"Good. I hope you enjoy it," Palasota went on. "Everything is of course taken care of, but if there is anything else that I can do for you, please say."

Kappler could not quite put his finger on it, but he thought he detected not so much a Sicilian accent as maybe an American one.

How could that be?

"That is most kind of you," Kappler said. Then, testing, he added, "So you have spent time in our happy home of Deutschland, Signore Palasota?"

Palasota, hands on his hips, shook his head.

"Not once. Never been near it." He glanced at Müller, then said: "I'm told constantly that it's a lovely place."

"That it is!" Müller put in.

"Then you're a native Sicilian?" Kappler pursued.

Palasota nodded, bending a bit at the waist as he did so. "Born right here in Palermo," he said.

"I see," Kappler said. "But you must forgive me. Something does not quite fit. Perhaps it is my poor hearing—I had a long drive from Messina in a very noisy little Fiat this afternoon—but I do not detect a Sicilian accent."

Palasota shrugged.

Kappler went on: "Again, forgive me, I mean no insult whatever—and most would indeed take this as an insult—but I think I hear what could be the accent of an American?"

Jimmy Palasota grinned broadly.

"Close. A *former* American."

"Former?" Kappler repeated. "How is that?"

"I was an American citizen. I spent many years in New York City before being asked to leave. They took away my citizenship."

"Really?" Kappler said.

He thought: *Just like Hitler did to Fritz Thyssen.*

"Really," Palasota said.

"Educate me, if you would, please. What does it take for one to be 'asked to leave' and then have one's citizenship revoked?"

"Well, I wasn't asked to leave right away. I spent a few years behind bars. And after I got out, and they said I hadn't learned my lesson, they deported me back here."

"And then they took away your citizenship."

"And then they took away my citizenship."

"May I ask why you served time in the prison?"

Palasota looked at Sturmbannführer Müller for a moment, then back at Kappler as he mentally chose his words.

"Running businesses that were frowned upon," he said as he glanced at the hookers. "Girls, for one."

The two young women looked at each other, sensed that they were the subject of conversation, and giggled.

So he ran whorehouses in New York? Kappler thought.

And now he runs one here?

"And such an enterprise as that gets one deported from the United States of America?" Kappler said.

Jimmy Palasota chuckled. "No. Not that alone. I guess I shot one guy."

"Only one?" Kappler said.

"One guy too many."

Müller, sipping at his wine, put in: "Shot or killed?"

Palasota raised his eyebrows.

"Okay," he said, "killed."

"How many did you kill?" Kappler said.

Palasota's eyes wandered around the room. He crossed his arms and shrugged.

Müller, his tone suddenly icy, said: "He asked how many. Tell the obersturmbannführer how many you killed!"

Palasota met Müller's eyes for a long moment, then he looked at Kappler.

"Let's just say more than one, Herr Obersturmbannführer."

Kappler nodded as he thought, *Very interesting. The body language suggests this Palasota does as he pleases. And he is completely uncowed by Müller and his temper.*

Müller, his tone now lighter, raised his glass in toast toward Palasota.

"Very well, then! *Salute!*"

Okay, so now I understand what's probably the real appeal for Müller.

He believes that they are kindred souls.

Müller, the murderous bastard, has the reputation of being quick to the kill.

He glanced at the bar.

Which would explain the look those men made—they probably are university professors.

Oskar Kappler had had no choice but to oversee Hans Müller when the SS had transferred the germ warfare experiment to Palermo from the Dachau concentration camp.

The program used live humans as hosts, injecting Sicilian prisoners with extract from mosquito mucous glands to develop strains of yellow fever. When the sickened hosts eventually died of malaria, new hosts—often members of the Mafia brought in from the penal colonies off Sicily—were injected.

It had been no secret to the SS that everyone approached at the University of Palermo to contribute to the experiment had been shocked and disgusted that the Nazis had come in and inflicted such a horrible program upon Sicilians in their own country—and, pouring salt in the wound, had done so in a villa named for Archimedes, who was widely considered the greatest of all Sicilians.

And so Müller had gone directly to Dr. Carlo Modica, the brilliant seventy-year-old mathematician who had served as the head of the university for a decade. He explained to the gentle Modica that, if one in such a prestigious position participated as the figurehead of the experiment, it would send a positive message to others at the school and elsewhere.

Modica of course balked, but Müller coerced him. Then Modica, while injecting prisoners with the extract, managed to infect himself—and died.

Müller planned to replace him with two of Modica's colleagues—Dr. Giuseppe Napoli, also in his seventies, and Professor Arturo Rossi, a metallurgist who was fifty-five. He wound up shooting Napoli—and did so in front of Rossi. Rossi disappeared—the SS still hunted him—and shortly thereafter the villa exploded.

Müller blamed Mafia sabotage for the explosion. Kappler didn't care what the cause. Privately, he was very glad it was gone. He believed—and felt sick to his stomach for having had any connection with it—that what had occurred at the villa was equal to the atrocities he heard were being committed at the Auschwitz concentration camps. Word was that Josef Mengele was conducting dispassionate experiments, treating humans, many of them mere children, as if they were laboratory rats. Worse than rats, in fact, because he was dissecting KL prisoners while they were alive—and without use of anesthesia. It was so barbaric and disturbing that in order to get German soldiers to serve at the KL required bribing them with bonuses of cigarettes and salamis and schnapps.

Kappler saw that Palasota had more or less ignored the praise from Müller.

"Again, Herr Obersturmbannführer," Palasota said, "it is an honor to meet you and have you here. Now, if you'll excuse me—"

"We're about to have dinner," Müller interrupted. "You must join us."

"Thank you, but I can't," Palasota said, then looked at the young women and then at Kappler, and said, "I hope you all enjoy yourself."

As Kappler watched Palasota saunter across the lounge then disappear through the doorway behind the long wooden bar—greeting the two professors drinking there as he passed—Kappler wondered even more about the man.

He must have something on Müller. Something good . . .

"Well, then," Müller said, "shall we buy our ladies dinner?"

"Is that a good idea?" Kappler said.

"What harm is it if the ladies join us for dinner? Is life not better when in the company of lovely women?"

Damn it, Kappler thought. *The reality is that I cannot talk business with him in his condition. And we sure as hell will not discuss anything important in front of these hookers.*

As the Romans themselves slurred here so long ago—"In vino veritas." Maybe a drunken Müller will run off at the mouth and reveal something the bastard otherwise wouldn't.

And I'd sure like to know what the hell is going on here.

Kappler nodded, then said, "Yes, what harm indeed? And then I am going to retire immediately afterward. We have a big day tomorrow."

Müller grinned broadly. "Yes, of course."

Two hours later, Kappler was walking alone up the stairs, holding the railing for balance while waving down at Müller. He stood in the lobby with Maria and Lucia on either side of him.

"It is your choice, my friend," Müller called after him, barely able to speak. "But not one I would take."

Kappler ignored him, then made the turn for the next flight of steps, and thought, *Except for Lucia playing footsie and rubbing the balls of her feet in my crotch, that was a rather uneventful meal.*

I got damn-near nothing out of Müller. He just got drunker.

All I know is that he said he's squeezing Palasota, just as the Mafia has forever squeezed others for its money.

What was it the bastard said? "Ah, the irony. We take our percentage in cash and sometimes in trade." Then he goosed Maria, who squealed, to Müller's delight.

What he's doing at "our hotel" is no different than what he's been doing at the docks, taking cash and "accepting as a personal courtesy" the occasional skim of what passes through the dock warehouses—from fresh food to cases of wine. Which was how the bastard came across those Tabun rounds in the warehouse. . . .

And that was it. Then I drank far more than I should, trying to drown him out while trying not to dwell again on Father's letter.

As Kappler reached the third flight of stairs, taking each step with care, he thought that he saw someone coming down the third-floor hall, walking toward him.

"Herr Kappler," he heard Palasota's now familiar voice call out.

Damn it. I do not want to speak with anyone else tonight.

Especially not with me drunk.

"Herr Palasota," he said. "Good night. I am retiring."

"Alone?"

"Yes," Kappler said with a chuckle. "Alone. I do appreciate the thought, however."

And I appreciate that you could be trying to get me in a compromising situation. Something to use for leverage later.

Nice try, but I made my no-whores decision a long time ago.

"Please, call me Jimmy."

"Very well," Kappler said, holding out his hand. "And I am Oskar. Good night, Jimmy."

Palasota took the hand, and gripped it tightly.

"Look, Oskar. I am not judging, but if I may say so, you looked rather tense when we met earlier. I am sure that an important person such as yourself has many difficult things weighing on your mind. A little companionship is good for the soul. And it takes your mind off those things. These are very nice women. You will be pleased, trust me."

Kappler chuckled. "Again, thank you. I do appreciate your concern. I simply need some sleep. Good night."

There was moonlight coming in the bedroom window of Kappler's suite, and when he went to close the blinds, he glanced out. The city was dark. There was little to see, even in the soft moonlight. Just as he started closing the blinds, he noticed in the harbor that the new T-dock was empty.

So, the S-boots are out on patrol.

Tomorrow, when they are back, I should visit with their captains. Anything for an excuse not to suffer more time in Müller's company.

Five minutes after Kappler had crawled into bed, he heard a faint series of taps on his door.

If I ignore it, it will go away.

He rolled over.

The series of light taps became more persistent, then the tapping became continuous.

"Damn it!" he muttered, then threw back the sheet.

He went to the door in his boxer shorts and pulled it open enough to see who stood in the hall.

"Lucia," he said softly.

She held a bottle of cognac and two small glasses.

And she had changed into a sheer nightgown. Even in the dim lighting, he could make out the naked curves.

She is stunning! But . . .

"*Grazie*, no," he said, holding his hand up, palm out.

She smiled, then before he knew it, she turned and smoothly slipped in through the gap.

Damn it!

He sighed.

Okay, one drink, then I send her on her way.

After Lucia drank almost half of her glass of cognac, she went and sat on the edge of the bed. And smiled seductively.

I am too drunk and too tired to throw you out, Lucia.

And perhaps my new friend Jimmy Palasota is having my room watched to see if you stay.

But that's okay because nothing more than you staying is to happen.

Oskar then walked over and, using his hand, made a chopping

motion down the center of the bedsheet. He pointed to the side of the imaginary line where Lucia was, then pointed to her. And then he pointed to his side of the imaginary line, and pointed to himself.

Lucia frowned, then nodded her understanding. She drained her glass and crawled under the sheet on her side of the imaginary line.

Oskar thought, *Well, that certainly went better than I expected.*

He drained his glass, then got in under his side of the sheet. On his back, he looked at the ceiling a long moment, then closed his eyes.

In the quiet darkness, Oskar could hear Lucia's soft breathing.

Their combined body heat was quickly warming the sheets, and with that Oskar noticed that he could now really smell her.

It's lilac. So fresh . . .

She moved to adjust her pillow, and when she did more of her warm scent seemed to engulf him.

Oskar felt himself inhaling slowly and deeply.

Then he felt a stir in his groin—and, a moment later, the sheet directly above his groin slowly began to rise.

The movement did not go unnoticed.

Oskar felt her hand slide over to him under the sheet, then wrap around his penis. She stroked and he was suddenly extremely hard.

She giggled—and then her head disappeared under the sheet.

Ach du lieber Gott!

What the hell!

I may well be in a concentration camp tomorrow.

"Oh, Lucia," he said softly. . . .

[TWO]
Palermo, Sicily
2335 30 May 1943

"We don't want to stay on the air a second longer than absolutely necessary," Dick Canidy said. "Always a chance someone is listening, and I've about had enough excitement for one day without some SS bastard trying to triangulate on our signal."

"Understood," John Craig van der Ploeg said, his voice sounding genuinely tired. He yawned. "And agreed. I'm exhausted."

Exhausted and he looks like shit, Canidy thought as he pulled a fat cigar from his pocket, unwrapped it, bit a hole in its closed end, and then lit it.

Small wonder. He's been throwing up since we went wheels-up. He got smacked around really good landing in that tree. And now he can barely stand—never mind walk—on that busted ankle.

But . . . whoopee! Lucky me . . . I'm stuck with him for the duration.

John Craig was sitting on the floor by the window. Canidy had taken parts of one of the busted beds and with them fashioned short legs for the wooden bedside table that also had been broken. The result was a bit wobbly, but the lower height was close to perfect for John Craig to get his hurt foot under and be able to comfortably work the SSTR-1 wireless telegraphy set.

What would have been better was the location.

John Craig sat an inch from where the pool of blood and brain matter from Mariano's head wound had dried on the wooden floor. It had a distinctive foul odor, and John Craig's stomach, though absolutely empty after the last series of dry heaves, still was sensitive.

Canidy saw that John Craig regularly looked to see that he was not in fact sitting on the dried blood.

Still, Canidy knew nothing could be done; there was only the one window, and the W/T antenna went out it.

And I really tried to make it right. . . .

After Canidy, with some effort, had turned the chair and Mariano upright, then slid him over by the stairwell, he had taken one of the torn bedsheets and covered the dead man. Then he had taken another bedsheet and scrubbed at the dried pool. All that that had accomplished, however, was to break up the caked blood and tissue—and stir up the fetid odor. The room smelled worse.

Frustrated, he threw open the window. As a warm breeze floated in, he walked over to the broken beds.

"The SS think they're tough, huh?" John Craig said as he watched Canidy work.

Canidy, puffing heavily on his cigar, grunted.

"With an organization as large as the SS," he said, "headed by the sonofabitch Himmler and charged by Hitler to protect the Nazi state at any cost whatever, they are tough. And the sense of invincibility they get from that machine makes them more dangerous. Makes them damn mean"—he gestured with a piece of wood at Mariano—"sadistic even. But separate the man from the machine, and he discovers he's not the tough guy he thought."

Canidy began sorting through the wooden pieces, and said, "General George Washington said that to be a good leader, an effective one, people don't need to love you, or even like you, but they need to respect you. And that's the chink in the SS's armor. Being feared is not the same as being respected."

He looked at John Craig, and added, "Eventually people choose not to take counsel of their fears and rise up."

"Like the resistance fighters training at your throat-cutting academy," John Craig said.

"And the Polish underground I told you about. They are tough and determined, even if they have to fight alone," Canidy said, still looking at him. He glanced at Mariano. "And he was tough to the end. And Charley Lucky is one tough sonofabitch."

"Who?"

"Luciano. He's the New York Mafia boss I was going to tell you about. He's currently serving thirty-plus years—and remarkably still running his gang, and helping us—at New York's Great Meadow prison."

"Running the mob from prison? And helping us how?"

"I'll get into that in a minute. You know what *omertà* is?"

"Sure. The Mafia's code of silence."

"If you never heard of Charley Lucky then you probably never heard of how he, when left to die, took *omertà* to a remarkable level."

John Craig shook his head.

Canidy found four more or less even lengths of wood. As he carried them over to the window, he began, "Giuseppe 'Joe the Boss' Masseria—a ruthless guinea gangster who was born on the coast about forty miles from here—we damn-near flew over Menfi tonight—fled Sicily to avoid murder charges. He wound up in New York, and eventually became a Mafia don, the *capo di tutti capi*—"

"Boss of all bosses."

"—Yeah. And Masseria's mob made a lot of money. Then a hotshot named Charley Lucky became his number two, and he made Masseria even more. Luciano had a lot of ideas and smart connections—his most trusted friend going back to childhood is Meyer Lansky—and suggested to Masseria that they diversify, do business with gangs that weren't Italian." He paused, then added, "Now that I think about it, Lansky is another tough Polish Jew, so that had to influence Luciano's thoughts."

Canidy walked back to the beds, found the busted side table, and carried it to the window.

"Anyway," he went on, "Luciano was already envisioning a nationwide syndicate. He not only wanted to do business with gangs that weren't Wops but with gangs that weren't Wops and weren't in New York City. Despite Luciano's pushing, Masseria was having none of it. Worse, Luciano's hunger for even more power made him paranoid. This was October 1929, and as Luciano stood on the sidewalk in front of the Flatiron Building, there at Broadway and Fifth, a car pulled up. He was forced into the backseat, and the goons bound and gagged him. They took him out to a Staten Island warehouse, where he was strung up with rope, then pistol-whipped and stabbed. Before they left him for dead, they slit his throat."

"But you said he's serving time. So he's still alive?"

"Let me finish," Canidy said, fitting the wooden boards to the tabletop. "Charley Lucky, living up to his name, managed to work free of the ropes, then crawl to the street. Cops from NYPD's 123rd Precinct found him. Of course they knew who the hell Charley Lucky was, and after they got him stitched up, they made all kinds of threats to get him to tell who tried whacking him. He refused to rat out the goons."

"Omertà."

Canidy looked up from his project.

"*Omertà* in a big way. The cops, having no choice, let him go. Charley Lucky found out who ordered the hit, and settled the score—without breaking the code of silence. Now, that's goddamn tough."

John Craig looked at the dead man.

"And you think the same about Mariano?"

"Absolutely. He didn't tell them anything they wanted to know. If he had, he would have the bullet to the brain but still would have most of his fingernails intact. And next to none of those bruises. They wouldn't have wasted their time and energy—the SS are lazy bastards—beating him head to toe with a cosh."

John Craig nodded.

"You said something about this Charley Lucky helping us. We're working with the Mafia? Those guys don't even like each other. . . ."

Canidy nodded. "They're cutthroat and worse. But as General Donovan told me, 'Sometimes we have to dance with the devil.'"

"But . . ."

"But nothing. We have to do whatever's necessary. Churchill really put it in perspective when he said, 'If Hitler invaded hell, I would make at least a favorable reference to the devil in the House of Commons.'"

"Huh," John Craig said, unconvinced.

"Look," Canidy said, an edge to his tone, "the mob has its hands in everything in New York. We approached Charley Lucky's lawyer, who passed to him our request for help hunting Nazi sympathizers there and for getting us connections here. Luciano hates Fascism—particularly Mussolini, whose vicious secret police, the OVRA, Organization for Vigilance and Repression of Anti-Fascism, swept through Sicily arresting suspected mafiosos—and agreed to help us. A mob guy named Joe 'Socks' Lanza—who's the union leader who runs the Fulton Fish Market—introduced me to Francisco Nola. Lanza, by the way, is the wise guy who had the stolen Johnny guns; that's where I got mine. Anyway, Frank Nola—whose wife is Jewish and who had relatives arrested by the OVRA and thrown in the penal colonies on those small volcanic islands north of here—helped me (a) rescue Professor Rossi and (b) in the course of that rescue, helped me discover that the goddamn Krauts had—and probably still have—plans to use nerve gas." He caught his breath, then ended with, "So *that's* why 'but nothing.' Sometimes we do have to dance with the goddamn devil."

John Craig, clearly exhausted, was expressionless. He simply nodded.

Canidy then dug into his coat's inside pocket and produced an envelope.

"And this is why," he said, holding it out.

John Craig opened it and found a letter folded inside a handkerchief.

"Be careful with that," Canidy said. "The letter's a little ragged around the edges from the last trips here."

John Craig saw that the letter was written in English and again in Sicilian. He read both, and saw that they were the same:

March 1943

The bearer of this letter is Mr. Richard Canidy.

With this letter, the bearer brings to you my many good wishes.

It is requested of you in turn that the bearer be given the same respect and considerations that would be given if I were to personally appear before you.

Your friendship is appreciated and it will not be forgotten.

Charles Luciano
(Salvatore Lucania)

"What's with the handkerchief?" John Craig said, handing it all back.

"It's from Luciano's family. It will be recognized, establishing our bona fides, and it may damn well be key to finding Tubes."

Canidy returned the envelope to his pocket. Then he stood, tested his work, and announced, "Your desk, more or less, is ready."

Even though Canidy had at least fifty pounds on Mariano, John Craig could see that he was having trouble getting him down the stairs. The rigor mortis had set in while Mariano had been tied to the chair, and his muscles now rigidly held the body in the seated position.

Ten minutes later, Canidy reappeared alone at the top of the stairs, grabbed the dirtiest sheets, then went back downstairs.

When he came up the next time, he found that John Craig had opened the suitcase and dug out its contents to reach the false bottom, then taken out the transmitter, the receiver, and the power supply. The three instruments were now on the low wooden table, connected by two thick black power cords with chromed plugs.

After hooking up the antenna—a six-foot length of thin, dull, bare wire—John Craig had run it out the window, attaching it along the plant shelf there.

Canidy walked over to the two shredded mattresses and dragged them to the front wall.

John Craig yawned.

Canidy saw it and said, "There's your luxury five-star accommodations—but not before you get your ass on the air."

John Craig, sitting on the floor, put his fingers together as if in prayer. He interwove his fingers, then stretched his arms, palms out, causing at least a half-dozen knuckles to make rapid popping sounds. Then he separated his hands and exercised his right hand, wiggling his fingers and rotating his wrist.

Canidy watched the ritual with mild amusement. He had seen Tubes do the same in the very same place.

The transmitter and receiver had black Bakelite faceplates with an assortment of switches and dials. The bottom right-hand corner of the transmitter featured a round key on a short shaft that resembled a black drawer pull handle.

After a long moment, he finally looked up at Canidy, who was puffing on his cigar.

"Ready when you are. Do you want to send encrypted?"

"No, out in the open is fine. Message: 'Hail, Caesar! We have checked into the Ritz, and are partaking of local wine, women, and song. Tell Hermes thanks for the lift. Send our mail in next five minutes, or tomorrow. Jupiter/Apollo.'"

"Hermes is god of—?"

"Flight, of course. He's also the god of thieves and mischief, which nicely fits Darmstadter. Stan'll figure out that part, no doubt."

John Craig made a weak smile, then looked serious.

"You're not mentioning me, landing in the tree and screwing up my foot? And screwing up the mission?"

"Well, you haven't screwed up the mission. Yet. And what can they do about your foot? It's our problem."

John Craig nodded, then held one of the headphone cups to his ear with his left hand. He looked at the W/T transmitter box and put his right index and middle fingers lightly on the round key, and began rhythmically tapping out the Morse code.

After a minute, he said, "Done. I added 'confirm receipt.'"

Then he threw the switch to RECEIVE.

Almost another minute later, with the can still on his ear, he heard the receiver tap out, "Apollo. Receipt confirmed. Good to hear your hand. Be safe, buddy. Daffy."

John Craig put down the headset, grinning at the mental image of Bob Duck, his deputy in the OSS Algiers commo room. Eighteen-year-old "Daffy" Duck took great delight in mimicking the voice of cartoon characters. He did it as skillfully as he tapped out Morse code—and often did it at the same time, ending more than one string of code by filling the commo room with his lively version of Porky Pig's *Tha-tha-that's all, Folks!*

"There's confirmation," he said. "Guess we have no mail."

Canidy snuffed out his cigar and put it in his pocket. "Then shut it down and let's get some shut-eye."

"You don't have to tell me twice. . . ."

As John Craig reached for the power—and in his head heard Duck's voice saying, *Tha-tha-that's all, Folks!*—the receiver came alive.

"Oh, shit!" he exclaimed, reaching for the cans.

Five minutes later, after pulling out the codebook and writing freehand on the transcription pad, he had the message decrypted.

He tore out the sheet and handed it to Canidy.

"And, no," he said, "I did not make up the second part."

"What?" Canidy said as he began reading:

30MAY 2345

To Jupiter

From Caesar

Neptune says he will pick you up per usual. Contact him on Schedule EO-1.

Good thing Neptune will, because I have to ground Hermes for what I guess is excessive drinking. He won't quit telling wild story about Apollo shooting down Nazi Giant bird with tiny gun. More soon. Check six.

[THREE]
OSS Algiers Station
Algiers, Algeria
1201 31 May 1943

Stanley Fine was eating a grilled tuna steak on a hard-crusted roll at his desk while reading the overnight messages—and rereading the ones from Wild Bill Donovan and Allen Dulles, and shaking his head—when he heard a knock at his office door.

Oh, hell, he thought when he looked up. *What does this sonofabitch want?*

"Colonel," Fine called out formally. "Nice to see you. Please come in."

Fine was amazed at how the tall, slender, balding man looked uncannily like his boss—*despite the fact that the clean-shaven Ike doesn't have that ridiculous-looking "toilet seat" male-pattern baldness.*

Intellectually, however, they had next to nothing in common.

A brilliant soldier, General Dwight David Eisenhower was commander in chief of AFHQ, and already had been tapped to command the even more important invasion of Normandy. Meanwhile, his aide Lieutenant Colonel J. Warren Owen was an Ivy League–educated world-class bullshitter whose only redeeming quality was his ability to recite chapter and verse of military protocol—then force it down others' throats. He was prone to pretension, and always quick to remind everyone who his boss was, and thus, when he spoke, who he spoke for.

Some of Owen's detractors devoutly—if not hopefully—believed that Ike kept Owen around because of the resemblance, and thus made for a convenient decoy—if not a bullet magnet.

Owen entered Fine's office, seemingly awaiting Fine's salute of a superior officer. When Fine simply stood and smiled, Owen unceremoniously held out a manila envelope.

"The General asked me to offer you his warm personal regards," Owen said officiously. "And this."

"Thank you," Fine replied, taking the envelope.

Fine began to sink back into his seat. He did not bother opening the envelope but instead casually tossed it on his desk. He absently motioned for Owen to take the chair before his desk.

Owen's expression made it clear that he did not want to do anything at the suggestion of a lowly captain, but reluctantly he took the seat and somewhat awkwardly crossed his long legs.

"The General," Owen then said, snootily, nodding at the envelope, "asked me to hand deliver to you the details of the bombing plans. He's concerned, of course, about your station there."

Stan Fine, more out of hunger than thought, automatically reached down and picked up his sandwich. Then he made eye contact with the disapproving Owen.

"Forgive me," Fine said. "I should have asked if I could interest you in some lunch. We have a very nice kitchen and a terrific chef. I'm told that this tuna was swimming this morning. Now it's lightly charcoal-grilled—I like my tuna rare—and delicious."

Fine did not think it necessary to share the information that the fish had arrived at Dellys aboard one of Francisco Nola's boats—and with three members of Nola's wife's family just smuggled out of Sicily. The family members were being interviewed at OSS Dellys.

Fine then saw the look on Owen's face and wondered if the idea of rare fish did not meet with Owen's palate.

"They can of course prepare it medium or better—"

"Thank you kindly," Owen quickly interrupted. "It looks delightful but I am off to luncheon"—he pulled back his left sleeve and checked his wristwatch, which Stan Fine saw he oddly wore with the face down, underneath his wrist, the clasp on top, and decided that was simply another example of Owen's pretentiousness—"in ten minutes, so you will understand my having to leave momentarily."

"Of course," Fine said.

He thought, *Thankfully.*

Owen nodded again at the envelope and said, "You're not curious about the plans?"

"No, not immediately. Should I be? I'll get to them shortly, I'm sure."

Stan Fine took a big bite of his sandwich and chewed appreciatively.

"But the General was concerned about the station."

"The station?" Fine said, trying to swallow. "Which station would that be?"

"Your intel station on Corsica."

"Ah. You're referring to Pearl Harbor."

"Yes, that's the one. The General is quite pleased with it. If you should have any intel from there for the General, I of course would be pleased to personally carry it to him."

I'm sure you would, you brownnosing sonofabitch.

And, if it meets whatever you think your needs are, you'll take the credit for it.

If it doesn't, you'll see that it's quietly tossed.

Never mind that my agent is risking his life every goddamn minute while you're "off to luncheon."

"I do appreciate that, Colonel Owen," Fine said. "But right now, nothing. As you know, that could change at any moment."

Fine took another healthy bite of his grilled tuna sandwich.

"Yes, of course," Owen said, looking somewhat uncomfortably at Fine's sandwich, "at any moment."

Lieutenant Colonel J. Warren Owen then stood.

Fine stayed seated and looked up at him from his sandwich.

"Well, then," Owen said, "one other thing before I leave. Any chance you might know about a station called 'Saturn' or maybe 'Mars'? Apparently there is rumor that one or both exist, either on or near Sicily. I know that after all the General has said about Sicily being off-limits, it couldn't be one of ours."

Fine chewed and swallowed.

Oh, absolutely not one of ours!

"Saturn, you said?"

"And Mars. That's what I heard."

Fine looked off in the distance, toward the operational charts hanging from the bookshelves, then looked back at Owen and locked eyes.

"No, I'm afraid not. Never heard of Mars or Saturn."

Owen nodded, and gestured toward the envelope he'd brought.

"Well, that's very good, because the early bombing that has begun on Pantelleria soon will move to Corsica—as well as Sicily and other islands. Softening them up. And as much as the General appreciates the intel he's getting, it would be tragic to take out our own people."

"Softening?"

"Softening different targets, of course," Owen confirmed, and said it with an arrogance that suggested he might be doing it all himself, "to confuse Hitler as to what our real target is next."

"When?"

"June seventeenth is the first sortie. Everything you need to know is in the envelope."

Fine automatically glanced at his desk, to where he had put the messages from Donovan and Dulles.

Jesus Christ! I've got to get Canidy to take out that SS bastard in Messina before we bomb the place? And he just got there.

Fine looked up to respond to J. Warren Owen.

He was gone.

[FOUR]
Palermo, Sicily
0810 31 May 1943

Dick Canidy tried to walk casually along Cristoforo Columbo while scanning the activity in the port. He followed nearly a block behind two men who carried a wooden crate by its rope handles at each end. In the ten blocks he'd just walked, he hadn't seen even a half-dozen soldiers, which he considered one of the first signs that the message declaring a half-million troops were pouring into Sicily was pure bullshit.

Canidy saw at the nearest dock that at least six stevedores were provisioning two forty-foot-long wooden fishing boats. Moored next to those boats was a rusty-hulled ninety-foot cargo ship.

Like the first one I blew up thinking it had the Tabun.

The cargo vessel had a small main cabin at the bow and a long flat deck with large hatches and a pair of tall booms. Through one of the hatches the booms were lowering stacks of wooden crates, much larger versions of the one the men ahead of him carried. Beyond the cargo ship, Canidy noticed there was a pair of hulking Schnellboots under armed guard. The S-boats were tied up at the end of a T-shaped pier.

That's a new pier. They finally replaced the one that burned when the cargo ship went up.

I wonder if either of those S-boats was the one that we watched machine-gun the crew of the fishing boat.

And I wonder if any of the fishermen here know that an S-boat did that.

Frank Nola damn sure saw it—"This day I vow to never forget," he said—and would have said something.

Canidy could not shake the image. They had been en route to Sicily aboard the *Casabianca*, running on her diesel engines near the surface to make better time while charging the batteries. It had been a clear, mostly moonless night, the sky filled with brilliant stars. Through the periscope, they spotted the S-boat alongside the fishing boat half its size, both silhouetted in the soft light of the night sky.

Nola took a turn at the scope to see if he could tell if it was one of his boats being shaken down—right at the time the Germans machine-gunned the fishermen. Nola became hysterical when the *Casabianca*'s captain ordered an emergency dive and heard that they could not shoot at the S-boat and risk themselves being fired on—and their mission blown.

At least L'Herminier put a torpedo in the S-boat that was escorting the ship carrying the Tabun that he took out with a second fish.

Two blocks farther down Cristoforo Columbo, he came to the single-story brick building that held Nola's import-export business office. It was where he had introduced Canidy and Tubes Fuller to the Brothers Buda.

Antonio and Giacomo—aka Tweedle Dee and Tweedle Fucking Dumb.

Canidy turned the corner and realized he now was walking through what at first glance was trash scattered all up and down the street. Then he looked closely at a couple of the eight-by-ten-inch sheets and realized they were familiar. He picked up one for a closer look of its sketch—a German soldier's helmet on top of a wooden cross and the word "You?"

Hank passed over Palermo all right.

Kauffman should've tossed them out a little more slowly so they didn't all land in almost one spot. Too bad he didn't dump these directly on the SS over in Quattro Canti Quarter. . . .

Canidy tossed the sheet back to the street and walked up to the door of the building. The weight of his .45 in the small of his back was somewhat reassuring as he stood to the side of the wooden door and rapped on it with his knuckles.

But I'd rather have the Johnny gun that I left with Apollo. . . .

An hour earlier, Canidy had walked out of the small crapper and found John Craig van der Ploeg struggling to get off his torn mattress. John Craig had pulled off his boots before going to sleep at midnight. His right foot had looked swollen then. Now, in the morning light, it looked both swollen and horribly bruised.

Rising to his left knee, he slowly tried putting weight on the injured foot—and his face contorted with pain.

"Damn it!" he said, shaking his head.

"As much as I hate to say it," Canidy said, "you're not going anywhere today. Even if you could manage to walk, you'd draw attention. You just need to give that damn foot time to heal."

John Craig van der Ploeg glanced over at the radio.

"At least I still can run that."

"Yeah, and it probably works out better that you do sit on the radio while I go see what I can find this morning. What is the radio schedule?"

"They're alternating ones. With Neptune, it's her usual Schedule OE1-0—odd-numbered days she will transmit and be available to receive at fifteen minutes after odd hours. On even-numbered days, it's fifteen minutes after even hours. With Algiers, it's Schedule OE3-0, which means we're available during the same odd/even setup, but it's fifteen minutes before the hour."

Canidy glanced at his wristwatch.

"Today's the thirty-first. And it's ten after seven. So Neptune should be on the air in five. Think you can raise her?"

John Craig nodded.

"If the *Casabianca*'s at periscope depth and ready to receive."

He stood, putting all his weight on his left leg. Sliding his hand along the wall, he started hopping toward the window, almost dragging the bum foot. It took a little effort, and a lot of pain, but he eventually got situated at the radio, carefully keeping clear of the dried pool of blood.

He then went through the ritual of warming up his right hand and wrist.

"Time?" he finally said.

"Sixteen after," Canidy said.

John Craig then tapped out Morse code alerting Neptune that Jupiter was standing by.

John Craig switched to RECEIVE, picked up the headset and put one of the cans to his ear, then reached into the suitcase and came up with a transcription pad.

Canidy and John Craig then stared at the W/T.

Nothing happened.

After four minutes, Canidy said, "It's seven-twenty. Try again."

John Craig nodded and re-sent the code, and threw the switch back to RECEIVE.

Again they stared at a silent W/T.

"Maybe they're sitting on the bottom," Canidy offered. "Give it another shot in two hours, I guess."

A second later, John Craig's eyebrows went up as the receiver lit. He held the can tightly to his ear and began scribbling on the paper pad. Then he sent a short series of taps acknowledging receipt, and shut it down.

He pulled out his codebook, decrypted the message, then tore it from the pad.

As he handed it to Canidy, he said, "Does that sound good?"

> *31MAY 0715*
>
> *To Jupiter*
>
> *From Neptune*
>
> *Expecting 24 hour delay of departure from Pearl Harbor.*
>
> *Will send ETA when en route.*

Canidy crumpled it into a ball and tossed it back to John Craig. He caught it and put it in his makeshift burn bag.

"Who knows?" Canidy said. "Maybe they just have to stay on

station at Corsica another day. Doesn't really affect us either way right now."

John Craig then brought the radio back up, switched to SEND, and tapped out another short string of code. Almost immediately after throwing it to RECEIVE, he got a reply. Canidy saw that it was a brief one, because he didn't bother writing anything before shutting down the W/T.

"Algiers?" Canidy said.

"Yeah. They have nothing for us now. I'll keep checking back. And I will see what kind of traffic I can create with quote Tubes unquote so that when you bring the gear with the radio direction finder, we might have some signal to home in on."

"The last contact with Mercury was when?"

"Last week. I think May twenty-sixth. The message that had the half-million-something troops and stuff arriving in Sicily."

"We're about to see how much of that is bullshit. This place should be crawling with Krauts if half of it is true. Speaking of whom . . ."

He paused, looked over at the machine guns lying by the mattresses, then walked over to them and took the Sten and put it within reach of John Craig.

"Okay," he then said, "you should be fine until I get back. If for whatever reason I don't come back, you're going to have to be creative."

"What do you mean?"

"I mean that because of your bad foot, you'll have to figure out how to get the hell out of here and to the *Casabianca*."

Canidy could see by the look on John Craig's face that he had not considered that possibility.

He ran his fingers nervously through his mop of black hair as he nodded thoughtfully.

Then he softly said, "How the hell do you do . . . well, do *this*?" He gestured around the room and up and down. "I mean, torture, killing, living in filth, and with a corpse . . . and God knows what else. *Why?*"

Canidy grunted.

"Standard answer? I don't have a damn choice. Last I asked, they won't let me out of the OSS. Not until we make some certain crazy sonsofbitches in Berlin and Tokyo history."

"No, that's not what I meant. You do have a choice. You had all kinds of valid excuses not to put this mission together, starting with Eisenhower declaring Sicily off-limits. And you're not supposed to be operational. You know too much. Yet . . . here you are."

Canidy said: "From all the Top Secret messages that you've seen in the commo room, you're not supposed to be operational, either."

"You're not answering my question."

Canidy looked at him a long time, then exhaled audibly.

"What? You want me to wave the flag and hum 'The Star-Spangled Banner'?" Canidy mimicked waving a tiny flag with his right hand and hummed, *Oh say can you see . . .* "Sure, there's patriotism. But it's really about not letting the bastards win—on a personal level, not letting the cruel sonsofbitches get to our families in the ways we've seen them do others."

He paused, saw John Craig nod his understanding, then went on: "Two years ago, with England on its knees, Churchill spoke at that London boys' school—what's it called? *Harrow*—and said something that's stuck with me: 'This is the lesson:' he said, 'never give in, never give in, never, never, never—in nothing, great or small, large or petty—never give in except to convictions of honor and good sense. Never yield to force; never yield to the apparently overwhelming might of the enemy.' "

John Craig considered that and said, "You mentioned earlier about not taking counsel of your fears."

Canidy nodded. "Right. There's no damn time for that. It's all about 'This is the lesson.'"

John Craig's stomach then growled noisily.

"Got your appetite back?" Canidy said.

He reached into the suitcase and pulled out a small paperboard box. It had olive drab print that read: DINNER and US ARMY FIELD RATION TYPE K.

John Craig took the box and tore it open.

"I'm starving. Thanks."

He dumped the contents on the table beside the radio. He picked through the round tin of ham and cheese and the packets of crackers and sugar and salt and powdered orange drink mix. Then he stuck the Peter Paul Choclettos candies, Dentyne chewing gum, and the four-pack of cigarettes and matches in his pocket.

As he worked the tiny key to open the tin can, Canidy said, "You should stay away from those Chesterfields. I hear smoking cigarettes stunts your growth."

John Craig grunted. "That'd be the least of my worries right now."

"You're right. So, be careful with that radio. You do not want to be found. Where's your Q-pill?"

John Craig suddenly looked up from the food.

"You're serious?" he said.

"You're goddamn right I'm serious." He gestured at the Sten. "You can shoot your way out only so far. So you either save a couple rounds for yourself, or you bite the pill."

John Craig dug in his pants pocket and produced the inch-long brass tube that contained the rubber-coated glass vial of cyanide.

Canidy nodded as he held up his tube. "Do I need to remind you about what the bastards did to Mariano?"

As Canidy knocked again on the wooden door of the brick building, he saw that the padlock hasp was empty and open.

So someone is either in there—or didn't lock the damn door when they left.

He grabbed the doorknob and tried turning it. It was locked and just barely budged. But he saw that the door did move somewhat, indicating slop in the lock's tang. He rapped on the door once more, waited a count of fifteen, then pulled out his pocketknife. He slid the knife blade in the crack of the door beside the knob. The blade depressed the tang, pushing it back into the door, and the door swung inward.

He pulled his .45 out as he entered, then pushed the door shut behind him.

Just as the last time he'd been there, Canidy found the same pair of desks pushed together back-to-back in the middle of the room, a wooden office chair at each, both piled high with papers. A row of battered wooden filing cabinets stood against the near wall. And random clutter—boxes of half-eaten German rations, broken wine bottles, overflowing cans of trash—was everywhere.

He then heard the sound of a deep snore. It had come from the next room, which Canidy remembered being a smaller office. He carefully pushed open its door, looked around the room, then slipped inside.

The room held a single desk with a wooden chair behind it. Against the far wall was a couch with a massive human form on top.

Ah, one of the Brothers Buda.

Canidy approached and could see that he was lying on his back, with one hand holding a wine bottle by the neck to his chest. He had pulled down his coppola just enough so that the traditional Sicilian tweed flat cap covered his eyes.

Canidy knocked the coppola to the ground.

Okay, which one are you?

I think Tweedle Dumb . . .

He aimed his .45 at the puffy chest, then sharply nudged him in the ribs with his knee.

The fat man snorted loudly, then cracked open his right eye. Both eyes then popped wide open. They were bloodshot.

No, maybe it's Tweedle Dee.

"Remember me?" Canidy said, and smiled.

[ONE]
Chemische Fabrik
Frankfurt, Germany
1445 31 May 1943

In addition to his luxurious office that filled the entire top floor of the Berlin headquarters of Kappler Industrie GmbH, Wolfgang Augustus Kappler, as befitting a company's chief officer, kept a private office at each of his subsidiary companies. None, however, was as well appointed as that in his headquarters building. They were purposefully Spartan by design, meant to give the visiting chief executive a highly efficient space from which to conduct what more times than not could be a brutally cold business. Kappler believed that a chief executive of a multinational corporation belittled certainly himself, if not his subordinates, by working out of a common area such as a conference room.

As Wolfgang Kappler entered what he still considered to be his personal office, despite Chemische Fabrik having recently been nationalized, he thought, *Battles are always best fought on home turf. And I have many, many battles yet to fight. . . .*

Early that morning, Kappler, traveling on papers of highest priority issued by the Office of the Reichs Leader and signed by Reichsleiter Martin Bormann himself, had secured at the last moment a very small but private compartment on the first Frankurtbound train out of Bern. Watching the springtime beauty of the Switzerland countryside go past had allowed him to consider without interruption all that he very well might have to do in short order. Then, at the German border, having that quiet time turned upside down by the arrogance of a Gestapo officer as he scrutinized Kappler's documents only served to put a point on it.

After finally arriving at the dreary Frankfurt Main Hauptbahnhof, he then came directly to his Chemische Fabrik office.

He wore a perfectly tailored dark gray woolen suit with an almost crisp white dress shirt, and matching burgundy necktie and pocket square. He had just put his black leather briefcase on the massive wooden desk when a plump fifty-five-year-old woman appeared at his office door. She had a very round face and wore her thin graying hair braided and rolled into a bun at the nape of her neck. She had on, over a basic white linen long-sleeved blouse, a plain brown woolen jumper dress, its hem falling almost to her leather flats.

Kappler knew that Bruna Baur was, like him, a devout Roman Catholic and, quite possibly, also an anti-Nazi. Especially after her only son, Otto Baur, fighting in vain with the Sixth Army at Stalingrad, had been killed in January. Bruna at first appearance seemed very simple. But Kappler knew that she was much brighter than most gave her credit for. She long had worked for him through Klaus Schwartz, and with Schwartz's departure she had more or less begun working directly for him.

"As you asked, I have Frau Kappler on the line for you," she announced. "I have placed a call to Herr Krupp's Berlin office. And Herr Höss said he is on his way."

"*Danke*, Bruna," he said, taking his seat behind the desk.

"Herr Kappler?"

He looked up. "Yes?"

"It is good to have you back," she said in a genuine tone that showed she appreciated the gracious gentleman that he was.

He smiled.

"Danke," he repeated, then he lied: "It is good to be back."

As Wolfgang Kappler picked up the telephone receiver, he looked at it and thought, *I do not know for certain if the line is being listened to by the SS, but Allen Dulles told me that I must assume everything I do is—"You cannot afford to take any chances whatever from this point forward."*

And on the assumption that my conversations are being listened to, I believe I will mention whatever I can think of that will confuse whoever is out there listening.

Kappler was tired, but made himself use a chipper tone as he spoke into the telephone. "My darling! How good it is to hear your voice. How are you and Anna? . . .

"That is wonderful, dear. And, yes, I know it has been two weeks since we have talked. . . .

"I understand. But I was out of the country on business—actually in Portugual first, and just now back from Bern—and simply unable to call. But that is why I call you now. . . .

"No, I have had no communication with Oskar in many weeks. I'm sure he's all right, my dear, and busy with the war effort. We would have heard otherwise were that not the case. . . .

"Yes, of course, I cannot wait to see Anna and you, too, my love. I need to be at my Berlin office, and will probably be up there in a day or so. Please be sure not to go anywhere until we can see each other. . . .

"Yes, to you, too. Good-bye."

Thank God I kept that short, before she had a chance to possibly mention the Ruhr bombings.

I wonder if she is even aware of that? If not, that is why I want to be the one to tell her, as well as what I've told Oskar. . . .

He hung up the receiver, then stood and went to the large plate glass window. It had a reflective film on the inside that allowed for anyone in the office to look out but did not allow anyone on the manufacturing floor to see what or who was behind the window.

As he looked out over the factory floor, he heard behind him a light rap at his door and then a familiar voice.

"Herr Kappler?" Walter Höss said, his uneven tone betraying his nervousness.

Kappler turned. "Walter. Please come in. How are you?"

Höss walked to the desk. He was a small-framed, frail-looking thirty-five-year-old who in his neat but bland two-piece suit and tie looked like the overly organized accountant he had been before Kappler had promoted him. Kappler towered over him, and it was obvious that he was made uneasy by Kappler's intense green eyes that were surveying him hawk-like.

"I am fine, Herr Kappler. We, uh, we were not given word to expect you."

We? The royal "we"?

Has your new temporary chief officer title gone to your head?

"Did my Berlin office not call ahead?" Kappler said. "There were instructions to do so."

Actually, I did not make that call on purpose, Walter.

Surprise visits from the boss can be quite useful for a number of reasons.

"No, there was no word."

"So you said."

Höss stared back awkwardly.

"Well, that's quite all right," Kappler said. "No harm done. I am here now."

"A lot has happened since your last visit—it's been at least a month—right before Sturmbannführer Schwartz's going-away party."

Kappler felt his skin crawl with Höss's use of the SS rank.

That's how indoctrinated that bastard Schwartz made everyone with that ridiculous SS costume.

Kappler forced a smile.

"I do well remember, Walter. And right after *Herr Schwartz's* party, I had you assume the duties of my assistant until we found Schwartz's replacement."

"Yes, sir, but I am not sure—" He paused, trying to find the right words, then hesitantly went on: "I'm not sure you're permitted to be here."

Kappler's eyebrows rose and his chest expanded.

"What the hell do you mean?" Kappler flared. "I have run this company almost as long as you are old!"

"But . . . but, Herr Kappler."

"I put you in your job. I can replace you, too."

"Yes, sir. Of course, sir. But you must have heard—"

"There is no but!" He pointed toward the door. "Get out of my office."

Höss looked as if he might soil his shorts as he stammered, "You do understand that I will have to make inquiries."

"Make all the damn inquiries you wish! I would suggest beginning with Reichsleiter Bormann himself!"

He went to his desk and opened the leather-bound address book there.

"Here," Kappler went on, picking up the telephone receiver, "I will personally place the call to Marty for you."

Kappler saw in the accountant's face that the absolute last person he wanted to speak to—and very likely incur the wrath of—was Hitler's personal secretary.

Kappler stood there for a long moment looking at Höss, then at the phone.

He appears to be terrified. Good.

I have won this battle . . . though with a bean counter it is not much of one.

This is someone who actually looks forward to long, dull hours of dealing with columns and numbers. He is unable to think beyond the obvious. And so ten seconds of human confrontation turns him to mush.

Now, I will give him a way to save face.

Kappler sighed audibly.

"Forgive me, Walter," he said evenly. "You must understand that, having lost to the bombing all of my Ruhr Valley operations—all seven were washed away in the flooding—I am under a great deal of stress."

Höss nodded.

"I heard. And I do understand, Herr Kappler—at least as much as I believe I am able. And I'm sorry. It is a great loss, for you and for the Fatherland. That must be disturbing."

I wonder exactly how much he knows.

He knows that this company has been nationalized—but what about others?

And as far as I know, I didn't lose all seven. Only five. Does he know otherwise?

Höss gestured at the telephone.

"That will not be necessary, Herr Kappler. Please accept my apology."

Kappler returned the receiver to its cradle.

Höss suddenly looked relieved.

After a long moment, he asked, "Is there anything that I can do for you, Herr Kappler?"

"Yes, as a matter of fact, Reichsleiter Bormann has asked for a report on our current operations. If you wish to be useful, I will need the last month's production reports. All of them. As well as projections for the next six weeks—no, the next six months."

"Yes, of course," he said, turning to leave. "Right away."

"But start with the next six weeks," Kappler called after him. "I do not wish to wait forever. I have other business to tend to, as usual."

An hour later, Wolfgang Kappler was flipping through a thick sheaf of reports that, in true Teutonic fashion, detailed literally down to nuts and bolts the last two months of production at the facility. As he scanned the pages, he ran his fingers through his short dark hair, then rubbed his temples.

Walter, despite his faults, has always been good about going the next step. Ask for six weeks, he gives you eight.

I'm sure that that has served him well with trying to please the gottverdammt *Gestapo.*

"This is a good start," Kappler said.

"These production papers, and plans for the next year, Herr Schwartz left in his office," Walter Höss said. "You are aware of them, yes? And that he still maintains an office here? A small one, to keep an eye on production."

Am I aware?

Not of one damn word!

That bastard!

Kappler nodded. "Of course. Schwartz worked quite closely for me, as you know. When was he last here?"

"Two weeks ago."

"Have you heard from him since?"

"No, sir. His next scheduled visit is not for another month."

Kappler nodded.

"I would have been happy to send these to your Berlin office," Höss said in what he hoped was a helpful tone, "and saved you the trip here."

Kappler did not reply to that. Instead, he stood and went to the plate glass window.

Chemische Fabrik Frankfurt consisted of two massive, fully enclosed manufacturing facilities. This part of the chemical manufacturing plant covered two full city blocks. The second, which was across the street, covered three.

Here, as far as the eye could see under the vast metal roof, stood shiny rows of twenty-foot-tall stainless steel cylinders that were connected by a labyrinth of heavy industrial-grade piping. On opposite sides of the building were railroad spurs. The spur to the left had flatcars stacked with crates that were being off-loaded by men in black-and-white-striped outfits under the watch of guards.

Those pitiful sklavenarbeiter . . . *I don't know that I'll be able to save any others now.*

None of us will survive unless I am successful.

On the right side, there was a conveyor belt that led to the other rail spur, where more *sklavenarbeiter*, also in black-and-white-striped prison uniforms, and under guard, hand-loaded small metal canisters into boxcars.

"What exactly are we producing today?" Kappler said, hoping to appeal to the accountant's ego.

Höss motioned at the sheaf of papers he had brought.

"As detailed in there, high explosive," Höss said, the pride evident in his voice. "One hundred twenty tons every twenty-four hours, which is twenty percent in excess of what has been ordered. As you know, we have not manufactured any nitrogen or phosphate products for agricultural use since last December."

Kappler gestured at the left rail spur.

"And this is what? Trinitrotoluene coming in from our other plant?"

"That is correct. TNT. It is added in this facility with ammonium nitrate to produce the high explosive Amatol. We have also, as backup in the event that components for the high explosive become rare, been asked to be prepared to gear up for production of the lower-grade explosives Trialen and Myrol."

"And these are being shipped to where?"

"I don't think I understand . . ."

"If you are manufacturing the high explosive, you must be shipping it somewhere."

"Yes, of course. These boxcars are locked and sealed here and then taken to the central Frankfurt railyard, where another locomotive takes them—among others—to their final destination, the assembly point. The railcars all look more or less alike, and there are at least twenty departures a day from the central railyard—so who knows which train carries what and to where? You can see why your question at first confused me."

He went over to the sheaf of papers and flipped through but could not immediately put his finger on what he was looking for, and clearly was embarrassed. He flipped through a second time.

"Aha," he said, removing the sheet. "And this is the Special Program order from Berlin, under the signature of Field Marshal Milch and General von Axthelm but also with that of Reich Minister Göring."

He held it out, and Kappler waved it away. Höss looked a little dejected as he put it back in the stack.

"I'll get to it eventually. Tell me its key points."

Trust me, Walter, I will read it very carefully when you have left.

Höss went on: "It states that the Luftwaffe requires an additional one hundred tons of high explosive each month. That is to be brought up to five thousand tons monthly by this time next May."

That's for just one program?

"Luckily," Höss went on, pointing out to the floor, "we had

begun manufacture of the metal casings to contain the high explosive—they are there to the right—before your steelworks were lost in the Ruhr bombings."

He paused and looked at Kappler.

"A terrible, unfortunate act," he added.

"Yes."

"We were not so fortunate with getting the casings made there for the T-83 material. The Tabun?"

Höss looked at Kappler, who nodded that he was aware of the code name.

"But as we have yet to bring the plant on line for the manufacture of the T-83, we have time to make them at another source. As one might expect of the brilliant Herr von Braun, the requirements are quite exact—with slight modification they are essentially the same as those for the high explosive—and I have full confidence that we will not only meet the production numbers but exceed them. And because the order for T-83 is a fraction of that of the high explosive, we accordingly need only to manufacture a fraction of the metal casings."

So the plant is being converted to make Tabun.

And for what? What is this Luftwaffe Special Program?

"How much T-83?"

"Not quite half."

Fifty, sixty tons of nerve gas each month? That is ten times what was used for the howitzer munitions!

This is insanity!

What the hell is this Special Program?

There must be a way to knock out the plant during the transition without there being suspicion of sabotage. . . .

Höss gestured again at the papers he had brought.

"The requirements are detailed in the order, of course," he added.

Of course they are!

We wouldn't expect less of "the brilliant Herr von Braun," would we?

Kappler nodded his understanding.

Okay, Walter, now you can get the hell out of my office.

They were quiet a long moment, then Höss said, "Very well. If there is nothing else you require of me for now."

"I'll let you know, Walter. Thank you."

Höss went to the door, stopped, and looked over his shoulder.

"Herr Kappler?"

Wolfgang Kappler looked up from the stack of papers, his green eyes staring intently. "Yes?"

"It is good to have you back. It's been very . . . very unnerving around here lately."

I don't believe a damn word you said, except maybe the unnerving part.

"Thank you."

Höss nodded and left, pulling the door closed after him.

Kappler quickly went to the stack of papers that Höss had brought. He had flipped through them and found the Special Program order when, a moment later, the door opened and Frau Bruna Baur appeared.

"A moment of your time, Herr Kappler?"

He waved her in, and she closed the door.

"I am not clear what I am to do," she began.

"About what?"

"I just received a call from someone who said they were calling on behalf of Herr Wernher von Braun."

"And?"

"They wished to speak to Herr Höss or whoever was now in charge."

Interesting that they understood the bean counter was serving temporarily until we could replace Schwartz.

"Ordinarily, I would have had Herr Höss take the call. But seeing how you are here now, I thought . . ."

Kappler nodded. "You thought correctly. Any idea what they wanted?"

"No idea. When I asked if there was a message, the reply was simply that the call to Herr von Braun's office should be returned as soon as possible."

What could that be about?

Maybe Schwartz is changing his scheduled visit here? Or did he get himself in some hot water?

"Very well. See if you can get them back on the phone. Also, any word from Krupp?"

"Yes, sir. As I said earlier, I called Herr Krupp's office and left your message. When the call was returned just now, by his assistant, she said that Herr Krupp appreciated your condolences for what happened to his people in the Ruhr bombings, that he offered the same to you for your losses, and that he would be pleased to meet with you the next time you are in Berlin."

"Very good."

"It is quite difficult to imagine what has happened in the Ruhr," she then said.

It is damn difficult even when you've seen the photographs. . . .

Kappler noticed that she held her hands together nervously. Then he saw that she held a very tightly folded sheet of paper.

"Have you seen this?" she said somewhat hesitantly, fumbling as she unfolded the sheet.

He looked at the paper she held out. It appeared to be some kind of mass-produced flyer.

"These began showing up here two days ago," she said. "I found this one on the floor of the ladies' toilets."

Kappler took the sheet and read it.

These must be what Allen Dulles said were going to be air-dropped.

"Is there any truth to what it says?" she said. "Are the Americans making those kind of advances?"

He looked up at her and said, "You do realize the grave danger of possessing something like this should the Gestapo find it? Or even Höss?"

She nodded. "And that would suggest that it's true. If it were lies, they would not care that we have it."

Kappler looked at her a long moment.

It is evident in her eyes. She does indeed still mourn the loss of her son.

As would I if something were to happen to Oskar.

Kappler nodded and said, "From what I understand, yes. They actually were British bombers. Thousands died when the floodwater escaped the dams. There is limited water. And without the dams' hydroelectric plant, there is no power for what homes and industries do remain."

"They said something like this could never happen, that it was impossible."

"Yes, they did."

"Just as they said we would not fail at Leningrad," she added bitterly.

Kappler made a face that he hoped looked sympathetic.

How many mothers must feel as she does?

"All lies this Hitler tells," she then said. "If the impossible has happened, then it could happen again. And that means the bombings . . ."

He nodded. "They could mean the beginning of the end."

Which very well could explain the desperate production rate of high explosive and nerve gas for this Special Program. . . .

[TWO]
Palermo, Sicily
0820 31 May 1943

"*Ciao,* Antonio," Dick Canidy said, aiming his pistol at the two-hundred-pound five-foot-five Sicilan lying on his back on the grimy couch. Antonio Buda's olive skin was coarse from a lifetime of wind and sea and sun exposure. He wore dirty denim overalls that fit tightly, bulging at his rolls of belly fat.

Wide-eyed, Antonio immediately let loose of the wine bottle neck as he held up his hands chest-high, palms out. The empty bottle clunked on the raw stone floor.

"Sit up," Canidy said, taking a step back and gesturing with the pistol.

Antonio swung his feet to the floor, then keeping his left hand up at chest level, used his right hand to push his massive body to the sitting position.

As he brought his right hand back up, he leaned slightly forward—and experienced an intense episode of flatulence. It went on deeply and loudly before finally ending.

Jesus Christ, Tweedle Dee! That was special.

But I guess that's to be expected of one so damn big.

What goes in . . .

Then Antonio leaned back—and there came a second episode, one lasting nearly as long.

Is he going to shit his shorts next?

What was that—from the wine?

Or from being nervous because he's looking down the muzzle of a .45?

Antonio then grimaced and made a shrug that could have been meant as an apology.

Canidy sighed. After a moment he reached inside his jacket.

He came out with the envelope containing Charley Lucky's handkerchief and letters of introduction. He gave Antonio the letter that was written in Sicilian.

Keeping his left hand high, Antonio took the letter in his right, read it, looked Canidy in the eyes, and nodded, then handed it back.

Canidy, after returning the envelope to his pocket, then carefully put his left thumb and index finger on either side of the hammer of his .45, squeezed the trigger, and gently decocked the weapon.

Then he motioned for Antonio to put down his hands.

When Antonio had, Canidy made a thumbs-up gesture, and as he did so, a wave of relief flowed over Antonio's face. He responded with a thumbs-up, and added a weak smile.

"Where is Francisco Nola?" Canidy said, remembering that the Brothers Buda understood a little English—very little.

"Francisco?" Tweedle Dee said, turning his head and seeming to somewhat understand.

Is Tweedle Dee now playing Tweedle Dumb?

"Francisco," Canidy repeated. "Where is he?"

Antonio shook his head and shrugged.

Oh, this is just fucking great. Conversing with Nola—who also has a room temperature IQ—was never exactly stimulating.

Is he saying he doesn't know where, or doesn't understand what I'm asking?

Now what do I do?

Oh, what the hell. It's worth a try. . . .

Using his left hand, Canidy then pointed at Antonio, then pointed at his own eyes, then said, "Francisco?"

Antonio stared blankly back with his bloodshot eyes.

Canidy shook his head.

Where is Marcel Marceau when you need the sonofabitch?

Canidy thought he then noticed a flicker of recognition in Antonio's eyes.

He knows?

And then Antonio leaned forward and had a short episode of flatulence.

Antonio shrugged and shook his head.

"No Francisco," he said.

Canidy exhaled audibly.

"No Francisco?" Canidy repeated.

Antonio shook his head again.

Canidy then once more pointed at Antonio, then at his own eyes, then said, "Tubes?"

Antonio shook his head.

Damn it! But at least he didn't let rip with another window-rattling fart. . . .

Canidy repeated the miming and said, "Andrea?"

Antonio's face seemed to turn sad at the mention of his sister. Then he shook his head.

All three of them? He hasn't seen a single one? Not even his sister?

What could that mean? Certainly nothing good . . .

And now where the hell do I look?

Maybe check the port and Nola's warehouse? Could ask Antonio if there's more T-83—what he calls "buh-lets." That has to happen at some point.

But then what? I guess just go back and see if John Craig has raised Tubes or whoever on Mercury Station, then try to track the signal.

Wait . . . the hooker!

John Craig said that Tubes wrote him about a whorehouse. Tubes didn't find that on his own. Nola had to show him. And if Nola knows where it is, so should his cousin.

Canidy then pointed again at Antonio, then at his own eyes . . . then paused.

Okay, how the hell do I mime "whorehouse" without looking like a fool?

In point of fact, how the hell do I mime anything without looking like a fucking fool?

He looked back at Antonio, who appeared to be waiting somewhat anxiously for his next clue.

Wait . . . that's it!

He then slipped the .45 inside his waistband at the small of his back.

Canidy then smiled and started over.

He pointed at Antonio, then at his own eyes, then with his right hand, he made a circle with the index finger and thumb and then poked his left index finger in and out of the circle.

"Sí?" he said, and repeated the poking motion.

Antonio's eyes grew huge and his body seemed to quiver.

Antonio then very loudly and very angrily said, *"Andrea?"*

Oh, shit!

Then, hands and arms flying, he let loose with a rapid-fire barrage of what Canidy decided were probably very colorful Sicilian longshoreman expletives.

"No, no, no!" Canidy quickly said, holding his hands palm out and shaking his head.

Antonio stopped his verbal salvo and stared intently at Canidy.

Now what the hell do I do?

What would— Oh yeah!

Canidy then held out his right hand toward Antonio, then repeatedly rubbed the tip of his thumb across the tips of all his fingers. Then he again made a circle with the index finger and thumb, then poked his left index finger in and out of it.

Antonio looked at Canidy's hands, then met his eyes.

Canidy saw that there now was a conspiratorial gleam to Antonio's eyes—*It's damn near a leer*—as he chuckled a knowing *Heh-heh.*

"Sí!" Antonio finally said slowly, smiling broadly.

He started to stand. The process of getting to his feet took a moment, and when he was finally up, he was not steady.

Canidy feared that the movement was going to trigger another episode of flatulence. It did not come to pass.

Antonio Buda led Dick Canidy—unsteadily at first, with only two comparatively brief episodes of flatulence—almost twenty blocks to Palermo's four corners city center. There they turned down an alley, and finally took some stone steps that led below street level.

We're entering a whorehouse through a secret entrance?

No, it looks like a service entrance.

There was a heavy steel door that had at eye level a smaller door behind metal bars. With his sausage-shaped knuckles, Tweedle Dee rapped out a series of three knocks three times. There was no answer, and after a minute, he sighed, then repeated the code, this time knocking harder and louder.

There was no answer still, and Antonio looked at Canidy and shrugged. They waited another minute, then an impatient Canidy hammered the code out with his fist.

The smaller door suddenly flung open, and the left side of what looked like a young woman's smooth-skinned face immediately filled it. Her big brown eye curiously darted between Canidy and Buda—then the face and eye were yanked out of the way.

That was a really good-looking woman, Canidy thought.

A pockmarked acne-skinned face with a hard-looking dark eye immediately replaced the first. The eye also darted between them, this one looking less with curiosity than it did with great suspicion.

Judging by how the face was turned to look up and out, Canidy guessed it was that of a boy.

He must be standing on his tiptoes.

And his haircut is about as bad as the Budas' bowl cuts.

The boy's face then quickly pulled back, and the small door slammed shut. There then came the sound of locks being turned, and the door was opened slightly. A small male arm then appeared in the opening, impatiently waving them to come in. Tweedle Dee had to push open the door more in order to fit though the gap. When Canidy had followed, the door was slammed shut and it was immediately locked by the boy. The woman was nowhere to be seen.

Canidy was surprised to see that the boy had a stub of a cigarette now dangling from his lips—and then realized that the boy wasn't a boy.

It's a fucking midget!

The adult male stood four-foot-four. He wore the pants and vest of a dark gray woolen suit, and a wrinkled white open-collared cotton shirt, its sleeves rolled up past his elbows.

And he's armed!

Canidy could see that inside the man's waistband, somewhat hidden by the vest and his suspenders, he carried a small-frame semiautomatic pistol. It was familiar to Canidy. The black Colt Model 1903 Pocket Hammerless, chambered in .380 ACP, was standard issue as general officers' pistols—and for officers in the OSS.

Should I be suspicious of where the hell Shorty got that Colt?

Hell, if he's Mafia, then he probably stole it.

But where would he get one here?

The midget then took a last long drag on the cigarette, tossed it to the stone floor, and stubbed it out with the toe of his shoe as he exhaled.

See, John Craig? Canidy thought, suppressing a chuckle. *Here's proof those damn things will stunt your growth.*

And they apparently cause craters of zits. . . .

Canidy discreetly scanned the room and saw that they were in some sort of a storage room. The wooden shelving along the right wall was stuffed with stacks of folded linens. Against the far wall were cases of canned food and wine in stacks five to six feet high.

Antonio Buda bent over to exchange pats on the back with the midget. Then they had a brief conversation, one with a great deal of gesticulating. The only thing Canidy understood for sure was the mentioning of Francisco Nola. The man constantly glanced at Canidy as Antonio spoke.

I wonder, since he's carrying that Colt, why he didn't see if I've got a gun.

Maybe Antonio's telling him now. . . .

Then Antonio pointed at Canidy's coat.

Shit, he is!

But then Canidy realized he was pointing to where Canidy had put the envelope. Canidy produced the letter of introduction that was written in Sicilian.

Here you go, Shorty.

He watched the man read it, raise his eyebrows, and nodded. The midget then looked up and studied Canidy for a long moment. He said something to him in Sicilian. Canidy was about to gesture he didn't understand when Antonio said what Canidy guessed was exactly that—he didn't speak Sicilian.

Then the man grunted and marched out of the room with the letter.

Now what?

I don't want that damn thing disappearing!

Canidy looked at Antonio, who shrugged but then put out his hands as if he were a priest blessing his congregation, the gesture suggesting *It'll be okay.*

Canidy raised an eyebrow and made a face.

It damn well better be.

Glancing around the storage room, Canidy saw nothing unusual among the shelves—until he came to two medium-sized cardboard boxes. One was labeled bluntly in black block lettering, the other in a flowing red typeface that was below a red cartoon drawing.

The black was in German. It read: LATEX FORSCHUNGSGEMEINSCHAFT KONDOME.

The red was in Italian—PER AMORE—and the drawing was that of Cupid putting what looked like a balloon on his blunt-tipped arrow.

Aha! Occupational necessity . . . condoms.

And guess which one's stick-up-their-ass Kraut-made and which one's Italian.

Five minutes later, the midget appeared at the door to the storage room and exchanged a few words with Antonio. He then looked at Canidy and motioned for him to follow him.

Canidy looked at Antonio and raised an eyebrow.

Antonio started with miming. He pointed to Canidy and gave him a thumbs-up. Then he pointed at himself, held his palms together at the side of his head, indicating sleep, then pointed in the direction of the import-export office.

Okay, so he's going back to the couch to sleep—and probably to fart. No surprise.

Canidy gave him a thumbs-up that he understood.

Then Antonio made the knowing leer again. He formed the circle with thumb and index finger and poked at it. He grinned and gave Canidy a thumbs-up.

What the hell? I'm not here to get laid.

He'd better not have given Shorty the wrong idea. . . .

The midget caught the exchange. He grunted.

"Prego!" the man said, gesturing impatiently for Canidy to follow.

[THREE]
Schutzstaffel Field Office
Palermo, Sicily
0905 31 May 1943

SS-Obersturmbannführer Oskar Kappler grinned inwardly watching the visibly hungover SS-Sturmbannführer Hans Müller desperately fumble as he closed the blinds of the window to his office. It had rained most of the night, and the morning light was especially bright, causing Müller to shield his eyes as he did so.

The office was very nicely furnished. There were fine oil paintings, thick rugs, and heavy ornate furniture. Müller clearly had helped himself to whatever he wanted in Palermo. Seeing that made Kappler remember the story his father had told about Göring's "sweetest dream of looting and looting completely"—and that that criminal mentality, especially at the highest levels, had been what motivated him to diversify the family assets in other countries.

Kappler sat on the leather-upholstered couch, carefully sipping coffee from a fine china cup. A china coffee service that had been brought in by SS-Scharführer Günther Burger was on the low table before him.

Everything about Müller looked worse than usual—he had huge dark bags under his unpleasant dark eyes, his paunch was distinctly bloated, his thin black hair stuck out at odd angles.

You look like shit, Hans ol' buddy.

And from all that booze you clearly feel like it, too.

Couldn't have happened to a nicer guy . . .

"Herr Obersturmbannführer," Müller said after he sank into the leather chair behind his desk and picked up his coffee cup. "I thank you for being understanding about having to postpone the review of the warehouse until later. I thought that they understood my orders to be prepared this morning. I will deal with them later, and I promise you it won't happen again."

Who the hell do you think you're kidding, you bastard?

We're not going anywhere because you're too damn hungover.

You're just lucky that I drank far more than I should have.

And that I did not actually get a lot of sleep.

If I felt any better myself, I'd insist we go just so that I could enjoy watching you suffer. . . .

"Very well," Kappler said, "but I will need to review it before my return to Messina."

Müller seemed to wince as he sipped his steaming coffee.

I bet you'd love to have a little hair of the dog in there.

Then again, for all I know, you do. Günther served you away from me.

As Müller closed his eyes and rubbed them, he said, "And when would that be? What I mean is, when do you plan to return? You have just arrived here."

"I am not sure at the moment."

Müller grinned as he opened his eyes.

"I trust then that you had a pleasurable evening?" he said.

Kappler met his eyes.

The last you saw me, you bastard, was as I walked up to my room alone.

While you stood in the lobby with both Maria and Lucia.

Did Jimmy Palasota report to you that Lucia shared my room?

Or is it you who has that suite watched?

"I slept well, if that is what you are asking."

"Yes," Müller said. "I'm sure that you did."

Did Lucia say anything?

Of course she did!

Mata Hari and so damn many others have proven one cannot trust women in bed, that anyone could be a spy.

Nietzsche said it: "In revenge and love, women are more barbaric than men."

Still, Lucia did not attempt any "innocent" pillow talk—and even if she had, I do not speak Sicilian and she does not understand German.

He took a sip of his coffee and had a flashback of their night.

Spy or not, what a delight that girl is!

"Müller, can you tell me what information you have gathered concerning the American invasion?"

Müller made a face.

"There is not any information," he said matter-of-factly, "because the invasion will not take place here."

Kappler stared at him, wondering, *Is that the alcohol talking? Or just plain arrogance?*

Pantelleria, only a hundred kilometers away, actually is being bombed.

I suppose I cannot blame him. Until fire falls from the sky, it must be hard to believe that there's a war going on.

Yet it is a fact that the Americans went into North Africa with enough forces to eventually rout the Afrika Korps. Our intelligence reports show that they captured more than a quarter-million of our troops.

And this shortly after Generalfeldmarschall von Paulus's Sixth Army was embarrassingly surrendered at Stalingrad. What was that? Another million lost?

So it's really no small wonder that there aren't troops massing on this shitty little island.

Müller went on, his tone sarcastic: "It is my understanding that we soon will have the honor of the Panzer Division Hermann Göring—with two battalions and ninety-nine tanks—and the Fifteenth Panzergrenadier Division, with three grenadier infantry regiments and a sixty-tank battalion. And of course our superior Luftwaffe forces." He paused, then added: "Forgive me, but I'll believe that when I see it."

"You will see it," Kappler said automatically, hoping he sounded convincing. "They are beginning to arrive in Messina. We have been promised that by early July there will be one hundred and fifty thousand Italian troops, plus twenty thousand German troops and that many more to support the Luftwaffe."

"Again, I'll believe it when I see it," he said, then drained his coffee cup. "As you may know, last night we were expecting the arrival of a *Gigant.* It never showed up. When I called out to the airfield this morning, all I got were runaround answers to my questions. The only thing I know for sure is the *gottverdammt* aircraft is not at the Palermo airfield. The aircraft was supposed to be transporting eighty-eights—packed with the big guns and ammo for our coastal defenses—and I'm betting that it was diverted, that it flew right over us and landed in, probably, Naples. Which is fine with me."

Kappler looked at him silently.

"Let them fight the damn war there," Müller explained. "I'm comfortable here."

Kappler then said, "Did you not get the intelligence report? That there was the bombing of Pantelleria on May eighteenth?"

Müller suddenly laughed, then looked sorry for having done so. He rubbed his temples and said, "Yes, to watch the troopers—

especially the Italians—running around here shitting themselves and ready to shoot at anything that moved—usually each other—was rather humorous. After a couple days, they calmed down." He chuckled. "That could be because a lot of them wore themselves out at the Hotel Michelangelo."

"They what?"

Müller nodded. "They were with the women and wine. Our hotel made quite a profit for nearly a week—until the troopers realized not a single bomb had landed anywhere near them."

Kappler grunted.

He said: "What about the intelligence report that states the same May eighteenth bombing of Pantelleria will commence here June seventh?"

This time Müller grunted.

"If one believes everything one hears, then the invasion itself is to take place on that date. We've been monitoring the radio traffic of the Americans and . . ."

"And what?" Kappler said. "You seem very sure of yourself."

Müller locked eyes with him.

"Would you like to know a secret?"

I'm your superior officer, you arrogant bastard!

I have the right to know everything that you do—and more!

"I suppose," Kappler replied, as he went to sip his coffee.

Müller stood, a little too quickly, and wobbled a bit, then motioned for Kappler to follow.

They went up a raw stone stairwell to the top floor of the SS Provisional Headquarters building.

They came to a wooden door that was locked.

"Open up!" Müller called, as he rattled the doorknob.

After a long moment, the sound of the lock turning could be heard. When the door swung open, SS-Scharführer Otto Lieber stood there.

What the hell? Kappler thought.

Otto stepped aside as Müller waved Kappler inside. Otto then closed and locked the door.

Kappler then saw Günther Burger sitting at a desk in front of what appeared to be a telegraph radio station. He held a headset to his ear.

Those switches and dials are labeled in English!

"An American wireless," Kappler said.

Müller nodded.

"Shortly after the explosions," he began, careful not to reveal anything to the scharführers, "I discovered a spy cell. Intact. We interrogated its operator—an American spy—and were then able to successfully convince his handlers that we were him. That he was us. That . . ."

"I understand. The Americans believe their man still is secretly spying."

"Exactly."

"Why am I just now learning of this, Müller?"

Müller seemed hesitant to answer, and glanced at the scharführers and then at Kappler.

"I will explain later, if that is acceptable."

Kappler didn't respond to that. After a moment, he said, "What happened with the radio operator?"

"I like to believe," Müller began, carefully choosing his words, "that I am faithfully living up to Der Führer's order about how enemy commandos are to be handled."

Immediately executed, Kappler thought.

Or, if interrogation is necessary, immediately after that.

With you, I should have known . . .

"As insurance, I have him locked up," Müller said. "To satisfy Der Führer's order, it is arguable that I continue with his interrogation."

Then you didn't kill? That's a first.

What's the real reason for that?

Müller then looked to Burger.

"Anything, Günther?"

"We got a contact this morning, Herr Sturmbannführer. It was not much but came in very clear and strong. That storm last night must have cleared the air."

"What did they say?"

"Just that they were checking in and would be in touch later with some important questions."

"What did you tell them?"

"That we'd be waiting. And that we'd probably need additional supplies."

Müller grinned.

He looked at Kappler and explained.

"Supplies are our little code word for more bribes."

Müller looked back at Burger.

"Let's give it a little test. When they contact again, Günther, send a request for an airdrop. Ask for some gold and Italian lire. Tell him"—he looked at Kappler and grinned—"that you're trying to bribe the head SS officer in Messina."

Here he goes again like Göring . . .

[FOUR]
Palermo, Sicily
0915 31 May 1943

Dick Canidy stood watching the midget knock on a heavy metal door.

The man had led him on what seemed a circuitous route from the storage room, taking what clearly were hidden passageways. They occasionally offered glimpses of the public spaces of the whorehouse.

After leaving the storage room, they first passed through a laundry room and then a kitchen. Some workers acknowledged the midget as they passed, but did not seem to pay any particular attention to Canidy.

It's as if Shorty does this on a regular basis.

They had then taken a back hallway, passing a couple of attractive young women. They exchanged greetings with the midget as they passed.

Was one of them the girl who opened the door?

Are they all hookers?

They then came to a stairwell and took it up one flight.

Okay, now we're on the first floor, street level again.

Walking down another passageway, Canidy briefly saw what looked like a bar—*A lounge?*—then some steps past that got a view of what looked like a lobby and the ten or so people in it.

Jesus! Those two Aryan teens sitting there could've been ripped from a recruitment poster for the SS!

The midget had then led Canidy around a corner and they finally arrived at the heavy metal door.

After the man knocked on it, he immediately opened the door without waiting for an answer.

Canidy could see that there was a somewhat cluttered office, and that a petite, full-figured dark-haired woman he guessed to be in her middle twenties stood before a large wooden desk. The casually dressed man behind the desk—he was about forty, muscular and rugged, with a warm face and thick brown hair—was handing her what Canidy decided was a small stack of cash. The man appeared to be showing genuine concern to the young woman. He spoke to her in Sicilian; Canidy couldn't understand it, of course, but thought that he said it in a soothing tone.

"Grazie," she replied softly, taking the cash and folding it, then slipping it inside the waistband of her skirt.

She nodded once and, head down, turned to leave.

Canidy saw that she, too, was attractive.

"Maria," the midget cordially greeted her, as Canidy had just seen him do with the others, as she passed.

When she looked up and smiled meekly, Canidy saw that she had a hugely bruised right eye.

What the hell? Did she get beat up?

Maria put her head back down and went out the door, pulling it closed behind her.

Canidy saw the man look from the door to him.

"Welcome to the Hotel Michelangelo," the man then said pleasantly, and in English, as he got to his feet.

Hotel? Canidy thought.

Canidy saw that on the desk before the man was his letter of introduction from Charley Lucky.

"Jimmy Palasota," the man said, and offered his hand.

After hearing Palasota fluently speak Sicilian with what sounded like a native's tongue, Canidy was surprised not only that he spoke any English at all but that he clearly was fluent in it, too.

"Dick Canidy," he said, realizing he probably was being repetitive as his name was spelled out in the letter of introduction. "It's a nice surprise to hear you speak English. I was afraid I was going to be flogging a dead horse trying to mime to get past the language barrier."

Palasota smiled, and motioned for Canidy to take a seat in the chair.

"It will be good to speak and hear English again," Palasota said as he sat back in his seat. He gestured at the midget, who now stood off in the corner, watching, and added, "Vito here says Antonio Buda brought you."

Vito? I like "Shorty" better.

Canidy looked at the midget, who was keeping an eye on him while pulling out a cigarette and then lighting it.

But something tells me that you wouldn't.

He then noticed that there were two Thompson submachine guns leaning upright in the corner within Vito's reach.

Even more American-made weapons.

Canidy looked back at Palasota and said, "Yeah. I met the Buda brothers through their cousin, Frank Nola."

"I am familiar with Francisco."

"You are? Have you seen him?"

"Not in quite a while. No one seems to have. I was wondering about that."

"I need to find him."

"You want to tell me what that's all about?"

Honest answer? I don't know. Do I?

And what exactly do I tell you?

I don't even know who the hell you are.

Be very careful, Dick, because you really don't know how much devil you're dancing with here.

Palasota picked up the letter.

"Okay, then you want to tell me where you got this?"

Canidy reached into his jacket and came out with Luciano's handkerchief.

"Same place I got this," he said, handing it to Palasota.

Palasota examined it briefly and nodded.

"Look," he said, tossing the handkerchief on the letter of introduction, "I'm not doubting these. I happen to know they're the real deal. I'm just asking for some background. You're American, obviously. But you're not one of Hoover's G-men."

"How do you know?"

"Trust me, I know. For one, they don't have the guts to be behind enemy lines. And even if they did, and they actually did something, J. Edgar couldn't call a press conference and brag about it."

Canidy chuckled.

"So," Palasota went on, "if you're not FBI, I'm guessing some kind of military intelligence. Am I close?"

"I'm a friend of Frank Nola, as I said, and I'm trying to find him. That's all I'm going to give you right now."

"Well, that much Antonio gave Vito. That and he said Nola told him that you have risked your life for the family and for Sicily. So, now you and I have an honorable understanding." He gestured at the handkerchief and letter. "Thanks to our mutual friends, that makes you *gli amici. Capiche?*"

Canidy grinned.

"You find something funny about that?" Palasota said evenly.

"No. It's just that that's almost the same exact friend-of-a-friend speech I got from a wise guy who runs Fulton Fish Market in New York City."

Palasota then grinned.

"Aha! So it *was* Tommy Socks who got you to Charley Lucky?"

They locked eyes a long moment.

"Tommy"? Canidy thought. *Is this a test?*

" 'Tommy Socks'?" Canidy repeated.

Palasota nodded. "Sure. Tommy Socks Gambino. You know . . ."

It is a test!

"No, as a matter of fact, I don't fucking know," Canidy said, sharply sarcastic.

Canidy noticed Vito, who picked up on his tone of voice, stand a little more rigidly, his hands discreetly crossed at his belly so that his right hand was on his Colt.

Canidy went on: "Where did you say you were from?"

"I didn't."

"Yeah. I know."

Palasota then broke eye contact and laughed.

Fuck it, Canidy then thought. *What's to lose?*

"It's Joe Socks," he said, "and you damn well know it. Lanza is my go-between with Luciano at Great Meadow prison. And for the record, I don't like being fucked with."

"Easy, my friend," Palasota said calmly. "Just take it easy. I had to make sure you knew who was close enough to Charley Lucky to provide those items. Tell me, how is my old friend Joey Socks?"

Canidy saw that Vito relaxed at hearing Palasota's calming tone.

"Last I saw him," Canidy said, "in March, he was having a little trouble at the docks and had to whack at least a couple bastards."

"That's Lanza. Damn good guy. I miss him."

"He was here?"

Palasota shook his head. "I was there, in New York City."

"Doing what?"

Palasota met his eyes again and said, "I'm Jimmy Skinny."

Canidy shook his head. "Sorry."

"Ah, how I've been forgotten so quick. I was Charley Lucky's chauffeur before he went to the big house. He taught me everything I know"—he snorted—"which I suppose is why I wound up in the goddamn slam, too, before I got deported in '35."

"Deported?"

Palasota didn't answer as he opened one of the deep drawers of his desk and reached in. He came up with a bottle of Italian grappa and two squat glasses. He poured three fingers of the pressed grape brandy into each, handed one to Canidy, and held his up in a toast.

"I think we might be able to help one another out," Palasota said, then added, his voice sounding on the edge of being emotional, "To Charley Lucky and Sicily!"

Canidy met his eyes.

And so, Jimmy Skinny, we have established our bona fides. . . .

Canidy tapped his glass to Palasota's, and they tossed back the brandy.

That booze is going to play hell on my empty stomach—and my thinking.

Be very careful, Dick. . . .

"Okay," Canidy then said, "you asked why I need to find Frank Nola. . . ."

". . . and," he finished ten minutes later, "now we've come back to find Frank and Tubes and get them the hell out of here before the invasion begins. I don't have a hard date for that—I've only heard soon—but be aware that the Allies started early bombing of Pantelleria and some other small islands a couple weeks ago."

"May eighteenth," Palasota said.

How the hell did he know that?

Palasota then grinned.

"You should have seen the Krauts, especially the local head SS guy, scared shitless, running around Palermo. You would've thought the bombs had hit here. We actually did a lot more business than usual for a few days after that. The Krauts didn't want to go meet their maker without a last couple good romps in the sack."

Canidy grunted.

"After they calmed down," Palasota said, "nothing much happened. Life went back to normal." He paused in thought, then went on: "I don't know about any more of the nerve gas, but we can quietly get word out. The information on military strength is easy enough. We know what's here—which the Germans are complaining is not much, and mostly just a bunch of Italian soldiers. I bet that explains why the news of Pantelleria and all its heavy defenses being bombed made them panic. And we have ways to find out about what may be coming."

Canidy grinned.

"What?" Palasota said.

"Sorry. That just made me think about Mussolini's bold declaration. He said that the heavily fortified Pantelleria meant that Italy unequivocally owned the Mediterranean. And then I thought of the Maginot Line. Some of those Germans no doubt remember it, too."

"I don't follow."

"France, in the First War, built a line of fortifications along its border, very heavy ones that they were absolutely convinced would keep the Germans out. The Krauts, however, immediately flanked the line and plowed right through, taking France in a matter of days. That miserable failure gave way to: 'What's the literal translation of Maginot Line?' "

"What?"

"Speed Bump Head."

Palasota laughed.

"Well," he said, and shrugged, "that looks like what's going to happen here, too."

"You don't seem to be too concerned about that."

"Look," Palasota said, "I learned a long time ago that I am nowhere near the sharpest knife in the drawer. But I am a survivor."

Yeah. A survivor just like your tough old boss.

But don't think you're conning me into thinking you're not bright.

You were damn quick and smooth with your little test to see if I really knew Joey Socks.

Jimmy Skinny went on: "I am biding my time until the Americans come. I can put together two and two and get, not four, but twenty-two, *capiche*? These Nazi officers are arrogant and love to brag. And I have ears everywhere." He waved his right hand above his head. "The girls, the waiters, the bartenders, everyone is listening. And of course certain rooms have been bugged."

You did learn more than a thing or two working for Charley Lucky.

The most important being: knowledge is indeed power.

Are you recording our conversation?

"I understand," Canidy said, then after a moment added, "This is none of my business, but that girl in here earlier . . . Maria?"

Palasota nodded. "A very nice girl. She is not available, but there are many others just as nice."

"That's not—"

"You want a girl?" Palasota interrupted. "Just pick one. Or two. On the house."

"That's not what I came for," Canidy said.

Jimmy Skinny laughed loudly.

"But that's what everyone comes for! And to be with one of these beautiful pinup girls for an hour, they happily pay fifteen lire."

Canidy did the conversion. *That's fifty cents.*

Palasota smirked and added, "When the Americans get here, the price is going up to sixty lire."

Canidy ignored that and instead said, "Maria is a beautiful woman. What I was going to ask is, who the hell hit her?"

Palasota looked at him a long moment, then nodded and said, "There's an SS officer, head of the Palermo office here—"

"Müller," Canidy interrupted, immediately understanding.

Palasota's face gave away that he was impressed.

"Yeah," he said, his tone now bitter and mocking, "*Herr Sturmbannführer Hans Müller.* He really is a mean bastard. And the one who was scared shitless about the May eighteenth bombings."

Vito, at the mention of Müller, grunted contemptuously.

Canidy glanced at him, then back at Palasota as he thought: *That's saying something coming from one who's known a mean bastard or two in his life.*

"I'd suggest that that's the understatement of the day," Canidy said. "I've seen his work. He's the sonofabitch who had the fishermen tortured after the cargo ship blew up in the harbor, then hung their bodies by wire nooses from the yardarm to rot. And he executed a professor from the university—at point-blank in front of Professor Rossi."

And I think Mariano is some more of his handiwork—or at least his men's.

Palasota looked at Canidy a long moment, then said, "I remember the bodies. Müller was ten kinds of pissed off. At the blowing up of the ship and the villa. He decided to send a message with that."

"So I heard."

"With such a hot temper, I do not think you will be surprised that he likes to smack around the girls. Especially when he's been drinking; he's one mean drunk, too. So, I pay the girls extra. Because of the abuse. And because they become damaged goods and can't work. They are lucky if it's just a bruise or two. That is what just happened with Maria. One girl was not so lucky after he ordered those fishermen hung."

He paused to let Canidy consider that.

I hear you.

You're saying I'm responsible for that collateral damage.

But you do understand the big picture. Otherwise we would not be having this talk. . . .

"Müller got pretty rough with her," Palasota finished, "and she wound up cracking her skull on a table corner. He called it just an accident. But she'll never be right in the head again. She just turned twenty."

Canidy had a sudden mental image of the birthday dinner at Claridge's that he'd had only months earlier with Ann Chambers—when they celebrated her twentieth.

Jesus H. Christ!

Rationally, I shouldn't feel bad for a hooker. What happened to her is what's called an occupational hazard.

But I do.

Especially after having almost lost Ann.

"And there's no telling the sonofabitch no?"

Palasota grimaced and shook his head.

"The real bitch of it is that it would happen anyway. He would just do it at the threat of gunpoint. So, we pretend that it is part of our friendly business." He paused, then pointedly added, "But, trust me, his time is coming."

"Why not just see that he has an accident now?"

"No!" Palasota said quickly.

Canidy studied him.

That was a fast response—maybe too fast.

What is that about?

Palasota, trying to appear casual, said: "What I mean is, better the devil you know than the new SS bastard you don't. Follow me?"

Devil? An interesting choice of word.

They say it takes one to know one, no?

Canidy nodded.

"This might sound odd," Palasota then said as he looked at him, "but you look like you did not get a good night's sleep. You got a place to stay?"

Canidy automatically rubbed his chin, and felt the heavy stubble.

"Yes and no," he said.

"What is it? Yes or no?"

"We could do better."

"We?"

"I have another man with me."

One whose ankle will probably become instantly healed when he sees all these attractive women.

Palasota has to have a doctor who can look at that foot if it doesn't get better.

"Then it is settled. You will stay here at the hotel."

What? And have all your "ears" listening to everything I'm doing?

And where the hell would we run the wireless?

"That's not such a good idea," Canidy said. "I saw some SS in the lobby. That's a little too close for comfort."

Palasota nodded thoughtfully.

"I can find you something else, then."

Well, we don't need to be in that shithole any longer. Not with Nola's dead cousin. Damn! The body . . .

"That would be helpful," Canidy said.

"È cosa mia," Palasota said finally, dramatically touching the fingertips of both hands to his chest.

Canidy remembered Joe Socks Lanza declaring the same to him—"It is my thing, leave it to me"—and Canidy had done that and Lanza had delivered.

"The last I saw Frank Nola," Canidy then said, "was at his cousin's house. Do you know them, too? I believe it's Mariano and Nicole."

Palasota shook his head. "Does not ring a bell. Got a last name?"

"I'm not even sure I have their first names right."

"Sorry."

Canidy nodded, and thought, *The Brothers Buda would recognize him, if that's who it is.*

Canidy went on: "Frank had brought the Budas' baby sister there to that house to hide her from the SS."

Palasota raised his eyebrows in question.

"Her name is Andrea," Canidy said, "maybe nineteen years old, a beautiful girl with dark hair and eyes."

Palasota nodded. "Yes, that's Andrea."

"You do know her?"

"Yes, she's here."

What? She's a hooker?

That's why Tweedle Dee looked sad. And then got pissed off when he thought I mimed that I wanted to screw her. . . .

But then he said he didn't know where she was.

Or was that just one more miscommunication?

"What do you mean she's here?"

"She's here working."

Then that's what Tubes said when he told John Craig about screwing a whore? It was Andrea. . . .

"Andrea is a . . . working girl?"

"Oh!" Jimmy Skinny then said. "No, not that. She's in charge of the maids. And she keeps an eye on the girls when they get hurt. She studied to be a nurse at the university. Maria saw her this morning, before she came to see me."

No shit!

"I need to speak with her," Canidy said. "As soon as possible."

Palasota turned to Vito, snapped his fingers, and in Sicilian rapidly gave what clearly was an order.

The midget nodded once and without a word went out the door.

Canidy looked again at the Tommy guns standing in the corner.

"Dumb question," Canidy said. "Where did all the American weapons come from? Those Thompsons, and I saw that Shorty—I mean, Vito—has a Model 1903 Colt."

Palasota chuckled. "You are lucky he doesn't know English. If he heard you call him that, he might use it."

"That doesn't answer my question," Canidy said. "Most Model 1903s I've seen have belonged to general officers. Shor— *Vito* isn't quite in their league."

"Actually, the real story is I've got more Berettas and Lugers than I know what to do with. They're worthless pieces of shit, as far as I'm concerned. Worse than that compared to the Colts. As for them being carried by officers, that may be true, but first guy I saw packing a 1903 was in Chicago—Alfonso Capone?"

Jesus. All these wise guys are connected!

Canidy grunted.

"Yeah, I've heard of Al."

"So I've been having Colts and Thompsons, same as I carried in New York, shipped here since I arrived. Joey Socks gets them, then Francisco Nola, until he disappeared anyway, was smuggling them for me."

No surprise there . . . Lanza's office is where I got my Johnny gun.

Need to change the name of that place from Fulton Fish Market to Fulton Black Market.

There was a knock at the door, and the door immediately swung open.

Vito entered, trailed by Andrea Buda. Canidy saw that she was nicely dressed but not in anything revealing like the hookers wore. There was something different about her, then he realized that she had had her shoulder-length thick chestnut brown hair cut short.

Changing her appearance on purpose?

Better to hide from the SS?

The shorter hair seems to accentuate those breasts. . . .

Her dark almond eyes glanced around the office.

When she saw Canidy, he started to smile and was about to say *"Ciao"* when he saw her eyes grow huge—and furious.

She began screaming at him, then lunged. Vito, trying to restrain her, grabbed her around the waist and dug in his heels—but only managed to get dragged across the office.

Canidy caught her wrists as she started hitting him openhanded on his chest.

"Andrea!" Palasota yelled.

[ONE]
OSS London Station
Berkeley Square
London, England
1410 31 May 1943

"That's right, General Sikorski," Colonel David Bruce said into his telephone as he made notes on a legal pad. "Sausagemaker confirms that they got the latest delivery. I'll let you know when I know more."

Lieutenant Colonel Edmund T. Stevens—standing at the desk and holding a stack of manila folders—watched Bruce hang up the phone, stare at it a long moment, then grunt.

Bruce looked up at Stevens and said, "We could turn over the entire U.S. Army and Navy to Sikorski and it wouldn't be enough. That makes their third supply drop for May, right?"

"Yeah," Stevens said. "His Tourists distributed the first two to underground cells in the north, and this third went to Szerynski in the south. It had the usual five thousand pounds of"—he flipped open the top folder and read from a sheet—"four Browning thirty cal machine guns, forty-four thirty cal carbines, fifty-five Sten submachine guns, and just over forty thousand rounds of ammo, plus a couple hundred pounds of Composition C-2."

"How much more can we get our hands on, and how quickly?"

Stevens looked back to the folder and began flipping pages.

"Two more on hand. That's an additional five tons' worth. And enough coming in today to put together another." He looked up. "I can't say exactly how long it'll take—a day or three? Sometimes longer—to requisition more."

David Bruce noted that on his pad.

"See what you can find out soonest, Ed, and let me know so I can relay that to Donovan. He says to send more immediately."

"Got it. I'll get working on the two we have on hand, then start the paperwork for more."

"Anything else?" Bruce said somewhat impatiently.

"Szerynski said that he is taking a team back to that camp they found the Germans building in southern Poland. They want to see what's happened since they took out the train carrying Wernher von Braun's assistant, and see if there is anything else that they can sabotage."

"They're going back that soon?"

"It has been seven, eight days."

"Dulles says that the Germans have not even mentioned the sabotage, let alone the loss of that assistant . . . Schwartz?"

"Yes, SS-Sturmbannführer Klaus Schwartz, the chemist."

Bruce shook his head. "What could the rocket scientist's chemist assistant have been doing that would warrant such silence? Even Dulles's connections in the Abwehr can't find out—not only what he was up to but that he died doing it."

"I don't get it either," Stevens said. "Normally, Hitler's High Command would be ordering some ridiculously extravagant service, the casket covered in medals, to honor one of their fallen great SS heroes."

There came a rap at the open door, and when they looked they saw the commo room chief in the doorway.

"Colonel, sir," Captain Tom Harrison said, "another Eyes Only Operational Immediate for you. Busy day, huh?"

"You don't know the half of it, Harrison," Bruce said, waving him in.

Harrison purposefully marched in and went through the ritual of extending the clipboard for Bruce to sign the Receipt for Classified Document, then Harrison handed him the document with the TOP SECRET cover sheet.

Harrison saluted, then after seeing that Bruce's attention was on the message, gave up waiting for it to be returned, and marched out.

"Oh, what the hell?" Bruce said after he'd read the first two paragraphs:

TOP SECRET X STATION CHIEF
OPERATIONAL IMMEDIATE FILE
COPY NO. 1
OF 1 COPY ONLY

31MAY43 1630
FOR OSS LONDON
EYES ONLY COL BRUCE, LT COL STEVENS
FROM OSS ALGIERS

BEGIN QUOTE

DAVID,

GOOD NEWS OR BAD NEWS, YOU DECIDE. WE ALREADY HAVE AGENT IN-COUNTRY FOR ALLEN DULLES'S REQUEST.

JUPITER, UNKNOWN TO AFHQ AND AGAINST IKE'S WISHES, HAS BEEN IN SICILY ALMOST 24 HOURS. HIS MISSION: (A) LOCATE AND RESCUE MAXIMUS AND OPTIMUS (B) LOCATE AND DESTROY ANY NEW TABUN MUNITIONS (C) DETERMINE VALIDITY OF REPORTS OF UPWARD OF HALF-MILLION ENEMY TROOPERS. AND NOW, IN RECEIPT OF MY MESSAGE TODAY, (D) LOCATE AND BE PREPARED TO ELIMINATE SS-OBERSTURMBANNFUHRER OSKAR KAPPLER SOONEST BUT BY 7 JUNE.

LT COL J WARREN OWEN -- KNOWING NONE, REPEAT NONE, OF THE ABOVE -- TODAY INFORMED ME THAT AFHQ BEGINS SOFT BOMBING OF SICILY ON 17 JUNE, AFTER DIVERSIONARY SOFT BOMBING OF SARDINIA, CORSICA, AND PORT OF NAPLES ON 7 JUNE.

LASTLY, AN INTERESTING PIECE FOR OUR PUZZLE. AS A WAY TO KEEP OSS BUSY -- AND PRESUMABLY THE HELL OUT OF AFHQ'S WAY -- LT COL OWEN HAS BEEN SENDING GERMAN AND ITALIAN GENERAL OFFICERS TAKEN POW IN TUNISIA TO BE INTERROGATED BY US AT OSS DELLYS.

OUR CHIEF INTERROGATOR IS CAPT JIMBO LINDER, A NORTH CAROLINIAN FLUENT IN GERMAN WHO WAS SCHOOLED IN SWITZERLAND AND UPON GRADUATION RETURNED TO STATES AND JOINED NAVY. LINDER, AS SHARP AS THEY COME, MISSES NOTHING.

IN THE COURSE OF INTERVIEWING AFRIKA KORPS MAJ GEN HELMUT VON ECKARDT, OF THE 5TH PANZER ARMY, LINDER

THOUGHT THAT HE WOULD BE CORDIAL TO THE GENERAL AND CASUALLY MENTIONED THAT CONDITIONS FOR VON ECKARDT SOON WOULD IMPROVE WHEN HE WOULD BE SENT TO BE INTERRED IN LONDON.

LINDER SAID VON ECKARDT DAMN NEAR CAME UNGLUED. HE TRIED -- AND MISERABLY FAILED -- TO CONCEAL DEEP CONCERN ABOUT THE TRANSFER. VON ECKARDT ANNOUNCED THAT HE WAS QUITE CONTENT WITH REMAINING IN DELLYS UNTIL WAR'S END, WHICH HE SUGGESTED WOULD COME SOON ENOUGH. WHEN LINDER ATTEMPTED TO FIND A REASON, VON ECKARDT GAVE UP NO CLUE.

LINDER KNEW THAT HE SMELLED A RAT, THAT IT WAS EVIDENT VON ECKARDT FEARED SOMETHING SIGNIFICANT. WHILE THE VILLA THAT VON ECKARDT SHARES WITH TWO OTHER OFFICERS, ONE GERMAN AND ONE ITALIAN, IS AS NICE AS ANY QUARTERS IN DELLYS, ALMOST ANYTHING IN LONDON WOULD BE A VAST IMPROVEMENT.

THE VILLA IS WIRED, AND WE MADE CERTAIN THAT COGNAC AND SCHNAPPS WERE IN AMPLE SUPPLY.

THE NEXT NIGHT, AFTER LINDER'S INTERROGATION OF AFRIKA KORPS COL LUDWIG MULLER, MULLER AND VON ECKARDT WERE HAVING AFTER-DINNER DRINKS. MULLER ANNOUNCED THAT HE WAS LOOKING FORWARD TO BEING TRANSFERRED TO LONDON. THEIR LOUD ANIMATED CONVERSATION THAT FOLLOWED, FUELED BY THE ALCOHOL, WAS CLEARLY RECORDED BY OUR LISTENING DEVICES.

```
VON ECKARDT TOLD MULLER THAT THEY QUOTE DON'T WANT
TO BE ANYWHERE NEAR LONDON WHEN WERNHER VON BRAUN'S
VERGELTUNGSWAFFE BEGIN FALLING UNQUOTE.

VON ECKARDT DESCRIBED THE V-1 AND V-2 AERIAL
TORPEDOES AS BEING ALMOST IMPOSSIBLE TO STOP, AND
COMPLETELY DEVASTATING, SUCCEEDING WHERE THE BLITZ
ON LONDON HAD FAILED. VON ECKARDT WENT SO FAR AS
TO SAY TO MULLER THAT HE WOULD TAKE HIS OWN LIFE
BEFORE BEING SENT TO LONDON.

LINDER IS NOW WORKING ON A METHOD TO FIND OUT
WHAT EXACTLY VON ECKARDT KNOWS ABOUT BOMBS,
INCLUDING CURRENTLY INTERVIEWING HIM ABOUT PREVIOUS
COMMANDS THAT MAY INDIRECTLY POINT TO HIS
INVOLVEMENT WITH SAME.

WILL KEEP YOU POSTED ON ALL THE ABOVE. AND LET
ME KNOW WHAT WILD BILL WANTS JUPITER TO DO
WITH KAPPLER.

END QUOTE
FINE
TOP SECRET
```

Bruce passed the message to Stevens and angrily said, "That damn Canidy is back in Sicily! What does he think he's doing?"

Stevens read it, then said, "Dick has his hands full, that's for sure. I know you don't like what he tends to do, but you have to admit he gets the job done—"

"But at what cost? He's risking not just his life."

"—and if he can quickly get to Oskar Kappler in such a way that old man Kappler believes Bormann made good on his threat to harm his family, then the old man will really work to help us."

Bruce looked at him a long moment.

"Let's leave that to Stan," he said, then tapped his writing pad. "We have Kappler's wife and daughter to deal with."

Stevens nodded, then looked back at Fine's message.

"At least Ike having Jimmy Doolittle's bombers strike farther north will keep Hitler guessing—convince him we are softening them up and bypassing Sicily entirely. And maybe keep attention off Canidy."

"What do you think about that general? That's really the first word we've heard about the aerial torpedoes that's not been fed to us or been pure propaganda. Short of von Braun, it's right from the horse's mouth."

"Well, I've known Jimbo—call sign 'Limbo'—since he flew off-the-book ONI missions out of Miami," Stevens said. "He is a damn good guy. And damn bright. Stan is right that he misses absolutely nothing. I wonder what we can find out about this von Eckardt for him?"

"I don't know. But we have to try. It certainly looks like von Eckardt knows something that we needed to know yesterday. When Ike hears about this, we damn well better have some answers."

[TWO]
Palermo, Sicily
1320 31 May 1943

"No more screams, *sí*?" Dick Canidy said to Andrea Buda as they stopped before the faded yellow door of the house. He put his index finger to his lips.

"Sí," she said, nodding. To make it clear, she put her hand over her mouth.

Good. I wish I'd put my hand over your mouth in Palasota's office, Canidy thought as he pushed open the door and called out, "Apollo!"

"Andrea, calm down!" Jimmy Palasota had yelled in Sicilian over her screaming. "It's all right!"

It had taken some time to get her quiet enough so that Canidy could release her wrists and she would talk instead of scream. And then she had rattled off something in Sicilian as she waved her hands wildly.

"Jesus, Jimmy," Canidy said when she stopped and stood there catching her breath. "What did she say? All I recognized in that tirade was Frank and Tubes's names."

She glared at Canidy as Palasota translated.

"That she doesn't know where they are," Jimmy Skinny said. "And something about every time she sees you, someone in her family winds up missing."

"What the hell does that mean? I haven't done a thing to her family."

"Well, she made the point that Francisco is missing—"

"And so is Tubes!" Canidy interrupted. "They were working together, for christsake."

"—And, she said, they were with you shortly before you disappeared and then they did."

"If anyone is to be suspect here, it's her. She was with them—certainly with Tubes—long after I left here."

The last time that Canidy had seen Andrea Buda was when Frank Nola had brought her to Mariano's house, where Tubes Fuller had first set up MERCURY STATION. Nola had found her blocks away in Professor Arturo Rossi's home—disguised in Rossi's clothes—hiding from the SS, and convinced her she'd be better off at Mariano's. They learned that the SS was hunting her father, Luigi, because his fishing boat had left port the night that Canidy had blown up the cargo ship thought to hold the nerve gas. Shortly thereafter, with Rossi being smuggled to safety in Algiers, Müller had ordered two random fishermen tortured for the sabotage, and their bodies hung in the port by the burned pier.

Andrea's father and her twin brothers had avoided Müller's wrath—for the time being.

Palasota then said: "She also mentioned something about you letting the Germans machine-gun one of Francisco's crews."

Canidy's eyes darted between Jimmy Skinny and Andrea.

What the hell?

I knew Nola would repeat that story—but I didn't think that I'd turn out to be the bad guy in it.

"That is pure bullshit!" Canidy blurted. "What happened was we were under way, coming here, when we happened across an S-boat stopping one of Nola's fishing boats. The goddamn Krauts had the crew already lined up when we first saw them, and in almost the next moment they mowed down the crew. There was not one damn thing we could do but save ourselves." He turned to look at Andrea. "Frank saw that and knew that we later did sink an S-boat, maybe the same one."

Canidy looked back at Palasota. "Tell her that."

He did, and then Andrea studied Canidy for a long time.

Palasota then added something, ending it with, *"Capiche?"*

She then looked between Palasota and Canidy, and nodded.

"What did you just say, Jimmy?"

"What Francisco told me about you risking your life for our family and country. That you're doing it right now."

Canidy nodded.

"What was the cousin's name?" Palasota said.

"I don't think that's a good idea."

Palasota looked at Andrea and said what he wanted. All Canidy understood was "Nazi SS."

"Mariano?" she then said softly, looking at Canidy. Tears suddenly flowed down her cheeks. "I go."

"You really shouldn't," Canidy heard himself say. "Let Antonio or—"

"I go!" she repeated, this time angrily.

That is one tough young broad.

"Your English . . . it is getting better."

She nodded. "Tube teach me."

Yeah, I bet he taught you a thing or two.

Canidy led Andrea into Mariano's house, their feet crunching on the broken glass and plates. Andrea gasped at all the damage. Canidy closed the door then motioned for Andrea to wait in the kitchen. She nodded, then saw a straw whisk in the corner and started sweeping up small piles of debris.

There had been no response to Canidy's calling out, "Apollo!"

He looked around. The bicycle was where he'd left it. He listened carefully for a moment, then stepped around the bicycle, pulling out his .45 as he went.

"Apollo!" he called out again as he pounded up the wooden stairs.

He approached the top, turned to look toward the window—and saw John Craig van der Ploeg, still sitting on the floor, was bent over the makeshift radio table. The Sten and the empty K-ration box were on the floor beside him.

Canidy quickly scanned the room, noticed nothing unusual, then quickly crossed the floor.

He saw John Craig's torso slowly rising and falling, then heard his soft snores.

He's out cold.

Canidy put his .45 back in his waistband, then walked over, grasped John Craig's shoulder, and gently shook him.

John Craig awoke startled, groping around for the submachine gun as he sat bolt upright.

Then he realized it was Canidy.

"Damn it! You scared the crap out of me!"

"Welcome to my world. Hours of boredom punctuated by moments of sheer terror."

John Craig exhaled audibly.

"Actually," he then said, rubbing his eyes, "I'm glad you did wake me. I was having this really bad dream about that Luftwaffe transport. But instead of me shooting it down, it shot us up. Then I bailed out and as I popped my chute, the Giant circled back and came right at me. The last thing I saw was the pilot—who looked just like Mariano—screaming bloody murder. Then you woke me . . ."

Canidy grunted. "Either your bum foot must be making you delirious or you need to lay off those Peter Paul Choclettos."

"You find anything?"

"Yeah," Canidy said. "Jimmy Skinny's Whorehouse Hotel."

"What?"

After Canidy explained the connection, he looked over at the wireless.

"How about you? How goes it with the radio?"

"Good. On my third try, I got a hit on Mercury," he said, reaching into his coat and pulling out what Canidy recognized as a decrypted message. "But it was a new hand."

"You hadn't heard it before?"

John Craig shook his head. "Not this one. It wasn't so much heavy-handed keying but sloppy. Like they were new to messaging. Really like they'd just learned."

"What did the message say?"

"Next to nothing besides saying that they need more 'supplies.' I sent that we were just making contact, checking in, and that we'd have questions later. The signal was really strong and clear, and I wanted to wait till we got the RDF for when they're on the air longer."

"Good, but getting our gear won't happen until dark," Canidy said, then motioned at the message. "What else do you have?"

"We got another from Neptune."

"An update? They said that when they were under way—"

"But they're not under way," John Craig interrupted, shaking his head. "The update is that they now expect a thirty-six- or forty-eight-hour delay."

"Damn it! They were going to be on station tomorrow and the second. Now it's on the third and fourth?" He sighed. "It's two hundred and fifty miles from Corsica to here, which will take at least two, three days. So that puts arrival here on the seventh or eighth. That should make our life interesting . . . assuming we survive."

"What if it's longer?"

Canidy grunted again. "How's your backstroke these days?"

John Craig chuckled nervously, then said, "What about Hermes?"

Canidy shook his head. "It's one thing for Hank to drop us from those black birds at night, but it would be suicidal to land in daylight. We need stealth, and that's what boats, especially subs, offer."

John Craig nodded.

"Algiers sent two messages," he went on. "The first was short, and said that the Sandbox interview of the latest group that Nola's fishing boat smuggled out knows nothing of the whereabouts of Nola or Tubes."

"Shit. No surprise, though."

John Craig finally held out the handwritten decrypted message. "And, saving the best for last, this one is interesting."

Canidy took the sheet and his eyes fell to it:

31MAY 1145

To Jupiter

From Caesar

Wild Bill's orders. Your priority now is to locate immediately—and be prepared to extricate or terminate, if so ordered—SS Lt Col Oskar Kappler, deputy officer in Messina SS HQ.

Absolutely critical this mission accomplished no later than seven (7) days from this date.

If ordered to terminate subject, important but not imperative to cause death to appear as if an SS or OVA murder.

Wild Bill demands that you confirm receipt and your understanding of this order.

Canidy said, "What the hell?"

And then his mind raced.

I thought that this Kappler guy was okay. That he wanted the war to end.

Hell, he was the one who tried hiding that Tabun here.

Amazing how fast the rules change in this game.

How the hell am I going to get to Kappler in Messina and take him out? By—what?—June sixth?

Maybe if I go through Müller?

Yeah! I could get them both at once, maybe with some C-2.

Or make it look as if Müller got Kappler, right before Kappler shot him.

Everyone hates that sonofabitch.

"Message back: Wild Bill's orders received and understood—"

There suddenly came from downstairs the unmistakable sound of a young woman screaming.

Again?

But now she sounds terrified, not angry. . . .

John Craig stared at Canidy, who was pulling out his .45 again as he explained, "Andrea. I left her in the kitchen."

Then they could tell that Andrea's screams were getting louder and closer—and that she was running up the stairs.

Canidy pushed the Sten within John Craig's reach, then aimed his pistol toward the top of the stairs. As he strained to discern how many pairs of feet were pounding on the steps—*sounds like it's just her*—he stuffed the decrypted message into his pants pocket.

Andrea then appeared, alone, at the top, wide-eyed and tears flowing.

"Are you okay, Andrea?" Canidy said.

"It is Mariano!" she cried.

Well, that's what you get for not staying in the kitchen like I told you.

So much for being a tough girl.

She ran to Canidy, then buried her face in his shoulder and began sobbing.

Canidy looked at John Craig, who stared at Andrea.

"I think I'm dreaming again," John Craig said. "My God, she is more beautiful than Tubes said."

Andrea, her ample chest heaving, turned her head and dabbed her sleeve at her tears.

Then she seemed to notice John Craig for the first time.

She must have heard him mention Tubes.

"Andrea," Canidy said, "this is John Craig, a friend of Tubes."

"Ciao," John Craig said, and made a half-attempt to get up, then winced with pain.

As she started to make a weak smile in reply, her face suddenly showed great concern.

"Is bad!" she said, and quickly went to John Craig and knelt beside his deeply bruised and swollen foot.

Andrea Buda tried for what to Canidy felt like an hour to get him to understand what she clearly insisted was to happen next. All he knew for certain was that it had something to do with John Craig's foot—she pointed to it and repeatedly said, "Is bad!"—and that she wanted it done somewhere else but in Mariano's house.

Finally, she grabbed Canidy's hand and led him across the room. As she started to pull him down the stairs, Canidy called back to John Craig, "Sit tight, Gimpy. I'll get this figured out."

Canidy then guessed that Andrea was going to have him do something with Mariano. But then she led him, not to the living room, but to the kitchen, and then out the front door.

Ten minutes and five blocks later, they came to another residential street and then to another house. As Andrea pulled a key from her pocket, she pointed to the door and then to herself and said, "My *casa*."

They entered, and Canidy saw that it was more or less similar to Mariano's—with one main exception. It was not destroyed. It was furnished simply and very neatly kept.

They stood in the kitchen, which had a basic wooden table with four wooden stools. Andrea went to one of the lower cabinet doors and took from it a small black bag that she then put on the table. She dug into it and produced a roll of tape.

It's her medical bag.

She held it up to Canidy, then pointed in the direction of Mariano's house, then motioned from it to the tape roll.

"You want to bring Apollo here?" Canidy said.

She looked at him not completely comprehending, then repeated the gestures.

He nodded. *But it will have to be after dark.*

Fifteen minutes later, Andrea was again kneeling at John Craig's feet, her medical bag nearby. He was lying on his torn mattress. She had moments earlier just come out of the small bathroom carrying a large bowl of water. She carefully put the hurt foot in the water, then soaped a sponge and began slowly cleansing it.

From John Craig's expression, Canidy thought he looked like he'd died and gone to heaven.

"You going to be all right for a while, Gimpy?" Canidy said to him. "I need to go talk to Palasota about my new priority."

John Craig's mop of hair nodded as he gave Canidy a thumbs-up.

When Dick Canidy returned two hours later, he was still annoyed that going back to see Jimmy Skinny basically had been a wild-goose chase.

He's gone God Knows Where, and when I finally repeat "Vito" often enough that they get the goddamn midget to show up at the front desk, the sawed-off wiseguy hands me a note from Palasota with a hotel room key—after I specifically said that I did not want to stay there.

What a clusterfuck this is becoming!

Canidy again entered the house calling out, "Apollo!"

And again there was no answer.

And again he pulled out his .45 and went up the stairs, approaching the top cautiously.

"Sonofabitch!" he said as he quickly looked around the room.

There was no sign of John Craig van der Ploeg or Andrea Buda. The room held only the shredded mattresses and the makeshift table.

And the wireless is gone! What the hell?

He looked under the hidden door in the floor and found only empty space between the joists.

Damn it!

Canidy then pounded down the stairs and checked the rest of the house.

As he went to the living room at the back of the first floor, he realized something had changed.

Fucking Mariano is gone!

How did that happen?

I could barely move him. No way that John Craig or Andrea could have.

Canidy covered the five blocks back to the casa that Andrea had announced was hers. He knocked at the door, and when there was no answer, jimmied the lock, searched the house—but found absolutely no trace that they had been there.

When Canidy reached the single-story brick building that was Frank Nola's import-export office, the metal hasp on the wooden door was not only closed but had a heavy dull brass padlock securing it.

What the hell?

Tweedle Dee said he was coming back here.

Canidy looked around, then exhaled audibly.

I need to get my bearings and think this whole damn thing through.

And fast. I'm supposed to be—somehow—on my way to Messina. . . .

He reached in his pocket and pulled out the note and key from Jimmy Skinny.

Palasota had written: *Sorry. Best I can do right now. Get cleaned up, rested. Check back. –J*

[THREE]
Office of Chief Executive
Headquarters, Kappler Industrie GmbH
Berlin, Germany
1015 1 June 1943

"I have just come from the Reich Chancellery," Wernher von Braun announced in a tone that was anything but pleasant as he came through the massive double oak doors held open by Wolfgang Kappler's executive assistant. Inge Gelb was an unassuming, slender blond forty-year-old.

Kappler, seated at his desk, slid shut the top drawer that contained his Luger 9mm pistol, and stood. He noted that von Braun, in his SS uniform, had dispensed with greeting him with a stiff arm and a hearty "Heil Hitler."

"And it's nice to see you again, too, Wernher," Wolfgang Kappler said, purposefully sarcastic as he gestured for the assistant to close the door and told her, "Inge, absolutely no interruptions, unless it is Herr Krupp calling."

Kappler noticed that von Braun seemed unbothered by the mention of Krupp and the possibility of Krupp's call interrupting their meeting.

"*Jawohl*, Herr Kappler," she said, almost bowing as she backed out and pulled the two doors shut.

Kappler's wife had been responsible for the design of his luxurious office. There was a rich mix of dark-stained hardwood paneling and thick burgundy woolen carpeting, as well as grand oil paintings showing four generations of Kapplers. The furnishings were in the baroque style of Louis XIV, the ornately carved pieces projecting, she'd said, the majestic power that reflected that of the chief executive industrialist himself.

Kappler looked over at von Braun, who now stood by the wall of floor-to-ceiling windows that overlooked a bend of the meandering River Spree. He stood erect, hands on his hips, staring out at the gray and dreary day. Kappler, wearing one of his fine suits, could see von Braun's reflection in the glass.

He looks ridiculous in that SS uniform.

But I suppose he had to wear it to please Hitler—anything not to give him the slightest excuse to anger him.

Then again maybe, like Schwartz, he likes wearing it.

"And how was your visit with Adolf?"

Wernher von Braun turned and walked to the desk and took a seat in one of the leather-upholstered gilded armchairs. Kappler gestured toward the silver tray with the silver coffee service and, after von Braun nodded, poured them both cups.

"Let me begin, Wolfgang, by asking you something. Have you ever had the pleasure of being at the receiving end of one of Hitler's furious sessions? One in which Der Führer is so angry that his face glows red as a beet, his spittle pelts you in the face, and the climax of his screaming and yelling is when he rips the eyeglasses from his face and throws them across the room?"

Wolfgang Kappler took a sip of coffee as he thought, *I've always thought it a serious sign of abhorrent behavior that Hitler would even keep a stockpile of extra eyeglasses just so he could throw and break them. That's calculating. And sadly childlike, if not outright demented.*

"No, Wernher, I have not had the pleasure of being in Adolf's company in many years. And, even when I did—and I was around him quite a bit in those early days—he then was not prone to such dramatics."

Von Braun raised an eyebrow.

"I would suggest, having just experienced such a session and the memory of it rather fresh, that these fits of temper are not simply drama."

Kappler watched as von Braun pulled a white linen handkerchief from his tunic and delicately dabbed at his forehead.

Presumably at some of Adolf's spittle . . .

Von Braun went on: "There is genuine conviction in his behavior because he has a genuine conviction that Germany will be victorious. And, I might add, such conviction is infectious."

So you not only believe in that, you actively support it.

Kappler nodded, then said, "This I do not doubt. Even when younger, he showed that extraordinary conviction. I suppose that having such focus on one's goals—and, conversely, a dogged blindness to anything not fitting one's goals—is in large part how one rises to be in such a powerful position."

Their eyes met, and Kappler thought he could see von Braun wondering if that was also meant to describe him.

Yes, it was, Wernher.

You may well be brilliant, but you are no better than all the others in Hitler's circle. Clearly you are feverishly working to further a madman's failed vision.

A Thousand-Year Reich? It won't last another thousand days.

Yet you design more bombs—bigger and more deadly bombs—and use my labors, my companies, to ultimately further destroy our people and our country.

Just as has happened in the Ruhr Valley.

How very easy it would be for me right now to kill you.

But what good would that do? The programs would continue, more people would die—including me and, ultimately, my family.

Von Braun said: "After our meeting with Der Führer, Reich Minister Bormann suggested that I come see you. He said that you and he also go back a long time."

"Yes. We all do, actually. It was Bormann who introduced Fritz Thyssen and me to Adolf. You're aware, I'm sure, that Bormann named his sons after Adolf, Rudolf Hess, and Heinrich Himmler."

"I wasn't."

"And so they're all godfathers to their namesakes. And I was there when Adolf served as witness to Bormann's wedding."

"You do go back a long time."

And yet I am the one who supported them only to see them use that power and steal from me.

Von Braun watched as Kappler pulled back his left cuff to look at his wristwatch. Von Braun noticed that it was a very fine gold Patek Philippe.

"Wernher," Kappler said, somewhat impatiently, "I was happy to make a place in my schedule for you. But having just returned from a two-week trip, I have much to catch up on. Can we get to the point of this? I postponed two meetings and absolutely cannot miss my eleven o'clock appointment."

Wernher von Braun, not accustomed to being so ordered, made a face as he locked eyes with Kappler.

"Very well," von Braun said. "Tell me about Walter Höss."

Oh, he's a real winner. You can have him to go with Schwartz.

But then I'd have to replace him, and I already have him in my pocket.

The next man may not be as easy.

"In all honesty, Wernher?"

"Of course!"

"Well, while Höss is not in Schwartz's league—"

"Few are," von Braun interrupted. "You must miss him."

Oh, yes.

How I miss the bastard.

"—I believe him to be quite capable. He is doing fine in the job."

"Very good. Then there is no reason that the Special Program quotas cannot be met?"

What do I tell him?

"Well, Wernher, my friend, the first thing I am going to do when I am done in Berlin is rush back to Frankfurt and try to find a quiet way to sabotage the conversion of the plant from high explosives to nerve gas. Other than that? Everything should be fine."

"None that I know of," Kappler said. "Everything should be fine."

"Very good. It is critical that we remain on schedule. We have been dealt setbacks. First with the bombings in the Ruhr Valley. Loss of the manufacture of certain metals has required that I redesign airfoils among other parts. . . ." He paused, then went on, "I do not know why I tell you this, except having just now been on the receiving end of Hitler's temper I'm still mentally going over all that I now need to do."

"I understand."

"I presume your steelwork losses in the Ruhr are the reason for your meeting with Herr Krupp."

So he did put some thought into why I mentioned Krupp.

"Among other things, yes."

"You have my sympathies. I cannot tell you how upset losing Klaus has been," Wernher von Braun then said.

What?

"You *lost* Klaus? He no longer works with you?"

Wernher von Braun suddenly looked shocked.

"You don't know?" he said. "I must say that I am surprised—"

"I've been traveling a great deal, as I said. What about Klaus?"

"Klaus was killed by those *gottverdammt* Polish guerrillas!"

Kappler shook his head.

Who else knows this? Höss clearly doesn't.

"What exactly happened?"

Von Braun looked at him a long moment, clearly deciding what he should—and should not—share.

He then exhaled audibly and began, "Much of this is highly secret, but Reich Minister Bormann would not have sent me here if you could not be made privy to such. When Klaus was killed, he was traveling for me—I could very well be the one who could be dead right now. He was sent to inspect a manufacturing facility for the Special Program. The railroad tracks were sabotaged, and when his train crashed, Klaus was killed. The entire scene went up in flames."

"That is tragic," Kappler said, hoping his tone sounded appropriately concerned.

"It has been a significant setback," von Braun said.

Always about the work, Wernher?

"As you know, he left behind a wife and four young children," von Braun added almost absently, then sipped his coffee.

Kappler looked at him. *And how many more young families will be left behind because of your new bombs?*

"I do know the family. Sad," Kappler said. "He was traveling alone?"

Von Braun returned his cup to its saucer as he shook his head.

"With two SS scharführers on my personal passenger car. It was the only railcar, as it was a trip of the highest priority. We cannot afford any further setbacks—Der Führer has made it extremely clear that he wants the V-bombs falling on London immediately—and I have selected a manufacturing site that, unlike our current one, is far more difficult for enemy aircraft to reach. It would appear particulary imperative in view of the fact that the enemy now has struck the Ruhr Valley."

"I understand completely," Kappler said. "So we will be shipping the material to this new manufacturing site. . . ."

Von Braun nodded. "They have already repaired the sabotaged railroad track, and construction continues only slightly behind schedule."

"And this manufacturing site is where?"

You said the "gottverdammt *Polish guerrillas*" . . .

Von Braun looked at him another long moment, and Kappler could clearly see that he again was deciding what he should—and should not—share.

"I'm afraid that that currently is restricted information," he finally said. "I'm sure you will know soon enough."

Kappler raised his eyebrows and grunted.

Kappler then wordlessly reached across his desk. He picked up a large manila envelope, fingered open its brass clasp, and double-checked the contents. Then he slid the sheets back inside and flattened the clasp.

He stood and held out the envelope to von Braun.

"You will find all the production figures in there, both current and projected, not only meet but exceed the quotas required," Wolfgang Kappler said perfunctorily, then took a long look at his wristwatch, tapping its crystal with his index finger. "If there is nothing else . . ."

The look on Wernher von Braun's face showed that he did not appreciate at all being dismissed. But he took the envelope and stood, then walked to the doors without another word.

At the doors, he turned and said, "Wolfgang, I think it might be a good idea that when Reich Minister Bormann and I share news about the Special Program with Der Führer, that you accompany us. That way you may—how shall I say?—personally witness how fervent his genuine conviction is for this Special Program. If you take my meaning . . ."

He pulled open the door and went through it.

It had taken Wolfgang Kappler nearly fifteen minutes to walk from his headquarters office to the Bebelplatz, the popular Mitte district public square. The gray sky heavy with humidity, he had walked quickly, worried that it might begin to rain at any moment.

As he moved the folded newspaper under his right arm to under his left arm, he turned south, away from the wide boulevard Unter den Linden. He wound through the crowd, circling the square twice, finally stopping at a bench to retie his shoes while carefully scanning the crowd for anyone who might be following him.

So far it is good, I guess.

He checked to make sure that the newspaper was still properly folded—that the manila envelope it concealed was not visible.

He had placed the envelope inside the paper in what he hoped would appear to be a casual fashion, so that were he stopped and the envelope found it would not look suspect. While the envelope contained details on the Secret Program, it wasn't as if he was not supposed to have it.

Still, he knew that being caught with it and having to answer questions was something that needed to be avoided at all costs.

Kappler then walked past the State Opera building and headed directly for the far end of the square. He reached Saint Hedwig's Cathedral, and after he entered the copper-domed neoclassical structure that was modeled after Rome's Pantheon, he came to the holy water, dipped a finger, crossed himself, and silently said a prayer for his family's safety.

He skirted the sanctuary, glancing in and seeing a dozen or more parishioners dotting the pews, on their knees praying. He finally came to the door that was the first confessional booth, and entered. He pulled the door closed and turned to the wall partition. There was a wooden railing midway up the partition and a pillow on the floor, both for praying. Above the railing was a gap—just large enough to pass a prayer book and perhaps some rosary beads—and above that a small door.

As Kappler knelt on the pillow, the small door slid open.

In a Pavlovian reflex, as Kappler had done all his Roman Catholic life, he automatically said, "Forgive me, Father, for I have sinned. . . ."

Then he heard a deep chuckle on the opposite side of the partition.

Wolfgang Kappler angrily shook his head.

How dare he mock me!

And in the House of the Lord!

A small envelope then appeared in the gap above the railing. As he took it, he then heard a familiar voice.

"And what would you have for me, my sinful son?" Hans Bernd Gisevius said in a sonorous tone.

[FOUR]
OSS London Station
Berkeley Square
London, England
1110 1 June 1943

Not bothering to knock, Deputy Station Chief Ed Stevens walked quickly into Station Chief David Bruce's office and said, "I was just given this Eyes Only in the commo room. It's from Allen Dulles to us and Donovan. This is not going to be good."

David Bruce looked up from his writing and took the document.

"Another *fait accompli*, I gather?" Bruce said idly.

"Well, let's just say we're about to get busier."

Bruce flipped past the TOP SECRET cover sheet, and his eyes fell to the message:

TOP SECRET

OPERATIONAL IMMEDIATE

1JUNE43 0835

FOR

OSS WASHINGTON -- EYES ONLY GEN DONOVAN

OSS LONDON STATION -- EYES ONLY COL BRUCE, LT COL STEVENS

FROM OSS BERN

BEGIN QUOTE

GENTLEMEN,

I HAVE ALWAYS BELIEVED THAT THERE IS NO GOOD WAY TO ANNOUNCE BAD NEWS, AND ESPECIALLY NOT TO SUGAR-COAT IT. THAT SAID: HITLER DOES IN FACT HAVE AERIAL TORPEDOES -- THE FIESELER 103, HEREAFTER "V-1" -- UNDER PRODUCTION. THERE ARE DESIGNS FOR THE V-1 TO CARRY WARHEADS CONTAINING HIGH EXPLOSIVE AND CHEMICAL WARFARE AGENTS.

WHEN WE CAME INTO POSSESSION OF THE FILES SHOWING ACTUAL PRODUCTION DATA FROM CHEMISCHE FABRIK FRANKFURT A.G. FOR THE AMATOL AND THE TABUN, WE

FOUND THAT IT ALSO CONTAINED PRODUCTION DATA FOR THE V-1. THE EVER EFFICIENT SS-STURMBANNFUHRER KLAUS SCHWARTZ HAD KEPT THESE COPIES IN HIS CHEMISCHE FABRIK OFFICE, PRESUMABLY NOT EXPECTING HIS EARLY EXPIRATION (MORE ON THAT SHORTLY).

THE V-1 FUSELAGE IS ABOUT 22 FEET LONG, 3 FEET IN DIAMETER, WITH A 17-FOOT WINGSPAN. ENGINE IS PULSE-JET. MAX FUEL IS 160 US GALLONS OF E-1 AVIATION GAS. MAX CRUISE IS 415 MPH AT 4,500 FEET. MAX RANGE IS 130 MILES WITH A 1-TON AMATOL WARHEAD. (NO FIGURES FOR TABUN WARHEAD DUE TO NO TESTS CONDUCTED. BUT TABUN WARHEAD WILL WEIGH ABOUT HALF THE AMATOL, GIVING THE WEAPON AT LEAST GREATER RANGE AND VERY LIKELY FASTER MAX SPEED.)

AS WE WERE AWARE, THE FIRST V-1 UNPOWERED FLIGHT WAS IN OCTOBER 1942, LAUNCHED FROM AN FW-200 KONDOR. THE FIRST SELF-POWERED FLIGHT WAS IN DECEMBER 1942.

WE NOW LEARN THAT THERE SINCE HAVE BEEN EXACTLY ONE HUNDRED (100) TEST LAUNCHES OF THE V-1, WITH APPROXIMATELY ONE-THIRD (1/3) AIR-DROPPED FROM HEINKEL HE-111 AIRCRAFT AND THE REMAINDER LAUNCHED FROM GROUND-BASED CATAPULTS.

THE VAST MAJORITY OF THESE WERE, IN ONE WAY OR ANOTHER, FAILURES. ONLY ONE (1) IN TEN (10) ACTUALLY

PERFORMED CLOSE TO WHAT WERNHER VON BRAUN HAD EXPECTED. NOT ONE OF THE 100 MADE IT DIRECTLY ON TARGET.

IT WOULD APPEAR THAT EVEN ROCKET SCIENTISTS HAVE BAD DAYS, AS VON BRAUN DID NOT KNOW WHAT EXACTLY WAS THE ROOT OF THE V-1 PROBLEMS. NEWS OF THIS HAS MADE HITLER FURIOUS, YET HITLER WAS IN FACT PART OF THE PROBLEM BECAUSE HE HAS ORDERED VON BRAUN TO RUSH THE PROGRAM.

DUE TO THE RUSH, THE MAJOR COMPONENTS -- ENGINE, AIRFRAME, GUIDANCE SYSTEM, CATAPULT -- HAD BEEN TESTED SEPARATELY. WHEN THEY WERE ASSEMBLED AND THE V-1 TESTED, VON BRAUN FOUND IT DIFFICULT TO DETERMINE WHICH PART -- OR PARTS IN CONCERT -- WAS RESPONSIBLE FOR A PARTICULAR CRASH.

ONE MAJOR CAUSE WAS VIBRATION. AT FIRST, THE WINGS WOULD STRIP OFF, THEN THE FUSELAGE WOULD BREAK APART. IT BECAME CLEAR THAT THE MAIN SOURCE OF VIBRATION WAS THE ENGINE ITSELF. THE PULSE-JET IGNITES FUEL 50 TIMES PER SECOND, CAUSING A REMARKABLE AMOUNT OF VIBRATION. IT TOOK EXTENSIVE TESTING ONCE THE SOLUTION OF INSULATING THE ENGINE WAS REACHED. THEN THEY HAD TO FINE-TUNE THE WING DESIGN. BECAUSE THE NECESSARY TYPE OF STEEL IS IN SHORT SUPPLY, THE WINGS HAD TO BE CRAFTED OF PLYWOOD.

AND THEN THEY HAD PROBLEMS WITH THE LAUNCH DEVICE. A PISTON THAT CONNECTS TO THE FUSELAGE IS PROPELLED BY HIGH PRESSURE GAS. THEY FIRST HAD TO TWEAK THE PRESSURE OF THAT GAS TO THE FIRST TESTS. WHEN THE ROCKETS WERE MODIFIED TO ADDRESS THE PROBLEMS WITH THE PULSE-JET VIBRATIONS, THE LAUNCHER HAD TO BE RECONFIGURED. AND WHEN THE WOODEN WINGS WERE THEN MODIFIED, AGAIN THE LAUNCHER HAD TO BE RECONFIGURED. AND SO ON. THEY BURNED THROUGH THOSE 100 V-1S IN SHORT ORDER -- ABOUT TWO MONTHS.

HITLER AGAIN COMPOUNDED PROBLEMS BY DEMANDING THAT THE V-1 BE LAUNCHED FROM BOTH GROUND AND AIR IN ORDER TO DELIVER QUOTE AN OVERWHELMING PUNCH UNQUOTE. GEN MILCH DID NOT THINK THAT AN AIRBORNE LAUNCHER WOULD FUNCTION ON A HE-111 -- HE ARGUED THAT THE WEIGHT AND DRAG WOULD DANGEROUSLY SLOW THE BOMBER, MAKING IT AN EASY TARGET -- BUT AGREED TO DO SO WHEN CONVINCED IT WOULD CONFUSE THE ALLIES.

WITH THE BUGS NOW MOSTLY WORKED OUT, HITLER IS DEMANDING THAT PRODUCTION BEGIN IMMEDIATELY SO THAT FIVE THOUSAND (5,000) V-1S CAN BE LAUNCHED IN DECEMBER 1943.

IN ADDITION TO THE CHEMISCHE FABRIK STANDARD PRODUCTION OF AMATOL, THERE NOW IS A V-1 SPECIAL

PROGRAM ORDER -- SIGNED BY FIELD MARSHAL MILCH, GEN VON AXTHELM, AND REICH MINISTER GORING -- REQUIRING 100 TONS OF AMATOL EACH MONTH, RISING TO 5,000 TONS EACH MONTH, AND ABOUT HALF THAT OF TABUN.

AS TO THE EXPIRATION OF KLAUS SCHWARTZ, HIS DEATH BY THE POLISH HOME ARMY WAS CONFIRMED BY WERNHER VON BRAUN WHEN HE MET YESTERDAY WITH WOLFGANG KAPPLER IN BERLIN. VON BRAUN STATED THAT SCHWARTZ, UNDER HIS ORDERS AND USING HIS PERSONAL RAILCAR, HAD BEEN TRAVELING WITH THE TWO SS-SCHARFUHRERS (NOTED IN MY 28 MAY MESSAGE TO YOU) WHEN SABOTAGE BY QUOTE POLISH GUERRILLAS UNQUOTE DERAILED THEIR TRAIN. HE DESCRIBED THE TRIP AS ONE OF QUOTE HIGHEST PRIORITY UNQUOTE.

HE WOULD NOT REVEAL TO EVEN KAPPLER WHERE THIS HAPPENED. BUT SINCE WE KNOW IT WAS NEAR THE CAMP UNDER CONSTRUCTION AT BLIZNA, POLAND, I HUMBLY SUGGEST THAT THE CAMP IS CLOSELY CONNECTED TO ONE OF VON BRAUN'S PROGRAMS. AND AS SUCH, HAVING HAD ITS RAILROAD SABOTAGED, IT WILL BE MORE HEAVILY GUARDED THAN BEFORE.

LASTLY, WE HAVE WORD BACK FROM THE ABWEHR AGENT IN MESSINA WHO MET WITH OSKAR KAPPLER TWO DAYS AGO. THE AGENT TOLD BRIGADE GENERAL HANS OSTER, DEPUTY DIRECTOR TO ADMIRAL CANARIS, THAT SON BELIEVES AS HIS FATHER DOES.

IN LIGHT OF ALL THE ABOVE, IT IS MY OPINION THAT GETTING KAPPLER'S WIFE AND DAUGHTER AND SON TO SAFETY SHOULD TAKE PLACE AT FIRST OPPORTUNITY.

TO THAT END, I HAVE SENT, THROUGH THE MESSINA ABWEHR AGENT, A MESSAGE TO OSKAR KAPPLER -- UNDER WOLFGANG KAPPLER'S SIGNATURE BUT WITHOUT HIS KNOWLEDGE -- ALERTING OSKAR TO EXPECT CONTACT FROM OSS AGENT JUPITER FOR HIS EXTRACTION.

STAN FINE WILL LET ME KNOW WHEN JUPITER HAS THE SON. PLEASE LET ME KNOW WHEN YOU HAVE THE WIFE AND DAUGHTER.

END QUOTE
DULLES
TOP SECRET

"With a range of a hundred and thirty miles," Stevens said, "it would appear that von Braun really did design the V-1 specifically to strike London. It's right at a hundred miles between here and France's coastline. I wonder what Churchill's pompous pal the Prof will have to say if these bombs start hitting here. And in December?" He paused, then added, "This is Ike's worst fear."

"Using the five thousand figure," David Bruce said, "one-tenth means five hundred aerial torpedoes hitting London. And with 'the bugs worked out,' that figure could likely be higher."

"But it also said that not one of them hit close to its target."

"Moot point. Considering that each one is said to be carrying a one-ton warhead of high explosive—making the total five hundred tons—this may well be akin to horseshoes."

"Horseshoes?"

"As in: 'Close only counts with horseshoes and hand grenades.' And now with aerial torpedoes. Five hundred tons of Amatol blowing up anywhere close to target will serve the purpose of terrorizing London. And, as Ike says, jeopardize the cross-channel invasion."

After a moment, Stevens added, "Well, we now have a pretty good idea why the Germans are keeping Schwartz's demise very quiet."

David Bruce looked at the message again, then tapped it and said, "Hans Oster and Canaris have a long history. Oster is part of Canaris's Black Orchestra."

"So then you really think that Dulles is setting up Kappler for 'extra-legal' work?" Stevens said.

"What I think is that Dulles knows if Old Man Kappler finds that his family has suddenly disappeared, he damn well might be angry enough to do something like that."

Stevens considered that, nodded, and said, "I have to admit that I know I would."

"As would I."

Bruce looked back at the message, then said: "I don't need to await word from Wild Bill Donovan. Get an urgent sent to Stanley telling him to message Canidy that this Oskar Kappler is expecting Jupiter to contact him. Canidy is to get Kappler out of sight yesterday, and out of Sicily soonest."

"I hate to ask this, but dead or alive? Dulles said 'to safety.' "

Ambassador David K. E. Bruce looked at him a long moment.

"Do you mean what's the right thing to do?"

Stevens said, "No. I made that mistake one time, and Wild Bill handed me my head. He said, 'I'm surprised to hear you say that. I thought by now you would have figured out that "the right thing" has absolutely no meaning for the OSS. We do what has to be done, and "right" has absolutely nothing to do with that.' "

Bruce then said: "Which in this case means that Oskar Kappler dead would (a) serve the same purpose as his disappearance—as you said earlier, getting the old man to do what we need—and (b) make the mission much simpler for Canidy."

"And that is what I figured—"

"But," Bruce went on, "having a grateful SS officer in our pocket for Operation Husky, one who's been running intel in Sicily for the last two years, would be extremely valuable, too. So tell him alive if at all possible. But, paraphrasing Robert Burns, should the best-laid schemes o' mice an' men go to hell . . ."

Stevens raised his eyebrows and nodded.

[ONE]
Room 801
Hotel Michelangelo
Palermo, Sicily
0725 1 June 1943

Dick Canidy suddenly awoke when he first heard the banging, then, a couple moments later, pounding.

He sat up, groggy, and looked quickly around the room, trying to get his bearings. The early morning sun lit the room. He had on only a bath towel that covered his waist.

Shit. I fell asleep—and deeply.

Who the hell is doing that banging?

Pulling his .45 from under the pillow, he looked at the door and listened.

The hammering came again.

Not my door . . . it's coming from down the hall.

Jesus! Are they really at it again?

Talk about trying to get the most bang for your buck. . . .

He stood, adjusted the towel, and went to the door.

He opened it a crack and peered out and immediately saw two men in the hallway.

And what the hell are they doing?

Just before dusk the day before, Canidy, running out of immediate options, reluctantly had gone back to the hotel.

He found the lobby and lounge crowded. There were a few civilians. But the brothel was packed mostly with German and Italian sailors, all drinking and laughing too loudly as they got friendly with Jimmy Skinny's girls.

No one in the boisterous crowd showed any interest in Canidy as he worked his way through the lobby and started climbing what he realized was the first of seven flights of steps to the top floor.

As he passed each floor, there was at least one hostess leading her client in or out of one of the ten rooms there.

Reaching the top floor, Canidy looked up and down the hall. He saw that there were only four doors on the eighth floor, not one near the other. As he passed Room 802 he thought he heard from inside it the distinct sound of a woman's deep, rhythmic moans.

I'm not going to have to listen to that all night, am I?

He came to 801, fed the key into the lock, then pulled out his .45. He entered and checked the suite, looking inside its small empty closet, under the iron-frame bed, and then in the tiny full bath. He found nothing unusual.

He glanced around the room and decided that it was much better than he had expected.

Certainly a helluva lot better than Mariano's dump.

From the looks—there then came from across the hall the distant *bam-bam-bam* of a headboard hitting against a wall—*and the sounds of it—business must be good.*

The black iron bed frame held a full-sized mattress. When he pressed his open hand on it, he found that the mattress was reasonably firm and that the well-washed sheets were thin but reasonably comfortable. Side tables were on either side, one with a lamp and one with a box of wooden matches and a tin ashtray.

Canidy dug in his jacket pocket and fished out a cigar stub, and lit it.

He saw on the far side of the suite was a squat couch, the corners of its cloth upholstery threadbare. And, in front of that, a scarred wooden coffee table. His eyes lit up.

On it were two unopened liquor bottles, one of them of the same Italian grappa brandy that Canidy had had a toast with Jimmy Skinny and the other a red wine. Next to that was a plate with two kinds of soft cheeses, a small loaf of bread, a bowl of olives, and a glass jar packed with sardines marinated in what looked like olive oil. And two empty glass jars meant to serve as drinking glasses.

Canidy's stomach growled.

Jimmy Skinny really knows how to take care of gli amici.

Why did I even think of not staying here?

Simple. Because the clientele seemed to be mostly Krauts—and now the Italian Navy.

Then he looked around the room and then up, along the ceiling.

And because this place is probably one of the bugged ones.

But as long as I keep my head down, eyes open, and mouth shut, I should be fine.

He found a corkscrew, cracked open the bottle of wine, and half-filled one of the glass jars.

He grabbed a fistful of olives and popped a couple in his mouth as he carried the jar of wine over to the window. He saw that he had a clear view of most of Palermo and all of the port—and Civil War Major General John Buford, the Union Army cavalry officer, suddenly came to mind.

He puffed on his cigar and grunted.

"General, we have taken the tactical high ground, have a solid foothold, and the enemy in sight. All is well."

We may be one helluva long way from Gettysburg, General Buford, sir, but battles is battles.

Then he thought: *Where the hell are you out there, John Craig?*

And Tubes?

And I don't even want to think about that Kappler SS bastard.

He took a healthy gulp of the wine, then could not help but notice that there was only one S-boat at the pier—*and I don't want to try to think what that means*—and, moored opposite it, there now was an Italian submarine.

The sleek black one-hundred-eighty-foot-long *Ascianghi* had a complement of nearly forty crew and six officers.

Well, that damn sure explains all the drunk swabbies—shore leave. No coincidence that rhymes with whore leave.

He then had a sudden need to hit the head—*this wine is going right through me*—and made a beeline for it.

Fifteen minutes and one lukewarm bath later, he came back into the room with a towel around his waist, poured another half-jar of wine, then went and sat on the bed.

He took a gulp of the wine, put the jar on the side table, and leaned back on the pillow.

Setting priorities, he thought as he closed his eyes, *here's what I know . . .*

One, find Kappler, then await word as to what I'm supposed to do with the bastard. Killing him—or having it look like the SS or OVR did it—certainly would simplify that. But, failing that . . .

Two, in order to find out what I'm supposed to do with Kappler, I have to find John Craig and/or his suitcase radio to get my messages from Stan and Neptune or . . .

Three, go out and get one of the suitcase radios I stashed. And probably the C-2. And definitely a bottle of that scotch.

He grinned.

Not necessarily in that order of importance.

And then there's the original One and Two—now Four and Five—finding Tubes and Frank, and any Tabun.

Forget verifying the half-million troopers. Even Jimmy Skinny didn't seem to buy that bullshit figure.

Canidy had suddenly caught himself in a huge yawn.

What I don't know is if John Craig got nabbed like Tubes did . . . or if I'll find either of them.

He had yawned again.

Then he had fallen asleep.

And then, nearly eight hours later, the hammering started.

[TWO]
Room 802
Hotel Michelangelo
Palermo, Sicily
0725 1 June 1943

SS-Obersturmbannführer Oskar Kappler was gently awakened from a deep, contented sleep by soft snoring and warm breath on his chest. He looked down at the naked young woman wrapped in his left arm—and suddenly had extremely conflicting feelings.

Lucia, sound asleep, had her left leg intertwined with Oskar's. She rested her head and left hand on his chest, her fingertips lost in his chest hair and her wavy dark hair. The sensation of her warm body weight rising and falling with his breathing and the peacefulness of her beautiful face made him long for them to be in a far different time and place.

Would such a loving and innocent young woman be selling herself were it not for this damn war?

He inhaled deeply. The aroma of her delicate lilac fragrance mingled with the husky, sensual smell that had come from their repeated couplings—energetic, exhilarating, and ultimately exhausting—over the course of the last two nights.

Then he felt more than a little angry at himself—disgusted, even embarrassed.

I am an intelligent and educated man—yet now I really am acting no better than that bastard Müller.

The first night with a whore I could perhaps excuse to the alcohol and my weakened emotional state.

But now?

Now, I not only willingly went back to bed with a whore, but I went back enthusiastically.

Which means that I shamefully personify what it says in Proverbs 26 . . . and Father never believed that I'd actually read the Bible . . . "As a dog returneth to its vomit, so a fool repeateth his folly."

He looked down and stared at her peaceful, almost angelic face.

But this . . . this is different, is it not?

Lucia has been so wonderful, and being lost in this moment is sublime.

I never want it to stop.

But . . . with a whore?

Am I indeed a fool and this my folly? Am I losing my mind?

God damn this war for destroying so much!

And now what? What about Father? And my family?

Who knows what today will bring?

But at least we have right here and right now. . . .

He inhaled deeply, then slowly exhaled.

Because of the movement or because she felt his gaze, Lucia slowly opened her warm dark eyes, looked up at him, then made a small sweet smile.

She has the timeless beauty of a goddess.

He smiled back, then leaned down and gently kissed her on the lips.

As he started to pull away, she smoothly moved up a little to keep contact—and they remained with their lips softy locked for minutes that seemed to drift into hours.

Oskar could not recall the last time he had felt like this.

Such peacefulness. Such passion . . .

Then he felt the familiar stir in his groin.

Lucia became aware of the movement that followed, and slowly slid her hand down his belly—

And stopped when there suddenly was a knock at the door.

They broke off their kiss, then looked at the door, then at each other. After a moment, there came a heavy banging on the door.

Scheisse! Oskar Kappler thought as he reached to the bedside table and grabbed his Luger. Then he kicked back the bedsheet and pulled on his boxer shorts. As he started for the door, he heard the metallic sound of a key being slid into the lock.

"Was ist das?" he called out just as the door started to swing open.

Lucia screamed as Kappler raised his pistol.

Then Kappler sighed and lowered the weapon when he saw Vito the midget—and, towering behind him, Ernst Beck the Abwehr agent.

[THREE]
Hotel Michelangelo
Palermo, Sicily
0750 1 June 1943

Dick Canidy took the steps two at a time as he headed down to find Jimmy Skinny or, failing that, Vito.

Now that I know Shorty is nearby . . .

Canidy had carefully watched through the crack of his door as Vito and an average-looking dark-haired man in a sloppy suit had stood at the door to Room 802.

Canidy had had a sudden urge to ask Vito if he'd seen any of the Budas but knew that it probably wasn't the best time for that conversation—especially with their language barrier.

There clearly had been no adequate response to the first knocks, and Vito had made a fist over his head and was hammering on the door.

A minute later, Vito looked up at the man in the suit, shrugged and made a face, then pulled out a huge ring of keys. He fed one into the door lock, turned the knob, and pushed the door inward.

A woman screamed.

Vito, standing his ground as he pocketed the key ring, exchanged words with whoever had opened the door, then gestured toward the man in the suit, who in turn then made what looked to be gracious gestures of apology.

Both men stood there for a moment without saying another word, then looked at one another, then turned their backs to the door of 801.

Canidy could not figure out what that had been all about, and why they stood there for almost five minutes, impatient, with their arms crossed. He was about to quit watching when a man's arm appeared from inside the room and waved the man with the suit to come in.

Almost immediately after that, a nicely dressed beautiful olive-skinned full-figured young woman with rich wavy dark hair to her shoulders came out into the hall. Canidy saw that her warm dark eyes were sad, and that she was frowning.

Canidy smirked.

As the early Greeks here first said, "Coitus interruptus."

Does Jimmy Skinny issue refunds for that?

Vito nodded at her, then turned and headed for the stairs.

The young woman fluffed her thick hair, glanced sadly back at the door to 802, then followed.

Jimmy Skinny picked up the carafe from the tray that one of the big women from the kitchen had just brought to his office. In addition to stained china mugs, the tray held plates of fried egg, fruit, and pastries. Palasota poured coffee for Canidy, then himself.

"And how did you find your room?" Palasota asked.

"I just followed the stairs past what apparently was at least half the drunken Regia Marina, stuck a key in the door labeled eight-oh-one, and there it was!"

Jimmy Skinny chuckled, then thought about the Royal Italian Navy submariners.

"I hear they're pretty lousy at sea, but they do drink like fish when on land. And they're not shy with the girls. We're doing a very good business. Still, I will be glad to see all the Fascist bastards run out of town and good ol' GIs filling the streets. And my beds."

Canidy looked past where Palasota was standing and noticed that the two Thompson submachine guns still stood in the corner. But with them was a Johnson LMG.

So Socks Lanza sent some of the Johnny guns here, too.

Nothing surprises me anymore. . . .

"Look, I've got a curious problem," Canidy said. "A new—"

The door suddenly swung open, and Vito appeared. He rattled off something in Sicilian—*Did he just say Müller?*—and then Canidy saw Palasota's face change.

Jimmy Skinny replied in Sicilian, then switched back to English and told Canidy, "This should not take long. Help yourself to the food. I'll have more sent."

[FOUR]
Room 802
Hotel Michelangelo
Palermo, Sicily
0750 1 June 1943

Sitting on the edge of the bed and pulling on his pants, SS-Obersturmbannführer Oskar Kappler looked up at German Trade Ministry Director Ernst Beck.

"You found me . . . here?"

Beck grunted. "It is our job to have such information. You told me you were coming overnight to Palermo. You don't think that this is my first time here, or to the hotel?" He paused. "Or to have business with Jimmy Skinny?"

Kappler considered that, then nodded.

Of course. You're an Abwehr agent.

Get your damn head clear, Oskar . . .

Beck then grinned.

"You need not worry about me mentioning the . . . girl."

"I wasn't," Kappler lied.

Beck then said, "I have been here because we have a fairly healthy dossier on your man Hans Müller. It's important to keep an eye on the dangerous ones. Especially those who can be coerced."

Kappler looked at him but didn't reply.

He pulled on a T-shirt and yawned.

"Those details can wait," Beck said, reaching into his jacket and coming out with a folded thin sheet of paper. "This takes absolute priority."

Kappler's pulse began to race as he took the sheet and immediately recognized the now-familiar routing head:

HIGHEST SECRECY

TO–

SS-OBERSTURMBANNFUHRER OSKAR KAPPLER

SS PROVISIONAL HEADQUARTERS SICILY

THROUGH–

HERR ERNST BECK, DIRECTOR

GERMAN TRADE MINISTRY, MESSINA, SICILY

BEGIN MESSAGE

MAY 31ST, IN THE YEAR OF OUR LORD, 1943

DEAR OSKAR,

AS I FIRST WROTE, MY KARLCHEN, THE TIME HAS NOW COME TO PERFORM EXTRAORDINARY TASKS THAT OUR ALMIGHTY GOD HAS CHOSEN FOR ME.

WHILE THESE ARE DANGEROUS, I HAVE EVERY CONVICTION THAT I WILL BE SUCCESSFUL AND THAT OUR FAMILY SOON SHALL BE TOGETHER AGAIN.

FOR THAT TO HAPPEN, IT IS IMPORTANT THAT YOU AND YOUR MOTHER AND SISTER IMMEDIATELY PUT YOURSELVES IN THE CAPABLE HANDS OF AGENTS ACTING ON MY BEHALF WHO WILL SEE YOU TO SAFETY.

AS YOU READ THIS, AMERICAN AGENTS ARE IN THE PROCESS OF TAKING YOUR MOTHER AND SISTER INTO SAFE HIDING. KNOW THAT, WITH THE GESTAPO KEEPING REGULAR TRACK OF THEM, YOU PROBABLY HAVE A WINDOW OF 24 TO 36 HOURS BEFORE THE GESTAPO DECIDES THAT THEY ARE MISSING AND/OR ON THE RUN AND SENDS A MESSAGE TO SICILY ORDERING YOUR ARREST.

THIS IS THE REASON IT IS CRITICAL THAT YOU MAKE YOURSELF AVAILABLE TO THE AGENT AS SOON AS POSSIBLE.

IF YOU FAIL, THEN WE ALL FAIL. AND AFTER OUR ARREST AND INTERROGATION, I DO NOT BELIEVE WE WILL

BE ALLOWED THE LUXURY OF FRITZ THYSSEN -- THAT IS TO SAY, SPENDING THE REST OF THE WAR IN A KONZENTRATIONSLAGER -- BUT INSTEAD FACE SUMMARY EXECUTION.

THE AGENT WHO WILL ASSIST YOU HAS THE CODE NAME JUPITER.

YOU WILL EVENTUALLY BE REUNITED WITH YOUR MOTHER AND SISTER, THEN APPROACHED BY THE POWERFUL AMERICAN GENTLEMAN WHO HAS UNIQUE KNOWLEDGE OF OUR KAPPLER FAMILY BUSINESSES AND INVESTMENTS IN THE AMERICAS THAT I TOLD YOU NOW CONSTITUTE OUR FAMILY'S ENTIRE WEALTH.

IT IS IMPORTANT YOU ASSUME CONTROL OF THESE UNTIL SUCH TIME AS I CAN JOIN YOU. AS YOU KNOW, OUR COMPANIES EMPLOY MANY PEOPLE AND THEY ARE COUNTING ON US, NOW AND AFTER THIS MADNESS ENDS.

I PRAY WE ALL SEE EACH OTHER SOON. GODSPEED.

YOUR FATHER
END MESSAGE
HIGHEST SECRECY

"You have read the letter and are satisfied that you understand its content?" Beck said.

Satisfied?

Perhaps terrified is a more appropriate word. . . .

Oskar Kappler did not trust his voice to speak at first.

He cleared his throat, then said, *"Jawohl."*

Ernst Beck held out his hand.

After a moment's confusion, Kappler put the message in it.

Beck then went over to the side table and took the box of matches from the ashtray, struck one, and, holding the thin paper over the ashtray, put the tip of the flame to the paper. He let go of it just as it went up in a flash.

Oskar Kappler's mind began to race.

There is no telling how much time I have—when did that twenty-four-hour clock start?

And how am I supposed to find this Jupiter? Just go sit in my office at Messina and wait for the phone to ring?

Or wait for the gottverdammt *Gestapo to come arrest me first?*

And . . . what do I do about Lucia?

You fool—you do absolutely nothing with your folly!

Beck turned to him and could see that he was mentally distressed.

"I know this is difficult, Oskar. I am here to help, including now getting you to connect with this Jupiter." He glanced at his watch. "I believe that I need to return to Messina. Would you like a ride?"

[ONE]
Hotel Michelangelo
Palermo, Sicily
0905 1 June 1943

Dick Canidy had just finished eating the last of four eggs that had been on the plate and was draining his coffee mug to wash it down when there was a knock on Jimmy Skinny's office door—and it immediately swung open.

Canidy turned to see what he almost instantly realized was probably the same view that whoever was in Room 802 had seen an hour earlier.

Vito the midget stood there with a man in a suit towering behind him.

Jesus, Shorty! Is this all you do all day?

By the way, your boss ain't here. . . .

Vito hesitated entering, looking somewhat surprised to see only Canidy in the office. He finally walked in and motioned for the man in the suit to follow.

Canidy, now getting a better view, sized up the man. He noticed he had a white rose in the lapel of his rumpled two-piece suit.

What the hell is that supposed to signify? Anything?

He was around five-nine and 190, maybe thirty years old, and with gentle Germanic features. His longish thin dark hair framed a somewhat friendly but inquisitive face. As his eyes met Canidy's,

Canidy nodded once but said nothing as he turned his attention to refilling his coffee mug.

Vito then said something to Canidy. Canidy had absolutely no idea what exactly it was, but it clearly had the tone of an order.

Canidy looked at him and shrugged.

Vito motioned impatiently at Canidy, then pointed to the door and said, *"Prego."*

Oh! Well, Shorty, since you've told me "please," then sure.

Go take a rolling fuck at a miniature doughnut.

Canidy shook his head, pointed to the ground, and firmly said, "I wait for Jimmy."

The man in the suit looked at him as if he now understood that Canidy was here to get one of Jimmy Skinny's girls.

And I don't know who the hell you are, but (a) that ain't happening and (b) even if it were, it'd be none of your damn business.

Vito made a face, then walked over and motioned for Canidy to bend down so he could say something in his ear.

Now what? Are you joking?

Impatiently, Vito motioned again.

Jesus, all right! All right!

Canidy shook his head in disbelief as he bent over.

Vito whispered, "Andrea."

As Canidy quickly carried his coffee toward the door, passing the man in the suit, he graciously gestured for him to help himself to what items remained on the tray.

Vito led Canidy down a back stairwell to a room with a locked metal door. He knocked on it, said something that also sounded like an order but, surprising Canidy, did not attempt to automatically enter. After a moment, he understood why.

The sound of locks turning could be heard, and then the door opened. Andrea Buda stood in the opening, and hurriedly motioned for Canidy to enter.

As Vito wordlessly went back to the stairwell, Andrea closed the metal door behind them, then threw the locks.

"Hello," she said, smiled, and motioned for him to follow.

Andrea led Canidy past a row of olive drab cots, then around a wall formed by stacked boxes of condoms. He then saw John Craig struggling to stand from behind a small metal desk—the wireless was set up on it—then grab a pair of wooden crutches and lean on them. His right foot was neatly bandaged.

"Damn I'm glad to see you," Canidy said. "Now I'm going to kick your ass from here to Messina and back for making me think you got grabbed like Tubes."

John Craig made a face.

"Sorry, Dick. I did not do that on purpose."

Canidy gestured at the foot and crutches.

"You getting better, Gimpy? You're mobile."

"A little."

Canidy noticed that John Craig not only appeared freshly bathed, but his clothes were clean.

And getting taken care of, are you?

Better not let Tubes find out Andrea does this for all the American radio operators. . . .

"So just where the hell did you disappear to?" Canidy said.

"After you left, Andrea refused to stay in that wrecked house, especially with Mariano's body. She went and got one of her brothers, who I eventually figured out was Antonio. When Antonio saw Mariano, he went and brought back his brother and a pickup truck that reeked of fish. After a lot of emotional drama, and them swearing he would get a decent burial, they put Mariano, wrapped in more sheets, in the back of the truck. An hour later, they were back, and then we—well, they—loaded everything in the truck and brought us here."

I was back there in two hours. Must have just missed them.

"What is this?" Canidy said. "It looks like a makeshift infirmary."

John Craig nodded.

"Something like that. It's Andrea's office. I set up the station in here, then since I couldn't find you and it was dark and we had the truck, I got them to drive out to where you said you'd stashed the gear. It took a little time, but I eventually found one bundle, in a rock outcropping just as you'd described."

John Craig gestured to a corner of the room. Canidy saw one of the suitcases and a duffel and a wooden crate that held a hundred pounds of C-2 plastic explosive.

"So, we have something to work with," he said, as he reached back to the desk and picked up his transcription pad. "Which is good because these came in this morning."

As John Craig handed Canidy the messages, he said, "Apparently the delay in Corsica didn't happen. Neptune is en route."

Canidy read that message, thought for a moment, then flipped to the next.

After a moment, he said, "So now I'm ordered to get this Kappler to Algiers yesterday, and get him there alive."

John Craig nodded.

"Well," Canidy went on, "the timing for that should be about perfect. It'll take Neptune two, three days to get here, in which time good ol' Jupiter should be able to make contact with Kappler."

Canidy flipped to the next page, found it blank, then handed back the message pad.

"Any word from Mercury Station?" Canidy said.

"Not one. And I've had the Radio Direction Finder ready to go."

Standing near John Craig, Andrea leaned against the desk and pointed to the chair.

"Stay off foot," she said.

John Craig exchanged glances with Canidy and shrugged sheepishly. "She's been taking really good care of me."

"I can tell."

Canidy then walked over to their pile of gear that John Craig had brought, dug through it for a moment, then said, "Aha!"

He pulled out a bottle of the Haig & Haig Pinch Scotch Whisky and triumphantly held it above his head.

"I need to go talk to Palasota," he then said. "Try not to disappear again."

[TWO]

Canidy had found Jimmy Skinny alone in his office. He was sitting behind his desk when Canidy had knocked on the door and immediately entered.

Jimmy Skinny did not seem surprised that it wasn't Vito.

Maybe everyone does it.

"Sorry about the interruption earlier," Palasota said. "That Müller was getting in a pissing contest with Fiorini, the new captain of that submarine. The guy's a really wet-behind-the-ears lieutenant."

"Not a problem. I solved one of my problems in the meantime."

Canidy brought up the bottle of scotch, and Palasota's eyes grew.

"Where did you get that? Even with my connections, I can't beg, borrow, or steal good shit like that anywhere."

Canidy put it on the desk.

"It's yours—no begging, borrowing, or stealing. Friend to friend."

Palasota raised an eyebrow.

"Okay, what do you want? I'm already working on the other things we discussed."

Canidy pointed to the Thompson and Johnson machine guns.

"For starters, that's my Johnny gun."

Palasota glanced at it, then nodded at Canidy.

"I wondered where that came from."

Canidy went on: "I need to grab the SS guy, Kappler. And then I'm going to need a boat—something—to shuttle us out to our ride back to Algiers. All sometime in the next three days."

"You mean *Müller*?"

Why are these guinea bastards always correcting me, telling me what I think I think?

"No, goddammit!" Canidy blurted. "I mean Müller's boss in Messina. SS-Obersturmbannführer Oskar Kappler."

Palasota looked at Canidy.

"SS-Obersturmbannführer Oskar Kappler?" he parroted.

"Yeah. I need to get to Messina yesterday."

"You're shitting me. Right?"

"What are you talking about? How can I be any clearer?"

Skinny Jimmy Palasota then laughed out loud.

Canidy was about to blow his cork when he heard Palasota then say: "SS-Obersturmbannführer Oskar Kappler just walked out of the hotel."

"So you are the Messina Abwehr agent?" Dick Canidy said twenty minutes later to the man in the suit as they both stood in Palasota's office in practically the same spots as they had about an hour earlier.

Ernst Beck nodded and grinned.

"And you're Jupiter," Beck replied.

Canidy nodded and grinned.

"This is just fucking surreal," Canidy said.

"Now what?" SS-Obersturmbannführer Oskar Kappler then said, somewhat anxiously.

"Jupiter here gets you the hell out of Sicily," Ernst Beck answered.

"Whoa!" Canidy blurted. "Unless someone is planning on a long swim, we're going nowhere until the sub gets here. Which will be probably in three days. Meantime—"

"I saw the message," Beck interrupted, "and with all due respect, it is imperative that Oskar disappear now."

"As far as I'm concerned," Canidy shot back, "he can spend the next seventy-two hours polishing bedsheets with that hot hooker of his."

Canidy smiled knowingly at Kappler, who he immediately saw found no humor whatever in that.

What the hell?

"I admit to embarrassment and worse," Kappler then said. "I was a fool."

"I am not passing judgment," Canidy said. "Besides, we Americans have a quaint expression that covers that."

"Yes?"

" 'A stiff prick hath no conscience.' "

Palasota chuckled. "I should put that on a sign and make it the motto of this place."

Canidy then announced: "As I was saying, now that I have completed this part of the mission, I am not leaving until I have done the same with the rest of my original mission."

"Which is?" Beck challenged.

Canidy looked from Beck to Kappler and declared, "You know about the Tabun. You were in charge of it."

"Unfortunately, yes."

"Where is it?"

"There is no nerve gas," Kappler said. "It was lost in a cargo ship that was sunk."

Now is not the time to share just who exactly blew up that ship.

And the one in the port . . .

"Not the Tabun that was with the howitzer rounds," Canidy said. "The replacement Tabun."

Kappler shook his head.

"It is not here. Yet. There was some scheduled to arrive in the next few weeks. It is my understanding that it has to be manufactured, then it will be shipped."

Canidy locked eyes with him a long moment.

"Your understanding? Or is that exactly the situation?"

"Both."

He could be lying. But why?

He wants the hell out of here, and knows that I am his conduit to safety.

Canidy nodded.

"Okay, Item Two," he then said, looking slowly between Beck and Kappler. "One of my wireless radios is under enemy control."

Canidy thought that he saw Kappler react to that information.

"I don't give a rat's ass about the radio," he said, looking at Kappler. "I am looking for my man who was its operator. Him and Frank Nola." He glanced at Palasota, who nodded, then looked back at Kappler. "Nola had been running an underground cell, and now he's missing."

"I think I've seen your radio," Kappler said. "And I may be able to locate your operator."

"Just tell me who has the goddamn radio," Canidy said evenly, "and I can handle it from there."

"Müller," Kappler said.

"Müller!" Palasota repeated, his tone one of obvious surprise. He looked at Canidy. "Dick, I had no idea about this. I've been trying to find Francisco, too, you know."

Canidy nodded.

"You're sure it's Müller?" Beck then said.

Kappler nodded. "He showed me a wireless that has its labels written in English. It's in a locked room on the top floor of the SS field office. Müller's scharführer was working it."

Absolutely no surprise there.

John Craig has been convinced from the start that the station was compromised.

"Did Müller say what he did with the operator?" Canidy said. "That sonofabitch has a nasty habit of summarily shooting people point-blank."

"He said he had him quote locked up as insurance unquote. He did not tell me where. And he did not mention the other man."

Then Tubes is alive!

And if he is, maybe Nola, too.

"Can't you order Müller to turn him over to you, his superior?" Canidy said.

Kappler shook his head.

"If I did, he would ignore me, or kill your man, or possibly both."

"Then I go see Müller," Canidy said.

"If you do, then Müller will shoot him point-blank before you get past the front door."

Ernst Beck held up his hand, palm out.

"I think that we can get Müller to bring him to us."

"Well, then, what the hell are you waiting for?" Canidy gestured impatiently with his hand. "Tell us how."

Beck raised his eyebrows in question as he looked at Palasota.

Jimmy Skinny clearly nodded his agreement.

"Müller can be coerced," Beck said.

"I don't understand," Kappler said. "You mentioned that earlier."

Beck studied him a moment, then said, "Jimmy and I found Müller's Achilles' heel. Ol' Hans doesn't like the girls he beats up."

Kappler grunted.

"That is obvious. He's a mean drunk. That I have seen too many times."

"Oskar, he does not like girls. Period."

"He's a poofter?" Kappler blurted.

Beck nodded. "He tries to have sex with the girls here, but it rarely happens. He gets frustrated and drunk, then humiliates them . . . and worse. It's all a beard, because he lives in fear of having to wear a *rosa winkel* in a konzentrationslager."

That, Canidy thought, *explains why Palasota was so quick to say no when I said why not just whack the bastard now.*

He's had Müller terrified of being discovered and sent to a death camp with a pink triangle sewn to his chest.

"Wonder if that would come as any surprise to Günther?"

Beck grunted. "Who do you think we caught Hans with?"

Palasota, his face furious, picked up the telephone and dialed a short number from memory.

After a moment, he controlled his tone as he said into the phone, "Hans, something has come up. Are you busy? No? Good. See you in a moment."

Palasota stood, and everyone else got up at once.

"We cannot all go," Jimmy Skinny said. "It will spook him. Give me and Oskar twenty, thirty minutes with him, and then you can follow."

"I don't like it," Canidy said.

"You don't have to, Dick. But it is what has to happen."

Ten minutes later, Dick Canidy and Ernst Beck entered the ornate metal doors of the SS Field Office building. Oskar Kappler was coming out of a room to the right, wiping at his uniform sleeve with a hand towel.

There's blood splatter on his neck, Canidy thought. *And his clothes.*

Kappler saw Canidy's expression.

"Your man is alive. Hans told me where to find Nola—his body."

Shit, Canidy thought. *Farewell, Frank. We have the watch.*

Kappler nodded to a stairwell in the corner of the room.

"Follow me."

A flight down, Kappler led them through a heavy wooden door, then past one made of iron bars, to a space that clearly had been set up as a torture room. There were medieval racks. Rusty chains hung from bolts on the wall.

They turned a corner and Canidy then saw Müller lying on the stained coarse stone floor. A pool of blood drained from a hole in the back of his head.

Canidy then saw Tubes strapped to a rough-hewn wooden table. It looked vaguely familiar, and he remembered the tables Müller had used in the villa for the germ warfare experiment.

Tubes looked gaunt. His once thick blond hair was thin, dirty, matted. There were bruises visible up and down his body, but they did not look fresh. Canidy looked at Tubes's hands and feet and saw only crusted scabs.

Sonofabitch!

Palasota was undoing the leather straps at Tubes's feet. Tubes turned his head, tried to focus, then managed to form something resembling a smile when he saw Canidy.

"Fins!" he grunted weakly.

"Yeah, Tubes," Canidy said, his voice cracking. "Fins. But not anymore."

Palasota looked up. "Fins?"

Canidy cleared his throat, then said, "It was our O.K. Corral code word for 'everything's about to go to shit so start shooting every bastard you can.' Got said a little too late, it would appear . . ."

"God help him," Ernst Beck said softly.

"You're going to be okay, Jim," Canidy said. "You're going home."

Kappler then saw Canidy look at Müller on the stone floor.

"The sonofabitch did the same to Mariano," Canidy said. "And probably to Frank. Who shot him?"

"It was a lovers' quarrel," Palasota automatically said, clearly fabricating the story on the spot. "Poor young Günther lost his head. Tragic."

"Sorry," Kappler then said, looking somewhat guilty. "I now realize you probably were hoping to have that honor."

"No."

"No?"

"Actually, I was looking forward to seeing the miserable sonofabitch suffer a very slow and painful death. . . ."

[THREE]
Room 802
Hotel Michelangelo
Palermo, Sicily
1645 1 June 1943

Dick Canidy watched as Andrea Buda came out of the bathroom carrying another bowl of warm water to the bed where Jim "Tubes" Fuller was resting.

Tubes remained very weak but now, after Andrea had worked with two girls for almost an hour solid, he was clean and his wounds dressed.

The first glass of water that Andrea had given him he had immediately thrown up. But now he was able to keep down a very diluted mixture of sugar and water.

He's sleeping the sleep of the dead.

Or the damn near dead.

She's doing the best she can—the best she knows—but this ain't exactly the Mayo Clinic.

I want him back to the best treatment possible, and that's Algiers, then London when he's ready.

John Craig van der Ploeg, on crutches, entered the room and hobbled over to Canidy.

"Here's the sub's coordinates. Neptune is under way and standing by."

Three hours earlier, when they had first brought Tubes to the room, Canidy had then stood with Ernst Beck, Oskar Kappler, and Jimmy Palasota at the window. They all looked down at the port, the four men passing a single pair of binoculars between them.

Canidy had another flashback to General Burford at Gettysburg.

"We have the high ground," he said, "but no plan of attack."

"We just can't sit here waiting for the sub to show up, right?" Kappler said.

Canidy glanced at Tubes. "Right. Not good enough . . . fast enough."

"I have an idea," Beck said, pointing out at the harbor.

"Hijack the U-boat?" Canidy said, incredulous.

Beck shook his head.

"Too big. Too difficult. The other one I can run single-handedly, more or less. I was in the Kriegsmarine." He looked at Canidy and added, "And you were in the U.S. Navy, yes?"

"Yeah, but as an aviator," Canidy said, mimicked an airplane with his left hand, then looked back at the port. "So, you're going to steal that S-boat?"

He shook his head again. "Borrow it. I'll bring it back."

Canidy chuckled and said, "I knew I liked you for a reason."

He then said: "Serious question: How the hell are we going to approach the *Casabianca* with a fucking enemy S-boat?"

"Serious answer?" Beck said. "Carefully. Very fucking carefully."

He looked at his watch.

"The S-boat has a complement of twenty-four. After they refuel and provision the S-boat for its nightly mission—which will happen anytime now—the crew will then come ashore to dine, leaving maybe one or two sailors aboard on watch." Beck paused as he looked to see if there were any questions. There were none, and he went on: "Then the U-boat crew will be flooding in here as usual right after six o'clock—which is in an hour and fifteen minutes."

"What about her captain?" Canidy said. "He's not going to Jimmy's brothel."

Palasota, tapping his fingertips to his chest, said, "Leave that to me. He will be my guest as we celebrate the new command of Lieutenant Mario Fiorini of the Regia Marina."

Canidy considered that, then said, "How do we get Tubes aboard?"

They all gave that a moment's thought.

Then Palasota said: "Easy. Same way we got him up here. But this time we cover him up on a gurney and have two of my men carry the passed-out drunken sailor back to his U-boat. At that point, we'll get the S-boat sailors to lend a hand—and take over their vessel."

"Simple enough," Canidy said. "And how are we going to get Gimpy here aboard? Same way?"

"You're not going to," John Craig said.

"What?" Canidy said.

"All things being equal, Dick, I'd just as well not get on the sub. Do I have to remind you how well I did on Hank's Gooney Bird?"

Canidy looked at him a long moment.

"Dick, I'm staying behind."

"Are you crazy?" Canidy said, then noticed Andrea Buda was watching John Craig with a keen interest.

And there's something in her eyes . . . do they have something going?

"I can keep the station going," John Craig said. "We never had a resistance built; now we can, with Jimmy Skinny. 'This is the lesson . . .' remember?"

John Craig saw Canidy looking at Andrea.

"Look," he then said, "there's not been a good time to get into this. Andrea said Tubes never touched her."

"What?"

"All that he sent me in the messages was boasting—but it was about a hooker. He was coming here instead, and it's probably how the SS caught him."

Canidy looked to Palasota, who nodded and said, "Makes sense. He was here . . . then he wasn't."

Canidy exhaled audibly, then looked at John Craig.

"Go get back on the radio with Neptune. Message back: quote We have commandeered S-boat. Do not repeat do not let loose any fish. Vessel is number S-323. If you miss vessel number, look for the colors. We will be flying France's new national flag. Signed Jupiter unquote."

"Got it. What's this about a French flag?"

"Just do it."

"Aye-aye, sir," John Craig said, then exchanged smiles with Andrea as he hobbled out the door.

When Canidy entered the S-boat's bridge, the man in the Kriegsmarine uniform at the helm startled him. But when he turned and looked at Canidy, he suddenly looked familiar.

"Welcome aboard. Oberleutnant zur See Ludwig Fahr at your service," Ernst Beck said, making a motion that somewhat resembled a salute.

"No shit," Canidy said. "Where did you get the uniform?"

Beck smiled and pointed up toward the Hotel Michelangelo.

"Right now, or very shortly," he said, "there is a rather embarrassed—and buck naked—Kriegsmarine leutnant asking a hooker if she has perhaps seen his uniform."

Canidy smiled, then looked aft. He saw that Tubes Fuller was in one of two bunks on the back wall of the bridge. He was out cold.

"Where's Kappler?" Canidy said.

"Down below, staying out of sight until we're under way."

Beck made what looked to Canidy like the practiced survey of a professional seaman. Beck then made a final full inspection of the vessel's perimeter, and unceremoniously said, "All lines free, let's get out of here."

There were two groups of three levers each on the console. The forward three had black knobs, the rear group red knobs. He reached for the far left of the black knobs and pushed it forward, engaging the port engine transmission. The S-boat immediately began moving forward and away from the pier.

Beck glanced around the perimeter of the ship, said, "Well, we didn't bring any of the dock with us. That's always a good sign."

They were thirty meters under way when Beck reached forward

and pushed the other two black knobs fully forward. Canidy could feel the S-boat respond almost immediately. Its bow rose and the stern settled in a little as it moved forward faster.

Canidy watched Beck, scanning the harbor as he made gentle turns for the mouth, then wrap his fist in an extended fashion over the group of levers with the red knobs. As soon as Beck saw ahead was nothing but open sea, he pushed the three red knobs to about three-quarter throttle.

The triple two-thousand-horsepower Daimler-Benz diesels roared, producing a massive black exhaust cloud behind the boat.

The noise level at the helm was considerably louder, and when Beck turned to Canidy and gestured at the console, he had to almost shout to be heard: "Any idea which of these levers works the brakes?"

The S-boat banged through somewhat choppy seas for two hours. Kappler had come up to the bridge and with Canidy watched Beck's almost casual running of the vessel, working its radar and monitoring its radio. While Canidy had been duly impressed—he knew that anything that looked simple usually was exactly anything but that—Kappler became bored and crashed in the empty bunk above Tubes.

Beck, with his face dimly lit in the green glow of the control panel lights, looked at Canidy and raised his voice to be heard above the engine noise: "Should be about another hour."

Canidy nodded.

Then, ten minutes later, he saw Beck's expression change in the green glow as he rapidly tapped the screen of the radar.

"Shit!" he said. "We've got company."

Then the radio squawked, an urgent German voice repeating an order.

"What's he saying?" Canidy said.

"For us to identify ourselves."

Which if we do, Canidy thought, *we may get blown out of the water for having stolen the boat.*

And if we don't, we'll damn sure get shot at.

"Christ!" Beck said, pointing at the radar. "There's a hot fish in the water! We're under fire!"

Beck made a course correction, then reached up and threw two toggle switches. Lights above each of them glowed red.

"May as well get rid of some weight," Beck said casually. "Turnabout, they say, is fair play."

One of the lights turned green, then the other one did.

Beck hit one toggle—and the S-boat shuddered as a torpedo fired. After a count of three, he hit the second toggle, and there was another shudder. He then made a hard turn to port, started an evasive series of zigzags, and finally straightened out and pushed the triple throttles all the way forward.

He glanced at Canidy and grinned. The noise was now too great for anything said.

[FOUR]
39 degrees 01 minute North Latitude
12 degrees 23 minutes East Longitude
Aboard the *Casabianca*
Mediterranean Sea
2335 1 June 1943

Commander Jean L'Herminier, chief officer of the Free French Forces submarine, stood five-foot-seven and maybe 140. The thirty-five-year-old carried himself with an easygoing, soft-spoken confidence. He approached his executive officer—a frail-looking sad-eyed Frenchman a head shorter than the commander—who for the last hour had had his eyes glued to the periscope.

"Sir, I have visual on another S-boat," the executive officer said.

This made the second Kriegsmarine patrol boat they had picked up on radar in the last three hours.

The XO added, "It's too damn dark to make out her hull number, sir."

"Understood. Canidy's message clearly stated that confirmation of our target vessel will be that it is flying France's new colors."

"Yes, sir. I don't quite understand that, but I am looking. . . ."

After a moment, the XO exclaimed, "*Sacré bleu!* Those sons of whores!"

"What?" L'Herminier said as he watched the XO step back from the scope.

"They mock us!" the XO almost spat out, indignant.

L'Herminier stepped to the periscope and had a look.

The XO could not believe his eyes and ears the next moment when L'Herminier chuckled, then stepped away from the periscope and began laughing hysterically at what appeared to be a white bedsheet flying above the S-boat's bridge.

The memory of being under fire only six months earlier still was a fresh wound. Ignoring demands of the admiralty of Vichy France that French ships be scuttled at Toulon, L'Herminier had sailed for North Africa—saving his ship and men from surrender.

And now L'Herminier remembered Canidy's descriptive word for Vichy France.

The commander turned to his XO and ordered, "Prepare to surface and make contact. Signal code word 'chickenshits.'"

[FIVE]
OSS London Station
London, England
1200 17 June 1943

"And then they got out on a Kriegsmarine patrol boat," Lieutentant Colonel Ed Stevens was telling Brigadier General William Donovan, "one flying the new colors of France."

David Bruce grunted derisively.

As Donovan was about to say something, there was a knock at the door.

"Come!" Bruce called.

"Well," Wild Bill said, "if it's not our favorite loose cannon."

Dick Canidy wasn't sure how to respond.

"It's a pleasure to see you again, sir. My apology for being late."

"I'm just damn glad you're here," Donovan said. "And with Kappler safe."

"Yes, sir. Thank you."

"How is Ann doing?" Donovan went on.

"I just left her. Very well. Thank you."

"Dick," Ed Stevens said, "I was just telling the General about the S-boat you stole—"

"Borrowed, Ed," Canidy said, grinning. "I got word that Ludwig Fahr—the Abwehr agent—got it back to Palermo by dawn, then scuttled it on some rocks and literally walked back ashore. They never knew (a) that Fahr was gone or (b) that he was who'd 'borrowed' the boat."

"I was just about to describe France's new national colors," Stevens said, grinning and gesturing for Canidy to pick up the story. "And how you used them on the S-boat . . ."

Canidy, with a straight face, looked at Wild Bill and said, "Surely you've heard about the new flag, sir?"

Donovan shook his head, but the Irishman knew when he was having his chain yanked, and grinned. "I'm sure you'll enlighten me, Dick."

"It's a white cross superimposed on a field of white with a white star and white stripes," Canidy said, grinning broadly. "It really stands out on a battlefield."

Everyone but Bruce chuckled.

After a moment, Donovan said, "Well, judging by David's face, we have some serious business to cover. Not that I don't believe what you did, Dick, wasn't serious. Damn good work."

I guess the ends can justify the means, Canidy thought. *I'm not getting reamed for going back into Sicily.*

"Thank you, sir."

"Especially in light of the fact that Jimmy Doolittle has begun the soft bombing of Sicily today. David, bring Dick up to speed on why it was important to get Kappler out of there."

After five minutes of background, David Bruce then said: "And what we have just found out is that just about the time that Walter Höss was escorting Bormann and von Braun into the Chemische Fabrik Frankfurt plant to meet Wolfgang Kappler, Gisevius and Kappler had cleared the border, headed for Bern. A railcar of TNT then cooked off, taking out half of the production facility and narrowly missing Bormann and von Braun. So there won't be a full production of high explosive for a while and there won't be any nerve gas for the foreseeable future."

Canidy nodded. "That means there won't be the threat of Tabun for Husky. Oskar said there was none in Sicily; that the replacement had to be manufactured first."

"And now, thanks to his father, it won't be," Stevens said.

"What about Oskar's mother and sister?" Canidy said. "Where are they?"

"We got them to Dulles," Bruce said, looking briefly at Donovan, "and Dulles has them with Old Man Kappler in his Bern safe house. It's an ancient estate near the River Aare. We are having our documents section produce papers to get them out, after enough time has passed, to South America by way of probably Portugal."

"And Gisevius?" Canidy said. "He really did us a helluva job by sending Ludwig Fahr to me."

"Dulles is also hiding Hans in Bern from the Gestapo," Bruce said. He paused, and brought out the knives as he added, "That's the same scenario Dulles had set up with Sparrow—and the Reds got Sparrow. We can only hope that this time the same mistakes won't be made."

There was a long, awkward silence.

Stevens then said, "Dick, it was Old Man Kappler who got us the V-1 specs."

"So the Krauts really are going to do that?"

"Last word," Stevens said, nodding, "is that Hitler is backing Milch's desire to have fewer bunkers, but ones the size of the bigger bomb-proof kind—like those of the submarine pens in Brest. Hitler and Milch agree that those heavily fortified bunkers best resist our bomb attacks."

"Field Marshal Erhard Milch?" Canidy said.

"Head of the Luftwaffe production program," Stevens confirmed. "Meanwhile, Göring is going off half-cocked. For one, he told Hitler he'd have fifty thousand V-1s built a month. He's had to settle for a hundred a month—"

Donovan laughed. "Who among us would have wanted to be there when Göring had to tell Hitler that exciting news?"

There followed the expected chuckles.

Stevens went on: "That production figure would rise to five thousand per month by early next year. Göring also had to compromise on the bunkers—only four of the heavily fortified ones, along with almost a hundred smaller ones in the field, and the ones launched from He-111 bombers."

"More fun news to deliver to Hitler," Donovan said lightly, then his tone turned more serious. "Still, Ike is not going to be happy hearing any of that. I bet he will come knocking on our door, especially understanding what we've accomplished supplying the Polish underground."

Stevens looked at Canidy and explained: "We upped the supply drops to Poland. Tripled, so far. And last week, Sausagemaker's team took out the construction site that's set to build the V-1s. Half of his team got the prisoners freed."

"Great!"

"But there's bad news. Mordechaj was following Stanislaw Polko—"

Canidy nodded. "His lieutenant. One brave, ballsy bastard."

"—and they got trapped. He and the other half of his team . . . they were wiped out."

"Jesus Christ . . ." Canidy sighed. "Then we've barely slowed the bastards down."

"But we did slow them down," Wild Bill Donovan put in. "And eventually we will stop them."

"'This is the lesson . . .'" Canidy then said.

Donovan nodded.

"Churchill, despite occasional bad advice, does get it right."

After a moment, Canidy shook his head and chuckled.

"What?" Wild Bill Donovan said.

"I'll always remember the last thing that Szerynski, the poor sonofabitch, said to me. 'Two things I've learned, Dick. One, we make war so that we may live in peace.' . . ."

Everyone nodded solemnly.

"Aristotle," Wild Bill Donovan said.

Canidy nodded, then finished, ". . . 'And, two, never share a foxhole with some bastard who's braver than you.'"

AFTERWORD

As Allied forces attacked occupied France in OPERATION OVERLORD on D-day, 6 June 1944, Adolf Hitler ordered Generalfeldmarschall Karl Rudolf Gerd von Rundstedt to transmit code word *Rumpelkammer*—junk room—alerting the regimental staff to prepare to fire the first volley of *vergeltungswaffen*.

At the launch code word *Eisbär*—polar bear—Nazi Germany's retaliation weapons began bombing London six days later.

Almost ten thousand aerial torpedoes—averaging one hundred V-1s a day at the peak—were launched at England for sixteen months, until Allied forces overran the final launching site in October 1944.

During the first two weeks, more than one hundred thousand London homes were damaged or destroyed. V-1s in those sixteen months caused more than twenty thousand casualties.

Winston Churchill's personal assistant, Frederick Lindemann, had mocked the V-1 bombings, declaring, "The mountain hath groaned and given forth a mouse!"

But the First Viscount Cherwell, opinionated and arrogant, had been dead wrong in advising the prime minister that the Germans were unable to build such advanced rocket-powered weapons.

Almost ten months earlier, Allied intelligence, using 3-D viewers on overlapping aerial reconn photographs, had pinpointed Peenemünde Army Research Center—Wernher von Braun's rocket development facility on the northern peninsula of a small Baltic island.

OPERATION HYDRA bombed it on the night of 17/18 August 1943, killing V-2 scientists and destroying enough of the facility to delay the V-2 rocket tests for almost two months. The V-2 was designed to have far greater capabilities than the V-1.

Nazi Germany, undaunted, continued its V-1 and V-2 development programs at Peenemünde and deep in Poland.

Then OPERATION CROSSBOW, the bombing of *vergeltungswaffen* launch sites, commenced on 5 December 1943. U.S. Ninth Air Force B-26s struck Ligescourt before bad weather stopped the sorties for nearly three weeks. Finally, on Christmas Eve, almost seven hundred B-24 and B-17 aircraft attacked twenty-four other launch sites in France with fifteen hundred tons of bombs.

And on 8 June 1944—D-day Plus Two—Allied aircraft shot up a fuel convoy, burning three-quarters of a million liters of missile fuel, and took out Axis trains bearing additional missiles.

As the Allies advanced in OVERLORD, launch sites were abandoned without firing a single shot.

The V-1 had failed to cause the destruction Adolf Hitler demanded. But for the fortunes of war, it could have. And, albeit too late to stop OVERLORD, it did succeed in terrorizing England.

Nicknamed "Doodlebug" and "Buzz Bomb" because of the unique sound made by its pulse-jet engine, the bomb would fly to just shy of target, then the engine went quiet—and after terrifying moments of silence it would explode.

On D-day Plus Eight, General Dwight Eisenhower ordered his

deputy—Air Marshal Arthur Tedder, who had been his commander of Allied Air Forces in the Mediterrean—that the V-1 targets were "to take precedence over everything except the urgent requirements" of OVERLORD.

The Allies used a thousand heavy and light antiaircraft guns, as well as employed fighter aircraft, to shoot them down. During daylight, some pilots would match speed with the V-1 and, going wing to wing, tip the V-1, causing it to crash after knocking out its gyroscope.

When the Allies captured the V-1 manufacturing facilities, they found a number of variants of the Fieseler 103.

One was a would-be kamikaze missile, with rudimentary controls designed for a suicide pilot.

Another—assigned the military designation of Fi-103D-1—was specifically designed to carry a warhead of nerve gas.